Sweet CREEK

What Reviewers Say About BOLD STROKES Authors

❦

KIM BALDWIN

"*A riveting novel of suspense* seems to be a very overworked phrase. However, it is extremely apt when discussing Kim Baldwin's [Hunter's Pursuit]. An exciting page turner [features] Katarzyna Demetrious, a bounty hunter…with a million dollar price on her head. Look for this excellent novel of suspense…" – **R. Lynne Watson**, *MegaScene*

❦

ROSE BEECHAM

"…her characters seem fully capable of walking away from the particulars of whodunit and engaging the reader in other aspects of their lives." – *Lambda Book Report*

❦

GUN BROOKE

"*Course of Action* is a romance…populated with a host of captivating and amiable characters. The glimpses into the lifestyles of the rich and beautiful people are rather like guilty pleasures.…[A] most satisfying and entertaining reading experience." – **Arlene Germain**, reviewer for the *Lambda Book Report* and the *Midwest Book Review*

❦

JANE FLETCHER

"*The Walls of Westernfort* is not only a highly engaging and fast-paced adventure novel, it provides the reader with an interesting framework for examining the same questions of loyalty, faith, family and love that [the characters] must face." – **M. J. Lowe**, *Midwest Book Review*

❦

RADCLY𝑓FE

"…well-honed storytelling skills…solid prose and sure-handedness of the narrative…" – **Elizabeth Flynn**, *Lambda Book Report*

"…well-plotted…lovely romance...I couldn't turn the pages fast enough!" – **Ann Bannon**, author of *The Beebo Brinker Chronicles*

ISBN 1-933110-29-5
THIS TRADE PAPERBACK ORIGINAL IS PUBLISHED BY
BOLD STROKES BOOKS, INC.,
PHILADELPHIA, PA, USA

FIRST US EDITION JANUARY 2006

LIBRARY OF CONGRESS CONTROL NUMBER: 2005929169

CREDITS
EDITORS: JENNIFER KNIGHT AND SHELLEY THRASHER
PRODUCTION DESIGN: J. BARRE GREYSTONE
COVER DESIGN: SHERI (GRAPHICARTIST2020@HOTMAIL.COM)

Sweet CREEK

by

Lee Lynch

2006

Acknowledgments

Nel Ward, Sue Hardesty, Jane Cothron, Connie Ward, Shelley Thrasher, Sky Aisling, Leslie Hall, Carol Feiden, Kate Ryan, Mara Witzling, Joy Parks, Shawn Murray, Nancy Slobotna, Carol Seajay, Akia Woods, Darci Hering, Radcly*f*fe, Renee LaChance, Marilyn Silver, Wendi Richardson, Susan Dart, Melissa Hartman, Lyn Woodward, Katherine Forrest, Jennifer Knight, and David, Betsy, Carolyn and Kit Lynch—I LOVE YOU AND THANK YOU.

My special thanks to Diane Anderson-Minshall, who, as an editor of *Girlfriends Magazine*, asked for a column and gave me a novel. The short short stories which grew into this novel originally appeared, in different form, in *Girlfriends Magazine*.

FOR

MARCIA SANTEE

June 11, 1946 to June 14, 2005

YOU'RE IN MY EVERY BREATH

YOU'RE IN MY EVERY STEP

YOU'VE MADE MY LIFE COMPLETE

YOU ARE LOVE

CHAPTER ONE

Over the Pass

Chick was serving Clara and Hector White when the two city girls, hurrying out of the chilly December fog, tripped down the worn wooden step that led into the store.

One newcomer cried out, "Hola! Somebody's going to get totaled on this thing!"

The other looked up, lifted her backwards ball cap, ran a hand through her flattop hair, and grinned, looking sheepish.

Hector's brown eyes moved quickly away when they met Chick's. She knew he was trying to keep from laughing. Tourists were the only ones who didn't know about the step, and tourists, to Hector, were an endless source of mirth.

Chick had been tempted to do something about that step when she and Donny opened Natural Woman Foods on the edge of the town of Waterfall Falls eight years ago, but hadn't because it evoked for her the three-generation feed business that had preceded them in that old building. Sometimes, alone in the store with the hanging plants that festooned all the big windows, local handmade quilts suspended from the rafters, and a lazy fly looking for a way into the bakery case, she'd dream the stagecoach was on its way north from the port of San Francisco, coming over Blackberry Pass, laden with hungry passengers who'd seen a rainbow end somewhere on Stage Street.

Waterfall Falls, granted its first post office in 1861, now prided itself in year 2000 on its frontier character—and characters. Chick supposed she was one of them—a leftover gay hippie turned shopkeeper, she thought as she approached the booth Clara and Hector were sharing. She set down Clara's smoothie and salad and a sandwich for Hector, and waited for his teasing complaints. After eight years, she'd heard them all a dozen times each, if not about her food, then about Clara's cooking whenever she and Donny were persuaded to go for lunch or dinner out at the Whites' little ranch.

"You gave me the works again, Chick," Hector accused, examining sprouts that bulged from the bun like the fuzzy gray hair from under a cap that read, "A bad day fishin' is better than a good day workin'." Chick sold only wrapped sandwiches prepared by two enterprising women with a catering business in Greenhill.

"You eat that," Clara said brusquely.

Clara was too big for the booth, with legs that reminded Chick of small trees, shoulders that supported what would be respectable branches on any other trunk, and an incongruous pouf of home-permed white hair. Chick had scavenged the tall wooden booths, carved graffiti and all, from an auction and added two small round tables with mismatched chairs that she'd found at garage sales.

Hector, who matched Clara's six foot, one inch plus a basketball stomach, winked. "She thinks this rabbit feed will keep me jumping every time she gets a case of the honey-dos."

He took about a third of the burger in one bite and chewed it fast, biting off another piece like a ravenous woodsman. Clara was decorously removing her teeth into a napkin. She slid them into her coat pocket.

Chick checked over her shoulder for the city girls. The taller pale one in the cap rifled through bags of blue corn chips, jouncing a little to the electronic CD she played. The other, darker woman moved her fingers over an earth-mother image in the gift section. Both their bodies were turned away from the tableau at the booth, but broadcast alertness.

Outside, an empty wood chip truck rattled by. Until the rains started again, she guessed the mills would run at least two shifts. That would save a few jobs, but she'd come to dislike this time of year with its still, inverted air and an unnatural dryness that nurtured nothing but the decorative cabbages Donny had in her planters out front. This year the inversion had kept them fogged in for weeks. The whole town smelled like a pulp mill, and the air felt like suspended ice crystals that stung to walk through, as if the interrupted rain had frozen in place. People with allergies had trouble drawing breath and people with asthma were hospitalized. Burn barrels and old woodstoves filled the air with so many particulates that a warning system had been devised up in Greenhill—on "red" days only those with no other source of heat could burn.

She and Donny had traded in the huge old Earth Stove that had come with the building and put in a smaller, "high-tech" model which claimed to burn fuel four times—she had to laugh at what rural Northwesterners considered to be high tech. Chick missed the rain and feared global warming. She quickly banned such thoughts from her mind out of fear that her old depression would seep back into her, like this nasty constant fog seeped into walls.

She realized that Hector was waiting for her response and asked, "Honeydews?"

He was an always laughing, stalwart seventy-two. One leg jutted out from under the table, stiff from a logging accident. "Oh, you know," he said straight-faced, "honey do this for me, honey fix that?" His high-pitched machine gun laugh was a little ridiculous on a big mature man, but it was clearly genuine, shaking his whole body and rocking him, when standing, heel to toe.

Clara threw a cherry tomato at him. Hector caught it and popped it in his mouth.

The city girls had moved to the bakery case. They looked tiny compared to the old couple. Chick counted eleven piercings between them, that she could see, including a diamond-studded nostril.

"What's she do when she's got to sneeze?" Hector wondered aloud. By the look on his face, his question was real if rude.

Clara speared a squint at the city girls. "When I was that age, girls still wore white gloves to go downtown."

"We're about to start our second year in a new century," said Hector. "Like it or not, Mrs. White, New Year's Eve is only twenty days away."

Clara said, "We need to celebrate surviving the first year of that," with a gesture toward the city girls.

"I used to celebrate New Year's," said Chick. "Now I'd rather be sound asleep by the time midnight arrives."

"You and me both," Hector agreed. "But my party girl here always likes to start the new year awake."

"You know why. We need to be out with the animals when the fireworks scare them."

"You get fireworks out there?"

Hector told Chick, "You'd think it was the Fourth of July. That farm a ways up the mountain—I don't see any farming going on up there."

Clara interjected, "Maryjane. I bet you dollars to donuts it's maryjane they're farming. That's what they call it, you know."

Chick was afraid she'd burst out laughing. These were good people, Clara and Hector, but stuck in the days of *Reefer Madness*.

The darker, shorter city girl was inspecting the little goddess figurine in her hand. The fidgeter in the cap rolled a cold bottle of ginger beer between her hands as if she'd burned them. Chick couldn't tolerate their discomfort and wended her way to them, smiling when she noticed the way the fidgety woman was checking out her skirt-switching walk. It was how the women in Chick's family all walked, and she'd never regretted the attention it drew. She'd tested the mettle of a hundred butches by noting how frankly they watched her fat and provocative approach. She'd chosen a few lovers for their honest admiration.

"You two are a sight for sore eyes," she said with her gurgle of a laugh, her mother's laugh.

The woman who'd complained about the step had a hank of shoe-polish black hair overhanging the left side of miniscule sunglasses. She was the color of a tanned white person or maybe someone from Mexico. Her gaze was direct and challenging, yet her lips seemed set in an almost-smile that promised—Chick couldn't tell what, just that they promised. She wore a black turtleneck, a short black leather jacket, black slacks, and black thick-soled Doc Martens.

She stabbed toward the chocolate cookies with a slender finger. "Some of those." In answer to Chick's appraising look she added, "Please."

Chick eased a box of pastry papers toward them, and, with a finger tipped in glossy red nail polish, she slowly tapped the box, purring, "Help yourselves. Donny just baked them. Tuesday's cookie day."

"We'll remember that." The fidgeter set down the ginger beer and took off her cap to run her hands through her cropped hair again. She was dressed in over-sized cargo pants and a long-sleeved T-shirt emblazoned with a Day-Glo green kangaroo on a skateboard. She gave Chick an endearingly bashful grin as she reached to the post at the end of the bakery case and lifted a matching Day-Glo green Natural Woman Foods baseball cap from a display. She molded the brim until it was shaped like her other hat, then set it on her head and met Chick's eyes.

"Oh," Chick said. The blue of the woman's eyes seemed to leap out at her. Chick savored again the innocent surprise she'd seen earlier in those eyes as she sashayed to the bakery case. They always thought they didn't want a fat woman; Chick liked to change their minds. She'd begun making her own clothes long before plus sizes, when she was that rare creature, a lesbian flower-child in Chicago, then in San Francisco. She loved silken midnight blues, velvety deep greens, gauzy cottons wild with oversized flowers. She loved to see the look that came into her Donny's eyes at the sight of them.

She settled her cushiony bottom on the upholstered stool by the cash register and, trying to cool the excitement in her voice a little, asked, "You will be staying around here, won't you?"

Shoe-polish hair hesitated for a split second, then gave Chick a sudden brilliant, white-toothed smile that changed any assumptions she'd been about to make about the woman. Chick felt like she did when, in late afternoons on rainy days, the sun breaks through the clouds. "I'm Katie. This is Jeep."

"You've got good taste in women, Katie. I'm Chick Pulaski." With a laugh she added, "Like the highway. My father always said we owned it and—if we had a car—we could use it anytime we wanted—like everyone else in Chicago."

Jeep sauntered closer to ask, "Could we ask you for—ah—"

But Hector appeared at the counter, fishing through his billfold. "Hey, Chick," he asked, "why would a waiter rather serve six gals from LA bellyaching about Northwest rain than one from Waterfall Falls?"

Chick tried to glower at him. "Don't run these women off with your homemade riddles, Hector. I'd like them to stick around."

"Give a man a chance! Can you guess? It's because he'd get six times as much money!" He winked at Katie and Jeep. The man, thought Chick, would never learn lesbian rules.

"I only laugh because Hector's riddles are so pitiful," Chick told the new women.

Hector did a quick awkward shuffle from the counter and opened the door for three old women—two in Natural Woman Foods baseball caps (one neon yellow, the other neon pink), running shoes, and lined plaid flannel shirts stuffed into overall; the third in a skirt and cardigan sweatshirt embroidered with smiley faces—her hair, underneath a transparent plastic rain scarf, tinted blonde and beauty-parlor coiffed.

"Vivian! Myrtle!" called Clara. "Look at you, Naomi. I can't believe your little grandson's getting married this weekend."

"I need double ginkgo and glucosamine," Naomi explained, throwing wide her arms. "We leave for Coeur d'Alene in the morning."

Clara and her friends all talked at once as they headed for the vitamins via the day-old bakery specials.

"Gawd," Katie said when they were out of earshot. "I have never had so many retired breeders with motorized motels stuck in front of my car than on the trip up from the Bay Area!"

Jeep leaned over the counter and with a low voice said, "Solstice told us to stop here. She said you could give us directions to the women's land?" Laughing, she added, "Do you know how much that sounds like 'the promised land'?"

While the fog dampened the town outside, the smells from the baked goods case saturated the shop with cinnamon and warm honey perfume. Through the window Chick saw Sheriff Sweet, on horseback, ambling down Stage Street. The sheriff lifted her hat to the town councilman who doubled as the town barber and stood outside his shop. The sheriff generally ambled around town once or twice a week to exercise her horse and stay visible. The Chamber of Commerce provided free stabling because the tourists enjoyed this glimpse of the Old West and the shopkeepers appreciated such close monitoring. The sheriff only had one full-time deputy and ran things mainly with reserves. Donny was a proud reserve deputy.

"Who is that?" Katie asked, pushing her sunglasses down her nose. "I would so love to do a piece and call it, 'When the Law is a Lesbian.'"

"Our sheriff. Don't go pulling her covers."

Strangers were a treat, but some brought along a dangerous disdain for local customs. The long-closeted lesbians of Waterfall Falls were only in the past few years timidly mixing with some of the more established dyke immigrants who'd moved there during the early 1970s. During the northwest anti-gay ballot measure wars, the lesbian community had become increasingly visible and the Claras and Hectors had come to a startled acceptance of its members when they realized who their good if odd neighbors of twenty to thirty years really were.

Katie's manner made Chick cautious about giving these girls directions to women's land, but then she remembered that her own habitual come-on ways weren't much different from the sunglasses and haughtiness that were Katie's mask.

"We're lucky enough to have four of them in the county, and three more south of here. You probably want the bigger ones that have camping? That would be Dawn Farm or Spirit Ridge."

"Where Solstice lives," Jeep supplied, jingling her pocket change to excavate a folded slip of paper. "Spirit Ridge," she read.

Chick gave a helpless sweep of her arms. "I don't want to get you sweet visitors lost. The directions are pretty complicated."

Katie pulled pen and pad from a belt pack. "I find places for a living. Give me directions; we'll get there."

"That's city directions, honey. Here, I'd recommend catching up to your neighbors."

"Neighbors?" asked Jeep. "Did you ever think about that? Naybores?"

"It took me a minute," said Chick, laughing. "You're a punster. I guess you could have worse vices. But really, Clara and Hector are wonderful people. They'll lead you home."

Jeep stared at her.

"Don't look at me like I'm offering you as a sacrifice to straight rural America, good-looking," Chick said.

Katie removed her dark glasses altogether, eyes narrowed myopically, naked with alarm. "They know where the women's land is?"

Chick laid her fingers on Jeep's sleeve. "Follow them, honey. If you turn off on a muddy logging road by mistake, I don't think you'd be up for asking directions of some grubby guy killing Port Orford cedars with a chain saw."

"Gross." Jeep slowly pulled her arm away, like Chick's fiery fingertips could melt her bravado. Chick was reminded of Donny's butch arrogance back in Chicago—like Jeep's, only more so.

When Clara came to check out, Chick asked if the visitors could follow her.

"That would be no trouble," Clara said without hesitation. "You stick close behind Mr. White and me, girls. We're in the brown pickup with the volunteer fire sticker on the bumper. We'll let you know where to turn to head up the mountain. It'll be Northeast Blackberry Mountain Road you want." She paused and squinted at Katie. "You've got a four-wheel drive and heavy-duty windshield wipers, don't you?"

"Heavy-duty?" Jeep asked.

"You won't be on any super highway," Clara warned.

Katie took Jeep's arm. "We're going to be okay. My little Honda can do anything."

"I hope you're right," huffed Clara. "You could sit for a week on one of those gravel roads before someone came by. Or longer if you slide off into a canyon."

After Clara left, Chick filled a bag with the blue corn chips, the goddess figure, the chocolate cookies, and two organic sodas. She told the newcomers, "Clara's one of those doom and gloom people. You'll want to drive carefully, but we've been going up to Spirit Ridge for years in Donny's little pickup."

She was about to make change when Jeep said, "Wait!" and asked Katie, "Should we bring real food? I mean, they may eat weird stuff like tofu and brown rice."

Chick watched their quandary.

"I don't think we can ask those people if we can stop for McDonalds on the way," said Katie.

"There isn't one," Chick told them, laughing.

"You're shitting me, right?" Jeep asked.

Chick shook her head. "And the women on the mountain are every last one vegetarian, some more strict than others. You could bring some Gardenburgers up with you."

"Retch," said Katie. "Sorry, I don't do frozen compost." She grabbed two boxes of macaroni and cheese from a display at the end of the counter. "We won't starve."

A horn sounded outside. "I think that's your pilot car."

Katie and Jeep hurried across the old wood floor in their heavy shoes. Katie carefully maneuvered the step. Jeep, trying to open the bag of chips, stumbled up the step. She turned and gave them that embarrassed grin again. This time Chick noticed the dimple it put in her cheek.

She watched through a window as the city girls clambered into the Honda—insolent with bumper stickers—then took off after the rusted-out pickup. She gurgled a laugh again and felt an expanding warmth in her chest. It was good Donny wasn't the jealous type, the way she fell in love with every butchy new lesbian in town. Within moments, though, she felt her excitement fade and the familiar melancholy start to gather inside her chest like rolling San Francisco fog.

Goddess, she hated this. She was so content here with Donny. Her life had finally come together like a story with a happy ending. Why did the dim moods, another family trait, return each winter? She used to fix herself by getting high, but marijuana had turned against her years ago, filling her with ugly fears instead of peace. Now she got high on the little joys of life, like the appearance of a couple of new girls in town.

She forced laughter and said aloud, "I hope they're not too cool to thank the Whites."

Donny, who with her dog Loopy had been perched high up in the shadows of the narrow stairway to their apartment for some time, said, "Gayfeathers. It'll be a while before they remember their manners."

Chick laughed again and walked to the stairs. On her haunches, Donny scuttled down a few steps. Chick reached under the rail for Donny's hand. She remembered how Donny had nurtured some gayfeather plants all the way from a community garden in Chicago. A gathering of them thrived in their little plot out back of the store, nodding their flowers at the slightest summer breeze, like wild purple flags of encouragement. Donny had taken to calling gay newcomers to Waterfall Falls "gayfeathers." She squeezed Donny's cool hand in her own.

"Those two remind me of us when we first came," Donny said. "We thought we wanted to be country too. Remember when we found out that we got only two snowy TV channels and there was no Chinese restaurant up the street? They may go running to Clara and Hector to get rescued once they find out they're going to have to cook that mac and cheese on a woodstove."

"Or not," Chick said, moving back behind the checkout counter to slide onto her stool and pull an order book out from under a stack of recycled paper bags. "Neither of these gayfeathers looks like she'll scare off easy."

"Maybe," Donny conceded. "But I wouldn't look for them to stick it out side by side."

"I guess we'll see, honeybunch."

CHAPTER TWO

Goddess Country

R's fingers were so long, so quick on the drum that they, not the bonfire, seemed to spark. Her long earrings caught the light and drew Katie's eyes. She was aware of a half dozen women in the shadows, women who lived on the land and swayed, hummed, or beat smaller drums to R's rhythm, shifting with the stinging smoke, fragrant with sage that had been dropped on the fire, the only light in the damp nighttime woods. Chick from the store was there too, drumming, sweating by the fire.

"Not our cool Katie," mocked R.

Katie had carefully constructed her image. It brought beaucoup dinero on the local TV stations where she'd worked for the last eight years, starting with an internship while she was a senior in college. To tone down her off-camera, driven energy, she'd adopted a sexy slouch that telegraphed both indifference and allure. But her hair, which was severely parted and fell in a short stark black frame around her glasses, was the real knife-edge Katie. Except for giving up the on-camera contact lenses, she'd kept her Katie-self intact these three months of living here with Jeep, and she'd been ready to flee back to the Gen X scene any time. But around R, this magnificent matriarch who seemed to define not only Spirit Ridge but women's spirituality—meltdown.

Sweaty and shivering, dazed by the firelight, she stumbled on roots and rocks, following as R glided into the quiet piney night. She could still turn back. "She wants more than your nubile bod, Kate-o," Jeep had warned. "She wants your soul." Katie hadn't exactly told Jeep that she wanted R, but Jeep had guessed right.

She squatted near R. As they peed, a bullfrog harrumphed in the woods. The night was chill and she pulled her jeans up quickly. Rain gathered into large drops in the trees above and dropped to the forest floor around them. R's smile was serene. Something about that serenity agitated Katie—because she wanted it? Because she was scared of it? Because she feared it was a mask?

Inside her yurt, R fed the small woodstove with deliberate, flowing movements.

Katie spoke to quiet her yearning silence. "You're a really hot drummer." The wood snapped as it caught. Its heat did nothing for her shivering.

"Hot buns!" shrieked Toto, the brilliant blue, yellow, and scarlet macaw that R had taken in when its gay male owner died.

Katie had never seen R embarrassed before. "Don't be offended. He's a very loving creature, but otherwise typically male." R broke up a rice cake. Toto sidled onto R's shoulder, rubbed cheeks with her, and took the snack in his foot. "My drum is another voice. Before I found my lesbian self and began drumming, everyone told me I had no ear. They were right. Patriarchal music is noise to me."

Jeep wouldn't recognize Katie. She'd say she'd morphed into a clueless chick, frantic with desire, reading off some alien teleprompter. Katie was feeling for a new language and finally sensed what Jeep's fumbling beneath the surface of language was all about. The words she tried on felt clumsy. "I could see your spirit dancing over the bonfire."

R seemed to accept this as homage due. "I wondered if she'd dance for you. She's very ancient."

"How old are you?" Katie asked. R's earlobes looked like they were permanently elongated from the heavy earrings she wore.

R hesitated just enough that Katie knew she'd stepped over a boundary. Even the community's nickname for R, Rattlesnake, belonged to a creature whose first line of defense was a courteous warning. But it was hard to stop asking, asking, asking questions. She'd always been like that, even before asking questions became a career. If you had all the answers there were never surprises.

R held her hands up to the woodstove, turned them this way and that, reaching out. Katie felt pulled into her force field. R reached over and removed Katie's glasses and set them out of reach. "You don't need these."

Instantly Katie was a scrawny light brown girl again, with the still, expressionless posture of an invisible child. Her shivering was deep inside. The year she'd started school, her father hadn't come back from Mexico. She'd secretly memorized the eye chart because she didn't think her gringa mother could afford glasses. The blurred teachers never knew what to make of the Delgado girl—so bright, so slow, so creative, so secretive.

"What brought you to Spirit Ridge?" R asked while Toto gently groomed her hair with his formidable beak.

Katie took her time answering. First, when she heard about the new school shooting in Santee, California, this month she'd felt such relief that she didn't have to go down there and cover it. School shootings really got to her. But what had brought her here? She remembered once, when she was very small, going down to Mexico to see her dad's family. The Virgin Mary statue and the candles impressed her and she'd been fascinated by her old, old great-grandmother's ceaselessly clicking rosary beads. She'd wanted some of her own. The memory glowed like some sacred journey she'd taken, perhaps an initiation rite. The two Sundays they were there, she'd gone with the grandmothers and all her cousins to a small country chapel. It was white-hot, and the holy water her grandmother sprinkled on her at the door was a cool benediction.

"I've been living lies since day one. School was this I'm-just-like-the-white-girls trip. What was I thinking? I lived in a lousy trailer park! TV land is all hype—sound bites, putting a spin on reality, packaging tragedy to entertain. Being nice to boys even when they treat me like a hooker on retainer. I learned to do all that real young."

"What a horrid way to live."

Bull's-eye. She'd finally found someone who thought like her. She needed a moral compass to point her way or her ambition would take her over—or was she only about ambition? "I first started looking at Oregon as a story because I saw that a cottage industry had been created around ballot measures—homophobes were supporting their families by fundraising from people's fears. It's the women who'll save the planet, you know." Even on the land, in this hiatus from the fast lane, her enthusiasm came roaring over her like the flames consuming the kindling in the woodstove. "In the name of Christianity a handful of gluttonous people were calling for ridiculous laws and taking gay rights and abortion as platforms because they knew these would get people going. Why wasn't anyone talking about this? These men were using a religion that grew out of love and celebration to make money off of hate." R added a small log. "They were arsonists—starting fires of hate. When sacrificing gay people and pregnant women stopped bringing in enough money they threw in taxes and anti-government initiatives. It was so clear to me! I wanted to tell the story and debunk the whole operation."

"Men have perverted spirituality for all of history to get power and money."

"Well, duh, I started to see that. And people like me have been exposing them at their stupid hate tricks just as long. But it'll never stop. I could never uncover all the wrongs. We just hit a new century and everything was the same and I wasn't going to change anything with a story or by being a national TV news anchor. All of a sudden I was dead in the water."

"Many women return to the land to escape something."

"It's not about escape for me, R."

"Oh?"

"I've been intimate with the evil that men do out there—crime and criminals, political deals, natural disasters, abuse of kids, animals, women. It's numbing. It's been corrupting my sense of purpose. I need some moral grounding because I don't think I ever had a personal sense of what's right and wrong for me. And that's something you need in my business." It frightened her to even think it, but she said, "If it's still my business. I'm thinking I don't have what it takes."

"Or you have too much."

"Meaning?"

"Don't they call newscasters 'talking heads'? Implying empty heads? Surely you can do better than that."

Did R really believe she could do better? "Some of them primp and read the prompters, but I know fine investigative reporters who also read news into the cameras. Don't believe everything you hear, R."

"I know only one investigative reporter whose personal ethics and spiritual journey have led her to Goddess country. That doesn't recommend the group to me as a whole."

Katie wanted to run out and find a few more to prove there were good people in the broadcast field. Why did she feel she had to apologize for her profession to this woman? "Goddess country. I like that. I need to write it down." She fumbled in her jacket pocket for the packet of index cards she carried. "I really have to get out of this habit of taking notes on everything. It's a compulsion."

"Or your work." Was R condemning her again or was there a note of admiration in her voice?

"I can't live so compromised any more, R," she said, wondering if she wanted too much.

"Do you think you've found a place without compromises here?"

She wasn't that stupid, but she wanted to believe it. "Haven't I? Look at you. No men in your life, living on your own terms, at a subsistence level maybe, but tell me you're not independent. And here, the word goddess has nothing to do with sex goddesses. I need to be in your Goddess country, to breathe in the air of this free place, to know free women. You're not about money and power and fame. You're about getting away from all that."

"I'm honored that you include me in such idealized company."

Katie felt like a little kid again. "Am I idealizing? That's what I see. You're a beautiful, strong, and free woman." She was sounding like R again. Didn't she have a language of her own?

R bowed her head. "Thank you. I honor your courage in leaving work you no longer believe in."

"This is strange, but I love it when you talk like that, all formal."

Toto screeched, "Talk dirty, talk dirty!"

R kissed his gaudy head and put him in his cage. "My heart speaks."

"At first I thought you were way corny, but feel." She dared press R's hand against her pounding heart. "I think it's because I actually found someone on this planet who's comfortable inside her own skin."

R's eyes were both powerful and placid. "I only know how to listen to…" She opened her arms as if to include the universe.

"The factory I came out of forgot to give me those instructions."

"Do you really think so poorly of yourself? I see a self-possessed woman. A woman who watches. That's what attracts me to you." With no warning, R pulled off her sweater and the white thermal underwear she wore, then pressed Katie's hand against her bare breast and drumming heart.

"You're awesome," said Katie, lips not quite touching R's. She began to shiver again, but she felt flushed from head to toe. This woman, this woman. Was it love she felt for her or greed for what R was?

R's face and breasts glowed in the firelight. "I can't give you anything you don't have."

"I have nothing of value. I'm a bottomless pit." She sounded like R again, but she did feel empty, dizzy with possibility and self-doubt. She wanted the woman's quiet power, and she wanted to be rid of her own chatter and constant motion. She wanted to change the disk from Nine Inch Nails to goddess chants. The rational Katie knew no one could do this for her, but for once in her life she refused to listen.

R dropped their hands. Was that firelight in her eyes or anger? "And you want me to fill you up."

"No, I don't."

"Oh yes you do."

Light-headed with desire, Katie groped her way behind R up the narrow wooden ladder to the sleeping loft. She drank R in like water. She couldn't make her hands stay still, couldn't keep her whole thirsty being from this great oasis. Was this sex or some sort of worship? Maybe there was something to the term *sex goddess*.

"You're so cold," she told R under the pile of musty-smelling covers. "Let me give you my heat."

R took it.

CHAPTER THREE

Getting Up Again

"This sucks. You know that, don't you?" Jeep said, slapping a piece of firewood on the two cords she'd already stacked. Sweat ran into her eyes and tickled her rib cage, and her hands prickled with the wave of heat that traveled to them when she was upset.

Katie, in her ice-queen mode, sat on the top porch step, out of the incessant drizzle. She blew the long hank of black hair out of her eyes. "Truth? It's not like we said forever, Jeepers."

No, they hadn't, but wasn't that why you got together with someone, to start your forever? Jeep couldn't say her heart was broken. It was kind of like she felt stripped of who she thought she was, stripped of purpose and focus. She was lost in space.

After nearly three months on women's land, Katie had finally agreed to move out of their tent to town, and Jeep had put the last of her savings on her half of the firewood and rent for this moldy oldie mill cottage. What could she find in town that was cheaper now that she was alone? She didn't even have enough for a Greyhound out. If only her old tin can Chevy hadn't died back in Reno. She slammed another log onto the pile.

Katie cried, "Look out!"

The woodpile wobbled, then pitched over.

Jeep jumped, but took one on her right foot. With her back to Katie, she squeezed her eyes shut until she could balance without screaming in pain. It wasn't a hand, it wasn't a hand, she chanted, small comfort though it was.

Through tearing eyes she saw Sheriff Sweet patrolling on her horse. "Get it over with, Katie," she managed to say through clenched teeth.

Katie obliged. "I have to do this, Jeepers. It's not the sex. You and I were great in bed. And nobody's ever made me laugh like you do. But R puts me in touch with my spiritual side."

The thought that Katie didn't want her any more had Jeep on the edge of howling in protest and begging her to stay. "This is completely cheesy," she said instead. "Spirit stuff goes here." She held out one hand, palm up, and then the other. "And sex and laughing go here?"

But Katie wasn't listening. Her eyes were following the sheriff, and Jeep could hear her thinking, "That sheriff's hot." Now she felt rage. Katie had never stopped cruising women in all the months they'd been together. Jeep had thought it was a game; now she knew better. "Go genuflect to her genitals then."

Katie picked the wrong moment to ask, "Are you going to be all right?"

"Just *go!*"

And she did. Super cool, super sexy, killer fun Katie Delgado, who'd rescued her from terminal loneliness and sleazy Sami. With that girly swivel in her walk that always made Jeep want to do something outrageous, like grab her ass, she went quickly to her red Honda. Her Katie, who'd thanked Jeep for being nuts enough to run off with her and help her get off the media merry-go-round.

A few months ago, after they'd bummed around the West and Midwest so Katie could go on interviews at a few TV stations and get disgusted with their corporate mentality, they'd headed to women's land in Waterfall Falls to visit Jeep's old music shop customer, Solstice. They'd both been seduced by the clean air and back-to-basics way of life. She hadn't imagined that there could be a life without Eminem's lyrics assaulting her ears everywhere she went. Being away from m.e.n., period. Katie's stuff was still in storage in the Bay Area, locked up. Now Katie had locked herself up too, driving off to Spirit Ridge with the few belongings she'd had in the rental. Driving off to R—who actually liked being called Rattlesnake behind her back. R, with her drumming and her coiled gray hair, who wore inner peace like a sexy nightgown yet could lash out like her deadly namesake.

Her non-stop tears felt like the fabled winter rains they'd endured in a tent that first month. She hobbled through the mud in the backyard to resurrect the fallen logs, but the pain in her foot made her gasp. Why bother? Why stay in this dyke Siberia with the crunchy granola set where a gay film fest meant *Mrs. Doubtfire* at the drive-in forty winding miles away and she got to play fiddle before no brighter lights than a campfire? Why bother moving away, for that matter? She'd still be Katie-less.

Jeep eased herself into a seated position on the back steps and took out of a back pocket the small harmonica she'd had since before she'd even started taking violin lessons. She played a wistful tune that sounded to her like the whistle of a train headed out of Reno into the desert. God, she'd hated the grimly hot desert. So had Sarah.

Hot or no, she was thinking she'd been better off back in Reno where every day after work she'd race Sarah across the hot, dry parking lot of their apartment complex into the dingy courtyard tiled in orange and aqua. Their mailbox had been layered with the residue of decades of gummed labels that had come before their own: G.P. Morgan and S. Teitel.

Nestled in the junk mail and bills one day was the white envelope she'd been waiting for.

"Is this the scoop?" Sarah had asked in a whisper. "Finally?"

At their door, Jeep gave her the keys and said, "My hands are shaking. I haven't been this scared spitless since—remember when my roommate decided to skip class and walked in on us with our blouses undone?" She watched a stray dust mote drift by. "What a weird word, 'blouse.' It sounds like what it covers—round, round, round, you know?"

Sarah laughed as she swung open the door. "That was as far as we'd ever gone—open blouses. I had no clue how much more we'd do!"

The late afternoon sun shone in a wide sheet across their scuffed hardwood floor. Sarah moved through the light, long silver earrings flashing, and Jeep thought she'd never seen anyone lovelier. So what if she wasn't invited to audition for the Reno Philharmonic? She had Sarah, sunshine, her violin. Her fiddle! If this letter didn't take her along the flight path she and Sarah had planned, then a fiddle it would be again. She'd go electric.

"Open it, Jeep."

"This is, kind of like, so heavy." She tore through the envelope with a forefinger, unfolded the light blue Philharmonic stationary, saw the word "sorry," and felt herself sag. She handed the letter to Sarah.

"Oh, my poor Jeep."

"I guess Mr. Beethoven and his cronies will have to get along without me."

A sideways smile lifted Sarah's grand crown of brown curls. "These people are a bunch of snoots, Jeep. I don't understand why they won't even listen to you."

"They probably heard how totally lame I was at the one audition I did get."

"You were nervous."

"Does this mean we have to move to Idaho?" Jeep asked. With no more prospects in the city, Sarah had been lobbying to return. "It's too cold there."

"Desert rat! It's deliciously chilly." Sarah hugged herself as if she could feel the mountain air. "Since you never see your family even though they're right here, my family would love to have us nearby. I'm not sure I could take living that close to them." She looked thoughtful. "No, I love the mountains and the country, but that's no place for a lesbian to live. I had to come to school in Nevada to find out I love women—and you."

Sarah's parents were college-degreed old hippies who'd gone back to the land, but left organic farming to open a family counseling practice in their home. Now her dad headed up the county mental health program, and her mom had become the discharge planner at the medical center. She'd told Jeep that they'd farmed, canned, built their own house, and made their own clothes long enough to give Sarah a taste for the country way of life, and then turned into boring solid citizens. Jeep, when she'd visited them, thought they were pretty affected, hicks who ordered fancy coffee by mail and covered their coffee table with Robert Maplethorpe and Ansel Adams books. Their CD player filled their ranch house with Tibetan monks on bells and aboriginals on dijideroos. Sarah was into the home arts in a major way, but kept trying to fit into big city life. That she wasn't quite sophisticated enough for Reno told the whole story, Jeep thought.

"I wouldn't fight landing someplace less like a frying pan than Reno, but your family thinks I'm a no-talent after I blew the audition they finessed for me over there. I really let them down. And there's no good old-time music in Idaho."

"Old-time music? I thought you decided that was tatty antique music, Jeep. You haven't played any in ages."

Jeep felt a sulky look take over her face. Sarah hated the thought of her going on tour, which she might have to if she was playing old-time music. So Jeep had been concentrating on music she could play for a living in Reno. "You're so freakin' certain I'll find a way to do what I love close to home, but who has time to hold down a job, try to break into the straight music scene, and play what I love?"

Sarah looked hurt. "I didn't know you were so unhappy, Jeep. Maybe we should consider Idaho. If we lived in the mountains you'd find an old-time music audience. You could give lessons and make money buying and selling instruments on line. And doing repair work—you said your father taught you a lot. And for once my family came through when I asked them to support you too. Didn't they all go to hear you, Jeep—Mom, Dad, my grandmothers, my grandfather, my brother's fiancé? My sister's dumb-as-a-rock boyfriend thought you were great."

"Right. They were here for your graduation. I was in the orchestra."

"But they came to the casino too and thought you were terrific."

"My big three-bar solo? I really thought I'd be showing them my stuff in the symphony next time. It's been eight months and four days since we left Miners' U, and I'm no closer to supporting myself with music."

"You are such a snob, Jeep. You don't need to play classical to be a great musician."

"I thought that was what you wanted me to do."

"It seemed like the best way for you to get what you wanted. And why do you use those put-down names for the U? What's wrong with going to a school with a seismology lab?"

"The Mule Team String Quartet is not exactly the fast track to the top, Sar. Reno's a famous backwater, but it's still a backwater."

"Give me a break, Jeep. Having Julliard or the Berklee College of Music on your résumé wouldn't guarantee you work."

"This town is a closed shop, but it would help. I've tried the opera company—well, you know, I've tried everywhere." She'd tried for too long not to feel discouraged, but what was the use? Why hadn't she been born with a burning desire to be a wife and mother and maybe a cage cashier for a casino? That would have been an easy tune to play in this town. Sarah's family, like hers, said they were okay with her being gay, but were concerned she'd end up old and alone. She could read between those lines. Like men didn't die long before their widows. If that was their reasoning, they should be glad she liked girls. No, she didn't see moving to be with family.

At the coat closet, Sarah pulled out a tangle of wire hangers with an irritating jangle and wrestled to get one free. When they fell, she kicked them inside and slammed the door shut. "Dorky things."

Sarah seldom got rattled like that. "Aw, Sar, I'm being a flake. Reno's not gay Paree, but we've got our privacy—finally. I've got you to myself—finally. We can conquer the world tomorrow." She held her arms open. The word "finally" was a code word for them and always made them laugh and hug, like they'd finally found each other.

Sarah stepped out of her pumps and leaned into Jeep's embrace. Her hair smelled faintly of pear shampoo. Jeep rocked her, saying, "You're so soft. See that little bird out there flitting up and down in the bush? That's how your fingers feel when you touch me."

She kissed Sarah's neck, right in the curve that felt like home. How could she get annoyed at a woman whose skin smelled like fresh bedclothes when you were really really tired? She was looking past her un-trusty old light blue tin can Chevy Spirit hatchback which was barely a vehicle and to the border of the lot, with its hardy shrubbery and newborn leaves. She reached under Sarah's skirt and slid a hand up her thigh, drumming it on the soft, smooth, cool skin below her panties.

"You always say I'm a bird," Sarah accused, voice light again, and pirouetted away from Jeep's hand across the bare wooden floor, her long dark hair lifting off her shoulders.

She loved to touch Sarah. A part of her would be happy to do nothing but touch Sarah and play fiddle for the rest of her life.

"Ouch!" Sarah cried. She held one foot in her hand, balancing, then pulled off her knee-hi nylons.

Jeep moved quickly to help. "I'll sterilize a needle."

"No, prop me up while I get to the chair."

She watched as Sarah pulled a big splinter from her heel. "We could use that rug your mother offered."

"We'll have our own soon," Sarah predicted and limped to the table in the dining nook where her tilted drawing board was kind of a member of the family. On the board lay an unfinished plan of the house Sarah was designing for them to live in when Jeep came into demand as a musician or they won the lottery. Sarah looked from it to the kitchenette at the end of the living room, then took a metal tape and measured the refrigerator.

That, Jeep thought, as she sat two years later on the rotting steps of the house she'd shared with Katie all of, what, maybe a week and a half, was the memory of Sarah that never failed to bring tears to her eyes. She knew the damage she'd done when she betrayed Sarah's innocent trust that they had a future together. Betrayed it even while Sarah tried to fit a rehearsal/music lesson/instrument repair space into that dream of their house. She feared neither of them would ever again trust a dream.

With disgust at herself she burst out of her gloom and stood upright. "Oh, geez!" She'd forgotten her foot. It was her toe, the big one—it hurt like a son of a gun and she couldn't bend it. She gritted her teeth against tears, but they weren't only about her foot and there was no stopping them. *Why isn't there anybody to tell me what to do?* She reached inside the front door to grab her skateboard and hopped off the porch, trying to stem the tears with anger. She slammed the board to the road. Though she was only a block from the main drag, there wasn't even a sidewalk.

She wiped the harmonica with the American flag bandanna she kept in a back pocket and started toward town through a driving drizzle. She was wrung out. The emotions that raced through her at any given moment this week left her feeling like a space wreck. It was awkward, using the skateboard left-footed, but there was no way she could push off with her bunged up right foot. She could feel her toes swell up even on their wooden gurney. She rolled past the sprawling mill. It was an abandoned dusty shadow of itself, the bitter workers competing with her for jobs at the remaining mills, Dairy Queen, and the hardware store.

Maybe she truly was a space wreck. Alone now, with no Katie, no Sami, no Sarah, she was floating outside the atmosphere, a battered, unrecognizable object equipped with a temporary and obstinate consciousness. Someday, without warning or after a long agony, her lights would shut down. *Space junk, that's all I am,* she thought. A cast-off scrap dyke unmoored in a galactic ooze of emptiness.

"Do not forsake me oh my darlin'," she hummed.

She should never have left Sarah. Except—she hadn't known any other way out of Reno and—into life. The five-minute skateboard ride to Natural Woman Foods took fifteen because she had to rest her foot so frequently. She'd wanted to hang out at the store from day one, but it'd been hard without wheels of her own. Since moving to town and catching on to Katie's roving eye, she'd been like some kind of scrap attracted to a magnet, but felt too humiliated to admit Katie had dumped her. Now her need was greater than her shame.

Donny's dog Loopy was in her customary spot outside. She stroked the dog's cowlicked fur, resting so she could lose the limp before she went in, but then focused so hard on looking good that she forgot the old wooden step, tripped through the door and, unable to balance because of her toe, fell, her skateboard flying down the main aisle of the store while her cool shattered into a million shards.

"Yo," she groaned to the long skirt and floppy chinos that hurried her way.

"Honeybunch, this is one of those new city girls. Did I tell you they moved to town?"

She'd forgotten the warm slow voice that flowed from Chick.

Donny, in her overalls, asked, "Don't know how you stood it up at Spirit Ridge so long. Can you get up, kid?"

Jeep cursed herself. Off-key dweeb. "Of course I can. But give me one good reason why I should."

"There might be a customer," Donny said mildly. "At least I *hope* there'll be another customer."

She felt four strong hands lifting her. The door was still open and that silly-looking Loopy was standing, staring at her with what looked like alarm on her face.

"Whatever." Jeep struggled to the wooden stool Donny offered. Donny had skin the color of brown chalk, a non-stop wide delighted smile, seriously short hair, and green eyes that seemed to beam amused love. Oh, mortification. She'd been introduced to the mythic butch Donny in passing the few times they'd come to town, but had never been this close before. It was like meeting a movie star. She'd sort of timed her visits this past week so she'd miss her and get Chick all to herself. Chick made her feel like she could do no wrong.

Now Chick carefully removed Jeep's Doc Marten and handed it to Donny. "About time you came back to see me, dreamboat."

"Ow!"

"Maybe a broken toe. Donny could swing you over to the clinic, but they can't help that toe."

Another wave of weeping threatened and Jeep just managed to whisper, "I don't have insurance anyway." Stop feeling sorry for yourself, asshole, she thought.

"Strap it up with adhesive tape till you can walk on it," Donny suggested.

"It's a good thing you're not still up at Spirit Ridge," Chick said. "You'll need to be icing that foot, and you couldn't exactly freeze anything there."

She didn't even try to swallow her bitterness. "Could we get anything *but* ice at Rancho Rattlesnake? It was so freakin' cold in that tent—that's why we moved to town. Now Katie's headed back to be with that bizarre character. I'm wondering if Katie didn't engineer the move to get rid of me."

"You poor little thing. I don't know how any woman could leave you, you're so cute." Chick pressed Jeep's head against a well-cushioned chest that smelled of clothing dried in fresh air.

Like Sarah, she thought. Life had been so much simpler with Sarah. Maybe I should call her.

Donny asked, "What happened to your buzz cut? Your pierced … everythings?"

Jeep jingled the change in her pocket. "I moved to Style City. If by some miracle there's one decent haircutter here, I can't afford her. And I'm tired of backwoods adolescent boys asking where else I'm pierced."

"The bitch hit on Chick too," Donny complained, but her eyes were kind.

"R? That's sick. Can't she tell the difference between butch and femme?"

Donny looked pleased and reached to squeeze Chick's shoulder. "I think I'm going to like this kid."

Chick laughed her syrupy laugh, leaning into Donny's hand. "Do snakes care who's butch?"

Jeep thought for a moment. "They might."

Chick laughed again. Her face was heart-shaped, with a soft sag under the chin and skin the color of blushing cream-colored blossoms. "She's so serious she's adorable."

Donny grinned. "Welcome to Waterfall Falls. You've become an official native. Dykes move to the country and break up. It's an initiation rite."

"Not you. You two didn't," said Jeep, a little nervous at even the thought that they might. She needed this to know forever could be done.

"When we first got here—" Chick threw a teasing look at Donny and touched her own honey-brown hair which was tied back with a wide black ribbon, "—we were just friends. That's the trick—don't bring a lover with you."

"No? How about if she follows you later?"

"Jeep," Chick said with a smile only in her eyes, "I made that up. Don't worry about it. If you want to import someone go right ahead, but

I want the right to inspect her, interrogate her, and withhold my stamp of approval."

Donny shook her head, smiling. "Of course you do. You're the femme in charge," she said and, first quickly kissing the back of Chick's neck, hefted a sack of beans. The sound of beans rattling into a barrel soon came from the south end of the store.

On the wooden stool Jeep fidgeted, foot throbbing, stomach grumbling at the smell of Donny's homemade pastries. She was fresh out of cash and couldn't buy one. She thought of Sami's exorbitant Starbuck's habit. What the fuck am I still doing in Waterfall Falls? Even now Katie was being seduced by burning sage and mantras. I'm out of here, she vowed. Jeep Morgan and her fiddle could find work somewhere else, where there were twenty women waiting to jump her bones like Lara had.

The door flew open. A small woman with hair short on top, long down the back, in cowboy boots, a blue-checked shirt, a bandanna tied at the neck, and red denim overalls called out, "Wish us luck!"

Her clothes reminded Jeep of the getup she used to wear to play at the roadhouse in Reno. Did women really dress like that here? And how did these locals always manage to look dry? They seldom wore rain gear.

"Make 'em dance till they drop, babe!" shouted Donny through the store. Chick lifted the crystal around her neck and blew a kiss through it.

Through the side window Jeep could see a van load of women pull onto Stage Street. Loopy watched after them too. Jeep liked the look of the old yellow bus, lavender guitars painted on its sides.

"That's Muriel with Imagine My Surprise, the old-time music band," explained Chick.

Donny said, "They advertise to the straights as Surprise, but we know what the surprise is."

"They won't play without our blessing. Today they audition for Senorita's, the only place in town with live music."

Jeep stared after the truck. "An old-time music band?"

"They call themselves a banjo blues band," said Donny, "but I think they're a wannabe blues band. They're more into that old-timey white stuff."

"Incredible. You mean there's a whole other layer of dykes around here?"

Donny's eyes were full of laughter. "Another? Every time I try to figure out how many I lose count, and I've been around eight years. Help me here, Chick. There's the land women, the music crowd—"

"The softball players and the artists and writers."

"The professionals—"

"The wannabe teachers and financial planners and social worker types—"

"The blue collar dykes who pump gas and paint houses—"

"The druggies—"

"And there's always some overlap, like lesbian welfare moms who write poetry and hang with the jocks."

Chick managed to curl herself inside Donny's shoulder. "Don't forget the small business women."

"That would be us."

"In this little hole in the mountains?" asked Jeep. They had to be putting her on.

Donny startled her. "You need a lift home, kid? You're still sopping wet from skating over here. Come on, we'll take a ride and I'll show you where—and how—some of the dykes live along the way." She turned to Chick. "You don't need me for a while, do you, babe?"

"Home?" Jeep was saying, confused. "I never thought of Waterfall Falls as home." She had a vision of a small storm of space junk, all the scrap dykes coming together, clang, clang, clang, and settling in to orbit this silly little town. "Would you show me where that women's band plays?"

CHAPTER FOUR

Breakdown

Donny kicked the damn truck. The last thing she wanted to do on this hot fall day was walk up this particular driveway in this particular county and ask this particular jive white man for help. Where was her diplomatic Chick when she needed her?

The rain had dried up for a few days, so she'd taken Jeep fishing at dawn and was heading back to Natural Woman Foods when the truck died. She and Jeep had taken up fishing soon after the breakup with Katie. Fishing was her therapy and she'd thought it might help the kid, who acted so lost. Hell, maybe Jeep would be better off going back where she came from, but Chick acted like the kid was her firstborn, so Donny had set out to bust up Jeep's melancholy. It had paid off. When the sheriff wasn't available to go with her out to Sweet Creek, which was most of the time, Jeep made a tolerable fishing companion even if she did throw back what she couldn't eat.

The road was on an incline here, with shoulders eroded from runoff. The best they could do was to coast into a driveway.

"You want me to come with you?" Jeep asked her.

She laughed aloud. "'Cause you're a white girl? A crew-cut city dyke in a leather jacket isn't going to hack it. Maybe I look like a backwoods drag king, and maybe I've been butting heads with Mr. Homo Phobe for years, but at least he knows this enemy. He might shoot you on sight."

Jeep looked worried. "So he's like, one of those militia crazies?"

"He's one of the fools messing with this anti-gay shit around here. You know what bumper sticker I want? 'I Don't Brake for Bigots.'"

Donny grabbed the lavender bandanna from her back pocket—she owned seven plus a purple for dress up—and kneeled to rub a new scuff mark off the white-tooled violet boots a local shoemaker custom made for her little feet. Donny still owed him another year of birthday cakes for his entire family.

"I thought your ballot measures were ancient history?"

"Not to me they're not. Or to this guy." She let a panting Loopy out of the cab on her leash and led her to a patch of scrub for a quick pee. "Every big election there's some bullshit to fight. We almost always win, in the courts at least, but these organizers got the taste for power. They send out mailings and make appearances in little towns like Waterfall Falls to stir up the angry laid-off mill workers and the retired California Republicans like these jerks who think they've found white het paradise in the Northwest. The purses and wallets open up, and cash falls out to do the Lord's work. Well, if that isn't an insult to the Lord, acting like He can't do his own work, it's an insult to be saying He made a mistake by inventing queers in the first place." She peered along the road in both directions. *Was this a damn hot flash coming on?* She hated the things, but not as much as she'd hated her monthlies. "Where are the logging trucks with the CBs when we could use one? Come on, Loopy, get in the truck."

"You don't carry a cell phone?"

"What am I going to do with a cell phone—lug it everywhere in case I break down once a year? I'm not on the internet either, and I can't be bothering to learn to operate Chick's remote control. I'd rather walk across the room to change the channel or, better still, read a good western novel."

"You read westerns? Zane Grey? Bill Crider?"

"I'll take any of them. If I lived in the olden times, I would have been the first black lesbian sharpshooter in the West." She took a gunfighter stance, pulled invisible six-shooters from holsters at her hips and spun them, shot each toward the sky while she made popping sounds with her lips, blew smoke from the barrels, and slid them back into the holsters.

"Oh my god, oh my god! Aren't you the notorious Donny Derringer?"

"None other, my good woman. How can I be of service to you?"

Jeep swiveled her baseball cap forward and shaded her eyes from the sun with its brim, then brought an imaginary fiddle up to her chin. She sang,

> *"There was a villain in Waterfall town,*
> *Puttin' all the gay folk down."*

Donny stomped one foot to keep the beat.

"The faggots and the dykes all lived in terror
Till out of the sunset appeared Donny Derringer!
Bigots, they ride over Waterfall Pass,
And here comes Donny to kick some ass!"

Donny hooted with laughter, and Jeep joined in with her unexpected hee-haw of a laugh. Loopy, excited by the sounds, balanced on the edge of the truck bed as if hopeful that someone might be calling her.

"You're a keeper, kid," Donny said. "We're going to have to find a way to tempt you to stay around." She held up a hand. "Car coming."

Jeep's worried look returned. A shiny black Blazer cruised into view around the bend from town. He already had his blinker on to turn into his driveway—the driveway Donny blocked.

She sneezed from the road dust. "Looks like we caught us the big one. Mr. Homo Phobe himself. Whatever it takes, we have to get going. It's delivery day. Without me at the store when the grocery truck gets there, Chick's a one-woman show. You keep a low profile and let me handle this."

"No problemo. Is he going to get, like violently mad that we're in his driveway?"

"He's mad that we're alive and breathing his air. Damn, I wish I knew something about cars. I never had one in the city or I'd out-mechanic any ten lazy-ass men."

John Johnson advanced on them chewing a toothpick and adjusting his Exxon cap. He was a big bent-forward hulk with white hairy shelves for eyebrows, nostrils and ears frothing with surly white hair. He'd sold his gas stations in southern California and built this showy retirement home right near her favorite fishing spot on Sweet Creek.

"What's the trouble now, Donalds?" Johnson asked in an irritated tone, eyes traveling from her purple cowboy hat to her black Henley and faded overalls, to her boots.

She wondered what the big deal was—she always dressed the same. Long ago she'd decided if she was going to be about the only black person in town, she'd do it in style. A few years after her arrival, the most radical of the high school girls took to wearing bright leather boots and fringed vests. Now such outfits were a common sight in town, and she'd noticed a postcard at the Thriftway Market of a horsewoman wearing Donny drag. A white woman, of course. Although she was nervous around horses and had no more fondness for cows, she liked to think of herself as a cowdyke.

Fists on hips, too aware that while he was older, she was half his bulk, she glanced at her raggedy red Datsun pickup, its hood gaping open in what would be clear to the stupidest man on earth was a gasp for help. "I could use a phone."

He adjusted neatly pressed work pants under his hanging belly. "We can use my bag phone. You want a tow truck?"

"Like I'm made of money. I was going to call a friend," she said, thinking she'd ask Chick to look up Hector White's number. She pulled off her hat and gave it a punch. Chick would be able to suggest something.

Johnson glanced toward the Datsun's tailgate where Jeep sat, one arm around the dog, as still as the nine-mile marker across the road, her eyes comically big. "You girls check the battery?" he asked with sour-faced contempt. "If that is a girl you're with. I can't tell with you people."

She ignored his baiting. "The battery's charged."

A big mocking grin spread across his face. "Anything in your tank?"

Back in Chicago Donny and the gals she ran with would have torn off his head. "Full up," she said.

She didn't know whether he was condescending to her as a woman, as a person of color, or as a dyke and decided that her color would put her at the bottom in his world. This set off all the usual alarms in her and she felt her blood heat up. She was angry at the racist white world, and she knew she would always be angry at the racist white world. How dare they think they were better than her because of an accident of color? Yet even as that old tape played in her mind, she knew she had to get into doing something about this instant rage, even if it meant changing herself inch by inch, because she took it out on people she loved when the anger had nowhere else to go. When it did have someplace to go, like at this critter, there was no longer a gang and she wasn't in Chicago. Her head-tearing-off days were over. She tore up nothing but herself.

She could see Johnson wrestle with his bad old self too. His foot was tapping like she was some cockroach he itched to squash, but these boys, they liked to show off. He'd owned gas stations—he knew something about cars.

"I'll take a gander at her," he announced.

"Twist my arm," she said and smacked her hat back on her head.

A mud-spattered two-ton pickup sped past with a bearded long-hair at the wheel. Sheriff Sweet was on his tail in her cruiser, red roof light blinking, but Donny saw her take note of their little tableau on the way by. The sheriff would circle back to see what was going on, but who knew how long that would take. Once Sheriff Sweet was in pursuit, she was In Pursuit and nothing much would take her attention away. Donny imagined the sheriff felt like she had to prove herself with every incident—prove that a woman could do the job as well as it could be done. Loopy let loose a series of low hoarse barks. She heard the sheriff whoop her siren once in the distance.

Jeep gave Donny a smart-ass look as Johnson bent his big be-hind to peer under the hood. "Maybe," Jeep called to her, "I should hitch a ride to work?"

Johnson straightened. "You stay put, little lady. Hitching's a damn stupid thing to do with all the weirdos around here."

Donny guffawed. "Say what?"

Johnson glared. "There's weirdos and then there's weirdos. She may be one of your kind, but she's still some mother's daughter."

Loopy was straining at her leash and whimpering in the back of the truck. Donny knew better than to let this fool get her going and tried to summon up Chick to calm her down, but she couldn't stop herself. "We're every one of us somebody's child, Johnson. Why don't you treat us all with that kind of decency?"

His jawline looked like it had turned to stone, leaving his lower lip jutting aggressively and foolishly out. She had him. He'd treated one queer like a human being for one second, and she'd caught him at it. She felt like she'd grown a foot in height.

His eyes backed away from hers and he muttered, "I never said to go out and kill homos."

"No?" Donny jabbed back. "Whose talk stirs up the sickos?"

"You people bring it on yourselves."

Don't jump all over his case, be gracious, Chick would say. *He's going to fix your truck, and he knows he showed himself up.* Chick would never advise going in for the kill, although if there was any joy in these exchanges that would be it. "Not your fault our store window got smashed the night you lost the vote on your anti-gay ballot measure? Not your fault somebody tore up Clara and Hector's garden for backing us? You're innocent as a newborn when you say people are going to get AIDS at Natural Woman Foods?"

His hand was a fist, twisting back and forth against his other, open palm. "It's plain wrong what you people do," he said and turned to prod the truck.

Her voice was sounding tinny to her, like it did when rage took her over. "It's nobody's business but our own what we do and you know it!"

She jumped when Jeep touched her elbow. "Chill, Donny. Delivery day, remember?"

Johnson held up a hose. "Here's your problem, girls," he crowed.

She'd been about to light into Jeep. Damn, this temper would drive away everyone yet. "Say what? I just put in new hoses!"

Johnson smirked. He was top dog again. "Like I've been saying, you don't have the right equipment." He paused. "Here, you need a clamp to hold this on. Reach me some duct tape from the back of my Blazer."

"I carry my own. And I guess I can manage the tape job, thank you."

He ambled away while she stomped to the toolbox in the bed of her truck and clanked through her rusty screwdriver collection to fish out the tape. *Why hadn't she spotted the loose hose and saved all this trouble? Goddamn if her mind wasn't going down the tubes.* Sweat beaded on her forehead and dripped onto the motor. *She needed the deodorant stone pretty badly. The damn flashes always came at the wrong time. She wanted to take off her hot vest, but it covered the fact that she didn't wear a bra. It was none of this lowlife's business that at this age she was too big to go without one. Damn body made her feel soft as her grandma, though come to think of it Grandma Donalds had a fighting spirit. Till the day she died of the sugar she chased junkies, gang boys, and drug dealers out of the store with a broom.* Donny had to stop herself from chuckling at the memory.

She hated to owe the man—and Chick would have her head for making things worse. *Breathe,* Chick would tell her. She added a skirting of tape around her first seal and signaled Jeep, who gave a cheer as the truck started right up. Johnson, leaning on his Blazer, arms folded, looked smug.

Relief replaced anger. "Thank you," she told the man, which should have been enough. Why couldn't she leave it alone? "Duct tape," she laughed. "Think we could mend this little town with duct tape?"

He started jiggling his foot again. "It's not the *town* that needs mending."

Donny wiped her hands on her lavender bandanna over and over, looking toward the heavens for gumption without anger, because she knew she was nothing but a coward unless she was spitting mad. "Tell you what." She dredged up words from some deep pocket of hope, maybe channeling Chick. "I appreciate your help. You and the little woman stop by the store for some of the best coffee and pastries you ever tasted. On the house."

His eyes said, "That'll be a cold day in hell." As she drove away he got smaller in her rearview mirror, but he never budged.

CHAPTER FIVE

The Last Forever

I admired Donny for months before she'd even notice me,"
Chick said, ladling thick rosemary-scented pea soup into
flower-patterned bowls. She kissed Donny's head as she passed her a
steaming bowl.

She was with Donny and Jeep in the huge kitchen upstairs from
Natural Woman Foods where daily Donny baked, cooked gallons of
vegetarian soups, and squeezed fresh carrot juice. Downtown Waterfall
Falls was quiet outside save for an Astro gas station, an occasional
vehicle on the freeway, and a steady light rain on the roof. When Jeep
had arrived half an hour ago, skateboard under an arm, tiny hailstones
fell from the top of her crew hat, shoulders, and violin case.

Donny sliced a loaf of zucchini bread. "You never let on to me."

"You were playing hard to get, good-looking. I did everything but
take my clothes off to attract your attention."

"I know, I know, I was there. I had to take them off for her," Donny
joked to Jeep. "You know The Devon Avenue Neo Diner?"

Jeep ate like she did everything else, fast, earnestly, by turns
nervously focused or at a dead stop, dreaming, her spoon midway to the
bowl. "Chicago's ultimate dyke dive? Katie was jazzed about taking
me there when she interviewed for some Chicago station." Jeep spoke
with such enthusiasm she propelled her spoon, soup and all, across the
scuffed oak table Chick had nabbed at a yard sale. "Oh my god. I am
such a slob. Let me—" She knocked over the salt, pepper, and garlic
shakers in her haste to mop soup with her napkin.

Donny whipped a lavender bandanna from her overall pocket.

"Thanks, honeybunch," Chick said, adding it to the clump of
napkins. "No harm done, Jeep." The poor child, she was one of those
women who didn't think about things, just did them, landed on her feet,
and wondered how she got there.

"But I never got to the diner," Jeep told them as the mess was
cleared. "We were going to celebrate her getting the job, only she hated

the interviewers. Get this—they wanted to know if she was married and when she said she wasn't, if she was gay. They'd recently cut loose a guy who was caught with little girls and didn't want another scandal. She was way past corporate games by then. We got the hell out of Dodge and came directly here."

Chick smoothed her long corduroy jumper under her as she sat. She knew she didn't easily draw the attention of the boyish types she liked—whether Donny at fifty-five or Jeep at twenty-four—so she allowed herself a secret feeling of joy at the little crush that gave Jeep ten thumbs. Donny's eyes were as confident as ever. "Of course they all want you," Donny had once told her when Chick asked if she felt threatened by the occasional admirer. "You know I've got good taste in women."

She leaned back and fingered the small crystal necklace Rattlesnake had given her the first time Chick went to Spirit Ridge to drum. Listening to Jeep she remembered that she and Donny had talked long into the night about this young woman. Jeep was still having a time of it trying to earn her rent in Waterfall Falls. Her rebellious buzz cut had grown into a shaggy homemade do. They fed her whenever she had nothing left to swallow but her pride, and they wondered what kept her in Waterfall Falls.

Loopy barked in the yard. "Hush up down there!" called Donny.

Chick felt the stab of anxiety that had visited her all too often recently, and went to look down at the street. No one there. She exhaled.

"What kind of dog is that silly Loopy?" Jeep asked.

"Who knows," she answered. "I think she's a Lab-loopy mix."

"Lupe like in wolf?"

Donny laughed. "No. Some little kids brought her by the store when she was about six weeks old. They had a purebred Lab, but she'd gotten away from them for a few days and then this litter came along. Some of her siblings have major curl to their coats. Hers is a little long. You can see she's slighter and more long-legged than most Labs. Anyway, the kid said she had the most Lab in her of all the siblings, but was a little loopy. So we call her half-Lab, half loopy. They were desperate to find homes for them before their father took them to the county."

"And you were desperate for a puppy."

"More like desperate to save a puppy," Chick said.

"So you met at the Neo?" prodded Jeep, her little round glasses steamy from blowing her second bowl of soup cool. "This is outstanding grub."

Donny was only halfway through her first bowl. Chick had long ago decided the woman was as skinny as she was because she never sat down long enough to eat a full meal. "Chick was the hungriest woman I'd ever seen. Spent more time making me feel like some fine chef than she did waitressing."

"Honeybunch, I'd still be cleaning houses if the smell of your baking didn't draw every passerby off Stage Street. And a lot off the freeway too. We do pull in the dykes, don't we?"

"Remember the two who had a restaurant in New England? Nellie and Rusty?"

She smiled. Donny's memory was shaking loose. "Diner, not restaurant. And it was Dusty and—give me a second—Elly. They were from Connecticut and driving the coast from Seattle to San Francisco on a vacation, but came inland to check us out. I'm not likely to forget that Dusty any time soon."

"You'd do well to forget her right now, babe." Donny gave her that warning smile that set her blood coursing. She blew Donny a kiss. "They sent us Jody," Donny went on. "She's this cross-country truck-driving dyke. She parks her rig by the park and comes in to shoot the shit when she's in the neighborhood."

"We get them from Montana, Florida, Texas. We've even had dykes from Amsterdam come through. We list in *Lesbian Connection* so we net all the lesbian voyagers."

"And California," Jeep pointed out. "I'm a voyager to your space station too."

Donny cocked approving eyes at Jeep. Chick was pleased that Donny had taken Jeep under her wing; it was time she got to act the lesbian elder. "I'd worked for the owner of the Neo off and on over the years at one restaurant or another," Donny said. "And after I retired from my security job at the museum I went full-time for what—four years? When I got roaming feet, I put my savings into a seventeen-foot trailer. You've seen it parked out in front of the trailer park on North Stage Street. The tiny orange one. Miss Chick volunteered to help drive west."

"I hadn't crossed the country since my hippie days. I wanted to do it sober. Besides, I was sweet on this tough-talking, playful butch."

"We were just friends," Donny emphasized.

"We saw every wonder west of Chicago," Chick said. "The Painted Desert—"

"West Hollywood—"

"The Grand Canyon—"

"Castro Street—"

"Donny hadn't been anywhere. You should have seen how excited she was. Watching her discover the rest of America, I finished falling in love."

"Not me," Donny said, pulling the woodstove fire forward, adding two new logs, and clanging the iron door shut. The rain had turned to hail and back again.

"You fell for the road." Chick gave Jeep a look intended to unmask silly Donny's years of denial. "Or so you thought."

"Then Chick decided she wanted to stay out West."

"I was flirting with adventure."

"You were flirting with danger. That town had a sundown law. I don't think they'd be able to think up something ugly enough to do to gays."

"Seventy years back."

"I wanted my homegirls—bulldaggers and queens who didn't take no mouth off nobody."

"She left me behind," Chick said, forcing away the drowning feeling she'd had, stranded in that rainy lonesome town an hour south of Waterfall Falls all over again. She slipped the crystal between her lips and rolled it.

Donny looked defiant every time they reminisced about those days. "You wanted to come for the ride. The ride was over."

Chick drew Donny between her legs, pressed her cheek against that little belly she loved, trying to press the sadness away. She was perfectly happy. Where were these feelings of despair coming from? "The Goddess and I had a long talk when Donny left."

"I went to Reno," Donny said.

Jeep cried, "My hometown! Maybe I saw you!"

"I like that Reno doesn't pull up its sidewalks at six. And my black money was as good as anyone's."

"It's a weird town, Reno," Jeep said, frowning. "Too weird for me. It's like, everything's for show, for the tourists. There were so few people there who I could relate to. I don't know, maybe someday I could go back there, but, like, my family fits right in and I don't." She seemed to return to them, fully engaged, but the lost look had returned to her eyes. "So you came back broke?"

"Hell, no! I came back a rich woman."

"Don't you exaggerate, Della Donalds."

"I'm not just talking money, babe."

Chick forced lightness into her voice. "Doesn't she say the sweetest things?"

"After Reno I had $53,284.76 in my pocket after gas and groceries."

"No shit," Jeep whispered.

"I bought a fancy pair of cowboy boots to wear when I blew into the Windy City. I was going to show the old gang a good time."

"Then," Chick pushed the last of the bread toward Jeep, "the Goddess kept her promises."

"The damn $300 boots hurt my feet."

Chick pulled Donny onto her lap, running a palm across her grizzled hair. She forced a smile although the plains wind had found all her chinks and was wafting in. Had trouble passed outside? Maybe M.C. was chalking up their sidewalk again. Someone kept doing it, writing "queer-owned," "les be friends," and other dumb remarks. Donny had been going out even on days she wasn't baking and using a wet push broom to scrub the words off. She suspected it was the man she'd been shocked to run in to at the pharmacy.

No one had liked M.C. back in San Francisco, least of all her. He'd thought it was his privilege to treat the women in her little circle of friends as his private harem because he was their dealer. He bothered her even more than he did the others because he knew she was gay. Not only did she resist him, but he considered her competition. One of her friends told her that M.C. liked to talk about Chick and what she couldn't do that he could when he was having sex. Chick and M.C. had had a showdown one day, in front of everyone, in which he'd apparently felt humiliated. After that, their group started buying from someone else. She'd never seen him again until that run-in at the drug store, a few months back. M.C. had apparently settled in peaceful Waterfall Falls. The chalking had started soon afterwards, and she'd caught him more than once following along in his pickup as she walked down Stage Street, making kissing sounds from his open window. Now, it seemed, he wasn't after sex, but some kind of revenge. And her world lost its light when she thought of him.

She forced her attention back to the kitchen. Donny was still telling Jeep tales of Chicago. "I kept thinking that the old gang wouldn't be the same without Chick, but then I saw we could be our own gang—with Chick I was homegirl enough, bulldagger enough for me. I came to see that I didn't need any street-wise crazy-ass sidekicks egging me on. Only I still do miss those queens."

"Point of clarification," said Jeep, who talked like the college graduate she was when she wasn't trying to impress her hero, Donny. "A, why didn't you tell me you have so much influence with the Goddess, Chick? B, didn't you live in San Francisco? How did you come to be working in Chicago?"

Chick laughed, partly to recapture the lightness she'd felt earlier. "I moved back to Chicago when my mother got sick. There was no one to take care of her. I tried working in jobs my two-year social service degree got me," she told Jeep. "I made better money waitressing, to tell you the truth. Social service work, as far as I can tell, has become the job of an accounting clerk. I know I did more good in an apron than I would have behind a desk filling out papers for people who needed money."

"She was always taking strays home from the diner," Donny said.

"After she died, I stayed on at my mother's apartment, the same one I grew up in. It had two bedrooms. Even I couldn't take up that much space."

"Was Donny one of your strays?"

"You must be wigging out!" Chick answered, laughing at the thought and surprised at her laugh. The wind was withdrawing.

"She stole me away from—"

"I didn't steal you, Donny, you jive-ass little bulldagger!" She laughed again and felt like she was developing the consistency of lemon meringue, all airy and light. Thank you, Goddess, she thought.

"Hush, now, my sweet chickadee."

"I didn't see Denise Clinkscales jumping into your trailer to join your odyssey. I don't imagine she was crying her eyes out in Chicago at the thought of you traveling with me, the way I cried my eyes out here imagining you going back to Chicago and her."

Jeep's mouth was open in the way Chick noticed when the kid was trying to keep focused. Her blue eyes went from one of them to the other, her hands across her lap as if to hold in all the dinner she'd eaten.

"The woman was no good for my Donny," Chick explained. "She was still married."

"But I thought she'd tear down Chicago she was so mad when I told her I was leaving town with you."

"She had no right to a good steady woman. Either stay married or claim the prize."

"You got the prize all right!" Donny declared, leaping off Chick's lap and beyond arm's reach.

"So you've been together how long now?" asked Jeep.

Donny returned and stood behind Chick, playing with her hair. "Not long enough."

"Listen to her, trying to prove what a prize she is. It's been a little over eight years, hasn't it, honeybunch?" Chick felt Donny's hand, out of Jeep's sight, sneak under and cup her bottom like she owned it. She gave a quiet little purr for Donny's ears alone. She'd purred like that for the first time the day they'd finally gotten it together. She let herself remember the surprise and desire it had brought to Donny's face. And she did remember it—every detail, she liked to think, of the hot fury of love that marked their first time.

She'd felt so cold while Donny had been away, as if the chill Midwest winds were blowing across the plains and valleys of the country and finding her, desolate in the mountains she'd wanted to share with Donny. Her little apartment, half of an old mill cottage someone had renovated, was poorly insulated if at all, and the electric heater was a bust. She'd hugged herself night and day until she found the job at the old-fashioned drugstore that drew travelers and townies alike. She worked the soda fountain, laughing with the customers and feeding them sweets, while the serious business of the pharmacy went on a few counters away. She made good tip money from the tourists, but mostly she took their warmth. She grabbed it from their laughter hanging in the air like her own hot hopes; she took their jokes and thank yous, and she wrapped them around her shoulders, wearing them home where they turned to vapor and drifted away.

Like Donny had done. Then Donny had called her, once from Las Vegas where she said she was just passing through, and once from Chicago where she sounded like she'd been drinking for a while and the sounds in the background convinced her that Donny had been swallowed up in the bar life again. Donny, she'd wanted to cry, get your shit together. You don't belong in that threadbare world where girlfriends wear out and you poison yourself with booze to survive. She'd been so sure there was more to Donny, that given a hothouse she'd bloom, given a devoted woman who wanted to do more than look pretty on her arm, handsome Donny would be the most steadfast and solid citizen on earth, more than a good catch, a mate. Chick had known by then that she wanted a woman who could take care of herself, who would find it a luxury to be fussed over, and who would do some fussing over Chick herself, in her own way.

Oh, Donny, she thought, watching her teach Jeep how to tie a fly. Chick had despaired of ever getting the home, the woman, the work she wanted, and had shivered even under the covers at night, covers she'd thought she'd be sharing with Donny.

In those early months on the rural West Coast, she had made ends meet by cleaning rental units for a property management firm out of Greenhill. That had been a scary yet freeing time for her. She'd known it wouldn't last forever and had waited, excited, for her new life to take shape.

And then Donny had called from another pay phone at a campground in Iowa. She'd left Chicago and was once again heading west. She'd called again from Wyoming. It was still winter in the valley, but Chick had felt trickles of spring in her blood. She realized she'd been making plans for Donny's homecoming all along. She knew immediately what to do. That big old mill town would never be warm enough for her, even with Donny, and on her days off she rented a little pickup truck, the cheapest thing available, from Bargain Wheels near her rental and drove to explore every little name on a map, checking out the forgotten towns that no one cared to retire to, that tourists only passed through. Most were nothing but two-block main streets or a cluster of offices and a general store around a storefront post office. The bright local boys stayed and proudly took to logging like their daddies rather than learn a new trade they could ply only in the cities. Girls who wanted to act and sing would find places in the local theater and chorus, or return from college with a husband who would eventually leave her and the kids behind in her momma and daddy's house. But Chick had seen that a handful of hardy newcomers would settle in each of these outposts, learning and loving the land and fitting themselves in with people who only understood family and adopted their friends for life.

Her search seemed to take forever, and there were times she regretted having left the Chicago snow behind. It felt more honest than the dry wintry fog somehow, an honest winter so windy and filled with snow that the whole city stopped. Here the trees turned to ice sculptures and the rain, when it fell, refused to turn white. Instead of the visible threat of snow-covered roads turned treacherous, on its shaded north side every pass was slick with invisible black ice. More than once as she'd hunted for home the light truck had spun out on her and she thought she'd lost her footing in the world altogether.

She'd found Waterfall Falls that way, driving the length of Stage Street—renamed Stage Boulevard when the casino went in, but none of the locals called it that—then nosing up and down the short side streets. The town looked western, with new facades to attract tourists, but facades tacked onto buildings that had stood since the late 1800s, often serving the same functions they'd served then. Even the doctor was in the old infirmary building.

Chick didn't decide that first day, though. It wasn't until the third Sunday, a wintry afternoon with a trace of falling snow and the service station offering to chain up her car because—the fellow pointed to Blackberry Mountain and she saw a line of cars barely crawling up the pass. "Black ice up there is bad today," he told her.

She'd chosen the motor court north of town instead of that drag of a drive home and got to talking with the couple who'd owned it since the mid-sixties. They were too old for the housekeeping chores and were looking for someone to clean rooms and sit at the front desk. Once they broke her in, they planned to visit their grandkids out of state a lot. She could have the room closest to the office plus some wages. By the end of the week she'd bought their old car and they'd caravanned with her to the mill town down south to return the Bargain Wheels rental and fill the back of their pickup with her things. It was as if they'd found long-lost blood, the way they helped her and trusted her from day one. They hit the road two weeks later.

Her trailer court room got downright hot when she'd settle in at night, achy from the room cleaning, but filled with her own heat too as she imagined Donny on her doorstep, Donny stepping in the room, softly kicking the door shut behind her, arms open.

She would be standing by then, roused in a long flannel nightgown, half-listening for the rumble of Donny's little motor home outside. No—she corrected her fantasy—she'd go to the dresser and pull out the slinky gown, the one she'd bought before Donny left, when they'd been so close to becoming lovers.

With the fabric at her cheek, she'd imagine Donny's hands on it, snagging a little from sandpapery fingertips, because Donny worked those hands hard cooking for a living, fixing the motor home, driving the balky old thing. Donny wasted those hands on women who didn't appreciate her beyond them. Would she touch Chick now? Why else was she headed back? Chick was so hung up on her, she sometimes wondered where she wanted Donny to touch her first. Times like that the image of Donny would come in so clear, be so powerful she thought she wouldn't be able to stand the sensation of those strong brown fingers grazing her nipples or slipping into her so politely while her whole body sighed to receive them. She would hold the gown to her chest as she felt her insides clutch with anticipation of Donny's fingers, release them, draw them deeper.

Of course it didn't happen like that. Donny pulled in two days later, just as Chick finished cleaning a hairy mess of a bathroom, and was carrying a heavy basket of wet cleaning rags, towels, and cleansers. Her long hair was in a sweaty tangle, spots of water slopped all over the worn balloon-legged pants she should have retired years ago.

She looked up and there was Donny, backing out of the side door of the motor home like she'd spent the night and recently awakened. Donny, in a short black denim jacket she hadn't seen before, black jeans, and a white turtleneck sweater. She turned, saw Chick, grinned, and started toward her. She looked too thin, like the trip had somehow chiseled her down to her essential self, naked now of city artifice, a woman on her own in a world with sharp edges. Chick loved to watch Donny move, all smooth and liquid saunter one minute, then leaping into a coordinated frenzy the next. Nobody could handle as many activities at once as her Donny, whether she was all at once cooking or driving/sipping coffee/telling a story/drumming a finger on the steering wheel/taking in Chick with quick glances stolen from the road.

Chick dropped her bucket, flung down her rags, and walked as fast as she gracefully could toward Donny, arms open. She could see Donny hesitate, like she might head back to Chicago any second, and then stand her ground. By the time Chick reached her, Donny was rooted and took her in her arms like a cottonwood tree drinking rain through all its surfaces.

"Ah," she said. "Ah, my Chick."

Chick felt a jolt of fire under her breasts at the word "my."

They were the same height. When Chick leaned back she saw wetness around Donny's eyes. Whatever struggle had brought her home was washing out of her. Chick had no doubt she was Donny's home. Donny pulled her close again, body gone soft except for her arms which felt sturdy as branches.

Without more than a smile, they went together to pick up the cleaning supplies. Chick led the way to the laundry. The last dryer load sighed to its hot stillness inside the machine. The room was steamy and smelled like home. Chick pulled sheets out and wondered, as she let Donny help her fold, still wordlessly, eyes on each other more than the task, if they would be a good fit for lovemaking. It didn't always come easily, she'd learned, and some women had rhythms so different from her own that touching became an irritant. She had a feeling she and Donny would be a match.

Donny's deft fingers pulled and tucked the sheets with the efficiency of movement that seemed to come so easily to her. When the linens were settled on their shelves Chick laid a hand high on Donny's chest to stay, then hurried next door to the office to put up the Be Right Back sign. She was done until new guests arrived in the late afternoon.

Donny lounged against the porch rail, a somber look on her face. Worried, Chick reached out, watched Donny's eyes roam her face, linger on her body. She closed her eyes to better relish the feel of that gaze. Going without a lover, her life had at times felt like a house on the plains, chilly winds stealing through the chinks of her walls. She needed someone to care for, to build her days with, or she felt a great gaping hole in herself. She'd heard this called relationship addiction, but she knew it was no addiction; it was the way she was made. The way most women were, she guessed, although the usual solution was to raise children, not something that had ever appealed to her—why bring another troubled little boy like her brother into the world? Even aware of Donny before her, she felt sadness threaten to overtake her, as it had so often before they met. She hoped that loving Donny would crowd out that creeping ivy, sadness. She wanted a companion who needed her too, who filled in the gaps in her walls.

Chick opened her eyes and recognized that Donny's look was not somber at all, but intent with desire. Her breath caught at the thought and she stood, lips parted, shocked by the honesty of Donny's want.

She laughed as she took Donny's hand and led her across the

gravel. Gotta have this woman, she exulted in silence. Gotta have this woman in my life. So Donny Donalds had decided. And on her—the fat, white, aging flower child who wanted a new life out West. The one who would lead her away from the city, the people, the life she had known.

Chick wasn't kidding herself. She knew the attraction was a package, not only a person, and that, like herself, Donny wanted to marry a life, not just a woman. This might be a midlife crisis for both of them, finally striking out on their own, casting off the lives that they'd been handed for one that better suited their aging selves. Donny could no more keep up with the mind-bending night life she'd always led than she could deny the arthritis she'd confessed had settled in her knees and made dancing or cooking a full shift too hard on her. The why didn't matter—the Don wanted to settle down, and Chick was more than ready to be at her side. She had exhaled the last cloud of this sadness attack and gestured toward her door. Donny opened it for her, followed her in, and gave it the little backwards kick Chick had imagined. Now, she thought, her breathing going choppy with excitement, now it begins.

When Donny moved toward her all scheming for the future—the future itself—stopped. Her heart felt as if it was squeezing open and shut. This is surreal, she thought, steeling herself so she wouldn't come the second poor Donny touched her.

But Donny didn't touch her with her hands. She stopped, tilted her head, and leaned forward, eyes closed. Chick felt all her blood, her life, her soul flood to her lips for Donny's first kiss: light, brief, broken when Donny pulled back and met her eyes.

Donny's voice was hoarse. "This okay with you, Chick?"

Her eyes were an olive green, not brown at all, Chick thought with surprise as Donny's arms went around her. She gulped air between kisses. Donny's hands were, finally, on her. Her face, her neck, her waist, her shoulders and back. Donny pulled her closer until their bodies pressed together, mound to mound, and she knew she was losing it, lost it, ground into Donny and called her name, called it into her mouth.

"Chick. Yeah, Chick," Donny breathed to her. "I'm sorry I took so long to figure this out. I'm here to stay if you want me."

She felt like some quivering femme in a lesbian romance novel. "Want you," she managed to say, and then said it, groaned it, whispered it as she kissed Donny's face and neck and hands, oh Donny's hands.

"You want me to close those curtains?" Donny, sounding breathless, asked.

"Oh, Goddess, I forgot."

Donny pointed to the bed. "Stay put, I want to undress you."

She sat, too stoked, too weak to do anything but comply.

Donny struggled with the old drapes and Chick prayed the phone wouldn't ring, no guests would come early, no one's toilet overflow. Donny returned, already unbuttoning her own shirt, flinging it and a white undershirt onto the chair. Her breasts were little, the pendulous kind, and for some reason a complete turn-on. Chick wanted to stroke them as she felt Donny pull off her shoes and long socks, then unzip the jumper down her back, but she felt shy as a bright, shiny new baby dyke.

Donny had raised an eyebrow and Chick stood to step out of her jumper. For a moment she felt horribly fat, but Donny was touching her immediately, covering her nakedness with her half-clothed body, praising her softness, her warmth, her wetness. She'd told herself to get over it, smiled and pulled Donny down to the bed with her. And Donny had stayed.

Now, eight years later, watching those fingers with the little fly, watching how she enjoyed teaching a baby butch, she thanked the Goddess for sending her Donny. Yet as always, as soon as she thought about how lucky she was, she feared the onslaught of one of her terrible sad moods. What were they about? Was she kidding herself, calling the status quo happiness? Sometimes these uneventful Donny years, both behind and ahead, got a little daunting in their sameness. At other times she was dazzled by the brilliant wild flowers that cropped up in what threatened to become a bleak landscape. What was the happiness everyone raved about if not this peace and contentment? So what if serenity held little excitement? When she'd craved and found excitement it had been no more than a Band-Aid over emotional wounds which still seeped. Was the sadness getting worse?

"Eight years is a long time," Jeep told them with somber respect. "An even longer time in lesbian years."

"Lesbian years?" asked Donny.

Again Chick recognized Jeep's open-mouthed, blank-eyed, lost-soul gaze as her way of concentrating. "Our accelerated relationships," Jeep said. "Does a lesbian marriage last half as many years as a straight one that has society's stamp of approval? Or is it so good it goes by twice as fast?"

"You do have a novel way of seeing things, Jeep," Chick said. "Like my brother." Donny gave her a sharp glance. "No, not exactly

LEE LYNCH

like him—he's schizophrenic." She felt her anxiety level spike like it always did when she told people about his diagnosis. She knew she talked about Martin too much, but by keeping him aired and exposed her fear of becoming like him seemed to lessen. He'd told her that he, too, was at times drenched in sadness. "It's called depression, little sister," he'd said, but she dismissed that term. Sadness was a little romantic; depression was a diagnosis.

"Original," she told Jeep. "Your thinking is original like his, but you're bright and funny, while he's bright and down, down, down."

Jeep looked as if she was working on thinking of something comforting to say.

"It's okay, sweetie. He's got it under control with drugs. He has a job again, supervising sorters at a recycling center. He's a master collector, organizer, and sorter, always has been. He was studying botany in college when he got sick, so he's okay with the job."

"I was going to tell you that I had a special sister," Jeep said, her voice strangely thin. "Jill was autistic. Not brilliant autistic, a little slow. She had these major, kind of like tantrums. One day in the middle of a tantrum—she was twelve, I was ten—instead of getting on the school bus she ran out into the street. Boom, right in front of a speeding commuter. No more Jill."

"Poor Jeep." Chick couldn't stop herself from going to Jeep and enfolding her. She was interested in all these white-light, chakra, giving-energy-business ideas, but so far, there was simply nothing she could do for another woman that was better at transmitting love than holding a fragile head to her softest place. "Did you see it happen?"

"No," Jeep said over her shoulder. "I was oblivious, practicing upstairs before school and only half-watching Jill. I wasn't supposed to be watching her, but I always kind of did. I was the oldest of all normie kids, you know? And my parents never told me I was in charge of Jill, but I could tell they kind of expected it, always asking me how she'd behaved and if I was taking her along somewhere. I was in middle school. I mean, I loved Jill but she was a royal pain, and I escaped the house whenever I could. I was in the school orchestra and the glee club and the church choir. I did music for the school plays, and I played square dance music for the Dosey-Doe Club at fairs and demos at the mall and at retirement homes."

Chick let her go on, but kept touching her hair. "You blame yourself, don't you?"

Jeep was looking away. "My whole family blames me. I was supposed to be practicing, but really—" The thinness in Jeep's voice was stifled tears. "Really, Dad had left for work and it was Mom's week to get the little kids to the grammar school. I should have been at the bus stop with Jill, but I was really sneaking in time to play old-time music along with this old tape of Mom's." Jeep's voice was almost a whisper. "For Mother's Day, you know? I had to have it down by that Sunday so I could play it for her."

"Jeep," she said, "you had to have a life too."

"I know, but everything changed after that. My dad still kind of won't meet my eye and Mom…well, she had the three younger kids to take care of, and it seemed like after that she never asked me to baby-sit the others, not that I blame her. After Jill got killed, she kind of lost interest in music, in my playing."

"So you took the blame on."

"I kind of wondered a lot. If I'd waited at the bus stop with her, I mean, don't you wonder if you'd done something a little bit differently, if Jill—or—"

"—Martin."

"—might have been all right?"

"Yes, yes, yes. I used to worry that little rag of guilt to tatters. It's only human to feel like that."

"Or, like, what if I'd gotten twenty points less on my IQ, would Jill have been smarter? I could have gotten by fine, and Jill might have had a life. I get worked up thinking she'll never see a flowering prickly pear cactus or eat a raspberry or hear old-time music again. She loved bluegrass. Jill and me were the only ones to get Mom's bluegrass gene."

"Shit happens, doesn't it?" Donny said. The mournfulness of her tone somehow told its own story.

Chick expected Donny to talk about her alcoholic twin brother Marcus Junior, but Donny had been keeping quiet about him since he was diagnosed with advanced cirrhosis of the liver on top of diabetes several months ago. As far as Chick knew, Donny hadn't even cried yet. She used to act proud of his drunken antics, but the thought of losing him may have become too painful.

With an effort that made her realize how tired she was—and at only seven thirty at night she ought to be ashamed of herself—Chick pulled herself out of her funk again. "This wild woman didn't make it back to the two-timer in Chicago. She came west and handed me every last cent of her winnings."

Donny said. "Chick had a dream I could get behind."

"Over the next two months we combed the area for a place to put Natural Woman Foods."

"That's when I knew I really loved the lady, not just the land," Donny explained. "I wouldn't have done this kind of shit on my own. Chick convinced me that only about two-thirds of the people we met wanted to run this dyke out of town." Donny gave her quiet laugh. "I can live with two-thirds. What's hard for me is sorting out which are the good guys. Chick tended my soul-bruises at night."

"We played doctor."

Donny gave her a soft slap on the hand. "This store was one of the first places we'd seen, but we thought we wanted to be farther off the beaten track. When we came back to check it out again, the sellers convinced us we had to be near I-5 to get the business we'd need. And they said the fishing was good."

Chick spread her arms. "Can you believe we had no idea about all the women's land around here?"

"This was Lesbianville West," Donny exclaimed. "You can't tell me we settled here by chance."

"You think the area is like, a dyke vortex?" Jeep asked, her eyes wide. "We passed signs for some kind of backwards-running creek or something on the way up. I've been here for three months now, and I keep finding more dykes. Maybe the inverted energy draws us."

"A dyke vortex. I like it." Chick made a mental note to suggest it to the sheriff, a native who was completely baffled, and not particularly pleased, at the disproportionate numbers of lesbians in Elk County. "Lesbians are supposed to flock to urban areas."

"Cool beans! I moved to the poor dyke's Palm Springs."

"Yeah," added Donny. "We don't golf, we fish."

Chick laughed. "And eat what you catch, too."

Jeep, with her straight-faced humor, said, "You can't chew golf balls."

A timer went off and Donny leapt up again. "Damn, you made me forget those cookies."

"Molasses, from the smell."

"Double-molasses coconut date. You like them hot, Jeep?" A horn blared as it passed the store. "I need to find out who's making that racket out there about every night. Did you hear it at two this morning, Chick?"

She shook her head, but she was lying. The car horn had woken her up, and she had lain there petrified with fear for nearly an hour, listening to Donny struggle to get back to sleep. She knew who it was, and she knew the horn was meant to disturb her, to make her aware that he was out there.

Donny brought a tray from the oven, and Jeep looked as if she was going to cry. She took one, studied it, then broke off bits with her lips and seemed to suck the flavor out. "These are as good as Sarah's. Better than my mom's. Mom never could cook. The best we got was when my little sisters baked chocolate-chip cookies with that ready-made refrigerator dough."

Chick encouraged Jeep to take another cookie. "You're not homesick, are you, Jeep?"

"No! Well, maybe a little. Well, I kind of miss my family, and Sarah, but I kind of ran out on them all without any notice so…you know what they say about how you can't go home again."

"Not true," Chick advised. "Things may not be the same, but your family would rather have you than lose you."

"That I doubt, but if they did, I'd want them to move here. There were things I loved about Reno. I loved the neon at night, living by the railroad tracks, a clear view of stars, but it's getting bigger and bigger and, with global warming, hotter and hotter." Jeep licked crumbs from her fingertips. "It's not where I want to be. I never learned music so I could play in casinos. I'd rather keep doing this landscaping work than do music like that." She took another cookie and, typical of her habit of deflecting attention from herself, said, "So you got to Waterfall Falls and there were, like, no sundown laws?"

With customary quick jaunty grace, as if moving to some inner music—probably an early sixties girl group, Chick thought—Donny had cleared the table of everything but their mugs and a platter of the dark sugar-shiny cookies. Then she sat, took one and said, "Waterfall Falls is a mixed bag. Descendants of a black cowboy own the huge sheep ranch east of town. The barbershop's always belonged to a Latino family. The Job Corps Center contributes all the colors of the ex-city kids who've gone native and their mixed-blood babies are all grown up now. There's leftover hippies from sixties communes. We have a

Japanese-American dentist, a motel owner who immigrated from some little Middle Eastern village, and a sprinkling of people left from the days when the railroads and gold mines exploited the Chinese. And suddenly the Native Americans are God's gift because they built a casino that pays living wages. Gays are the last minority here struggling for at least token acceptance. Yet we stay scattered. I don't kid myself that the straights would welcome a real melting pot. They're still the majority and like it that way."

Jeep always joked about singing for her supper. She wiped her fingertips and reached for her fiddle case, asking Donny, "So how did you figure out that Chick was the one?"

"Excuse me." Chick felt herself color. She always got teary-eyed at this part. She took another cookie and bustled away from the table to fill the sink with sudsy water.

"Once upon a time I thought love happened between the sheets," Donny said, shaking her head. "It happens when you're stripping wood floors side by side, and on your way to meet with your small business advisor, jittery as June bugs against a screen."

"You think?" Jeep asked. "I've been thinking that myself. It's like, with that varmint Katie, I was all of a sudden on fire for her. I couldn't stand it sometimes, I was so charged. But with Sarah, well, we did strip the floors in our apartment. And sat and watched TV at night with that wood glowing up at us. I miss that. I don't miss the all-nighters with Katie one bit."

"There you go," Donny said. "The next one, you ask her to strip. If she takes her clothes off, run the other way. If she knows where to rent a floor-stripping machine, you've hit pay dirt."

Jeep's laugh was shy, but unruly. Chick had wondered if it was the reason she was so serious most of the time—to muzzle that laugh. It was infectious, though, and Chick joined in as Donny helped the string mop do a little strip tease.

"I'm so glad you're in our lives, Jeep," Chick managed to say. "We must have had a very boring time of it before."

The kid looked at them, said, "That I doubt too," and launched into a galloping tune. Usually Chick and Donny just listened, but tonight Donny whirled her, sudsy arms and all, around the round oak table while Jeep's violin drowned out the sounds of the rain.

A minute before, she'd wondered how she would manage to drag herself to bed when Jeep left because she felt so drained. Now she was flushed with the music and ready for more. But, she worried, what would she feel ten minutes from now? If only she could dance with Donny forever so this endless sadness would never cascade over her again.

CHAPTER SIX

Honeybee Dance

Jeep and Donny straddled the rough pole railing on the porch outside of the Grange Hall and watched women hug and eye new arrivals. Donny was doing a running commentary, as if this were a night at the Oscars. These were, Jeep supposed, the town's dyke celebrities, so she'd better take notes and do a who's who for—for herself; who else was there? She imagined pointing everyone out to Sarah. By the time the movie started, Sarah would have invited half the audience to dinner. Funny, Sarah was kind of like Chick that way.

Chick was inside popping corn for the Monthly Movie Mixer. She could smell the stuff out here. This was too weird. "Is this for real?" she asked Donny. "Dykes meeting in an all-American Grange Hall? I thought these things were reserved for Future Farmers of America."

With a chuckle, Donny said, "Takes me back to Black Panther days when the white liberals were falling all over each other to hold fund-raisers in their fancy houses. I'd go along just to be a black bulldagger in a radical's beret, drinking Chablis from a long-stemmed crystal glass in the billiard room, or whatever they called those fancy rooms bigger than the whole apartment I grew up in."

"I remember reading about the Black Panthers in a twentieth-century history course I took. You were one of those?"

"You could say I was in the gay ladies' auxiliary. One of my gayboy friends took me to a couple of the happenings as his home squeeze. I didn't have to dress in girl-drag because I was a revolutionary. He couldn't let on that he really wanted to be one of the brother's ladies."

"Cool." She felt her awe of Donny go up another notch.

They watched the crowd a while longer. It looked like the hellos were the deal here, not the film. As usual, most of the women ignored the misting rain and stood out there unprotected. She noticed a woman striding across the lot, thumbs hooked in her belt loops, a light nylon jacket flapping open. Instead of hugging her, the other women seemed, without looking, to move back to let her pass. Jeep nudged Donny.

"Single," Donny muttered. "Name's Cat."

"Single? Total babe. Dish, Donalds—what's her fatal flaw?"

Donny elbowed her. "She's too hot for anyone around here to handle."

Jeep straightened, jingled the change in her pocket, wished she had cash for a class haircut, and caught the babe's smiling eyes. "Anyone?" she asked Donny. Donny looked like she knew something and wasn't talking. "She's not traveling with the Birkenstock Brigade?"

Donny chuckled. "Doesn't fit in. She works full-time at the grammar school. Phys ed. She doesn't have time to play at lesbian utopia."

Jeep smiled. "Play" wasn't exactly the right word to use for the land women. Some of them didn't have jobs, but they built their own little cabins, learning from each other, from books, and by trial and error. They grew some of their own food, kept their roads in reasonable shape, produced their own entertainment, cooked and cleaned in primitive conditions, and sometimes held a job or started small businesses to support themselves. Yet she kind of knew what Donny was saying. The life was pleasant compared to, say, working retail where you were on your feet all day with no time to run to a bathroom, a line of impatient customers, and someone on your video screen acting like a shoplifter while you wondered if the security people at their videos were watching you not catch him. But play? She guessed maybe some of them.

"You don't think much of the land women, do you?" she asked Donny.

"Deep down, Jeep, I'm a practical person. I saw what happened to black folk who thought they could change the world. Burned out in Philly. Suicided in Guyana. The brightest and strongest—like Eldridge Cleaver—locked up, or like Angela Davis, making her way telling it like it is again and again to white college kids. Sooner or later you've got to get real before reality gets you."

She wanted to ask Donny a thousand questions about how she should live her own life, how she could have a relationship like Donny and Chick's, but she didn't even know enough to frame the questions. She skipped back to what she did know. "She looks better than any gym teacher I ever had."

"Have many?" Donny joked.

Jeep felt her hands start to glow with the warmth of embarrassment, but she grinned. Donny was so cool for an old dyke. "Not enough," she answered, working at being cool back.

"Look at that parking lot," Donny said, pointing to the two rows of vehicles arranged on the pot-holed gravel and along the verge of the road. "It's practically split, half nineties Hondas and Subarus, half clunker pickups. And one bike couple."

"The Honda girls are closet city and the Subarus are out?"

"Some are, some aren't. They're alcohol counselors and teachers. Find the Forest Service workers."

"No-brainer. That row of dirty mini-pickups with the federal parking stickers and big dogs in the cabs. Is that the third half?"

Donny laughed and said, "It's what makes us dykes, that third half."

"Like the extra chromosome that makes us gay?"

"Is that what does it?"

"Sure. Gay guys are XYY and dykes are XXX."

"Triple-X rated! I like it!"

"You ought to see the K-Ys!"

The woman who'd parted the crowd moved into sight again when she stopped to talk with a small animated woman. "What does Cat drive?" Jeep wanted to know.

"Guess."

"The little LeBaron convertible?"

"You read that one wrong. Try the old yellow Ford F-150 that looks like a classic pickup freak refinished it this morning."

"No way. She's too much of a girl."

"A girl from a tough pioneer family that settled this valley. She's got her feet so solidly on the ground they're a root system. Look, there's her dog. George is Loopy's sweet, cuddly little pit bull pal. Cat named her after some girl in a kid mystery book. That is the best trained dog I ever saw."

The woman was petting and talking to the brown and white dog in the cab of her truck, and Jeep felt herself falling in—in love? That wasn't it, exactly, though she'd let herself in a flash. More like in admiration. The thought of love put her in mind of Sarah again. Maybe tonight when she got home she'd write to her. But where to send it? She could start with their old apartment. Was Sarah still coming home every day to the honey-colored sunlight on their old wooden floor? She felt a tug of anxiety. Coming home to their apartment with another woman?

"Does Cat live with anyone?" she asked.

"She's all alone in that big old house her great-granddad built.

She's asked us to keep an eye out for the perfect roommate. Someone pleasant and steady who can help her around the place without coming on to her and who's independent enough not to make a lot of demands. Oh, and maybe has a kid or two. She likes kids."

"So why doesn't she fill the house with her own?"

"Says she's not ready for that."

"She doesn't want a girlfriend?"

"Long story, Jeep. One I've been told not to pass on."

"Oh." Cat was making her way to them.

"How old is she?"

"I don't know exactly, maybe late twenties, early thirties."

"Like Katie, only from here she feels older somehow. Like she was born knowing how to get along."

"I believe some people are. And Cat may be one of them."

"The sheriff feels kind of like that too, but I thought it had to do with her job."

"Could be people with something to teach—and good cops like Sheriff Sweet have taught me a thing or two—are drawn to those occupations."

"No wonder I never wanted to be a teacher."

Donny looked at her. "You just think you're a know-nothing. You're learning quick."

"Me? I feel like I know less every day." It was true. She'd be feeling good and then all of a sudden it was like the ground went out from under her feet. It didn't take much either. A Saturday night alone, bad news on the radio, a stupid letter from her mom nagging about getting a phone or e-mail when she didn't have money for an ISP connection, much less a phone line or a computer. She'd left her computer in Reno, but had used Sami's, then Katie's. She asked Donny, "When am I going to know what I know so I can use it?"

With a laugh, Donny said, "I never knew till one day I looked over my shoulder and saw my backside running from trouble, trying to push me along. That's when I realized I just had to listen inside myself. What else are you needing to know about life?"

Jeep laughed too. "What to do when trouble catches up."

"You stand aside and get out of the way. If you're on the tracks when the train comes through, it's nobody's fault but your own."

She had a feeling she wouldn't understand that one for a long time.

The porch had become too crowded to rag without being heard, so she just watched. A place could not be more different from San Francisco.

Her time in San Francisco had been like its strange weather. Even when the sun showed up, the air always felt chilly against her skin, kind of like wearing short sleeves while hugging a tuba in a Thanksgiving Day parade. She'd done that once, learned to play tuba so she could go to Indianapolis for the regional championships with the band. It had been an extremely cold experience. In San Francisco she often wished either the sun would shine or it would rain, she didn't much care which. She went from hot Sami to cool Katie like the city changed weather.

Sami had this killer apartment on the top floor of the building the shop was in. Not an easy thing to find, but Sami had connections. In this case, she traded the building's owner maintenance for the apartment. Then Sami traded stuff out of the shop for someone to do the work. Musicians all over the Bay Area bought used gear at Muse Music, which Sami's father had started as a head shop called Muse back in the mid-sixties. Later, he'd gone into some kind of stock and bond work and turned over the shop to Sami, but he couldn't be getting much money out of it with all the bartering Sami did.

She had been down to Reno on a buying trip when they met, and Jeep had hitched a ride west with her, taking along only her fiddle, last paycheck, some extra clothes, and her skateboard. She hadn't been into waiting around for Sarah, to discuss splitting; Sami's van was loaded and idling out front. She wanted to kiss the bricks of their building goodbye, one by one. But then she was in the van, and before leaving felt real to her Sami was driving, one hand on the steering wheel, one on her.

Nothing but a crappy little Post-it note for Sarah. She hadn't known what she was doing, so what could she write? Sami was six foot, one inch and hauled heavy amps and stage monitors around like they were feather pillows. Jeep was a little flattered and a little repelled, but Sami was wonky about music and thought Jeep was a genius as well as adorable, so she had let herself be hauled away too.

Before long, she was ready to pack it in with Sami. Maybe the hardwood floors in Sami's apartment reminded her too much of the place she'd had with Sarah. Maybe Sami's pawing was getting real old. For a while, she stayed on mostly because she didn't have a clue where to go.

"Dude," she'd said to the guy in dreadlocks who came in the shop door during the week that would turn out to be her last with Sami. She even remembered the music that had been playing because that was the day she'd discovered Aaron Copeland's clarinet concerto. The thought of that music gave her chills down to the calves of her legs. Why did they call them calves anyway?

"Need some sticks," he told her.

"Are you ragging the customers again, Jeepy?" Sami had finally gotten out of bed and strutted through the back door.

The dude smiled brightly at Sami and beat a tattoo on the doorframe with his sticks. "Wish you were queer for me, Sami."

"If I turned bi for anybody, it'd be for you, Ahmed."

When the guy left, Sami lifted Jeep off the ground in a bear hug, wetly kissing on her.

"Give it a rest, girlfriend," Jeep complained.

"That's for opening up," said Sami with a dragon-breath yawn.

"You were still snoring."

"Why don't you get me some wake-up, Jeepster."

She surprised herself when she said, "I'll go get you a Starbucks, but I'm not copping anything that comes in a vial or a plastic bag."

"Hey, this is Y2K. Ditch the attitude, my little off-road vehicle. I'm on empty and not in street drag."

"I'm not taking a chance on messing up my life so you can have a toot. I don't think they allow violins in the penitentiary."

Sami raised her arms, her slouch almost simian. "Didn't I rescue you from your little desert ghost town? Give you four walls and a job? Don't I get no freakin' respect?"

"You do, your habit doesn't. You can't even start the day without a hit anymore."

"What a little punk. At least you're not weak in bed."

Jeep had left the store, slapped her skateboard to the sidewalk, and pushed off toward Starbucks. That was the thing about Sami. When she liked you she gave everything she had to give. You had to be grateful to someone like that, but, Jeep realized—and maybe she'd made the decision in her sleep—that it wasn't cool to let Sami go too far. A person could lose her soul in the process. Since she played music from that same site, she wasn't letting anyone mess with it.

She wasn't letting go of her soul around these country dykes either. Uh-uh. What was right for them was right for them, but she got to say what was right for her. Rattlesnake's crowd scared her the way Sami had. She didn't know why exactly, but she knew she had to keep her deflector shields up.

"Cat!" called Donny with a slight thrust of her chin. "Want you to meet my buddy Jeep."

"Hey, girl," said Cat, the smile in her eyes like a secret code.

The babe was a little shorter than Jeep, about five feet, six inches, with trendy long blonde corkscrew hair. She wore a patchwork Mexican jacket, black jeans, and dusty Reeboks. Next to Cat was the small woman Cat had stopped to talk with earlier. Jeep recognized her now as the woman from the old-time music band, hair short on top, long in back, who'd rushed into Natural Woman Foods for luck the day Jeep hurt her foot. The toe still grumbled when she treated it roughly. Donny had driven her past Senorita's later, but since then she'd been too busy and too broke to check out the women's band.

"This is Muriel," Cat said, "our washtub bass player."

"You're the violinist!" Muriel said, straight to the point. She was probably in her forties, with an East Coast accent and East Coast nervous energy. "We could use a fiddler."

Jeep checked out Cat's grin. "Yes," her eyes said, "Muriel's pretty weird." Jeep grinned back.

"Can we hear you some time?" Muriel asked. She spoke in staccato notes. "Where are you living?"

"I moved to Donny's old trailer out at Wanderers' Wayside this week."

"Sure. Sure. The trailer park? I know it. The tiny orange job out front?" Muriel turned to Donny. "Do you still own that? No? I'll bet you keep track for these wanderers, though. I was going to see if it was vacant. For my nephew. I don't want him up at Dawn Farm when he visits. You'll keep an eye out for someplace else?" Muriel leaned close to Jeep. "Donny and Chick, they're the lesbian Chamber of Commerce. Food, housing, rides to Greenhill. What's next," she asked Donny, "matchmaking? So, tomorrow, noon?"

It took a moment for Jeep to stop avoiding Cat's eyes after the matchmaking remark and to understand that Muriel was waiting for an answer.

"I'm working. Five o'clock?"

"What do you do?"

Jeep rubbed her chafed hands, examined her dusty Doc Martens. There was nothing wrong with the work—she was glad to get it through Chick and Donny's customer connections—but she found it hard to admit to. "I'm cleaning houses, raking leaves till I get something better."

"And you skateboard. I've seen you around town. You're afraid you'll fall and hurt your fingers of course. I would be too."

"No, I don't do tricks. I just cruise."

"Okay," proclaimed Muriel, either ignoring or not catching Jeep's joke, "but we need to find you work that won't hurt those hands." She darted off toward someone's hug.

Donny and Cat were both looking at Jeep's long fingers. Jeep, who secretly thought of them as a great asset in lovemaking as well as in music, slid them into her pockets. "So you're in the band?"

Cat pursed her lips and made some little sounds. "Mouth organ."

Jeep felt a shiver at the base of her spine. Was there anything not sexy about Cat? "Maybe we could play a duet some time." She slid her harmonica out of her back pocket and brandished it.

"Sounds like a plan, amigo," Cat said.

"It's getting cold," Donny said, leading them inside the raftered hall. "I wish the rain would start. This damp fog gets into my old bones."

Cat patted Donny's short curls as they moved indoors. "You've got more pizzazz than half this gang. What are you, all of fifty-six? I remember your fifty-fifth birthday party. You in your new rainbow logging suspenders." Cat stopped suddenly and Jeep, who'd been checking the hall out, collided with her.

"Sorry." She realized her hands had grabbed Cat's shoulder and upper arm to keep from bending her bad toe. She let go quickly. "My bad foot," she managed to say.

"No, it was my fault," Cat replied, smiling as if she'd read Jeep's hasty release for the signals it denied. Cat eased them past the awkwardness when she asked, "What brings you to Waterfall?"

Jeep had noticed that the locals shortened the town's name. She wondered if she'd be there long enough to earn the right to do it too. "I met Solstice in the Bay Area. She said to come visit so I did."

"Solstice is one of the women on the mountain, isn't she?"

Jeep was a little surprised Cat didn't know, but then a native might watch the traffic on women's land with some skepticism, like any community with a lot of transients. Migrant farm workers, the homeless, hippie hitchhikers, hobos, and fruit tramps—the tradition stretched back to the Depression years when so many Americans were labeled this way. Here was a generation of women who'd pulled up stakes and, in their own way, taken part in a migration.

"Uh-huh," she answered Cat. "She spends time in the Bay Area too, temping for money to live up here. She calls it her city fix. I worked in a music shop. She used to spend hours in there looking through sheet music, admiring guitars. She never said she played in a band like yours."

"Who," asked Cat with a smile that erased all her sophistication and made her look about twelve years old, "would admit to that?" Before Jeep could answer Cat said, "You like it here?"

She gave Cat a purposely goofy grin. "It's excellent. Lots of women."

"All fifty-seven flavors," answered Cat, sounding like she'd savored close to that.

Jeep stared at her.

"A variety," Cat explained.

"I knew that," Jeep replied, but she couldn't look Cat in the eye. Of course Cat knew exactly what she'd been thinking.

"But not as varied as my classes. I'm learning Spanish so I can talk to some of the kids."

Was Cat checking her out? And for what, a lover or a roommate? Was Cat where she went from here? Was her whole life going to be this honeybee dance from one flower to the next? The thought filled her with despair. She wanted—what was it she wanted? She saw herself, some day, sitting in the sun, in a backyard, a bunch of kids playing around her. She'd be tossing a football to one, shooing another into the house to practice. And later a family band with an auto harp, a banjo, all the old-timey instruments, like her family before her sister died. But she was a dyke, she never wanted to be pregnant, and she still wasn't settled down at twenty-four. She hadn't a clue how to get from here to that sunny there. She'd never even told Sarah about her vision. It was like one of those past-life regressions some of the women were into, but instead she saw her future.

"Do you know what you're walking into?" Cat asked. Jeep was startled by the question. It was kind of like Cat knew what she'd been thinking. "This community can be stranger than strange."

"Oh, that. That's not news." Jeep spotted Katie in the first row with R. She felt so angry so fast she wanted to yank out R's fucking braid. She'd never seen them together before.

Donny, who had been talking to an old woman with long white chin hairs, returned and led them deeper into the room. Following

Jeep's gaze, she put a comradely arm across her shoulders and said, "My buddy Jeep is getting her feet wet. R stole her girl."

"Kill," Jeep was whispering over and over.

"Down, girl. They're not worth it. You're going to find someone who loves you good."

Cat added, "If your ex wanted one of that crew, you don't want her."

What would she have done back in Nevada if someone had stolen Sarah? The thought sent a pang through her. She was surprised how deep it went. Kind of like vibrations from bowing the G string real slow, only she was the string.

R must have sensed Jeep in the back of the hall, because she rose and seemed to float toward her, pausing to bestow a press of hands here, a long hug there, long silver earrings flashing light, always gazing deeply into the other woman's eyes.

"Damn slick bitch," Donny mumbled.

Jeep had expected to feel all broken up the first time she saw Katie with her new lover, but she only got more steamed. What did she do wrong? What part of Katie had she totally missed seeing? They should have chanted together or some dumb ass thing? She never said squat about wanting to be a witch, if that's what these women hiding out in the mountains were. "R's pulling some magnanimous scene here, right? Thinks she's the high priestess of Waterfall Falls?"

"You got it," whispered Cat.

"Jeep!" said R in a tone that implied it was an amazing joy to find the light of her life right there in the flesh. "You don't know how good it is to see you."

"So," said Jeep. Making her voice loud and challenging over the crowd. "The Goddess of Spirit Ridge goes to the movies." She sensed the three dozen women in the room chill. Well, she was a seasoned performer; she'd play R like a kettle drum and tighten her screws. She'd make her sing, and then mute her.

"You must be a Hepburn fan too."

"Truth?" Jeep answered, glad she'd adopted Katie's favorite expression. Let the bitch know she'd disrupted a whole history of love. "The lady weirds me out."

"How unusual."

R seemed to expect an explanation. Jeep, who'd been holding a fist full of the popcorn she'd grabbed from a passing bowl, carefully choose one kernel and bit it in half. She'd never encountered a person who would barge into a sticky situation like this. She guessed it was really, really important to R to make sure she confronted potential demons, even if it meant tromping on an insignificant heart she'd helped fracture. Maybe she was kind of like a politician, always looking for ways to make points. The woman could have approached her any time in private. She was looking for witnesses to her recital. Someone had way oversalted the popcorn.

R smoothed a wool shawl that Sarah would have saved a year to buy and then considered too good to wear to the movies. Did R have big bucks? If she did, then why did she live practically like a street person? She was studying Jeep's eyes, obviously looking for the note that would charm her. Cooler now, she said, "I hope you enjoy being with your sisters for the evening."

Jeep kept her eyes on R's as she let disgust take over her voice. "You are sooo seventies." Carefully, she put the other half of the kernel of corn in her mouth.

She heard the outside door slam. Otherwise the room was almost silent.

"Jeep, I'd be disappointed if we couldn't have peace between us," R said.

Jeep stretched her mouth into a mockery of the smile R had been soliciting. Fire, she thought. Fire all phasers. "Maybe you should've thought of that first."

It was like watching an ice age arrive on fast forward. Jeep's hands blazed with heat and her red alert flashed: Enemy Engaged. Proceed with Caution.

"Can any of us control our paths, Jeep?"

Yeah, I'd like to control yours, she thought. She'd never physically attacked anyone in her life, but if she had a light saber she'd do some damage about now. She pictured R's hands, severed, dropping from her wrists and herself yelling, "You'll never touch Sarah again!" Katie. She'd never touch Katie again. Why was she thinking of Sarah?

At that moment Cat pushed a full bowl of popcorn into Jeep's arms and, guiding her backwards as she pulled Donny along, said, "Fall in, girls. There's Chick. We've got to grab seats. Excuse us, R!"

Shaking, Jeep settled between Donny and Cat with Chick at the end of the row. She felt safely surrounded by rebel troops. Do not cry, she told herself. Do not fucking cry. Deep breath, she told herself and turned to Cat. "You were awesome."

Cat touched her arm. "You were amazing."

"Do not cry," she said aloud, teeth gritted. A post blocked her view of the terrible twosome.

"You pulverized that snake in the grass," Donny said.

Chick leaned across Donny. "What did you do to poor R? She's the color of the blank screen."

"Not enough," Jeep said for the second time that day. "Did I just make an archenemy? Do I need to find passage to another planet?" She'd never be able to call this place home if she left now.

"Oh, Jeep," Chick said with her loving smile. "R is my drumming friend, but she comes on too strong. You declared independence. Good for you."

"She's right," Donny agreed. "That was like the first day at school. You faced down the bully in the schoolyard."

"I did?" She saw that Donny and Chick were holding hands. She missed that, hokey as she'd always thought it.

"You did," Cat agreed softly. "I'm proud of you. For all she's supposed to have done for the women's community, someone's needed to stand up to that woman for a long, long time."

"She's so troubled," Chick said. "What she needs is someone to hold her until she feels loved enough."

"For about ten years. In East Peoria," said Donny, but Jeep was admiring Chick's big heart.

Chick looked sad, watching R stand and turn to the audience to introduce the film. "That would be a good start."

How did Chick manage to care about even R?

The film was *Little Women*, circa 1933. Jeep had never known what people saw in that shrill-voiced Hepburn who always sounded on the edge of hysteria, and this copy was so scratchy, the women's voices so strident, the action so crazed, that she wasn't alone in her derision. First the audience squirmed, then giggled. The woman behind Jeep gave an alcohol-fragrant wolf whistle, and the laughter began.

Jeep joined in quietly at first. She was the new kid and had been conspicuous enough tonight. She was so pissed at R that her heart had hardly been bruised from seeing the two of them together. She felt happy, damn it. How could that be? Friends, she realized. Chick and Donny had become her friends, and Cat—she might just be starting something with Cat too.

Donny elbowed Jeep. It wasn't R's night. She'd risen to her full height, like a portentous moon, and now gave an insulted toss of her braid. With a regal stride, she left the hall. Quickly, head down, hands in the pockets of her leather jacket, Katie followed.

That's when the popcorn fight broke out. Jeep didn't start it, but, when Cat let fly with one well-aimed kernel that got her on the chin, she let herself whoop with laughter, and flung handfuls at everyone between herself and the door.

CHAPTER SEVEN

The Rain Never Stopped

The rain never stopped.

R and Katie climbed in silence along a narrow path above Spirit Ridge. Katie's TV news career had beamed her to a lot of places, none of them this deep into the natural world. She said, "I've never seen a place so consistent about raining while the sun's out."

With her staff, R pointed in the direction of a double rainbow.

"Awesome." Katie squeezed R's arm. She'd been watching her feet which still tripped or slipped on these wet trails if she didn't pay close attention to where she was going. Sometimes she worried that she'd caught Jeep's chronic imbalance, though Jeep's falls seemed to go along with her passionate and sometimes off-putting enthusiasms. "This place is enchanted. It's—" R pulled away and walked uphill.

They went on through a dripping patch of evergreens, past madrone trunks losing their bark in camouflage patterns, under the naked live oaks and aspen.

When they stopped again, Katie breathed deeply. "This is how the world should smell. All pine and earth, like an all-natural room deodorizer. And mushrooms? These are platters. Are they edible? Do people get high on them or am I thinking of the Southwestern kind?"

"Kate. You're chattering again."

She stifled a flash of annoyance. "Bummer," she said as airily as she could. "I think aloud, don't I?"

No one had ever complained before, but then she'd never had such a silent lover. R couldn't even tolerate Katie moving to the music on her headset. She'd tried playing Melissa Etheridge for R, but she'd covered her ears with her hands and looked more like Katie was stabbing her, than sharing an incredible song. R seemed to love her own thoughts more than—truth?—more than Katie.

"You make me feel like some little kid when you shush me like that, R."

"I don't make you feel anything. Own your emotions."

Katie started to protest, but stopped herself. She'd always been the trailblazer. First in her family to go to college, first woman news anchor for one station, first Latina for two others. Here, R was the leader. That was okay—following was cool. She had things to learn, but did R have to be so dismissive?

They turned onto an even rougher logging road. Deep furrows of half-dried mud ripped into the earth by heavy trucks and equipment made walking more difficult.

R stabbed her staff into the muddy ground. "Rapists. If you could have seen the land a few years ago you'd feel sick. That was all green. Now look at it. This violation is slightly above Dawn Farm. When the rains come, the topsoil will be washed from their gardens, the cabins may flood, and their spring—they may have to drink bottled water. We're building a cabin for a chemically sensitive woman over there. She is one of the creatures who've had their immune systems compromised by the male greed that's destroying the earth. Men are impervious to the wreckage they leave behind."

Katie realized then that R hadn't been showing her the rainbow, but the stripped hillside across the way. "Oh, gak. Is that a clear-cut? You're right, it's sickening. Why didn't they bomb it and save themselves the trouble? Why is this total logging allowed? I feel like doing an expose for national TV—from a feminist perspective." Immediately she saw herself in front of the cameras, earnestly clear-cutting forests of viewer ignorance. Awards would come; she'd thank R as she accepted.

"Women birth life. Boys destroy it."

"Testosterone—Can Our Forests Survive It?"

R's smile was teasing. "Do I smell one of your sound bites?"

She examined R for a sign that she was making fun of her. "You think I live and breathe stories. I was trying to be succinct and, like, lose the chattiness." Did she really think in headlines? "I can't win with you."

"Are we competing?"

She closed her eyes and shook her head. Sometimes R could be so discouraging. She was like a sniper who knew exactly how to aim at Katie's shakiest points. "You're always doing Ms. Rita Right," she told her, "full of brilliant insights and incisive comments."

R whirled on her, lifting her staff. Katie fought back the specter of terror so far inside her she was barely conscious of it, so her fear seemed out of proportion. Against the backdrop of heavy equipment tracks, uprooted brush and tree stumps from two to over three feet across, R spread her green poncho like wings. Her hood fell back into an aura that spotlighted that pale, serene face now handsomely flushed from the hike.

"Kate," R proclaimed, "I'm passionate about you, your enthusiasm, your energy, your millennial vision." She enfolded Katie in her arms. "And I'm a crone who loves her forest solitude."

"You told me it's healthy to let my inner child speak!" She'd never heard herself whine the way she did around R. "Now you think you've created a monster. Tell me to shut up, R, okay?"

R pressed her closer. The heat of anger re-formed to a cloud of excitement. My beloved, she sang to herself. She thought their explosive lust would flare here in the midst of the delicate hanging lichen and the hundreds of small mushrooms thrusting up through the earth all around them. She wished she could offload these emotions and the confusion they created in her.

Gunshots burst into the quiet.

"Mira!" Katie cried.

R moved quickly away from her, waving her arms and shouting, "Hello! Hello!"

A deer, two fawns whose spots had not completely faded, a stag, then a younger stag bounded from the woods to their right and stopped short at the sight of them, ears twitching, eyes staring.

"Run!" cried R, waving her arms and lunging toward them.

The deer leapt the road and vaulted over dense brush toward the steep mountainside above them. R seemed to grow taller and broader. Her reddened face turned toward the sound of snapping twigs. Katie's fear blossomed again, and again she shoved it back down with a vicious caution.

From their right came a man, rifle balanced casually under one arm, and behind him a boy, knees bent as he walked, his own rifle clutched Rambo-style as if he expected an enemy to leap at him.

"I was afraid you were going to shoot us," said R in her tightest disapproving tone.

"I hope you ladies will think about wearing brighter clothing."

"It's not," pronounced R, "hunting season."

The father laughed at her. "I'm showing my boy the ropes. Don't make a federal case of it."

"Look, Dad! Scat!"

"That's my man. They broke this way." With a smirk he tipped his hat. "Have a nice walk"—he paused a second too long—"ladies."

The rain was really letting loose now. Katie's suede-brimmed cap kept raindrops off her glasses, but the knees of her jeans were like iced gel packs. She was cold right down to her soul as she watched those men jog away. "I've interviewed murderers who felt less evil than that man."

"Men take life for pleasure."

Katie shivered. "Can't you stop them from killing on your land?"

"This is Forest Service Land. We're walking a logging road."

"And the Forest Service doesn't care?"

"Care? These agencies will sometimes pay a bounty to men who keep certain animal populations down."

Gunshots rang out again. Katie had been less upset in sniper and hostage situations with SWAT teams deployed all around her. She aimed her anger at R. "But you said it's out of season. We can get Sheriff Sweet out here. We can do something!"

"That sheriff is probably married to a hunter. She won't stop it. We can and do circle. We ask the Goddess to protect the land and our furred, finned, and feathered neighbors."

"That's not going to fix anything, R. Look at the Kyoto Agreement that wacko in the White House reneged on this month. The environment is big-time news. The peaceful nature-lovers, the crashing dozers, the fawn-murderers. News is education."

"Kate, women's spirit is so much more powerful than journalism. Publicity would martyr the land. The boys would at most compromise, and then the creatures would have lost ground because of our interference. That's always the way."

"So this is one of the compromises you live with here. There's a price for serenity, isn't there? I'll tell the story of women on the land, women who thought they'd find sanctuary from violence in the peace of the forest, but instead are disturbed and endangered by weekend warriors hunting for terminal fun."

R said, "There you go again, writing copy instead of talking about how you feel, filtering your emotions through chatter. You said you'd come to escape your media circus." She turned away and walked uphill.

The guns were silent now, but so was the forest wildlife. In her head Katie answered R, no longer sure enough of herself to speak aloud. Yes, she'd come seeking clarity, serenity, the company of peaceful women.

She wanted to belong here. Yet there was no way she could turn off the excitement that bubbled as she trod this sodden, somehow sacred trail. She wanted to burst into song with "His Eye is on the Sparrow," that Lauryn Hill/Tanya Blount gospel song from *Sister Act II*. Had R even seen *Sister Act*? Instead a bird broke the silence, its call like Woody Woodpecker's—was there really a Woody Woodpecker bird? "What was that?"

"The bird? They're called pileated woodpeckers, gorgeous, prehistoric-looking creatures."

"Wow." Katie decided not to mention the cartoon character to R. And squelch the *Sister Act* song, she told herself. Instead, she offered, "Growing up, Mom and I talked about almost everything. There weren't enough minutes in the day to say it all."

"Ah! You're looking for another mother. Did you have a falling-out?"

"Never! We're okay, Mom and me. She loved that stupid chihuahua in the ads. She used to say, 'We didn't need no steenkin man.' She didn't marry until last year. Her feet were wearing out, so she took the best offer. She loved her catering business, said she always felt like she was going out to a party, not working, and she earned more tips than you can imagine, enough to buy our trailer and send me to college. Her customers were always proposing to her. Bob was her insurance agent for over twenty years and getting ready to retire. He can't believe she finally married him, and he treats her like his own personal movie star. She can't believe she landed a nice guy with a great house and enough money in the bank that they're traveling all the time. Before Bob—BB, we say—I was back there once a month to see her."

They hurried through an open space where the roadside dropped steeply to one side and was sheer cliff on the other. There were only scraggly scrub oaks and manzanita bushes here, exposing them to the rain.

"Look!" R cried, and Katie saw the huge woodpecker and heard its beak drumming at a dead tree.

"That's fantastical."

"You must miss your mother," R said, once again under the evergreens, trilliums dense on either side of the path.

"Truth? It's kind of freeing. I love seeing Mom, but it was hard to take that much time from work."

"Did she like your little friend Jeep?"

Katie laughed, remembering how her mother had hugged Jeep, then pronounced her too young a catch and told Katie she'd have to throw her back. And she had been right. Jeep had all those rough edges and made love with the excessive passion of a kid. "Mom thought she was cute as a button." A tumultuous button that rolled every which way and threatened to pull everything it was tied to into some vast chasm of lost buttons. Katie couldn't afford the distraction and had done what Mom said, thrown her back.

"Will I meet your mother?"

She felt a rush of hope that R might be serious enough to want to meet her Mom. She could see herself with R years from now, like Chick and Donny, having little traditions with each other's families. "If she comes up this way. Unless you want to come to California with me for the holidays. I promised I would always be there for Christmas."

"The thought of leaving this sanctuary during the most patriarchal and commercial season isn't appealing. I would be interested in knowing what she thought of me. Not cute as a button, I suspect."

"You called that right. And you'd totally hate hearing us chatter together. There's always so much to catch up on. Now I get the scoop on Bob's kids, their mother, and all his relations, while I'm trying to tell Mom the behind-the-scenes details that never get on TV."

She stopped while R bent to examine a cluster of mushrooms before slipping them into a small mesh sack. "Wow, R, look at the size of that pine cone! This whole forest is prehistoric. I need to send one of these down to Mom. She'll never believe me otherwise. I expect to find giant woodpecker eggs next." Her mother was a little like Jeep, careening dangerously over her edges and onto Katie's. But Katie could handle her—a shut door, a warning word was all it took to stamp out her hot spots. "I suppose," she went on, "it's why I became a newscaster. In my job I can chatter to the world. But I need breaks from it, slow quiet times, women like you. I can do this, R, be in the stories I write."

R said nothing, but turned and led the way deeper through the ancient pine, cedar, and hemlock trees. She thinks I'm crazy, thought Katie. Does she have a clue what I'm talking about?

She tripped on a broken root, its end jutting into the air like a tough, defiant reminder that it had once lived deep under the floor of the forest. She caught herself before she fell, but the loss of balance left her breathing more quickly. As if I could ignore a story like this. It had all the elements: a range of people, cute animals, conflict, politics, moral issues. The strutting family man and his child versus the rebel women and Bambi. She forgot the damp, her chill. R was a disappearing beacon ahead. She'd buy a camera of her own; she still had enough in savings and had had her eye on a Sony mini-DV cam for a while. She'd film this commanding woman, her lover, striding with her staff. She'd interview the men who hunted and who fed their children by stripping the land of trees that were irreplaceable in their lifetimes. She'd show the deer running, the women drumming for life.

Priority numero uno—she'd find a way to make R listen to her.

CHAPTER EIGHT

Bulldagger

Donny left her pickup about three-quarters of a mile from the main road. She strapped on her leather tool belt and folded a pair of work gloves under it, then started walking uphill the rest of the way to Dawn Farm.

It had rained all week, but today you wouldn't know it, she was thinking as she took a deep breath of the piney air and passed from cool shadows into pools of light that lifted a thin steamy mist from the muddy road. This felt like the first day of spring, although that had come a couple of weeks back. It was time to start going for walks again with Chick. They loved to walk over the wooden bridge in the park and watch the creek splash along the rocks. This would be a good time to hike to the waterfalls, too, when there was still plenty of runoff from the snows on Blackberry Mountain. The sound of boots jogging heavily toward her cut short her dreaming. Harold and Joe appeared around a bend.

"Hey, gentlemen," called Donny, "did I miss all the action? My truck had indigestion. As usual."

Big Harold, a massive muscled man in the logging drag of high-water jeans, red suspenders, and dirt-smudged white thermal jersey, leaned over to hold Loopy's muddy paws away from his jeans. In a nasal whine he said, "I won't work with those women one more minute!"

"It's roof day, Harold. Practically every faggot and dyke in town pitched in on this project at one time or another. You can't quit now or we'll take away your queer union card. Loopy, off!"

Harold put an arm around Joe's shoulders. Shy, plump, broad-shouldered Joe wore shorts on his bowed legs year round, with a down vest so often repaired it had a patchwork pattern.

"Donny," Harold said, with a gay man's mannered exasperation, "you know we're into respecting the Mother. We don't hunt. We don't cut old growth. We don't even look at riparian zones. We always replant, and only money-crazed fools clear-cut." He scratched the stubble of red hair around his bald spot. "What is it with these women? They're acting like I don't know what, like we're Georgia Pacific storm troopers."

Donny sighed. They were finishing a chem-free cabin for Kimama. "Is it the Spirit Ridge gals? Is R micromanaging you to death?"

Big Harold said, "Muriel the Dawn Farmer is a major pain, but we're used to her. I feel bad for Kimama. She may have chronic fatigue and multiple chemical sensitivity, but I'm sorry, that R has chronic harangue syndrome and she poisons *my* environment. R's sidekick Turda or whatever she calls herself—"

"Why can't they just have names?" Joe complained in a small voice.

"Tundra," supplied Donny, tilting the brim of her hat to keep the sun from her face. Harold in bitch mode was as annoying as Tundra.

"Frozen Turda," Harold said. "*Not* the flavor of the week at my ice cream parlor. She acts like R is a goddess. Talk about encouraging the woman."

Joe shyly spoke again. He was no rocket scientist, but had a way of seeing clearly from his heart. "The women have to be nice to R even when she drives them crazy," he said slowly, as if he were working it out for himself. "They can't say anything to her—she's their landlord—lady—whatever. R's a nudzh, a total nag. The women get upset and take it out on us because we can't fight back without being attacked for our sex."

He'd pulled a roach from a vest pocket and now flicked a match to life with his fingernail, lit the roach, and drew deeply. Donny shook her head no when he offered it, and Big Harold waved it away. "We graded this whole road with them, put a culvert in the washed-out creek bed, and spread rock, but today it's civil war, baby."

"How," Big Harold ranted, "can anyone stand to have sex with such a bunch of crabby, stinky, bossy—"

"Loopy, get off Harold! Now! I mean it!" commanded Donny. "The women aren't like that alone with each other," she said, surprised to find herself defending women she usually agreed were crabby, stinky, bossy dykes or worse. Chick was forever pointing out that only one of them was generally stinky, exactly two out of all of them were bossy, and the crabby one spent most of her time by herself in her house up the Elk River. "I don't know if trying to change the world gets to people, or if you have to be kind of crazy to try and change the world in the first place. What went down?"

"Oh, nothing much," Big Harold said. "They insisted that to give Kimama's cabin pure female energy they had to put the ridge pole in place themselves. Joe and I were asked to take our testosterone elsewhere." He raised a hand. "I understand. If we didn't have our own place we'd live at the men's land. But why not do it before we got there? Or R *could* have skipped her morning rude pill."

Joe had swallowed the last of the roach while they talked, then knelt and took both of Loopy's ears in his large hands, caressing and scratching behind them. These two men were a walking history of gay Waterfall Falls. Joe's family had pioneered the little valley shortly after Cat's had. Harold's father had found it while wandering after World War II. Joe and Harold fell in love on the wrestling team at the district high school and started an herb farm in the 1960s, employing first the hippies who lived at land collectives and now lesbians from Dawn Farm and Spirit Ridge. The women thought $8 an hour wages from gay employers who let them play in the dirt all day was heaven. Harold and Joe had spent many long winter evenings over the store or out of town at their double-wide manufactured house, playing board games and dissing the community.

"I've wanted to slap R upside the head myself a time or two," Donny reminded them. "Chick keeps telling me it's bad karma."

"Bad karma," said Big Harold, "is what put somebody like R in my life in the first place." He waited a beat, placing one fist on each of his hips and raising his chin in a queenly manner and added, "Anyway, they dropped it and put a crack in it."

"Say what?"

Joe had a stick and threw it far up the road for Loopy. She took off after it on feet as oversized as a puppy's, picked it up, and headed back downhill with long pauses for distracting smells.

Harold said, "Putting that in is a hell of a job even for a crew of, ah, individuals born with—ah, who had the opportunity to, develop their upper body strength."

"You're talking about the less-equal gender? About you boys?"

Joe said, "It fell on that chinquapin tree stump Dee uses as a table, but didn't even dent the thing. You can't buy a table that good."

"I'm gonna cry," said Donny. Loopy reappeared, dropped the stick at her feet, and panted up at her.

"Kimama did," Harold told her.

"Couldn't you save it?" She was thinking about the way Chick would hoot with laughter when she told her about this later.

"With what, Gorilla Glue? We offered to cut a new pole. 'You just want an excuse to rape the forest, to take another sacred tree off Dawn Farm,'" Harold mimicked. Joe launched the stick again. "What did you do," Harold asked, "train that dog to break the speed of fetch? I've never seen a slower, sillier-looking animal."

Donny was still trying to come up with something that would explain the women's behavior when the three of them started laughing at Loopy's antics. Hell, why should she defend them? They were brought up to be polite like her and purposely acted ugly to men.

"Was I supposed to train her? I never had a dog back in the city—I didn't know how. Loopy had to train Loopy. I was too much of a gay dog myself," she said with a wink.

Joe smiled at his shoes. "Gay dog Donny."

The men seemed calmer now as Loopy alternated between bringing the stick to Harold and Joe.

"It's true," Donny said, "that green wood can make MCS people sick. That's why we dried the pole all these months."

"So can green lesbians make you sick," Harold said. "Excuse me for trying to help the bitch out of a jam, Don."

"That's a bitch," Donny flared, pointing toward her dog. "R's loopy too, but tell me you're perfect."

"Was there ever a doubt in your mind that I wasn't?" asked Harold.

It was hard to stay mad around these two. While Joe played tug-of-war with Loopy for the splintering stick, Harold said aloud what Donny was wondering. "I thought we got over this man-hating separatist business when we fought the ballot measures together. We need each other." He gave a deep sigh. "We'd better go before they spot us loitering and accuse us of insensitivity to homicidal lesbians. Thanks for letting us play with your gay dog. She's very therapeutic."

"I like to be with Loopy when I'm upset," Donny said. "I'm a happy animal when I'm around such a happy animal."

"You lucked out. She's got a little bit more oomph to her than a purebred Lab."

"Like me," Donny boasted. "Did I ever tell you that my mother comes from Ethiopian royalty and my grandfather said an Irish pirate married my great-great-grandmother off a slave ship?"

"Only thirty-three times, Don. And even you don't believe it."

She could have sworn she kept that iffy family story to herself around the boys. "Princesses and pirates—sounds like an instant dyke mix to me," she said.

"Have your writer give you some new lines, girlfriend."

"Let's go back up," said Joe.

Harold shrugged. "I'm over it. We might as well."

"Not quite yet," Donny urged. "Not all lesbians have my royal blood. Most of us are still pirates. Go see Chick at the store. Tell her to feed you. Go on." She made shooing motions. Something to eat and Chick's laughter would mellow these two out before they stirred the pot back here at Dawn Farm.

"Yes, your Highness," Harold said with a wide grin.

Joe mumbled, "Maybe she's got some of that tofu loaf today."

Donny tromped up the hardening mucky ruts. Steam rose between the twisted branches of a stand of manzanita and madrone. Farther on, the scrub oak and pines took over again while the last spring mushrooms poked through clumps of fragrant earth. When they'd very selectively cut down the trees where Kimama's cabin was to go, and set them to dry inside the pole barn last October, there'd been gay guys up from the Bay Area with gym-chiseled muscles pretending they didn't want to break their nails, and dykes teaching them to use chain saws while policing the trails to protect wild flowers and endemic ferns from big male feet. There had been none of this nasty sniping. With the rains, only the locals remained and the party mood was gone.

The sound of hammering, women's shouts through the woods, and the sound of a patiently wielded saw grew louder as Donny approached the tarped common kitchen, then passed a fenced garden with a perpetual crop of kale and green onion nestled in the weeds. In contrast to the better-planned Spirit Ridge, Dawn Farm was a bedraggled do-your-own-thing effort. A half-dozen shelters made of wood, corrugated plastic, and stone, some abandoned, dotted the thirty-two acres. Women came with their dreams, left after a week, or stayed for years. The resident dog, Maat, an old girl, lumbered over to Loopy and licked her face. Loopy tried to interest her in playing, but she went back under the shade of a sugar pine, one of the few untouched by the white pine blister rust that plagued these woods.

There was Kimama doggedly preparing window frames. She could work about half an hour at a time. Her cat, Muse, a white-and-black

Japanese bobtail that didn't set off her allergies, watched her from a good-sized boulder.

As a clot of women slid lumber up a skid, Muriel and Tundra pulled with rope while R, visiting for the day, directed. Solstice, also over from Spirit Ridge, was sawing wood, and the tall new kid, also from Spirit—was it Tree, Timber? Spruce, that was it—she was working on a threshold with a plane. The notorious ridge pole was not in sight. She took off her hat and fanned herself.

"Hello, Donny," said R, a sugary tone in her voice and an appraising look in her eyes. "Have you come to help me?"

She was glad Harold and Joe weren't hearing this woman because they'd about-face and walk again.

"I'm here to help Kimama," she answered pointedly, but couldn't resist adding, "Aren't you?"

R looked into her eyes for a long moment. "Chick said you have a problem with anger. Have I done something to make you angry?"

"Chick told you that?" Donny blurted. Where did Chick get off telling R this kind of shit? Yes, it was true, she was angry, chronically, intolerably, always angry. It was exhausting, this anger. And she was angry at one single unchangeable fact—that she was and always would be the odd woman out here in Waterfall Falls and everywhere, but especially here. She was black in a white land, woman in a man's world, gay in a straight universe. She wouldn't be any other way, but she was permanently angry that neither would the world change. The anger spilled out of her and that was probably a good thing, or she would explode from it.

R was watching her. "Shouldn't I have said anything? I thought you were talking with each other about your problem. You should be talking to someone. It rushes out of you. Maybe one of your so-called butch friends? Katie's ex probably needs a friend."

"So-called?"

"Clearly, you're in the mood to feel offended today. You don't intimidate me like you do many of the women, but for Kimama's sake let's pretend I never said a word, shall we? I see you have your own tools. I'd like to get the roof completed today."

Intimidating? R was the intimidator around here. Donny was too mad to think what to say to the woman. R reminded her of a pimp she'd come into too much contact with in Chicago. He ran a string of transvestites who at least pretended to adore him. When he'd walk into a bar trailing a "girl" or two, he acted like he owned everyone in sight. He was so far above them all that he'd clear a bunch of dykes out of a booth with a sweep of his hand. Then, too, she'd been too infuriated to protest.

She followed R's line of vision and saw the ridge pole. "What the—"

"Aren't women resourceful? When the pole broke they lashed it together."

"This is bullshit," Donny said. "That jerry-rigged thing won't last through the first wet snow. Do you know how hard it's going to be to fix? Did you stop to think that roof might crush Kimama in her bed? What is wrong with you people?"

"Donny," R said in a calm and quiet voice. "You need to know that I find the term 'jerry-rigged' highly offensive to the German people. Your color doesn't excuse that kind of slur."

The anger stretched her skin till it felt like a mask across her face. The woman was out of line, wasn't she? Donny couldn't tell any more whether her anger was righteous. She was so mad at so much. As a kid she'd been mad at black people because everything wrong in her world was their fault for being poor and uneducated. In the sixties and seventies she was mad at white people because everything wrong in her world was the oppressor's fault. She'd seriously wanted to be a Black Panther.

"I don't need to know anything from you, R. And why don't you let the Germans take care of themselves? I find it highly offensive that you fucked up this woman's roof and disrespected my friends Harold and Joe. They've taken too much of your holier-than-thou, anti-man attitude over the years. You may have the rest of these women fooled, but not this bulldagger."

R was stillness itself. She might be meditating, not acting like a human shredder. "This is old territory between us, Donny. You know I don't think the term 'bulldagger' appropriately describes who we are. Please control yourself or leave us to work in peace."

"Why? Because I'm the only one around you can't control? Not my problem. You're in rare form today, R. Harold and Joe were right on to offer a new pole. What were you trying to prove?"

"I refuse to listen to your abuse. You have got to get control of yourself."

"Baby, I am controlling myself. You don't want to see me when I lose control of my bulldagger self. And by the way, I wasn't inviting you into the bulldagger home-girl club." Two women began to nail rafters at the top of the cabin. "What're they doing now?" If R thought Donny was going to let her mad go and start bowing down, she had another thing coming. "When that pole collapses it's all going to have to be taken out and redone, probably in pouring rain and heavy winds, and then where is that child going to stay?"

"Isn't she beautiful?" came a soft, very young voice behind her.

Donny turned to Kimama's beatific smile. Her round face and albino coloring gave her a cherubic air, despite her years as a street kid. Kimama was Shoshone for "butterfly," and the name fit her well. She must not have heard what was being said over the hammering and the saw.

Kimama asked, "Did R tell you the ridge pole crashed this morning? Lucky Muriel was a Girl Scout."

Donny could feel her face relaxing, the skin giving up its tautness. "That's one bad-ass lashing job."

"I need to go zone out." Kimama looked up with that happy grin. "And dream about my—almost—roof."

The last of the fight went out of Donny. She looked around at the woods, at the blue sky, the air so clear she could see buds on the trees. She should holler to shut down the job until it could be done right, but this trusting baby dyke needed her space yesterday. She'd talk with Harold and Joe about ways to make it safe. With any luck R would be running some other crew of women ragged on her own land when they came back out to shore it up. Maybe they could prop it with a couple of sturdy posts. Chick would like that—it would give Kimama someplace to hang herbs to dry and her washing in winter.

Did she intimidate Kimama? "It'll be a whole roof by tonight, no sweat, girl."

"I can see why Chick snapped you up, Donny."

"For my brains and good looks?"

"No, silly, because you make everything sound doable."

"Well, it is. Just about everything is do-able."

"But poor Harold and Joe. The women weren't very kind to them. They've helped me from the start, and they'll be mad if they're not in on the finish."

"Harold and Joe will be fine. They'll be back in a little while." There she went, reassuring this sweet young femme again. It was a reflex.

Donny unbuttoned her vest and answered the work crew's greetings. She wasn't much of a hugger herself, but she put up with some hugging. Maybe she should do more of it, make sure she wasn't intimidating anyone. That crack stuck in her craw, damn it. Was it her anger that scared them? The floor of the cabin was slick with sawdust. Five minutes later she was straddling a rafter, high on working hard and quick, hoping her creaky joints wouldn't disable her tomorrow. She used her grandfather's hammer. He was the one who taught her about tools as he made repairs on his store.

She wasn't even going to bother to hash out the boy issue or talk about repairs with Tundra and Muriel. They always sided with R, except when the three of them went at it among themselves. Still, as exasperating, brash, and contemptuous as they could be, she had to love them: their hair slicked back with sweat, lips clenched on nails, skinny white arms working those hammers to build a new world. She'd get Harold and Joe out here this summer. Maybe Jeep and the sheriff would help too, although as far as she knew, the sheriff had not set foot on women's land except during the black helicopter scare when the women living at Dawn Farm thought they were being spied on.

Donny couldn't budge these political types with their attitudes, but there wouldn't be women's land without them. Dykes had some choices besides the bar scene because of those attitudes. Chick would help make peace between them and the boys. She was probably loading up Harold and Joe right now, sending them back with lunch for everyone.

"I'm putting on my working music, women!" she called out.

"Did you bring your disco tapes?" asked Kimama.

"Why? Do you want to dance?" she asked and snapped her fingers.

"Not to that old music!" Kimama said with a laugh.

"It may be old, but it's not that trashy rap."

While she worked she imagined in turn dancing with Kimama and watching Tundra and Muriel whup that old pimp's ass.

CHAPTER NINE

Pensioners' Posse

The streets of Waterfall Falls were as wide as they had been in the days cattle thundered through. Natural Woman Foods was the last business at the south end of town, and the last with a roofed sidewalk. When she'd first seen the store, she knew it was the one she wanted if for no other reason than that wooden false front. This was the Wild West whose images she'd grown up with, and it fed some hunger in her for adventure. No matter how strung out she was from this persistent depression on any particular day, Chick never stopped being enchanted by her lonesome outpost. On days like this one, with wetness from the last rain shower sparkling in the pine branches to the south of the store, she felt like the luckiest woman on earth.

She moved from the window to the little nook of the store that made so many of the townspeople curious and a little nervous. Here she sold crystals and amethysts, unscented candles, and mother-earth necklaces. Here were the healing books, the We'Moon calendars and the chakra charts, the anthologies of women's spirituality, and the herb bags which at times brought her so much comfort, and which some of the older customers bought as sachets. Rattlesnake came in for bundles of sage and complained that Chick abused them by storing them in plastic. Chick laughed and said even the Goddess would sneeze at their smell. This was not merely a display of New Age sidelines; it was her altar at work.

The altar she'd made upstairs, on the secondhand oak hutch Donny had secretly refinished and given her one Christmas, was more personal. There were pictures of Donny, of Donny and herself, of the bluegrass band in Village People costume, and of Blackberry Mountain with a bonnet of snow. The store altar did in a pinch, and she'd already dusted in there twice today.

Despite facing the shelves, bagging the day-old baked goods, making up dozens of packages of seeds and nuts, waiting on customers, and making half a dozen pots of coffee before ten o'clock, it wasn't until Clara and Hector White arrived in their rusted pickup that Chick discovered what a truly sorry state she was in. Clara barged inside with Hector limping several feet behind. Would she and Donny look like that in twenty-five or thirty years? Chick careened toward them, arms out, thirsty for hugs and suddenly enveloped in the mugginess of a hot flash.

"Twenty-three years since that old branch snapped back at me, and I still feel her right here," said Hector, rubbing his arthritic hip. He hugged her, then held her at arm's length. His fuzzy white hair was bunched like a clown's around the base of his Ford cap. She could see the top of his long underwear shirt where his collar opened. "You look like the rain's getting to you too."

"You know she loves the rain," snapped Clara.

Chick settled them into seats, pouring coffee with an unsteady hand. "It's *him* again. That sleazeball M.C."

Hector said, "Forgive an old man his memory, but this guy was what, family? A friend?"

"Just a creepy guy who was part of the crowd I hung with."

"Lordy, lordy, doesn't that fool know you can't stand the sight of him?" Clara asked as she patted dry her face and the white hair that escaped the frayed oversized men's handkerchief she used for a kerchief.

"He's wanted to baptize me a born-again straight person since my Chicago days."

Hector looked puzzled.

"Get me into bed," Chick explained. "Just saying it turns my stomach." She left out the part about fooling around with Pennylane. "M.C. chased every woman that passed in the street, but Pennylane was the only one he called his old lady. He used to tell the story that he'd fallen in love with me when I smashed a cop in the nose so hard all eight of us were able to bolt from the paddy wagon. M.C. included."

"I hope he doesn't have the arthritis in his nose," said Hector. "I hope he still has a nose after you got through with him. That was the time you kids got caught smoking funny stuff in the park?"

"It wasn't toking that got us in trouble, it was M.C. dealing to an undercover."

Clara looked up from folding the handkerchief and said, "Why didn't you run and let him take what was coming to him, the dirty dope pusher? Not that I think you ought to have got away with what you were doing either, but at least you weren't getting schoolchildren hooked on dope."

"They took us by surprise. The cops were doing a sweep. One word on the undercover's walkie-talkie and the uniforms were on top of us, their wagon right behind them. We lucked out when another something happened across the lake and they left those two poor drivers to take care of all of us."

"What did you do," Hector asked. "Hog-tie them?"

"Too bad we didn't have you there to show us how," Chick said with a laugh. "We didn't have to. Eight longhairs, eight directions, dozens more freaks in the park that day—by the time the cop up front in the driver's seat realized his partner was in trouble, we were scattered in the fog. M.C. even managed to grab his stash back."

"Men," Clara speared at Hector, though they'd been married fifty-two years.

Clara had said the same thing, like a call to battle, that day a week or so ago, when the pension posse went up the mountain to talk sense to M.C.

Hector had told her, "M.C. was our original ratty-haired redneck hippie. There were a bunch of them that moved into the hills from the cities, addle-brained from dope. The fool still booby-traps his land and greets folks with a shotgun. You wouldn't catch him in town till lately. Always sent his faded-looking worn-out hippie wife, that black-headed woman I understand is her sister, and their vanload of ragamuffins."

Chick sat down as she did now, smoothing her voluminous skirt around her, holding her crystal pendant with all the fingers of her right hand. It had dawned on her one day as she held her crystal that the reappearance of depression in her life, the worst since her teens, might have something to do with approaching menopause. Life was such a trip. Because she'd rejected M.C. when she'd been wild with the hormones that had probably attracted him, he was avenging himself as those hormones disappeared.

She'd told them, "I never would have planted myself here if I'd known M.C. was up on Mule Butte."

Clara had patted her hand. "What's M.C. stand for anyway? Mr. Cuckoo?"

Chick's gurgling laugh had escaped, but ended in a shudder. "No. It stood for Mission Control. You went to ol' M.C. for liftoff."

"A dope code," Clara said, punching the air with her index finger. "Didn't I tell you, Pa?"

"What brought him down to make trouble?" Hector wanted to know. "He's the one got the town to put up that sign: 'Patrolled by the Waterfall Posse. Persons breaking our laws will be remanded to the authorities.' Horsefeathers."

Chick hugged herself. "I'm afraid Donny will turn vigilante too if I tell her he's bothering me, but she knows something's happening." Donny's temper was scary. Not because Donny would ever hurt her, but Chick feared she would get into such big trouble while in a rage they'd have to leave Waterfall.

"How'd he spook you this time?"

She'd been shivering as she'd answered. "He said he was in charge of pushing snacks at the basketball game that night and wanted to show them what a moneymaker it could be. We worked out a discount and he said if they made this a regular thing, I'd be pulling in gold, not only with the basketball sales, but with all the parents who'd come into the store once they knew how out-of-sight the munchies were—he still speaks in hippie. Then he had me wrap *all* the baked goods, while he scooped pounds and pounds of bulk foods into bags. 'For my brood,' he said. I caught on when he gave this evil laugh. 'April Fool's, babe!'"

She covered her face with her hands. "I went for it. I still haven't got it all put back. I feel like I'm being stalked!"

"There you go," Hector had said solemnly, drawing her be-ringed, braceleted hands into his big sandpapery ones. "You called it right. That's exactly what's going on."

"Don't give her the heebie-jeebies, you jackass," Clara scolded.

He'd floundered. "It seems to me that if a person was to get to know you, like we did, then it doesn't matter that you're, uh, different. You're a nice gal and you—"

Clara butted in as if to forestall some passionate declaration. "—don't deserve this."

"Hey, this will cheer you up" said Hector. "What's green and lives outside?"

"This is no time for one of your riddles, you old fool."

"Patty O'Furniture!"

Chick had given him a weak smile in response. How many times had she come right up to the edge of telling Hector and Clara how homophobic they could be? Why couldn't he say gay? But she loved them for being so naively well-meaning. "Nobody deserves hang-up calls, screaming drive-by insults, notes under the door. One day he threatens to steal me, the next, to kill me. He gets me so off balance, I can't keep my mind from imagining what he'll pull next."

"With you woolgathering all the time, Donny must wonder if there's someone else." Clara shoved her uppers in place with her thumb, eyes on Chick and Hector's still-clasped hands. "I would."

Chick had drawn her hands from Hector's and went back to worrying her crystal. Of course she flirted with Hector; that was her way. With a sudden flush she remembered she'd even flirted with crazed M.C. way back when. Why had she even associated with slime like M.C.? She'd done some stupid things in her San Francisco years to surround herself with people and stop her terminal aloneness.

She'd lamented, "Twenty-five years ago M.C. didn't seem so much evil as wacko. Crazy was cool."

"There's something wrong with a man who acts the way Mr. Cuckoo does," said Clara with ardor. "You always see the best in people. That man's caught you on your blind side."

Soon afterwards, the first of their cronies had arrived.

"Malcolm," called Hector, "Got one for you!" Malcolm waved him off, but Hector went right on. "What's the difference between a mouse and a beautiful girl?"

"You want me to tell you in front of the ladies?" Malcolm said, elbowing him.

"The mouse harms the cheese, and the girl charms the he's!"

"Good one!"

It was a Tuesday, senior discount day, and sunny off and on so there were a slew of customers. If this kept up, they'd have to hire someone to help her as Tuesday was usually Donny's day up in Greenhill, getting their town supplies. Hector and Clara had discovered Natural Woman Foods first, and gradually, over a year or two, their whole crowd followed. To this day they acted as tour guides, proudly proprietary, unnecessarily parlaying questions back and forth between their friends and Chick. They were shouting interpreters, as if they were the only ones not hard of hearing. That day, even the old folks' cheery greetings failed to spike Chick's adrenaline.

Clara, like a hummingbird in a garden, had gone from a couple to a widower to two spinster farmers Chick hadn't been able to draw out. Maybe they really were sisters. As more seniors arrived, they were greeted with whispers.

Hector came over and talked about the antics of his brand-new foal, and Chick had forced herself to respond because she knew her laugh tickled these customers. She'd noticed that the baked goods she'd so carefully wrapped and unwrapped hadn't been snapped up by the usual sweet tooths. The ever-popular wheat bran and prunes lay in their bins untouched.

Several minutes later, Clara had briskly borne down on the checkout counter and announced, "There's nineteen of us here today." Slowly, the others had congregated behind her. "And plenty more where we come from. We'll be visiting Mr. Cuckoo tomorrow bright and early. Let's see if we can't step on his corns."

"You mean about—"

"The stalking," Hector supplied. "Some of these folks are in the church he's started going to."

"Church! What a hypocrite!"

"Be careful," advised a small woman who'd nodded at mention of the church. "He may be planning a hairy Christna coup like that guru who took over the town in Oregon."

"A Baptist coup?" Hector had whispered to Chick. "They'd have to have too many fund-raisers to pull that off."

She'd laughed genuinely then. The local Baptist Church was forever coming by to request a donation for one project or another, assuming that Chick and Donny were as anti-gay as their congregation. These people were serious about confronting M.C., though. "What in the world will you say to him?"

A man on a walker had informed her, "Never you mind what we'll say. The fella's getting too big for his britches altogether, and the Pensioners' Posse is going to cut him down to size on a whole passel of matters."

"I'd love to be a fly on the wall," she'd said. Donny had made their side door accessible, particularly for this fellow and the lady in the wheelchair who sometimes came in.

"You stay right here, young woman," Clara commanded. "He won't know you've had a thing to do with this. We aren't trying to make it worse for you."

There were many confirmations of this and pats on the arm or shoulder as the Pensioners' Posse hotfooted it to the aisles, piling the goods they'd been neglecting on the counter. Hector came behind the counter and bagged the groceries beside her to handle the rush. Chick made transactions as fast as she could with her eyes so misted up she could barely see. She'd come to love her senior customers.

When her pickup truck cavalry had gone back into the hills to recruit more to its indignant army, she finally finished cleaning up M.C.'s mess. Donny came home an hour later with sacks of potatoes grown by a local organic farmer. In the back room, Chick had ravished her with a lusty kiss born of feeling a little bit safer because all those people cared.

"Is my lady really back?" Chick very specifically remembered Donny asking. She'd felt as if she might have returned from the land of fear. Since then there had been no sign of M.C. Still, she felt most comfortable when someone else was in the store with her. This morning, she was trying to keep Clara and Hector as long as she could.

"Men," Clara said again. "They don't have the sense they were born with." She went back out to their car for the shopping list Hector forgot.

"What made you decide to marry Clara?" she asked him, watching Clara stride across the sidewalk and yank open the truck's heavy door.

"Oh, I liked my drill sergeant in the war too," he admitted with a laugh. "A sharp tongue strengthens character." He looked at the floor and became serious. "That old lady's been a fine helpmate, a hard, thrifty worker. It's not every woman that will take a man who can't have kids, you know. Something happened to me in the war that makes your Agent Orange look like a Kool-Aid attack."

"But you have kids."

"When we first started spending time together I told her what the Army doctors told me in the hospital, that it wasn't going to happen. Eight years after we married it did happen. I didn't know whether to accuse her of fooling around with the milkman or to declare a national holiday. I doubted it was the milkman, though. Clara and me aren't exactly the best lookers in town. When our boy started to shape up into something halfway human he looked a lot like me."

"He was born bald with a baseball cap?"

Hector grinned his gap-toothed grin. "That was the good news. He was fuzzy-headed, and you could drive a Mack truck between his front teeth, too."

Clara returned and scribbled something on her list with the stub of a pencil. "Is this the first time Mister Cuckoo's been back since we talked to him?" she asked.

Chick smiled at the nickname. She'd been calling him that to herself and found it took a little bit of the demon out of the man. "He hasn't even called and hung up on me."

"Was he doing that too?"

"I assume it's M.C. I don't seem to drive anyone else up a wall like I do him. What went down?"

"We gave him what for," Clara said. "Told him he was abusing his authority in the vigilante group if he thought he could go around town bothering young ladies."

"Far out," Chick said, amazed at their chutzpah. "You are beautiful people."

Hector grumbled, "Sounds like we need to do it again."

"We were too darned nice. I told you that, mister."

Hector ignored Clara. "We elected Malcolm to do the talking. He's a retired union leader."

"The man on the walker?"

"That's the one. He appreciated M.C.'s community involvement half to death—"

"Nearly turned my stomach," said Clara.

"—and then told him about some others we appreciate, including you."

"You may think we're old and decrepit, Malcolm says, but we stick together. Malcolm said you, for example, were like one of our kids, and we'd take care of you like one of our own."

"Meantime," Clara said, "me and a couple of the ladies kind of wandered off, seeing what we could see, but M.C. started on his own little speech about respecting privacy. We had to pretend we were too feeble to stand there and went back to our cars. Didn't see a thing except for all the old trailers and shacks he's got spread around the place. And his kids weren't anywhere near school, at least not any of the older ones. How many does he have?"

"I haven't got a clue."

"Too many," decided Clara. "He could have his own little dope farm up there with all that help."

"Probably does," Hector agreed. "I could see cleared spaces in the forest. I doubt they're corn patches."

"You're mind-blowing. I don't know how to thank you."

"Don't be ridiculous!" chided Clara. "This is our town, not some nasty character's territory."

Hector said, "It's our way of thanking you."

"Until today, I've been more calm this week than I've been in a long time."

"You leave this to us."

For a moment Chick believed they were that powerful, like a kid who still thought her parents had super powers. She half-hugged, half-clung to both of them at once. Slowly, she remembered that her protectors were a couple of eighty-odd-year-olds who planned to move into the retirement housing across the freeway in a few years. They were a lot more likely, as her mother had been, to need caretaking than to be able to take care of her. If only she could rely on Donny to help her fight off M.C. without ruining everything by losing her temper.

The thought scared her and she fought a downpour of despair. She didn't live alone and naked on a rocky mountaintop crag, but Goddess help her, that's how she felt.

CHAPTER TEN

The Quiet Drummer

Jeep and the little blond, round-faced boy sat on the classroom floor at Waterfall School. He beamed up at her.

"He don't talk," scorned his half-sister, barely a year older than little Luke's four.

"How come?" Jeep asked Luke, who watched with solemn interest as his sister flounced away. "How come you don't talk?"

He looked at Jeep again, his eyes pools of trust. He wouldn't talk to her, but he was tapping a kind of Morse code rhythm on his knees with the heels of his hands.

A maelstrom of preschoolers in pastel spring dresses and shirts swirled around them. One girl in a pink dress hurried on Canadian canes toward the windows. A precociously handsome boy with neatly combed hair sat at a tiny desk that almost hid his leg braces. The boy at the next desk rocked himself.

Arlene, the other teacher's aide, led singing while Dottie, the legally blind teacher, bent low over her paperwork despite the commotion.

A child playing in the pink plastic log cabin yelled, "P-U!"

"Whoops!" Dottie cried, instantly abandoning her desk to wheel a wailing little girl to the bathroom. Frequent incontinence in the classroom could get a kid banished. That was one of the standards for attending; they would never make it into a regular classroom until they were potty trained.

"Can you say your name?" Jeep asked.

Her nightmares these days were about multitudes of children with overwhelming needs and herself neediest of all. She dreamed that she was trying to teach impossible tasks to too many children. In the dream they had no eyes, no limbs, only wordless voices that were never silent. She'd awake with her hands sweating and swollen. Even awake she felt a constant imperative to know everything she needed to know, to give them everything they so badly needed all at once. There was no yardstick, like continence, to measure her readiness for this classroom.

The job scared her. Donny had said people who had something to teach were drawn to teaching kinds of jobs, but she'd never thought of herself as having anything to teach. These were preschoolers, though, preschoolers with a strike or two against them. She guessed she might be able to teach them some of the essentials. She'd watched her mom so patient all those years with her sister Jill.

Luke reached with a tentative hand to Jeep's buzz cut and pressed softly on it, as if expecting sharp points. He flattened it and smiled an entirely pleased kind of smile. With her first paycheck she'd gone to Arnie Herrera, the town barber, and described her old haircut. He'd tried, but she'd ended up with something that looked more flattop fifties than nineties neopunk.

"Bad haircut," she told Luke.

Dottie had told her there was no physical reason Luke couldn't talk. He was the sweetest kid, kind of like love on two feet. What had happened to him? What would happen?

"You know, Luke," she confided to the boy, "this is the last place in the galaxy I thought I'd find myself. And you—you're some advanced being luring me to Planet Bliss. Right?"

Luke startled her with a smiling nod, like a wise little alien.

"Wild. Who am I evolving to?"

While Luke tapped the toy piano next to him, she remembered that rainy day a month ago when she got started on the road to this job.

"Being poor is depressing!" she'd griped to the bluegrass band's sexy harmonica player. She was hanging her laundry on a line she'd strung across the tiny trailer when Cat knocked at the door, her pit bull George at her side. She was there to rehearse a harmonica duet Jeep wanted to add to one of the band's songs.

"Never doubted it," Cat had replied, ducking two damp flannel shirts to sit at the fold-out table. Jeep's eyes kept being drawn to those excellent breasts underneath Cat's bright white hooded sweatshirt.

"See?" demanded Jeep to distract herself. "I'm hand-washing everything. Laundromats are too pricey."

Cat leaned against the back of the countertop refrigerator and stretched her long legs across the bench. George was exploring all the new scents. Like the other locals, Cat wore Wrangler jeans, but she bought hers at the tack shop south of Natural Woman Foods on Stage Street, not at Wally World in Greenhill. Jeep had gone over to the tack shop with her and had been sorely tempted by a black cowboy hat with a lavender band. In Reno it had been mostly tourists who wore cowboy hats in air-conditioned casinos, but here, with all the rain and as hot as she was told the sun got, she could use a hat with front and back brims. Cat was sorely tempting too, even if she did smell kind of horsey today. Except, Jeep was *not* about to fall for anyone. She was just fine married to her solitude and her freedom.

"You're bragging on your poverty," said Cat.

"No way. I'm not your downwardly mobile type. I was brought up middle class. True, there were a lot of us, and the family minivan was always secondhand, but we at least had a minivan and our own Sears fucking washer and dryer, thank you very much. This scrimping on food or eating handouts from Chick and Donny is getting real old, even though I know it's some kind of worshippy-spiritual gig for Chick. Every time I thank her she's kind of like telling me, what goes around comes around."

"You're not the first one they've helped out."

"No? Who else?"

Cat was so good to look at. She could be a model for that Title Nine women's catalogue she and Sarah used to get. Meaning, she thought, strong-looking, healthy, and capable, like she wouldn't need anyone to help her change a tire on the freeway. Cat had started coming over to give her a ride to band practice, then hanging out afterward. She always brought in homemade date bars or oatmeal cookies she stashed in her truck. Jeep had laid in some of that mild green tea Cat drank all the time and put the kettle on now, wondering whose story Cat would tell her today. Donny and Chick had probably helped out half the dykes in town.

"Me for one," Cat answered.

"But you have a job, a nice house." Donny had driven her by Cat's house one day, and she'd felt herself gaping at it.

"I wasn't a financial rescue." Cat put her hands behind her head to cushion herself from the refrigerator. "Love was my problem."

"Been there, done that, did you get my postcard?"

Cat smiled, scratched George's back, and was silent so long Jeep wasn't sure she was going to tell the story. Then she saw her take a deep breath. "I fell in love with a woman and couldn't imagine a way to make a life with her. Or without her."

Jeep held her breath. Was Cat talking about her?

"So when she made her move, like a jerk I said no."

Her hopes, like a pretty little bubble, popped. Of course it wasn't her. She hadn't really thought it would be. She knew she wasn't really in love with Cat, but with her grounding. She wanted to have roots she was comfortable with too.

"We wouldn't be together now except for all the nights Chick and Donny sat and listened to me, used up boxes of tissues on me, and helped me see my way. If I'd let her go," Cat said, slowly shaking her head, eyes closed, "it would have been the biggest mistake of my life. This isn't just an attraction. We were born to be together."

Cat definitely had a girlfriend then. Yet Jeep had never seen her with anyone. She couldn't help but say, "You fell for the invisible woman? No. Wait. For Ellen, and she lives in southern Cal. Of course! Why didn't I figure that out before?" She pretended to smack herself on the forehead with the heel of her hand. "Does she fly in for holidays or what?"

Cat laughed. "I must sound crazy to you. It's nothing like that. She's got this job where either she has to be totally closeted, or totally out. And if she's out, there's going to be a big hullabaloo, and if that happened, I'd probably lose my job."

"Okay, so you're both in the closet. Sounds like a match to me."

"Jeep, this isn't a closet, it's deep cover. We can't live together, be seen together, even go to a restaurant together."

"Vacations? Long weekends?"

"It'd be noticed if we always left town at the same time, though now and then we do."

"There's someone with that high a profile in this town? No, I know, she's the resident FBI agent and needs to live like a mole so she can spy on the white separatist community living in an isolated enclave just over the mountain."

Cat sat up and looked her in the eyes. "No guessing games. We agreed we wouldn't say who we are aloud to anyone. If we don't say anything, we can't be quoted. Our closest friends will figure it out over time, and that's okay. You can't quote a guess, even if it's right."

"She must have a hell of a good job."

"It's not that so much as the fact that she believes in her job. It's who she is. I would never do anything to interfere with it." Cat laughed quietly. "It's one of those jobs that keeps her away half the time anyway. At least this way I won't worry so much."

Jeep was feeling a warm glow that Cat had kind of called her a close friend. Maybe she really was checking her out as a roomie. But, sorry, Dory. I don't have any kids to fill your house. "Me neither," she pledged. "I wouldn't want you to suffer over my big mouth. I don't even want to know who it is."

"At the same time, I need you to know that you shouldn't hesitate to trust Chick and Donny and let them help you out. That's what they're about."

Immediately, Jeep was plunged back into her own situation. "Right. But for what? So I can get arthritis freezing my fiddling fingers at the car wash? I used to know what I wanted to do with my life, Cat. Or I thought I did." She looked out at the row of trailers and the mountain behind them. "Maybe I was a little vague about what exactly, but for sure I was going to support myself playing some kind of music. That's not something I'll ever be able to do here." She looked back at the appealing mix of sultry and athletic that was Cat. "Why am I still here? There's really nothing to keep me."

Cat gave Jeep a long-suffering smirk. "Okay, fiddler-woman. Let's change the channel. While you're figuring it all out, there's an opening at Waterfall School where I teach for a preschool teacher's aide. The class is for kids with disabilities."

"Right. Me and kindergartners?" What a bogus idea, she'd thought to herself. "I can see the personnel recruiter banging on my door— we want a dyke musician with funny hair and piercings teaching our defenseless kids how to—what the hell can you teach disabled rug rats anyway? How to use a wheelchair?"

Cat looked at her with one eyebrow raised and she heard herself.

"Ah geez, I'm sorry. That was one of the most inane questions I've ever asked. Can you pretend you never heard it?"

"No problem, Jeep. I actually think you'd be good at it. That's why I'm telling you about the job. Muriel would kill me if she knew. She wants her nephew to get work and stay here. He's this genius kid who flunked out of his freshman year back East, and she thinks Oregon will fix him up."

"What is it with you and Muriel? You're kind of mismatched friends, don't you think?"

"I think I'm learning that no one's an unlikely friend," Cat replied with another smile. "It's true, I've never known anyone like Muriel. We connected because she started the band. I like that she's so totally self-involved. It means she doesn't pry. She knows lots about worlds I want to learn more about—music and art and good books. She used to teach music history and culture at Berkeley."

"Muriel?"

Cat nodded. "Her specialty was American music history."

"So that's why a bluegrass band. But you want me to try for the job, not her nephew?"

"You're a natural, Jeep."

"I am?"

"You are. I see in the band how playful you are, and focused too, open to anything unless it doesn't contribute to the session. And you're patient. Most professionals would have walked out on us really fast. I'm not the only beginner."

"It's about having fun," Jeep objected. "Why should the audience get to have all of it?"

"That's exactly what I mean. It's the attitude you need to have with kids. Girls in my classes who hate to play volleyball may love modern dance or running laps. As much as time and equipment allow, I encourage them to do what feels like fun. You could be trying to cram serious music lessons down our throats, but instead you're just being a band member. I'm learning a lot more following your lead than I would in some stuffy music class." Cat stopped, took a quick breath, and said, "Plus it'd be great for you."

Cat had really been thinking about her. "Wow. I didn't know all that about me." She admitted, "I guess a steady paycheck does have its appeal."

"You're going to love these kids. They don't let a little thing like non-functional legs or rejecting families or blindness stop them. They use what they've been given, no questions asked. They are wild on the playground, let me tell you."

"You think I need the inspiration, is that it?"

"I don't know, Jeep. Something's holding you back, isn't that what you were telling me? I'm having trouble believing it's the end of your relationship with Katie. Do you really think that was a match made in heaven?"

"It doesn't much matter what I think. She was just fun and exciting and—"

"A great lover? I've heard that line before. I've said it. That's not a formula for anything lasting. It's a formula for a love affair. Hell, my horse is fun and exciting. Plus she's never left me for another woman."

"And the sex?" teased Jeep.

"My horse is celibate."

"I knew that."

"So, will you at least apply for the aide job? These are kids that are being prepped to mainstream into kindergarten, then first grade. Not all of them will make it, but with the right help, a lot will."

Jeep hung the last of her socks. Could she help them? She dropped onto the bench across from Cat and felt the trailer shudder. "You're really wacked, Cat, you know that? Me and kids. I'd probably trip over a tiny tot and break it—day one."

"Afternoons only, five days a week, $9.25 an hour, pro-rated bennies. They have separate funding for classes in the summer too, so you could work year-round. No experience required."

"Oh, I have a little experience," Jeep said, remembering her sister's classmates. "But they'll never hire a queer."

"Am I the gym teacher there or what? In education it's don't ask, don't tell, and if they find out they may or may not fire you, like in the military. But I have to warn you, if there are more budget cuts this year, your class would be one of the first to go. You could claim unemployment though."

"You think? They denied me this time around because I didn't work last quarter. Teacher's aide. It must be the last open job in town."

The next week, Jeep went for the interview and tryout day. Dottie, a plain flabby woman in her thirties with twinkling eyes behind Coke-bottle glasses, liked her. Jeep had figured she could endure a lot for one-eighty-five a week. Indoors and dry.

And just like that, here she was, watching Luke feel his way on the toy piano. Another little guy snapped her attention back to the classroom when he bolted into the hallway. Jeep went after him and, as he opened his mouth to give his usual piercing screech, caught him under the arms and swung him around until they faced the classroom door.

"Left," she commanded. "Right! Left! Right!" It worked, as always, and they marched back in together. Jeep was awed that she was actually good with the Barney set.

Dottie clapped her hands. "Time to go see The Magic Show! Come on, the magician is waiting!"

The kids made their awkward way through the halls to a special assembly. The other pupils stared or averted their eyes.

In the auditorium, Jeep sat with her charges. Cat, unattached to a specific class, but a frequent visitor to Jeep's, leaned against the paneled wall. She wore red nylon running pants with a white stripe down the side, and a school football shirt that couldn't hide her breasts.

Okay, Jeep thought, so the babe had a girlfriend. She guessed she could use a few more friends like Cat.

Luke took Jeep's hand, patted it, and beamed. Cat was watching, her smile as big as Luke's. He just kept patting.

Jeep sighed and thought, look at me—no girlfriend, I live in a tin can, have rug rats on the brain, transplanted myself from the desert to mushroom country—and I'm so content I could sit here and cry. What am I going to do without this if they ever lay me off?

CHAPTER ELEVEN

Fishin'

Donny hadn't been surprised the first time she happened on the sheriff fishing at Sweet Creek. In thin-kneed jeans, high rubber boots and a faded black polo shirt, Sheriff Joan Sweet looked as if she'd spent half of her life on that boulder in the honeysuckle-scented air, casting her line for trout.

They shared silence well. It had become their custom to fish together once every couple of weeks, when Chick was handling the store and it wasn't raining too hard. They would split their catches. The sheriff still lived with her father, the former sheriff now retired on disability, her California-born mother, who, eighteen years younger than her husband, was chronically ill, and two much-younger twin sisters.

As Donny prepared for her old friend Abe's visit, she laughed to herself to recall the sheriff's little April Fool's Day prank the last time they'd fished. They'd settled at their usual rocky little bend where the water slowed and some of the fish practically dawdled. Down the creek a patch of skunk cabbage had welcomed the spring with enormous open leaves.

"Snowbirds are back," Joan said, pointing the top of her fishing rod toward a small gray, black-headed bird rummaging under a fiddlehead fern on the other side of the creek.

Donny had never paid much attention to birds till Chick, who had brought a bird book on their way west and was all the time getting her to stop so she could figure out what they were seeing. After a while Donny started noticing them, too. The sight of the little things and their songs made her feel joyous.

"Life is a sweet creek," she remembered saying, the thought coming to her out of nowhere.

A while later the sheriff had responded, "It's mostly not about the fish, Miz Della Donaldson. Which is a good thing with the creek running this fast." The scrub oaks and madrone trees dripped last night's rain from their coats of pale green moss and lichen. The sky was gray but holding off on a downpour for the present time. "Being out here is like being in a mind Laundromat. Don't have to think about the big bad world. China shooting down our planes over there, us shooting down our own citizens over Peru, and Hollywood turning out war movies like *Pearl Harbor*. You'd think we liked all that fighting and killing." The sheriff paused. "None of that matters here."

With each cast Donny had felt calmer, more able to think about the words she'd had with Chick last night. Naturally she wanted to take poor Jeep fishing, but not on a day she'd already planned to go with the sheriff. Jeep stirred up the peace of the place, arguing with herself over why Katie had dumped her and sketching mad plans for the future, from a Waterfall Symphony Orchestra to enlisting in the Marines so she could join their band.

"Do they have fiddles in military bands?" she'd asked while fishing with Jeep last week. She had started crying so hard Donny had taken her rod for safekeeping. "If they don't, they should," she had sobbed. "Why don't I fit in anywhere?"

Donny knew it wouldn't help to remind the child that they loved her at work and in the band, and what about her and Chick, didn't they count? Jeep was downhearted and needed to weep and moan for a while longer, but, Donny told Chick, she could listen to Jeep just about any time; she wasn't about to ruin every fishing day by bringing her along.

The sheriff pulled something in.

"Too damn small," they both said.

Joan removed the hook and set the fish free. "I never expect to catch much."

"You and me both."

The sheriff's line snaked through the air. "Dad's expecting a fish or two to fry this evening." Behind them her horse whinnied and vigorously shook its mane. "Easy, Gal," she called in a soothing tone.

Horses were so huge Donny never quite trusted them, but she couldn't let it agitate her. She was agitated enough. She'd been able to get away well before seeing Chick because Thursday wasn't a baking morning. She didn't like being called an uptight, pig-headed hardnose. There were times a woman had no choice but to dig in her heels.

A "mind Laundromat." She liked that. "I'm gonna wash those cares right outta my mind," she warbled unsteadily and was surprised when the sheriff took over, her voice clear and startlingly low.

Donny didn't know but one line of the song, and was amazed the sheriff did. She sang like a boom box playing the South Pacific soundtrack without an orchestra. Every critter in the woods around them went silent, except for an early nectar-starved bee. Wouldn't Chick love to hear this big bird.

"Encore!" Donny clapped when the sheriff finished. With a caw, a crow leapt from a rock to a low oak branch. She moved slightly upstream and noticed clover the size of quarters crowding around her feet.

The sheriff whipped off her neon green Natural Woman Foods baseball cap and swept it before her in a bow. They smiled shy smiles at each other, and cast their lines out into the lively creek simultaneously. The forest erased its brief silence with chittering birds and grumbling frogs and the desperate bee.

Donny had finally been getting comfortable with the sheriff, and now here was this whole new side of her. "You're a Broadway musical nut?"

The sheriff did a few soft-shoe steps on her rock. "There was such a shortage of male talent at Elk High I got some great roles. Picture me as Ezio Pinza."

"'Some Enchanted Evening'?"

"That was hot, but try 'There is Nothin' like a Dame.'"

"You did that on stage? In front of—"

"Every girl in the school."

"You must have had them lined up."

"All except Catching Rinehart." Joan grinned a very unsheriff-like grin.

"Say what?"

"Cat."

The sheriff had never mentioned Cat before. Of course, she wasn't spilling many beans now either. For all she gave away, the sheriff could be straight. Except Cat had already told Chick and her about the sheriff. They were the only ones in town who knew.

"Catching? That's Cat's name?"

"After her mother's maiden name. Her ancestors on both sides settled this area for the whites."

"You mean took the land from your ancestors."

"I was pretty nasty to Cat in elementary school, even though I'm only half Indian."

"You've known each other that long?"

The sheriff smiled.

Donny felt proud that Joan was opening up to her and asked no more. She'd treat her like one of Chick's volunteer plants in the tiny garden out back of the store. They were best left alone till harvest. Maybe she'd bring Chick some of those pussy willows she'd passed walking in. That and confidential dish of this quality ought to smooth things over.

But the third time the sheriff messed up a cast, Donny wondered what was going on. Joan almost never fumbled casts. There was no smile now. A bullfrog under the ferns upriver sounded a damp gravelly warning. She slapped a bug.

"New fly?" she asked. It made Donny nervous that the sheriff seemed nervous.

The sheriff cleared her throat. "It's my old Soft Hackle." She showed the fly to Donny. "Maybe it's time for a new one."

The whir of their reels and soft plunk of flies on the creek soothed her again. She thought she might take a little nap—let Joan catch dinner.

Then the sheriff said, "Got something to run by you."

Donny felt a tug on her line, but lost it.

"The name Abraham Clinkscales mean anything to you?" asked the sheriff in a startlingly different tone.

Donny had heard her talk to people in trouble with that quiet, too-casual voice. She froze as still as the sheriff's boulder. And now she heard it. The sheriff had called her by her full name earlier. No one even knew her full name except Chick. Was her voice going to shake? "Denise, my ex, was a Clinkscales."

"Any relation?"

"She had a brother Abraham."

"Her brother was a dope dealer?"

"I wouldn't be surprised."

The sheriff sounded like she was reading from a criminal record. "You shouldn't. The Portland police were observing a dealer and pulled Clinkscales in during a raid. Apparently Clinkscales had already made his delivery because he was clean. Your name came up when they searched his record, and they called me. He claimed he wasn't dealing, he was on his way to visit an old friend in Waterfall Falls."

I'm going to kick the shit out of that boy when I see him. He's still up to his old tricks. "I haven't seen Abraham in a thousand years," she said too quickly.

Goddamn, she thought she'd left that mess 2,000 miles and eight years back. She was too old to live with this fear in her gut. Why was the sheriff messing with her head? It was bad enough her body wanted to give out on her—her casting shoulder ached after only an hour and her damn back was sore from standing. She'd thank the sheriff to not treat her like a criminal. Wasn't there a statute of limitations on this kind of bullshit?

Joan didn't say anything. Donny's hook caught between rocks. The more she tugged, the tighter her line became.

She'd only been Abe's courier for a short while. What had she cared about his reputation in that dirty business? She'd kept back a little here and there, sold it, and kept the change. The worst weekend of her life, those two days she'd spent in jail. She wished she'd stayed out West with Chick and thought of her non-stop the whole time. It was a first offense for a very small amount and the courts were choked with bigger cases, the jails crowded with real criminals. The incident got her a record, but she never had to do the time. She quit then, figuring she had enough to go back to the tables. She'd won that second time. Won big.

She tried stretching the line taut and springing it free. She'd never cared for drugs herself and hated what the hard stuff did to people, but this was blow for white college boys. They were going to get shit-face drunk if they didn't have it, so what harm was there? The sheriff might not agree. She might think Donny was a two-faced hypocrite with a lot of nerve to be acting like a friend.

Those boys were going to buy it somewhere, damn it. Donny had taken a temp job cooking at a little place popular with the college kids. One of the waiters, a student himself, had hinted around that he needed a source, and of course he came to the only black person working there. She'd only been trying to earn enough to come back out West to Chick. It had been so easy. Until the bust. Was she finally going to have to pay?

She looked over. The sheriff was tinkering with her reel. Donny valued her friend's good opinion. There was something about her that made you trust her to do the right thing, yet if the sheriff was so desperate to keep this town clean that she'd pick up any little speck of dirt, she'd fish alone.

Her line waggled loose. Damn. She'd been so sure those weren't white-girl eyes. She skimmed the filament across the water with a flick that should have parted her wrist from her forearm. Instead it sent an ache up to her shoulder so bad it made her half gag. A little cottontail dashed from a clump of huckleberries to a stand of thimbleberry. Loopy was downstream trying to catch water skimmers with her mouth, barking now and then in frustration.

"Good cast!" the sheriff told her.

"You know, Sheriff, these days, with this third-strike rule, people in trouble will give up their firstborn to save their backsides."

Sheriff Sweet took an undersized fish off her line and sailed it back into the creek, giving Donny a sideways glance. "I'm listening."

It was none of her damn business, but Donny offered, "Let me tell you a story." She took in a deep breath. The lemon mint she'd crushed moving around on her patch of creek bank smelled so strong she tasted it. "I used to know a bulldagger who wanted real bad to start a new life in a new place with a new woman who'd nabbed her heart."

The sound of a song sparrow in the forest seemed so innocent next to the tale she was telling, the sheriff so unsullied and noble up there on her rock.

"All the dagger did was try to win a gambling stake." Donny heard the whining plea in her own voice. To make it worse, Chick's dad had kept his family on the edge of poverty because of his gambling jones so she couldn't cry on Chick's shoulder. "She blew all her cash on the tables and crawled back to the city with nothing in her pockets but her big ideas. She thought she'd never be able to face the woman she loved or be part of her dream because it was important to the bulldagger to be able to pull her weight."

The sun had been full out for a while now. The sheriff rolled up her cuffs. Donny was hot too, her shirt and overalls a wet mess at the small of her back, but she wasn't going to show it. "So this dude asked her to help out with his—ah—small business operation. She never told a soul, even the new woman, that the money they used to set up their dream wasn't only from gambling."

The sheriff was turning toward her.

"The bulldagger wanted this one shot at a better life." She pointed her rod at the sheriff. "If that woman was a solid citizen type in your town today, what would you do?"

The sun was almost above them. If the fish hadn't started biting by now, it was time to give in gracefully.

Sheriff Sweet was looking at her, waiting, goddamnit. Donny couldn't see inside those eyes that caught everything—birds, clouds, people, the creek, and the sunshine. They were like mirrors. She wished Chick were here to help her get out of this.

Finally the sheriff answered. "An ounce of prevention is worth a pound of cure, Donalds. Your friend, after all this time, might get off with community service. It would only be fair, since her friend the dealer was turned loose by the Portland PD."

Donny reeled in, waiting for the sheriff to drop the other shoe.

"I need to deputize someone to run our DARE program," the sheriff said.

"Say what?" Donny hated these say-what days, when everything pounced out at her. What kind of friend was Joan? If she thought she could blackmail Donny into being a mouthpiece for that fool program she could shove it and shove what she knew. She cranked the handle with such violent jerks her fingers kept sliding off. Fuck you, she thought, and the horse you rode in on.

The sheriff was smiling. Her eyes didn't look mean. They looked like Chick's when Donny pulled something really dumb, kind of laughing, kind of loving. The woman meant no harm, but what a jive turkey. Then she remembered what the sheriff had said earlier. She'd told her something about Cat. Neither Joan nor Cat had confided in anyone else about what they were to each other—she and Chick would have heard. The sheriff had been setting the stage, announcing that she trusted her.

She began to laugh so loud the woods fell quiet again except for that bee. "Was that some kind of April Fool's Day joke or is this how you get your volunteers?" she sputtered with shock and relief. She pulled off her jacket and wiped sweat with it. "I love you, Joan baby, I surely do love you. All you had to do was ask."

"I know," answered the sheriff with her solemn face. "I know."

She wanted to ask questions as they packed their gear, Donny into her pickup, the sheriff onto Gal. Could the sheriff stand to be friends with a criminal on the loose? Would she tell Chick? Would she hold it over Donny's head forever? She asked nothing; Joan, so typical, offered nothing. They picked the pussy willows for Chick and for Sheriff Sweet's mother. Donny drove back to Chick's arms as fast as her little truck would take her.

Knowing that he was on the road, she wasn't a bit surprised to get a call from none other than Abe Clinkscales a few days after fishing with Joan. The surprise, when it came, took a very different form. Abe announced his imminent arrival, leaving her barely enough time to get everything nice for him when he got there.

She and Chick had been using the back room for storage. Jeep came by and helped her drag bags and boxes of stock and supplies out to the already crowded back end of the store. She expected this to be an extended stay and didn't want Abe in their faces the whole time, so they carried the mattress and box spring down from the extra room upstairs. They set up a shelving unit from the produce crates she'd been saving. By the time she got to the bus stop she was exhausted—and excited. Sometimes it got lonely being the only black queer in the county.

"Let me see you!" Donny had said, circling Abe at the bus stop. "You look gorgeous! What gives with traveling in drag, bro?" She wondered if the police were still keeping an eye on Abe and if he was trying to elude them.

"I'm not a brother any more, Donalds."

"Say what?"

Abe swirled. He wore tight black pants, ankle-high boots with gold chains, and a fuzzy purple jacket patterned with flowers. "This is no longer drag, girlfriend. You can call me Abeo!"

"Abeo? Is that a name?" She didn't know what to say. Abe had talked about changing gender a long time ago, but they hadn't been in touch much since Donny moved west. "You didn't tell me."

"Didn't tell nobody nothing once I decided. Why do you think I left town? I need to be in the world as the new me. I don't need postgame telling me I'm wrong."

"When did you do this? Did you get it done in Chicago? Nobody helped you? I can't believe you went the whole way."

"Sweet pea, when did you ever know me not to finish what I started?"

"That's not something I'd know. I was never into boys, remember?"

Donny's friend was still broad-shouldered, very short, chunky, and loud.

"Boy? Was I ever a boy? I'm me at last!" Abeo announced, flinging his—her—arms upward and twirling. "Did I tell you what Abeo means in Hausa? 'Her birth brings happiness.' My sister—you do remember good old Denise, your ex, don't you? Denise told me that."

"Your family wasn't Nigerian."

"You and your roots hang-up. What's that got to do with it?

Abraham wasn't exactly a black African name when they called me after Abraham Lincoln."

"That bible dude he was named for was likely blacker than me."

"Martha Stewart's practically blacker than you."

"But I've still got better hair than she does."

They grinned at each other in the white light of the street lamp, the bus still dieseling beside them. The night was mild and moist with a still fog that hadn't broken into rain.

Donny tried to get back her big anger about Abeo ratting her out up in Portland. "Why didn't you call from Portland to say you were coming?"

"Portland? I left Portland last week. I had a little business matter to take care of in Seattle."

"So you made a delivery as Abe, then changed into your girl clothes and got on the Green Tortoise because no one would think to look for you on a hippie bus."

"I don't do courier work, man. I told you I got out of that business a long time ago."

"And you think they won't think to look for you here either. Shit, I'll bet you're running from the cops and the goddamned dealers."

Even as Abraham, Abeo had always batted his eyelashes to good effect. This time she played it haughty. "I'm getting back on that Tortoise. You don't need to know my business."

"Hasta la vista, then. I don't want anything to do with hiding a fugitive."

Abeo shrugged and wouldn't meet her eyes when she said, "I was clean. They didn't have any grounds for arrest, but I could tell they'd think some up if I didn't name some names—or disappear."

"You're saying you didn't name names?"

"I didn't give them anything they could use, Don. Scout's honor."

"What kind of scout do you think I'm going to believe you are?"

Abeo danced back a bit and let out a peal of laughter loud enough to carry the length of Stage Street. "Do you remember? You joined that Girl Scout troop so I had to join the boys? And they threw me out when they caught me with that Eagle Scout?"

"Abe, I mean it. I'm not rescuing you this time."

Abeo fastened herself to Donny's sleeve. "Did I tell you? I ran into Mr. Eagle Scout in the Castro last year? Only the uniform was different?"

"I don't believe a word you're saying, child, so let go of my arm. My woman's going to wonder where I'm at."

"Donny, you're the only one I've got to take care of me. I want to grow into my new body where no one's watching."

It wasn't the first time Abe had pulled a stunt like this, and Donny was sure it wouldn't be the last. She'd always taken him—her—in. Abe—Abeo—knew her weak spots better than anyone.

The Green Tortoise driver had finally located Abeo's two suitcases and the bus strained away, a knot of riders waving through the windows.

"You going to miss me, girlfriends?" Abeo shouted.

"Terminally!" came a voice from the noisily accelerating bus.

When it was gone, Donny felt naked, alone in downtown white America in the now-drizzling dark with her once protégé and best gayboy buddy, Abraham, in his new post-op persona.

To make it worse, Sheriff Sweet walked out of a bar the next block up. The sheriff's eyes checked them out, and she gave a little wave as she mounted her horse. Donny had a feeling Joan would see through Abe's disguise pretty quickly.

"What are you staring at, Donalds?" asked Abeo. "You don't like looking at this pretty woman?"

"I was worried I'd have the jimjams if you ever changed, but you haven't changed at all."

"Now, now, Miss Thang, *certain* things are different." Abeo looked down Waterfall Falls' deserted main street and seemed to shiver. "Is this a safe place for you, Don?"

She felt warm around the heart from Abeo's concern. She'd been a long time without a black friend. She was too city for the local blacks. "It's not safe," she told Abeo, "to be black in the United States of America. I'm an extra-large target here because I take on the voting booth queer-bashers. Did you follow the shit they pulled with their initiatives? I wanted to file a class action suit and sue their asses for making us waste our lives to keep the ground we've got."

"I've been otherwise occupied," said Abeo. "As you may have noticed."

"Don't tell me you stopped voting when I left."

"What difference would my little old vote make?"

"Get with it, Abe. Safe doesn't just happen. You have to force it down their breeder throats."

Abeo's attention had wandered. "How long you going to treat your guest of honor like some hitchhiker?"

"Don't you have any fight in you at all?" She looked at Abeo, who had always put on party girl airs like a perfume. For some people, being in the world itself was a fight. "Get in the truck and I'll take you up the mountain."

"Ah-hem," Abeo responded, somehow eyeing her suitcase and the truck bed simultaneously

Donny balked. "I never had to treat you like a lady when you really were a queen. Do I look like your house slave now?" She wasn't about to admit that hauling shit at the store left her hurting too bad to be bending over and picking up a suitcase as big as a chest of drawers.

"Humph." Abeo, who was almost a dozen years her junior, flung the big bags into the truck bed with ease, then daintily entered the cab. "Why are we climbing mountains tonight?" she asked as Donny clicked her seatbelt into its slot. "Chick won't let this gender-freak in your home?"

"You know Chick better than that, Queenie. She's up at Harold and Joe's place and wanted me to bring you there first. You remember how the white girls and radical faeries love that drumming. The boys have a teacher staying all week."

"Drumming! That's exactly like your woman to remember how I loved drumming. It gave me a vision of who I really am. What are we waiting for, girl?" Abeo asked, hanging on Donny's arm.

She smelled like she really had taken a bath in some funky perfume. Donny said, "For you to let go. I can't drive with you playing whiney little girl all over me."

Abeo slumped to her side of the truck. "Never mind then."

"Damn! You look like some fine woman, Abeo, but maybe you ought to tone it down."

"Who all voted you Miss Manners? Give a girl a chance to fine-tune her new-lady self. I'm saving up for charm school as soon as they send my check."

"You still acting crazy for the government?"

"I'll be crazy until I find a husband to support me."

Donny turned off Stage Street toward Blackberry Mountain, grinning at the dark road ahead. "You don't need that charm school. Do you know any better femme-trainer than me?" She took her hand off the steering wheel to smack Abeo's palm. "Damn!"

"What's the matter, Don?"

"I missed you," she said quickly to cover. Her fingers were getting so gnarled up from the arthur the littlest pressure sometimes started a big ache. Dr. Wu told her not to be overusing her hands—like she had a choice—but she was damned if she was going to act like some old woman. She wasn't the retiring kind.

Abeo chattered happily about her trip from Chicago and their old Southside gang until Donny parked alongside the other cars that jammed the boys' driveway.

They could hear the drums.

"Oo, baby. That's my song. Do I look okay?" Abeo asked.

Poor Abeo. She'd never been model material. "Like my dream girl back when I was a young stud."

For a while Donny kept them in the shadows away from the bonfire. The drumming made her irritable. She'd thought drumming would be a body thing, like dancing with your hands, but she saw little of that in these circles. Now and then Chick let out a sound of what sounded like pleasure, and once a gangly kid got up, drum under his arm, and stomped, knees high, around the fire. The rest of the drummers were concentrating so hard it made them look like they were being faithful to some fancy white man's score.

It had surprised her when Chick took up drumming. Chick started messing with the little drums they carried for sale in the store, getting together with a handful of drum nuts once a month, then more often. She'd once told Donny that drumming took her so far inside herself the drum beats became her heartbeat, and that made Donny wonder what, on the outside, her woman needed escaping from. Something had been on Chick's mind and had been for a while, something she wouldn't talk about, but which had her lying awake at night and making mistakes during the day, taking away her sex drive and sending her drumming every chance she got.

"It's my therapy," she had told Donny.

"What do you need therapy for, woman?" she'd wanted to ask.

She wouldn't ask, though. The times they'd gotten into it with each other were the times Donny had pushed too far, asked too many questions about the deep-down Chick. Chick did not care to be pushed. If she needed to go far away, that was her business, as long as she came back. Chick had been drumming long enough now that Donny knew it could be a distress signal or it could be about high spirits. She went fishing and Chick drummed. It was one more way they were different, along with their colors, ages, even their sizes. Beanpole Donny called Chick her love pillow.

The wind carried bonfire smoke her way and she shifted around the circle. Uh-huh, some of these people were showing off or trying to fit in; Chick was into it.

At the first sign of quiet, Abeo burst into the circle and threw herself at Chick.

"Abraham!" Chick cried, opening her arms.

Donny heard a little yelp from a severe-looking young dyke she'd never seen in the store. They normally got them all stopping in at one time or another.

Chick gave her big open laugh. "This is our city friend Abraham! Remember him from potlucks at the faerie farm?"

Donny could see the unease on the faces of the women around the fire. They were used to the local gay guys, but here was Abe dressed like the kind of woman they refused to be.

"But this isn't Abraham anymore, Miss Chick. It's the new improved version. I am Abeo the Magnificent!"

Donny could tell Chick hadn't understood what Abe meant about improved. "Abeo has left her old gender behind," Donny told the group. "She's a sister now."

"I remember you from my last visit," Abeo said, pointing at R. "And you and you." She looked beside herself with excitement—and excitement, Donny remembered, was Abraham's food and drink.

R, who sat drumless, cape around her, on the log closest to the fire, gave an unsmiling nod in greeting. Donny wanted to laugh at her discomfort—the woman didn't want to play if she wasn't setting the beat. She watched while two of the younger women, the severe-looking one, who Chick introduced as Sandstone, and the short, muscular old-timer Alice, pressed close to R, whispering. R seemed to answer by raising her eyebrows.

"Abeo," R said, "we welcome you as a woman."

"I know what you're worrying about, you and the other gay girls. You're scared I'm a straight woman. Well, have no fear. Abeo does nothing halfway. I am through with men forever. I don't want to be one or be with one." She looked at Harold. "As lovers. I'm not the man-hating kind of lesbian. I've lived in both worlds now."

R seemed to study Abeo in silence, then said, "I hope you've also embraced the lesbian sensibility that comes with being a woman-loving woman."

"Don't you be telling her how to be a lesbian, R," said Donny. "You took your own damn time joining our club."

R's eyes took on an intensely sad cast. "I've been a lesbian all my life."

"Funny. So have I and I didn't spend any of that time sleeping with a man or raising his sons. You and Abe here have a lot in common."

Alice and Sandstone rose menacingly on either side of R. Donny could hear one of the men give a loud sigh and saw another roll his eyes. She ignored them.

"Can Abeo catch a ride back with you later, Chick?" she asked. "Nothing against drumming," she told the rest. "But knowing you women I'd be here half the night. Tomorrow's baking day."

"You're leaving your friend *here*?" asked Sandstone. Alice seemed to grow burlier beside her, knees bowing, hands turning to fists.

Donny threw a challenging arm around Abe's shoulder. "What can I do if she'd rather be with you than me? She's only my best runaround buddy who I haven't seen for three years."

"Uh, excuse me?" the kid said with annoying hostility. "I was at Michigan when a trans woman tried to invade outer space. As long as this isn't woman-only space I'm okay with it, but I don't think someone can change their gender inside."

The little shit might as well have slapped Abe in the face. That tight-skinned fire-spitting feeling spread around Donny's head. Her own hands began to fist.

It was Abeo who responded. "I'm as anatomically correct as Barbie should be. Want to see?" she asked, beginning to unbutton.

"Quit it," Donny ordered. "My friend is not going to expose her private stuff for any politically correct recovering G.U.P.P.Y. who wouldn't know what a transgender street person goes through without reading about it in a gay studies book."

By the light of the fire she could see panic flicker over the faces of the women. Donny had heard their discussions often enough to guess what they were thinking. Should they support Sandstone? Was Abeo really a woman? Was it all right to cross Donny, who was not only a pillar of the lesbian community, but a black woman? Was it racist to let Donny's and Abeo's color influence them? What was R thinking?

Harold stood too. "We only have our teacher this one weekend, folks. Why don't we do what we're here to do?"

Donny said goodnight and walked to her truck. She'd gotten over her mad old self about Abeo's big mouth. It hadn't got Donny busted after all. And they could get over themselves too. From the silence behind her as she walked away, she knew at the very least they were telling Abeo she had to sit downwind from them so Kimama wouldn't get sick from her perfume. All the way to the highway, over the clamor of her motor, she strained to hear the beat begin.

CHAPTER TWELVE

Two Worlds

Señorita's was a long, low, flat wooden restaurant and lounge painted turquoise except for its yellow doors and pink window trim. Striped pots of plastic fuchsia hung along the rail of a porch which stretched the length of the building. The place reminded Katie of the tavern next door to the trailer park she'd lived in during grammar school, a place that seemed so glamorous then because it was where the grownups went to have fun.

It was the weekend of the Honeysuckle Festival and she felt ridiculously excited. She'd gone on a wildflower walk to persuade the women at Spirit Ridge to come into town for the parade and the sidewalk sales. They complained that they weren't into watching an army of little kids dressed as wild red honeysuckle, orange honeysuckle, Japanese honeysuckle in kimonos, twinberries in matching red, trumpet honeysuckle tooting toy horns—even the blue honeysuckle berries no one could grow around here—escort the Honeysuckle Queen on her vine float. They spent too much time trying to get rid of the pesty stuff so they could grow a few vegetables.

"Two-step dancing! Music by our old-time music band!" Katie Delgado had tempted the Ridgers, sunglasses raised in her hand as she danced by herself to no music at all.

"Maiden blue-eyed Mary," R had said, pointing to tiny blue and white flowers. "And over there, scarlet fritillaries." Katie had zoomed in and shot them, with their yellow streaks, like Mother Nature had been about to paint them orange then decided she liked the flowers the way they were.

"Let's do it!" said one of the land veterans, twenty-nine-year-old Nitara, originally from Delhi, who'd moved to the Ridge for a junior year project at Antioch and returned after graduation. She was still living on grants and writing an extensive history of women's communes seven years later. "I've always wanted to barge in on a drinking hole full of straights. They probably think it's a regular babe band."

"Not any more they don't," Katie said. "I know the owners. I couldn't believe Eddy and Perlita hadn't caught on. They're extremely *padrisimo* about it."

"You outed the band?" asked Marge, shock on her face. "Are you out of your mind? That's their steady job."

R's hands were folded, a sardonic little smile on her face. "The owners will let that information get out. They probably think the novelty will attract more men. And they're right."

Aster, who had moved there from the university with Marge, mimed sticking a finger down her throat. "Like yuck."

R said, "Men are much closer to our animal past than women. They may also want power and money, but only because it will get them more sex."

"Don't be such a grinch," Katie had chastised R.

"They can't help it. They have that propagation instinct. They disguise it, protect it any way they can. Who popularized romance? It's the only aphrodisiac they found that works on women. Who created marriage? That's simply the institutionalization of free and guaranteed sex, a business proposal in which men buy a female and feed and shelter her by bartering for sex and child-rearing."

Nightfall said, "Can you imagine educated het women being suckered into going along with such a patriarchal agenda?"

"Dancing is a heterosexual courting ritual," R said.

"I never danced for a man," Marge told her.

"Double yuck. Me neither," agreed Aster.

"Let's go turn dancing into a homosexual courting ritual! Come on, R, support poor dance-crazed lesbians!"

"If it means that much to you, Katie, I'll consider it. I realize this lifestyle shift from urban to rural has been difficult."

"R," she cried. "I don't want you to do it for me. Don't you ever like to cut loose and party?"

Nightfall said, "R's idea of partying is the quarterly potlucks at the Grange."

"Those are cool," said Katie. "But truth? They don't get my blood pumping."

"And that's what you need to feel good, Kate?" asked R. "A rush of pumping blood?"

"What can I say? I'm your typical type A, Gen X adrenaline junkie." Confessions of weakness sometimes appealed to R when nothing else did. Katie thought of it as tapping into R's goddess side, the way opposite end of rational. It reminded her to do the same, to rely on her guts more often when reading people.

So every night that week Marge and Aster had coached their land mates in the rudiments of country dance. The Saturday of the Honeysuckle Festival they walked into a macarena number at Senorita's, the hub of nighttime entertainment for the festival. Onlookers shouted encouragement to the dancers. The band was in overdrive, trying to make music louder than the crowd.

Katie, walking backwards, swished her hips and led R by the hand. From the motor homes parked in the lot and along the sides of the road, she guessed the snowbirds were trickling up north from their winter RV parks. It wasn't the Bay Area club scene, but it was going to give her a hit of what she needed.

The group snaked its way to the stage. There were seven of them, and four joined the hooting and clapping. "Someone," she shouted to R, "ought to talk to the band about performing at a potluck. That would liven things up."

R, wincing as she tried to make herself heard, said, "They did play for us, but I go to potlucks to talk to women, not to shriek at them."

Hands at R's waist, she fluttered her legs against R's. R pulled back and asked, "What are you doing?"

"Dancing with you upright for once."

"I'm not comfortable doing that here," R said.

Katie dropped her arms and turned away. She wanted more than anything to be on R's wavelength and felt like such a d.u.h. dud each time she failed. It was like meditation. Goddess, how she longed to quiet her mind, but as R said, she chattered. She was ashamed how she filled up her head with noise even in her silences. Tonight her body wanted to get in on the act, but wasn't that natural with a band up on stage playing killer music like this?

She leaned toward Nightfall and asked, "Isn't that a Grateful Dead tune?"

Nightfall bobbed her head, her face transformed by a smile. "Pig music, but so good. It's like getting drunk—you know it's bad for you, you know you're going to suffer down the line, but it's worth every heave. Listen to that banjo! These women know their stuff."

They sang along with the chorus. "We can share the women, we can share the wine..." until they laughed too hard to sing.

Jeep was a better fiddler than she'd ever let on when they were together. And for sure the band, in their checked shirts, neckerchiefs, and red overalls, hadn't had a Dead song in its repertoire before she joined them. Jeep loved the Dead and had used them to chill out. She'd told Katie that they'd been her mom's favorite group so their songs were like lullabies to her. It was obvious that Jeep had quickly become the heart of the band, leaping around on stage with her fiddle like a crazed elf. How did she keep her cowboy hat—complete with lavender band of course—from falling off? Katie had heard that the other women were total amateurs, some new to their instruments, others to any instruments. She wondered how much their professionalism was Jeep's doing, because they were totally cool. Jeep had probably even gotten them this job.

"Share the women..." Jeep had played that song while they were together, would play it on her harmonica, croon it over dinner in a restaurant, take her in her arms and dance her around to it in a motel room before leading her to the bed.

Katie didn't dare look at R who must be having a fit at the lyrics. Too bad her path had led her away from Jeep. She'd had good, if puppy dog, energy, and, with her bad punk haircut, her long straight nose, and ever-smiling lips, they didn't come any cuter. Katie still wouldn't be able to keep her hands off the kid if she hadn't opted for R. She laughed. Did her own puppy dog energy and dogging footsteps bug R as much as Jeep's had her? Probably! Jeep had been a transitional indulgence, while R was a discipline. The thought crossed her mind that this made her a disciple, but she didn't want to go there.

Katie had watched a torrent of apprehension pass across the face of each band member as they noticed the dykes out there, but a couple of numbers in, they were fine with it, catching their eyes and grinning. When Jeep spotted Katie her fingers didn't falter and, for the first time since their breakup, she gave Katie a pained little smile. Katie hadn't realized how much she'd wanted that to happen. She'd always known Jeep was strong and would be okay, and since she wasn't right for the kid, leaving had been better for both of them in the long run. Still, she'd had to steel herself against guilt these last few months, and now she could look forward to letting that go. She could dance to Jeep's music.

At intermission, the lesbians in the band surged onto the floor, arms extended for hugs. Jeep stayed with the harmonica player, Cat. Harmonica lips and violin fingers, she thought, what a great combination.

Katie watched the other customers drift to tables and the bar, isolating the nest of lesbians, casting quick looks or staring at them. Had the scuttlebutt gotten out that over half the band was gay, or were they too obvious to miss?

On the stage, one of the women was singing "Muskrat Ramble." She shook her head. Imagine My Surprise was an eclectic band all right.

Katie wore her short black leather skirt with a tie-dyed, long-sleeved T-shirt she'd bought at Fina's Finery. The straights were in pressed jeans and fancy western-style shirts or T-shirts, the men's printed with trucks and rude slogans, the women's appliquéd with horses, birds, kittens, and flowers. Her land mates wore homemade outfits and ill-fitting thrift store finery that would not have been out of place on a soup kitchen line. Even R, so regal on the land, looked shabby in slacks worn thin at the knee and a peasant blouse too short at the wrists.

While R held court with the quieter dykes, Katie drifted away from the group. Sharing R came with the territory.

She hadn't been inside a honky-tonk bar since she'd left the trailer park. Except for the people, it was like a gay bar. The dim lights lent it glamour, but underneath were layers of cigarette smoke, spilled beer, and worn fixtures. It would make a good setting for interviewing a rustic local if she ever got her project off the ground.

She found herself thinking about how much time and energy she used at Spirit Ridge taking care of basic needs like getting wood in for heat and bathing. R had running water, but it was gravity fed and came out of the faucet in a thin, weak, often rusty trickle. Filling the tub was such an interminable task that they shared the water, and when it was her turn to go second—they alternated—the water was tepid. She never felt truly clean. R believed that bath time was yet another ritual, a cleansing ritual, that needed candles, Native American flute music, and intimate talk. She had a habit of touching herself in the tub, and reaching in to touch Katie under the water, which always led to a soapy taste in the mouth for hours.

A bearded man in a white cowboy hat and snakeskin boots approached Katie. He held out his hand and she automatically shook it. "Don't tell me a looker like you is with that crowd," he said.

He was obviously trying to tell her that he knew she was gay, but thought, like a typical non-gay, it would be impolite to come right out and say it. She'd gotten too much of that even before she'd come out because she was a mix of Mexican and Italian. People couldn't figure out what she was, but didn't dare ask. She was shocked at the softness of the man's hand. He looked like a logger, with jeans held up by suspenders, but from talking to the locals she knew not even an equipment operator would escape calluses so completely. He didn't smell like engine oil, or horse. He did smell oddly of patchouli.

"M.C. here." He looked around at the other lesbians. "You know a big gal named Chick? Gives off new age woo-woo vibes and runs the granola and sprouts store?" When Katie nodded, he said, "We go way back, Chick and me."

She somehow doubted that, but gave the fake cowboy the benefit of the doubt. TV professional or not, Katie remained cluelessly gullible at times. She suspected that it was an asset as long as she checked her facts later. People could sense that she believed their every word during an interview and were more forthcoming than they would be to a skeptic. For some reason that made them more honest too. She couldn't imagine Chick tight with this mangy-looking dude, but stranger things had happened.

M.C. was maybe five foot, eight inches, skinny, and in his late forties or early fifties. He had an unkempt graying Abe Lincoln beard that shot up under his cheekbones like shadows to give him a cadaverous look, and short, unevenly cut hair with long bangs that met straight dark eyebrows. When you added the bushy sideburns and full drooping moustache that merged with his beard, he looked really hairy. He was slightly stooped, his arms hanging forward like a *Planet of the Apes* extra.

"How come I haven't seen you around here before?" he asked.

Katie felt R's psychic pull trying to drag her away, but her curiosity was stronger even than R, and her chatterer was stuck at the on position. She answered him without hesitation. "I've never been here before. You're a regular?"

"I like to stop in now and then." He'd been studying her body, but now he spoke directly to her. "What are you drinking? Want a beer?"

Before she had a chance to answer, he handed her a fresh bottle and lifted his own to salute her.

"Why not?" Why wasn't she surprised that he'd come prepared?

"It'll get you into the mood."

"This is a good thing. I feel so out of it here in hicksburg."

"Man, if I didn't go down to the Bay Area now and then I'd be nuts."

They talked about the city. He told her he'd moved here for the easy life on the land. He was vague about how he earned a living, but full of stories about the locals. His quick watchful gaze seemed to take in everyone around him, and he had an anecdote about each of them, mostly unflattering. As uncomfortable as he made her, edging ever closer with the excuse of talking over the noise of the crowd, she felt that flame of excitement. She was gathering material again. New stories had a taste to them, round and nutty and satisfying like nothing else.

Was there a story here? She found herself talking aloud about the vague project forming in her head. Interviews with guys like him and with the local women. People who made their living here and people who chucked their jobs to migrate here. This place had a history which kept both the 1960s and the 1800s alive. Were the two times similar enough that all these people could co-exist in the twenty-first century? What drew them, kept them? It had to be an anti-government hotbed both with natives bucking against land use rules and with the commune-dwellers and retired hippies into living under the radar of rules and regulations. Why hadn't they clashed?

"Hey, little lady, you're going to stir things up if you put us on TV," said M.C. "This is live-and-let-live turf. Think of us as babes in the woods who are better off not knowing we should be fighting a civil war."

"I wish I had my Sony. That was great!" She searched her pockets for something to write on.

"What?" M.C. asked. His attention, which had wandered to the crowd while she was talking, veered back. "You want to quote me?"

Gotcha, she thought. She could see his vanity was now on full alert. "Quote you? I want to film you telling me what you said."

"That would be a trip." He eyed the crowd again.

Yeah, she thought, like you're too bored with the idea, macho man. Ka-ching. She knew her hook was in.

He turned back to her and whispered close to her ear, "So, do you live up on the mountain with all those sister-types?"

She tried to step away, but bumped up against the bar. She hadn't realized how far she'd moved from the women. "Yes, I do. How about you?"

He gestured upward. "I have a place in the hills. It's no place I'd take a lady, though."

Oh, here we go, she thought. I show some interest and this zurramato moves in. Goddess, men pissed her off. You couldn't have a conversation without a man thinking it was a green light to your bedroom. They were so obsessed with their ugly bodies. She was repulsed at the thought that she might have stayed in southern California and married some slick kid from high school, taking her sustenance from biological chance.

Fuck this shit, Katie thought, turning toward the band, which was assembling after the break. She caught Jeep's eye. "Play something fast," she mouthed. "Help!"

Jeep, squinting toward M.C. behind her, then back at Katie with a spare-me look on her face, played a few bars of "Do Not Forsake Me" on her harmonica, her cue for the band, then lifted her fiddle and led the band into line-dance mode. The woman who played the plastic Calistoga bottle moved up to the mike and got the dancers on their feet with some astonishing percussion.

Katie let M.C. swing her onto the dance floor, planning to melt into the crowd as soon as possible. If he wasn't lying, Chick could put her back in contact with him, and with a camera in her hands she'd be able to handle this clown.

As if he'd read her mind, M.C. asked, "Is my old friend Chick in on this with you?"

"Not yet," Katie answered him, her fixed public smile in place. She could see that some old guy was asking R to dance. R folded her arms, glaring. It was time to get back to her, but Nightfall was already dragging R away from the man.

The dykes attached themselves to the end of the line, R maneuvering next to Katie. With a sweet, carefully modulated voice that made Katie's jaw go tight, she whispered, "I didn't know you danced with them."

"Chill, R. I want him in my film. Scene—women greeting winter solstice with a dance on the Ridge and a huge bonfire. Scene—this cowboy raping the wildflower-covered spring earth with his earthmover."

"You're obsessed by that male career I thought you left behind."

"Hey, little lady," the cowboy said in the gravelly slow tones of a habitual dope smoker. God, was that what he did for a living? Arm across her shoulder, he was trying to steer her back into his sphere. "You can come on out and shoot me any time. I'm with you old-growth tree people."

"Cool," Katie said. "You're the first dude to sign on." She made a few more of the right noises, and when she looked back for R, she was gone. It took way too long to disentangle herself from M.C. and go after her.

She found Sheriff Sweet leaning in the back door of the van, her horse's bridle in her hand, talking low. The night was fragrant with wet earth, soaked with a steady drizzle that had started in the late afternoon. R sat inside, cross-legged, crying.

"Girlfriend!" She'd never seen R cry before.

"I'll leave you to it then," said the sheriff, pushing her lanky self off the van and leading her horse, who, except for a few brown patches, was a ghostly white in this light, into the dark. The woman could have as least stayed to explain what was going on, although Katie had a good idea what it was.

R's expression would have suited the prosecuting attorney in the trial of a serial child murderer. "You smell like that beer hall," she said. "I thought you left the cities to be closer to the Goddess. You came so open. You came with love."

Katie had also never seen R this furious. "Nothing's changed."

"You were flirting with him to get your story! I could see that. Men oppress us. They destroy the natural world and women as a matter of course. They're very simply the enemy. How could you?"

"Everything you say is true, R, but it's like thinking about death. It's unbearable. I have to be able to function in the world."

"I can't deal with your other side, Kate. Pushing us to go public about our struggle to protect the mother land. Pulling us down here to consort with men."

The door to Señorita's opened and country-western music jumped out, like a banned cowboy tossed onto the street. Katie became a little Latina girl outside the road house next to the trailer park. She was quivering. It always came back to living in two worlds, always. She lost her language again.

Then R, as if knowing there was no one left inside to scold, opened her arms. Katie lay in the van with her, surrounded by R's mountain, the sounds of music and the glow of neon gone faint as they had when that little girl had lived in the trailer parks.

After a while she smiled to herself. That roadhouse cowboy was outrageously perfect for her film.

CHAPTER THIRTEEN

The Age of Aquarius

Y ou know why I love loving you?" Donny asked above her.
It was late. She'd thought making love would help her get
some rest tonight. She sleepily held on tighter, and Donny gave a last
thrust, groin to groin, before moving onto her own pillow.

"Donny, Donny, you're too much. You make it go on and on."

"Do you know?"

Chick was heavy and felt light. Her mouth tasted salty. She lifted
herself, straddled Donny, and grazed her mouth with both breasts,
watching her little crystal against Donny's darker skin.

"Because I'm a ringer for Ellen Degeneres?" She could hear
Donny's grumble of laughter beneath her breasts. "You're not laughing at
me, are you? Because it wouldn't take much to smother you with love."

Donny widened her eyes and took the tip of a sizeable breast in her
mouth, then turned her head. "Who'd want that skinny youngster?"

"I love that you always say the right thing. So tell me. Why do you
like doing it with me? I've been wondering what keeps you around."

"'Cause you're always so wet." Donny dipped her hand between
Chick's legs and, Chick could tell, came up dry. "Until recently."

She could feel the circle of sparks in her chest that would ignite a
hot flash and moved to lie on her back. Her body had been giving her
away for some time now. She'd been surprised that Donny hadn't said
anything. She hadn't wanted her to know that sex seemed like another
chore except when Donny started it. Even then she sleepwalked her way
through, enjoying the sensations while following Donny's lead. Tonight
she'd felt livelier for some reason, maybe because the Pensioners' Posse
was keeping M.C. away, but she knew that he was no more than a leaf
on a noxious weed whose complicated roots wound inside her.

"You think I don't have eyes in my head, woman?" Donny propped
herself on one elbow to look at her. "Go to bed," she told Loopy, who'd
come to peer at them, chin on the bed, when they'd started talking. "You
think I don't see that my laughing, generous, loving Chick is having

trouble leaving her bed in the mornings? You used to hate it when I saw you with your hair uncombed, and now you don't get around to brushing it till you get downstairs. You couldn't stand to wear the same clothes two days in a row, and now you wear one outfit all week. You look miserable creeping your way downstairs like the executioner is waiting for you."

Donny was right. She'd get as far as the familiar, comforting motions of flipping on lights, changing the disks in the CD player, making coffee, and setting up the bakery, and then despair would drain her again. Sometimes she'd visit her downstairs sanctuary, breathe deeply from an herb bag, run her fingers over the curves of a goddess figurine, and feel stronger. On other days she knew there was no such thing as a Goddess within and felt such aversion to her store altar she couldn't force herself to go near it.

Bless Jeep. Now that the kid was working at the school she'd come in for breakfast and sing bouncy little tunes as she set up the shop, no questions asked, and handled the first customers while Chick did deep breathing in the walk-in cooler. Slightly buoyed, Chick would move to the bathroom, comb her hair, and draw her trademark smile across her mouth like lipstick.

"I know you, Chick," Donny was saying. "Something's bugging you big-time, and it ain't Shrub's tax cuts."

Although M.C. was the least of it, she wanted to keep the stalking secret. Donny, the street scrapper, would fight him, only to end up keeping Sheriff Sweet company at the lockup. A lot of good that would do. Sweat collected along her hairline and between her breasts.

"It's too mind-bending, sweetheart. I can't explain," she whispered, trying to hold back tears. Crying would alarm Donny more. She wished she hadn't put Neil Young on the CD player. He was too melancholy tonight.

"What can't you explain? Did you fall for somebody else? Don't tell me you're serious about Jeep."

"Oh, my poor baby. No. There's only you."

"Then why can't you tell me?"

There was no stopping the tears or the hysteria in her voice. "Please listen to me! I can't even explain what's happening to myself. It's beyond comprehension."

The stalking was on top, but underneath was the worry that she'd get as sick as her brother, the damned hormones ricocheting around inside her like pinballs ringing her bells, and the despair itself that left her exhausted and hopeless. To make this whole trip worse, M.C.'s appearance had triggered her old self-hatred. She'd been trying to kill her warming, cushioning fat body back in her hippie days, trying to stifle her gay soul with drugs and self-medicate herself out of depression. She'd lived on booze in the girl bars, then battled hepatitis for a year. Now she knew she'd been trying to die. Back then she'd thought she was having fun.

The heat left her body. Her sweat turned cold. And I'm getting old, she silently sang along with Neil Young. How could she begin to put all that into words? She breathed deeply, deeply again. She thought if she could spend her life doing deep breathing, everything would be fine.

"You're fantastic, lover. Just the fact that you're in my life keeps me going. If you weren't I'd be finito. I'm really working on getting more cheerful." She reached into the night table drawer.

"What's this?" asked Donny, examining the prescription bottle Chick handed her.

Chick gave her best chortle, but it caught in her throat and she coughed. "I've joined the designer drug generation. You know, better living through chemistry?"

Donny looked stunned. "You're jiving me. You, the laughing lady, on Prozac? Since when? This shit takes people over the edge."

"You liked me over the edge enough a few minutes ago, lover-woman," Chick said, rolling onto her side, rubbing her hand over the gray curls at the bottom of Donny's belly.

Donny ignored her. "I thought you were seeing Doc Wu about hormone pills for the change."

"They were a big zero, Don." She moved closer, belly to belly with her lover. "I got into a funk. Freaked when I couldn't get out of it."

The surprise in Donny's eyes turned to fear. "Am I treating you bad?"

"No, my egocentric little butch. It's got nothing to do with you. With us."

"Check this woman out. Then why have you been moping around, jumping out of your skin every time I walk through a door?"

"I'm strung out, lover, and down in the dumps."

"Why didn't you say something? I could've brought you flowers. We could've gone on a vacation. We still can!"

"Donny, Donny, the drug may be working. We only now made love for the first time in—"

Donny sulked. Loopy whimpered in her sleep, her paws running in the air. "Yeah, and next time maybe I better invite my pal K-Y over to help." She sat up and stared at Chick. "Or is that it? Abeo's stayed too long? You don't like my weird trans friend and all the ruckus she's stirring up?"

The hot flash sparked again. "Why is this turning into your problem, lover? It's something inside me, okay? I need you to love me, that's all, not beat yourself up."

"You didn't tell me."

"I was too down to talk about it. Haven't you ever felt like that?" Donny was a concrete wall when she wanted to be. "I didn't mean to hurt you or leave you out."

"But you did cut me out. This is some serious shit you're talking, woman. If you can't let me in at a time like this, then I'm thinking you never have."

"How can you say that, Donny? You know you zapped my heart and soul."

"I never asked for your heart and soul. All I asked for is a gorgeous, loving woman to share my life with, and now you tell me you're so damned miserable you have to take drugs to get by?"

"Is that what's flipping you out? That I'm doing a drug? It's not a high, my sweet worrier." Donny's back was to her and she slid her arms around her. She felt so cool and soft and smelled slightly minty. Maybe she'd leaned on a bed of mint while she was out fishing earlier with Hector. He was a twilight fisherman, willing to endure the mosquitoes because the fish loved them. "I'm cool, Donny. Taking chemicals for recreation doesn't do a thing for me anymore."

"I'm not flipped out," Donny protested, squirming from reach. "It's no skin off my nose what you do to yourself."

Chick could hear the fear, though. What a totally stupid thing to confess with Donny's brother in the shape he was in. "I battled Dr. Wu on this, Donny. It was my last choice. I need help shaking this melancholy I'm going through."

"You need help out of that bottle?"

"What could I have asked you for? You can't make me happy."

"You were always saying I did. What changed?"

Donny was right, but wrong. "You do make me happy. Or you make it possible for me to be happy when everything else is going right."

"Then tell me what's going wrong."

"Dr. Wu thinks it's some combination of hormones and missing serotonin. That's the chemical they think controls—"

"I know what it is. I read the paper. Another fancy new-age way the drug companies are making a buck. Way back when, it was Miltowns for your nerves. Now it's all about your nerve synapses or something. The way I see it, either you're content with what you've got or you're not, and no drugs, no alcohol is going to fix you if you're not."

"I didn't mean to hurt your feelings, Donny. Let me brew us a pot of tea and—"

"I don't want no cup of tea, Chick. Stop trying to take care of me. Don't you understand? You need taking care of sometimes too, and you've got to let me instead of shutting me out. They don't sell what I can do in any shape bottle."

That unnerved her. "Sometimes all the love in the world can't fix what's broken. Look at my brother."

"Your brother's got nothing to do with this. He's got his wires crossed. You're having a little down spell. We'll get Jeep and Abeo and a couple of the gals on the land to cover for us, Chick. We'll take a trip. A change of scenery, some moonlight walks, maybe palm trees and a boat ride. How about a cruise? We can borrow the money."

"You're so good to me. When this is over I'd love to take a trip with you, but not now. Leaving home would be the end of me. You and our friends and the store are my glue." She had a vision of M.C. hurting Loopy while they were away. "I'd fall to pieces without our daily routines."

Donny was at the side of the bed, sitting up, pulling on her shirt. "Who will you let help you? Who else knows what's going on with you?"

"Only Dr. Wu. It's too heavy to share with anyone but her—and you."

Donny stepped into her overalls. "It's not right. That's what I'm for."

Donny would for sure think going after M.C. was a help. Chick bit her lip. No matter what she did, whether she lied to Donny to protect her or came clean, M.C. had worsened the big depression. He'd stopped coming in the store to play mind games with her, but she'd heard that he was helping out with Katie's video project, connecting her with the straights, insinuating himself into the women's community, getting closer.

Thinking about it made her feel crazy. She wanted to get under the covers and never come out. She saw herself, naked, at the top of Blackberry Falls, sliding down the worn rocks, one with the water, riding the flow to the dark pool and letting it take her down the mountain, along Sweet Creek to the Elk River, the easiest ride of her life, swift and buoyant and free of herself, to the Pacific Ocean. She could hear the rush of the waters and the osprey crying when they mistook her for a giant fish. She felt the salmon as she slid past them in the blessedly numbing cold.

She needed to talk to Donny and forced herself to surface. Donny was gone. Where? How would it feel if Donny never came back? She told Donny everything else; why was she blowing this so badly? Because this wasn't her scene. She didn't want this ugliness that clung to men like a cloud of furious insects to spread to her life.

She sat upright, felt the chill in the room as the covers fell from her. Donny didn't have to leave—without going anywhere, the Chick Donny loved had split and didn't know her way back. Who would take care of her lost butches—Donny, Jeep, Sheriff Sweet, the very young land women who didn't have a clue about life? Her days of chasing them were over, but they remained a passion. She'd been born Wendy to every lesbian Peter Pan. She had to get it together.

It was too hard. Under the covers again, she stared at the motionless ceiling fan and remembered another night like this long ago. She remembered lying on the shore of Lake Michigan in the fall, chilled, without energy to put on her coat, hungry with no appetite, fatigued to the bone but sleepless, so stoned she wanted a flood of water to bear her away.

The lake was coming at her again, welcomed and feared. She was too confused to know the question, much less the right thing to do. K-Y, Prozac, and lying to her lover—is that what her Age of Aquarius had come to?

CHAPTER FOURTEEN

Lonesome in the Country

Jeep thought it would be a kick to visit dinky little Blackberry Casino on a Friday night, but the locals she'd want to go with had already checked it out. Tonight she was so desperate to escape the lonelies that she'd found herself pondering a move back to Reno where she had even more nothing than she had here. If nothing ever happened in Reno, what was she doing in Hickrock, Nowheresville? Donny and Chick were visiting Clara and Hector, Cat was M.I.A.—was she with her mystery lover?—the band didn't have a gig until tomorrow night, women's land was out of bounds for her as long as Katie was around, and she wasn't really friends with the people from school any more than she was with the band women. That left herself. She already knew she was no fun alone, but she'd have to do.

She put on one of the five faded rugby shirts she'd snagged at a garage sale for $2.50, grabbed her board, and glided alone through the misty night, skidding occasionally on sodden leaves. Somehow lonesome in the country was twice as severe as lonely in the city. Maybe that's why country-western music tended terminally toward the poor me's.

The bright blinking lights outside the casino and the roar of sound within immediately cheered her as she checked her skateboard and scoped out the machines. This was a taste of home, of Nevada, and not as little and dinky as she'd expected. Garish, obnoxious, but familiar. From an early age she'd been drawn to the neon—what a word: neo! on!—and the merrymaking crowds. Her family's old ranch house—operative word "old"—had belonged to generations of ranchers before they sold their land to developers and their house to the Morgans, Jeep's grandparents, who passed it on to her mom and dad. It was a rambling compound of add-ons and outbuildings, always in need of paint, completely different from the compact homes of her friends and set on a rise, like a standoffish neighbor.

A gang of kids from the subdivision around it would bike and skateboard into town, a mile north, on a Saturday afternoon in the fall or spring when it was cool enough to be fun. They indulged in minor mischief like chalking up the sidewalks and weaving through pedestrians on the sidewalks of the main drag. They were full of resentment that any grody out-of-town adult could go into the casinos while they, the natives, could only peer in through glass doors. Occasionally one of them would escape notice long enough to win a handful of coins from a grocery store slot machine, but they'd all get so excited and noisy that they'd be tossed out. Even the arcades got pissed at them. The best ones were at the casinos and hotels for out-of-town kids in their best play duds. The sight of a crew in old jeans with skateboards under their arms was a tip-off to the change dragon who would hover and interrupt until they left.

The Blackberry Casino gave her a whiff of the old cigarette-smoke-infused excitement. Gambling equaled adulthood to the local kids. No matter that their parents made fun of the losers weeping in the streets and shuffling into pawn shops. Games of chance had seemed like real life. As she got change from a machine she thought of the irony: a bunch of children could see that gambling was a shabby substitute for life, like life was nothing but a trip to a game parlor where you played till you died at tables that dealt love and money and bad breaks.

She glanced around at the wall-to-wall machines. Had the empties been abandoned by losers? Did these players know something she didn't? The place was wall-to-wall slots. Bing, bing, bing, bing—the electronic sounds could make you nuts. On top of the endless binging came the tunes the machines played every time someone got a win. The only thing missing was the rush of coins down a metal chute. Passersby were shouting to be heard. You never saw so many empty slots at one time back home.

She roamed a row trying to pick up a good vibe, then grabbed a stool in front of a machine with a Western theme. No cherries, only cactus, boots, Ranger hat, crossed Colts. This was cool. Not Reno, but here she was, rassling with a one-armed bandit again, excited that she might win some money, but more excited that she'd become the grown-up she'd imagined all those years ago and the lesbian she'd dreamed of becoming when she saw *Desert Hearts* at fourteen. She pulled down the arm of the slot for old-times' sake. The pictures spun. Nada.

She'd already had a girlfriend by then, a guitar player all of sixteen whose permissive parents let her play on the street for change. The first time she skateboarded by Mindy she'd skipped to a stop. She'd realized immediately that this was a place she could fiddle. She'd been listening to her mom's bluegrass tapes and playing along for years. After an hour or so someone in the house would cry, "Enough, Gina Pauline!"

The weekend after she found Mindy performing on a corner, she skated around town until she found her doing a classical guitar number outside a parking lot where tour buses by the dozen parked. She set her closed violin case next to Mindy's open, nearly empty case and began to play along with the guitar. Mindy scowled at first, but didn't send her away. When Mindy finished, Jeep asked if she knew "Beautiful Blue Eyes." Almost immediately after they began to play, money was tossed into the guitar case.

Over pizza that afternoon they named themselves Two Girl Dudes. A month later they were skipping the pizza and making out on a bench in the park along the Truckee River. That had been exciting—the girl, the music, the way people would stop on the street and tell one another she was a prodigy—they'd talk about her as if she wasn't there and guess that she was Mindy's kid brother.

"Assholes," Mindy would whisper.

Jeep loved it and let her hair grow a little too long. "I ought to be arrested for impersonating a male musician," she'd told Mindy. That's when she decided the word "impersonate" really meant "imperson," like "him-person," "ate," like consumed. Because the "him" persons of the world consumed it. Mindy called her a damn feminist.

Then Mindy started bringing big cans of beer in a paper bag to the park, then to the street, slugging from the bag between numbers. Jeep tasted the stuff and spit it out. That wasn't worth getting busted over, she'd tell Mindy. But she didn't mind kissing the smell at all and still tasted it sometimes even when she was with a woman who never drank. Too soon the beer got more important to Mindy than the kissing, and then it got more important than Two Girl Dudes and Mindy started flaking out on Jeep.

She got away with this for almost three years when somehow Jeep's parents, who were teachers and never came downtown, heard that their sixteen-year-old daughter was panhandling alone on the streets of Reno. Jeep tried to explain that it was the playing she went for, not the bucks, but Mom and Dad were afraid she'd get in with street kids and start on dope. She'd pictured herself aflame from a crack fire, like that comedian, fiddling till she dropped.

Those were her defining moments, though, playing old-time music for an audience lavish with praise and kissing a beer-breathed girl in the park. The memory of those kisses got her damp down under. She sighed and realized she'd been locked in a staring contest with the electronic one-armed bandit in front of her. She tried again and watched the Wild West icons spin. Nada.

Too bad Cat had been busy tonight. Kind of like Chick would say, she'd be a blast here. It was just as well she wasn't interested in a romance with Jeep. Even if she hadn't been clear about not wanting a girlfriend, Jeep would have hesitated, not eager to lose a fun chum. Gawd, she missed Sarah. Once in a while they'd take ten dollars and duck into one of the casinos to see if they could make their money grow. Even when they lost it was cheaper than two seats at the movies and usually more fun.

In their last months together, she'd become both restless and tired from managing the gift shop at The Lucky City Hotel and Casino. She'd worked there forever, starting after school in eleventh grade, then working whatever hours she could schedule through four years of college. The job market had been so bad by graduation that she'd jumped at the chance to be manager when her ex-showgirl boss retired.

Her work hours had been good for playing the shows for which she was sometimes called in, but she'd started wondering where temp gigs would take her. Did she want to be a full-time casino musician? In that world young was in; old never would be. There were a thousand musicians in Reno, and most of them expected to make it big tomorrow. She could see herself, age sixty-five, all wrinkled up from the sun, still breathing casino cigarette smoke, the oldest surviving member of the Lucky City Orchestra. Except they'd can her long before that.

There had been a railroad switching yard behind the apartment building where she lived with Sarah. It always got her dreaming of distant places. One day while she'd watched a freight train being assembled, the cars creaking and groaning and bumping with the effort, she'd said, "I was thinking about starting a band."

With a tone of loving exasperation Sarah called, "Tell me something new," and continued to rummage in the freezer.

"No, this is different. I need to face it, Sar. I'm never going to make it into the classical world. And I'm pretty good with that old-time music number in the show. The director gave me the solo last night. He's going to let me go electric tonight. If the crowd keeps liking me, it could turn into a regular routine."

Sarah had stopped what she was doing and moved quickly to Jeep, arms out to hold her. "You see? It's happening! You and your old-time music are going to make it. You're going to have a rockabilly hit, lover!"

"It's not a hit I'm after. It's the chance to play music. Electric violin is like beyond description, Sar. He went ape shit when I used a pickup on my acoustic, but I want to get the real thing, maybe a vintage Fender if I can find one on eBay. They are so retro." With a thump the engine connected to a length of cars. "Want to come hear me? My number's around 10:15, then 11:15."

"I wish I could. I've got a meeting with Housekeeping first thing in the morning—Management's changing our health insurance. With Benefits off on pregnancy leave, I'm it in H.R. Friday night if you're working?"

"Date."

"Date," Sarah agreed, smiling.

Jeep tried to stop her restless fidgeting. "I'm sure glad you like old-time music."

"Growing up on Mom and Dad's Dylan and The Band LPs sort of prepared me."

"You could be road manager!"

"Jeep, dearest, you hate the idea of touring."

"Not if you were with me."

"Right. Ms. Homebody '01 suddenly has roaming feet?"

"Probably not," she answered.

It was true. Normally she liked nothing more than coming home after work and staying there. She had so much she wanted to do. Find that old Fender fiddle for one thing. Practice, for another. She never missed practicing on days she wasn't playing. And her refinishing projects were getting stacked up—the blue ukulele stenciled with daisies she'd found on the sidewalk in somebody's trash, the $2 clarinet from a garage sale, and the ancient banged-up banjo one of her teachers at the U had given her. She'd learned enough watching her dad refurbish instruments that she was about ready to string it. She wasted a lot of lunch hours roving garage sales, picking up old sheet music, original tapes of local groups, and all manner of clothes she dreamed of wearing in an old-time music band—vests and hats, suspenders and striped collarless shirts. Sarah said she was her garage sale dyke. The memory made her smile. Part-time teacher wages didn't leave enough money to do much garage saling now.

Sarah slid a gordito covered with shredded cheese into the microwave, but Jeep's appetite had been whetted for adventure, not burritos.

"I am a homebody, but nada times nada happens here. If aliens were coming to earth? Reno would be their last choice for a good time. Let's apply for jobs at The Magnet in San Francisco. I'll bet there's a radical music scene on the Coast."

"Radical old-time music? That's an oxymoron. San Francisco," Sarah said slowly as if testing the words for flavor while she spun lettuce dry for the burritos, "it's really, really far from the mountains, Jeep, and nervous-making. My parents wanted me to go to school there. We went a few times when I was small, but even Reno's too big for me, Jeep. I never want to go back to San Francisco."

She'd tapped the floor frantically, practicing her solo in her head. Maybe someone in the audience that night would be out from Nashville looking for a techno-country fiddler. Maybe this wasn't such a weird idea, but, kind of like her destiny. She composed a newspaper item aloud: "Mr. and Mrs. Robert Teitel proudly announce the appointment of their daughter–umm—Sarah Teitel-Morgan to the position of Design Engineer for the San Francisco Magnet Hotel."

"Based on my vast experience?" Sarah asked with a laugh. She took salsa from the refrigerator. "And I am so sure there's a dire shortage of wanna-be architects in San Fran," she mocked. "Maybe the casino will give you more solos?"

"I don't want casino solos. I want to play real music with a real band and get out of that toy store for flabby tourists." Jeep clenched her fists. "It hurts, I need to play so bad. But you! You could go to the architecture school at Berkeley, Sar." She sniffed at the warm food smell venting from the nuker.

"Between tours?"

Jeep decided to work on that banjo tonight after practicing. She'd teach herself to play it. She filled her plate at the kitchen counter and took it to the window seat over the parking lot. Did she have to bail on Sarah to get where she was going? The food lost all its taste. She sluiced extra salsa on her burrito. "Maybe they have an architecture school in Nashville. You could design the Brand New Opry."

"Nashville? Are you totally out of your gourd?"

Jeep snagged a chunk of escaping avocado and pointed her green fingertip at Sarah. "Sarah, it's kind of like it'll never be a new century again in my life even if I live to be a hundred. It's a time when I want to do it all! You never even want to dream."

The big living room window faced the street. She watched as an office worker left through the glass front door of a spiff old-style building. Next door recovering addicts smoked on the steps of a drug and alcohol rehab house that needed rehabbing itself. Had she hurt Sarah's feelings? She had to say this stuff or explode. Maybe she had exploded. Poor Sarah. "Geez, talk about beauty and the beast. Somebody designed these fab twenties buildings and what happens? People grind out dirty cigarettes on the porch rails. It's like playing music to a casino crowd."

Sarah took her hand, kissing Jeep's knuckles and looking up shyly at her from under his eyebrows. "I do dream, Jeep. I still dream of getting work in Idaho and adopting a slew of kids to raise there. I haven't begun to show you how beautiful my hometown is. Mountains and waterfalls, cool air, green grasses, elk and bear. And you could fly anywhere to make music, or paint up a big bus like that old hippie writer and travel the country to old-time music festivals. And women's festivals, if you had a women's band. I'd be waiting in the house I'm designing for us. With a barn-shaped music studio, where your band could rehearse. We could even have a homegrown band like your family did."

The lights went off in the office building and, one by one, the rest of the staff dispersed through the summer evening to their SUVs and minivans. Soon the air outside the city would fill with the smell of mesquite charcoal burning in backyards.

"Yeah," said Jeep, made a little uneasy by Sarah's family talk, "we can turn our backs on adventure and devote ourselves to a quiet, normal life, sputtering out in Idaho."

"Can't we have both?"

Jeep watched a neighbor, an old dude on a walker, make his way along the street. "Don't you want everything on the menu?"

"I'm afraid of your dreams, Jeep. Afraid they'll take you away from me. Take these delicious fingers away from me too."

She felt a quake of love for Sarah. "I am absolutely warped over you."

"Still?" Sarah said in her sweetest small hopeful voice.

"Still." Jeep kissed her, but she wasn't at all sure she'd feel the same about Sarah-the-mom. And did Sarah expect her to enjoy having a houseful of screaming-meemie loud-mouth kids when she was trying to rehearse?

"Let's go country dancing this weekend!" Sarah cried with a chirp of laughter.

Jeep had darted to their CD boom box and punched buttons until the Dixie Chicks' high-energy voices propelled her into a jittery dance.

Sarah had slipped her hand into Jeep's and slowed her down until, pressed together, they danced.

"Nothing in the world will take me from you, Sarah." Jeep felt kind of weird, like she was saying something she only wanted to be true. She quickly pulled the shades on that thought.

The peppy little six-guns and cactuses on the slot machine came back into focus, and she found her eyes were wet. She'd had to leave Reno, she told herself. She had to get out into the world and see what she could accomplish. She shook her head and checked to see how much she had left to play. Here she was, looking for fun in front of a video terminal display again. She played a line. At least she liked her job here. Sarah had always said that teaching kids was for saintly people. She would be so surprised, but only if Jeep told her, and so far she didn't have the nerve to get back in touch with Sarah. What if she was living with someone new? The very thought filled her with pain. The whirling display stopped. She'd blown another dollar. Maybe she was blowing her life too, she thought with the hopeless bitterness that sometimes overtook her. Why wasn't there anyone to tell her what to do?

Dollar number three went the way of the first two. Number four. Hey, she was just warming up. A pop melody chimed up the row and a change dragon hurried over with a receipt for the player's winnings. Bummer. She liked the old coins better; there was a romance to games of chance. This was like going to the grocery store. Okay, her last dollar. She rubbed her earring for luck, crossed her toes in her muddy running shoes, and was about to drop the coin when she felt arms squeeze around her from behind.

"Holy shit!" she yelped. "Katie?"

"Yeah, sweetie." Katie kissed her very lightly on the cheek. "I couldn't believe it when I saw you here. Love the cowboy hat. You working on a new addiction?"

Now she felt embarrassed about buying the black hat with its lavender band. "Get over yourself. I was never addicted to anything but you. What're you doing here anyway?"

"Truth? Getting a feel for rural America. Talking to some folks."

"You mean being a journalist."

Katie's coy look still made Jeep's hands sweat.

"I stand accused. How'd you guess?"

"Duh. The Sony?"

A silence came between them. Jeep looked at the pattern of the casino rug, wanting instead to look into those always-burning eyes. She listened to the clatter and curses and yelps of triumph that filled the cavernous room, wanting instead Katie's love talk.

"I heard about your project," Jeep told her. "The land babes are coming into Natural Woman fuming about losing their privacy to advance your career."

"Why is it only dykes are slamming me about it? If I can get this story out—Jeep! It's not my career I'm working on here. Don't you think an epic human interest documentary would help stop the rape of the old-growth forests?"

Jeep was getting ready to play the last of her money. "Are you getting this wild gambling junkie action?" she asked with a sneer. "Maybe I don't think trees are more important than protecting lesbians. Hey! Turn that thing off!"

"Why? You're doing good. The first dyke to dialogue with me."

"You're using me, Delgado."

"Jeep, remember we didn't know why we wanted to do this women's land thing? We felt pulled here? I think this is my reason. I'm not looking to out anybody. There's a common denominator somewhere between the tree-huggers and the people losing jobs that, once I find it and get my message out there, may change our world."

The noise level around them had lowered with the camera's presence. Katie's charm level was at 300%. But Jeep was inured to that charm now.

"Why bug me?" she asked and turned her back.

"I miss you. I miss bouncing ideas off you. You have such incisive, cut-the-crap insights."

"Until your insight, not mine, that we were over. Until this insight that I should be part of your project whether I want to be or not."

A few months ago she'd been thrilled to be part of Katie's ventures. A few months ago she would have—and had—followed Katie anywhere. Katie was awesome at getting what she wanted out of people.

"I'm feeling beyond manipulated," she said.

Katie moved closer, whispering, "I'm not filming, Jeep. I'm trying to get some of the natives interested. If you'll work with me for a couple of minutes, they'll be into it. Please?"

Jeep shoved the electronic button instead of pulling the arm down. Nothing. She could hear voices coming closer, the curious crowd closing in. She felt so confused. How could she long for Sarah one minute and regret losing Katie the next?

As she took chances on her machine she could hear Katie telling the mike, "Many natives simply don't make a connection between the environment, a family-values agenda, and their own problems. Are their children's disabilities caused by a degraded environment? Can they accept making a livelihood inside a gambling establishment rather than continuing to gamble that Mother Nature and the increasingly multi-national timber corporations will provide? Could the drama of gay people in this state, where there are still remnants of attempts from the nineties to try to vote away the rights of gays, possibly be related to the anger and fear of generations of logging families now running clandestine dope farms?"

Jeep still had a last play and as she mashed the button, she heard the camera. Bing, loser! Bing, loser! "Damn you!" She felt about as smart as fish bait. Katie *was* filming. She stood.

Some woman, obviously clueless about Katie's ambush and purpose there, trilled, "Is this going to be on the TV, honey?" She planted herself at Jeep's machine.

Jeep was no more than ten feet from the door when she heard the woman whoop and call "Bingo!" Man, she thought, there must be a journalism muse who spent her life by Katie's side. That winner would tell Katie anything she wanted to know now.

CHAPTER FIFTEEN

The Leak

I don't know how to patch roofs!" Katie complained when they reached the last item and she still had no work assignment.

"Neither did any of us when we moved here?" said ever-tentative gray-haired Dorothea who made every sentence a question and was one of R's ex-lovers.

R asked quietly, "Do you think you're unique?"

Katie hated that she pouted around R. "I'll slide off the moss, I know I will."

Solstice, the out-of-town customer at Jeep's store in San Francisco who they'd originally come to visit, groaned. "Did you have to bring up the moss?" She tossed a log on the fire, but it was damp and smoke slid into the room. Katie coughed.

Seven women lived at Spirit Ridge—plus Katie. In the dry season came campers, goddess worshipers, and burned-out freeloaders. Best, Katie had been told, were the city Ridgers who helped support the land with donations and work party/vacations. They'd pitch tents in the field or under the trees, tear off their shirts, get sunburned and lusty, and make plans to quit their jobs, which some actually did. It blew her away that a few, for the sake of two or three weeks of pure women's space a year, went back to the cities and tithed what they earned there to protect the land.

Tonight, at the monthly meeting, the lodge's tiger cat sampled seven laps, kneading her claws into Katie's thigh along the way, before settling in her basket beside the woodstove. They were having a late spring storm. Rain pelted the roof with every gust of wind. People in town said it was supposed to snow above 3000 feet. All this talk of outdoor chores seemed pretty ludicrous.

She felt like crying. This was so cool, this homeland and these women like her who had made a sanctuary. She'd never even be able to conceive of such a place, and a handful of them had bought the land, built the structures, put in electricity, plumbing, the whole nine yards. It wasn't exactly up to subdivision standards, but who set the standards? The point was, they'd done it, back in the 1970's when she was an infant. They'd done it for themselves, and kept it going for her.

According to R, they'd been on the verge of losing Spirit Ridge when she came along several years ago. Katie had the impression that R had taken over the management of their funds and found new resources until it was out of fiscal danger, but no one talked details. It was easy to see that she was the big cheese here now, whether they called themselves a collective or not. They'd finally accumulated enough money to buy materials for this year's repairs. Only the roof lacked a volunteer worker.

Katie realized she'd been counting drips from the leaking communal kitchen roof. One hit the plastic pail every three and a half seconds. At each hundred she'd start over. It was a habit—a compulsion?—she'd used to distract herself from the terrors and tedium of childhood. Leaks, curse words, planes flying overhead, she'd count them all.

She was supposed to volunteer for the project list which had been drawn up last summer at the annual meeting, but she didn't have the kind of skills it took to do these things. She tapped her foot, counting one, two, three, four to some opening rock riff she couldn't identify.

"I like the moss," she told them. "The lodge looks like a gingerbread house. We're cozy with the big shadowy woods creaking around us and the wolves howling—"

"They killed the wolves off a century ago," Dorothea noted sadly. She was a tall, red-haired woman whose quick long fingers knitted bright yellow yarn.

Aster's voice got louder and deeper as she spoke, like someone who'd been screaming. "That's a whole other project. And we're not using poisons up there." She glowered at the group and turned back to Katie. "Poison is the quick method, the American way. But rain will wash the moss killer into the ground."

Spruce, the big, awkward, quietly butch kid, said gently, "When I put off a small job, it only gets bigger."

"Kate," explained R, "has never owned property. This is all new to her." R sat cross-legged in the middle of a sprung couch, back straight, writing notes of the meeting in a bold hand. "I have to agree with the rest, Kate. This is no fairy tale. Nobody's going to take care of lesbian roofs but lesbians."

"You're making me homesick for the trailer park where I

came up—flat roofs too dry for moss. The gringo manager fixed what got fixed."

"We don't want the man on our land. It's like R says," Solstice explained in a tone that hinted of deeply held beliefs, "the leak will get too big for us to handle and we'll have to bring a man up here. I think they talk about us in town enough."

She and Jeep had named Solstice the original retro queen because of her harem pants, Birkies, hemp pullovers, and boycott of deodorant. "So I volunteer. I'd probably make it worse."

"I could teach you how to do it right," said Spruce.

R placidly asked Spruce, "Is that your privileged white liberal guilt volunteering?"

Did R think Spruce was coming on to her? If so, it was the first sign of possessiveness she'd seen. R made a strange white knight. Before Spruce could respond, Katie tweaked R. "No. It's my kind of politically incorrect butch coming to the rescue!"

Only Nightfall laughed. R shook her head. Katie noticed quick glances toward R to see how she was taking Katie's rebellion.

Spruce, face red again, mumbled, "I was only trying to help."

She was pretty hot in patched jeans and a black T-shirt rolled up her brawny arms. Spruce was a good name for her. "How about if this magnificent mujer who actually likes this kind of work does the repair while I tape her?" Katie suggested. Aster laughed. "Spruce doesn't talk."

Spruce grinned, pretended to flex her biceps, and said, "Oh, I could talk into the tape."

"And I could interview you while you worked. How you got your skills, what projects you've done. What brought you to the land?"

"I've only been here eight months."

"Still," Katie insisted, although it was plain Spruce's shyness would spoil her as a subject, "why couldn't I, like, do an interview and paint the goat shed? I could handle that."

"Because it's too rainy? Painting has to wait until the summer," Dorothea explained. "And we have no goats anymore."

Katie read from the list, "Patch roof? Clean chimney? Be real! They used to make little kids do that in Dickens's books."

The group looked at her, but Spruce was grinning, eyes cast down. Katie wondered if Spruce was crushed out on her. She'd do the roof for her, no problem, and on the QT. Katie felt like a user, but the child would get her moment in the spotlight even though she wouldn't get the girl. God, she was really contemplating this rural film project, wasn't she? She was supposed to be freeing herself from being obsessively on the prowl for stories, but this project could be very different.

She'd felt so lost back in San Francisco, like the cities, always light, were really dark. Like her light inside had been turned off. Did she need to get out of the biz, or just the daily grind? There had been times she'd felt like she was suffocating—no, dying, and she was only twenty-nine. There was an old Stones song, "Nineteenth Nervous Breakdown," that she'd been unable to get out of her head at times. She'd needed to breathe clean air for a while and had been doing anything she could to get out-of-town assignments. Her boss had begged her to take some time off, not resign, but she'd needed to cut the ties. In the city, the work was the only thing that made her feel alive. She wanted to get her candle lit again. Would hammering nails into a roof do that for her? No, but filming a lesbian doing it would, with some working song in the background, something by Sweet Honey in the Rock, that group R played over and over on her mini-boom box. And, of course, Spruce would do it while Katie got her interview.

"Okay! All right!" she said. "I'll patch the roof. You think I'm scared? I've done interviews from cherry pickers. I've covered climbing expeditions. I can manage to throw a plastic tarp over a roof."

"Oh, no!" wailed Aster.

"Joke," countered Katie. "You tell me how, I'll do it, but I only work with a net."

The whole group laughed this time. Katie had agreed to the collective will. Did they find that validating or were they simply relieved that the new girl was doing the least popular chore and that they wouldn't have to toss her lazy ass out? She admired their ideas, but was too independent to ever sincerely pitch in and build a lesbian utopia. Spruce fiddled with the fire, pushed the still-smoldering, smelly log deep into the coals. The cat stood, licked a spot on her back, turned in her basket, and settled back down.

"New business?" asked Dorothea.

There was a shifting of bodies, plumping of pillows, then dead silence except for the dripping roof and Dorothea's sliding, clicking needles. The rain must have stopped. Katie munched a handful of cold popcorn, popped in olive oil instead of butter for the vegan in the group, but well salted. She counted thirty-two drops, and felt apprehensive. Were they going to tell her she'd done something wrong? She was clearly not cut out for collective decision-making, collective interpersonal intrigues, collective incest. The cat's ears twitched.

Finally, in a rush of words, Nightfall, who'd volunteered to prepare a new compost bin for spring, asked, "What about Chick and Donny?"

Katie was startled. What did Chick and Donny have to do with Spirit Ridge housekeeping projects?

"Why is it up to us to do something?" Marge asked.

"I agree," Aster said. "If they want help they'll ask."

"Women!" protested Dorothea, needles accelerating. "The word is they haven't talked to each other in two weeks. It isn't our business, unless we care about the couples in our community."

Aster said, "You are so seventies, Dorothea."

"And that," Nightfall responded, "is a good thing. We wouldn't be here without seventies feminists."

Dorothea smiled at her yarn and murmured, "Aster is also not historically correct. Exclusive coupling was frowned on in the seventies."

"Maybe one of them, Donny or Chick, needs a time-out. We could offer Star Light Cabin up on the hill until they sort it through," suggested Solstice. She always wore a little purple velvet spangled beanie.

Spruce murmured, "All couples go through things like that. Don't they?"

"In the straight world they have family and priests and other het couples to turn to," said Aster, arms folded, resentment clear.

"Or rabbis," Marge added. "And," she said, looking at Aster as if they'd discussed this before, "couples can get counseling."

Solstice laughed scornfully. "We sure don't have a community of long-term couple role models to turn to."

"It's something in the air," Marge ventured. "Couples don't last here."

"Incompatibility?" asked Dorothea, squinting at her stitches. "Infidelity? Changes of the seasons?"

Aster gave a nasty laugh. "Electromagnetic repulsion?"

Thinking that these women must have come from a microsociety she'd never studied in her sociology class, or were so bored they manufactured problems for themselves and anyone else they could think of, Katie suggested, "Not that I noticed a problem, but it could be something simple like that friend of Donny's overstaying her welcome."

"Abeo," Marge said in her thoughtful way, "does take up a lot of psychic space."

"She could stay here?" Dorothea suggested.

Aster glared at Dorothea. "Abeo's not a birth woman."

"Better!" Marge argued. "She chose to give up her male privileges."

Katie decided it was Marge and Aster who had relationship problems, never mind Chick and Donny.

"All right," R sighed, as if to quash Dorothea's idea fast. "Maybe we can resolve this some other way. I'll talk to them."

Again the group got what it wanted, someone to take responsibility for a nasty chore. Katie could feel their relief at R's words, as if an angel had appeared to rescue them.

Nonetheless, Aster jabbed. "With your track record, R? You go through relationships like women grow on trees."

Gawd, thought Katie, these snipe-happy women are not only from this planet, they're no different than people back in the city. R didn't answer but, with deliberate, slow motions, closed her notebook. Katie noticed how every woman in the room began to gather her things together. R might as well have announced that their meeting would soon be over. Her every move was commanding. What made her so powerful? Did all that meditation gather some pure kind of energy in her?

Only when it was quiet did R say, "I know something about harmony. Communication. Perseverance. Women mate with many things, Aster. The land, for example."

Solstice nodded with a solemn look. Could it be that these women, to whom she'd come for harmony lessons, were looking for harmony themselves? R began to sing. Katie had seen her defuse tense situations like this before with song, but never so disarmingly. In a clear, high voice she was singing a lighthearted piece called "A Proper Little Pot," which involved tongue twisters. She had it down perfectly, of course, but when the others joined in, they tripped over words and one another as they had throughout the meeting, but they laughed about it now.

At the song's end, R stood and stretched out her arms.

Quickly, Dorothea asked, "Any other new business?"

Katie moved next to R, still fascinated by her. The woman should be in show business. What a talent. When R abruptly stopped rancor with song, she not only showed the women how sour they were being, but how sweet they could be. Again and again Katie had seen R save the home they'd made not only for all these women, but for women to come.

The rest rose and held hands. R led a closing chant, adding, "May the energy of these women and this land bring healing to all women. I give thanks for the land itself and for the women who dwell on it with me. Blessed be."

While the rest repeated, "Blessed be," Katie wondered where it left her if R was married to the land. She might share R's bed, but she totally knew right then that she'd never get to keep a piece of the woman's heart.

CHAPTER SIXTEEN

Laughing

It was closing time when R, in her measured, smooth way, moved through the entry to Natural Woman Foods. Sheriff Sweet, with the store's last cup of coffee in hand, nodded a curt hello and on her way out stopped in the open side door to rub Loopy behind the ears. The dog was watching Donny's every move, waiting to get taken upstairs for her dinner. Joan was watching R, whom she had described as some kind of trouble she'd probably never know about.

Donny rotated the old packages of miso soup to the front of a shelf and slid the new stock behind. She had some of Chick's new-age music on and liked to make a little dance for this kind of work. Cha cha cha, she sang. Nice, working with light packaged soups, not those damn heavy cases of cans. She called up front, "We ought to give a prize to the last customer of the day, gang. Nothing personal, R, except it never fails. Someone always comes in after the cash is counted and the store's shipshape."

Abeo, sweeping a rag mop left and right across the floor and leaving behind a cloud of eye-stinging bleach, was belting out the chorus of an old sailor song. "I'll swab yer deck and ne'er tarry, but I'm not the man you want to marry."

"Hi, R," said Chick. She opened her arms for a hug. "Ignore those rowdies. We're glad you've come."

"I'm not here to shop," R announced with her usual curt tone, accepting the hug.

Donny pushed herself upright and sauntered to the front in a way that disguised her stiff knees. Why had Chick gotten tight with this feminist bitch-on-wheels? As Abeo launched into another raunchy verse Donny cried, "Get down, sistah!" People like R were made to be messed with.

R gave a weak smile, though her eyes looked more calculating than friendly. "I wanted to speak with you and Chick."

"Shoot," Donny told her. Maybe the woman was finally going to sign on to help them stand up to the town bigots. There was another proposal before the town council about pulling *The Children's Hour* and *Philadelphia* videos from the library collection. Like either of those would recruit their straight kids? These people needed to get lives. It had always annoyed her that R, who everyone knew was the real owner of both pieces of women's land, wasn't willing to do her bit. The kind of people they were fighting listened to landowners. But no, R wasn't here to help; she wanted something.

"I'll wait until you're finished." R's eyes were tracking Abeo.

"Abe's my bro. I don't keep secrets from her."

"That woman wants to earn her country vacation," Chick said with the warm, full laugh Donny hadn't heard in a while. No one could feel unloved around Chick when she laughed, Donny least of all. Keys jingling, Chick went over to lock the front door.

"Milk crate?" Donny offered.

"I'll stand," said R.

"So what's happening, R?" Donny prodded, sliding a crate toward her anyway. "You gals in some kind of mess only me and Chick can help you out of?"

Normally, she'd give Chick a conspiratorial look over the Rat's head, but she was walking on eggs around Chick these days. Whatever was still weirding Chick out, Donny was satisfied no cheating was going on. She could live through about anything else.

"The women of Spirit Ridge are concerned about you both."

"No shit. Us?" said Donny. Now the bitch wanted into her life? If R wasn't careful she was about to get another anger demonstration. But Chick was smiling at her with that worried sadness around the edges of her eyes, so Donny laughed instead of launching into R.

That didn't stop R. "We thought you might not see that your chronic depression and Donny's anger may be symptoms of incompatibility."

"Who asked you to be our family shrink?" A little intimidation here might be just what the doctor ordered, but she could feel the sweat rising at her hairline. Shit, a hot flash.

"Donny, I suspect if you let go of your system of automatic denial, there would be fewer surprises in life to upset you."

"You've got us all figured out, don't you?"

Chick's hands nervously worked her crystal necklace. Her voice stayed sweet and low. "Are you asking if we're breaking up?"

"To be perfectly up-front? Yes."

"Breaking up?" Donny exploded. "What have you been telling this woman, babe?"

Chick pressed a hand to her heart. "Why would we break up? Things don't get much better than what Donny and I have."

R dropped carefully to the stacked milk crates. Got you, thought Donny, who never let up on her battle to get R to accept butchly courtesies. "I'm here to offer help."

"You heard my woman. Depressed or not she thinks I'm top dog, leader of the pack, Pope Donny the First—"

Chick's old warmth was in her laugh now. "The greatest lover in the world will do."

"Only because you're my inspiration."

R sat with hands extended as if begging alms. Abeo had switched to an old Harry Belafonte tune as she packed a box of produce for the walk-in cooler. "Bay-O!" she sang, "Beautiful Ah-bay-o!"

Donny looked closely at R, wiping her sweating palms on her overalls. What did this woman want from them? She always had to remind herself that R was full of slimy, still waters.

"One of my land mates," R revealed slowly, as if savoring her moment, "heard you weren't speaking."

"Say what? She heard us *not* talking?"

Chick was no longer smiling. "R, that's the furthest thing from the truth. Maybe your land mate doesn't understand companionable silence? Donny and I sometimes spend hours in the store, or upstairs, or on the road, hardly saying a word to each other and feeling completely in sync."

"Do I need to be more clear? We believe an additional person in your household is putting a strain on your relationship."

"Abeo?" Chick exclaimed.

"Somebody call me?" Abeo asked, passing with a box of carrots.

"You can always hope," Donny said, smacking Abeo's butt. "You're cool. We can handle this."

But Chick stopped Abeo. "The women at Spirit Ridge think three's a crowd. They don't know what fun you are."

"Abe has the downstairs royal suite," said Donny. "She's not in anybody's way. You're probably out tomcatting all night, Abe, right?"

"That's Thomasina-catting to you." Abeo turned to R, jingling her bracelets with one hand while the other seemed effortlessly to balance the heavy box. "The doctors made me look like the woman I am inside, but do you think *I* can make a woman? Know any single butch studs looking for a hot femme?"

To Donny's surprise, R didn't look affronted, but intrigued. "It baffles me," R said, "why a gay man would want to become a lesbian woman."

"Haven't you noticed? It's who I am."

R shook her head, wincing.

"So, Miz Liberal," Donny said, "you just want the world to be big enough for your kind?"

"Hush up, Donalds," Abeo told her and turned to R. "Give me a week or six and I'll explain it all to you, up at your yurt."

"What a flirt you are, Abe. Listen, R," Donny said, but she was wondering again, was Abeo getting on Chick's nerves? Was that what was bugging her, not the change, not hitting middle age? "This is no hostage situation, and we allow guests to practice Falun Gong here. If you want to issue an invite, talk to Abeo."

"I didn't mean for him—her to—" As if to distract them from her mistake, R cleared her throat and turned to Abeo. "The living is very primitive at Spirit Ridge."

Abeo cried, "Am I hearing an invitation to stay with the mountain women? Am I hearing the hen is about to be let loose in the hen house?"

R opened her mouth as if to object, but only looked affectionately amused.

"No way she's saying that, Abe," Donny said. "Take your size-nine foot out of your mouth."

"I'm charmed and honored, Miz R. Living on women's land—tell me I haven't come a long way, baby! You don't mind, Donny? Chick? I'll get my toilette together and be ready to go in a jiff."

As if realizing that Abeo was serious, R's eyes and lips got radically narrow. "I'm afraid I can't formally invite anyone without—"

"Oh, honey, you don't have to get all formal for me," Abeo said, doing a little fluttery happy dance toward R.

Again, R made no protest. Her eyes danced with Abeo. What was happening here?

Donny jostled Chick with an elbow. "You know, Rat, maybe you and the Ridgers are right. Maybe we need to be alone for a while. You think, Chick?"

Donny heard Chick's words burble up through suppressed laughter. "If things don't work out up there, R, bring our friend—"

"Oh," clamored Abeo, "I will please the misses, any way I can. Only give me a chance to show them my loveable girlish side." She switched from boastful to pathetic in a breath. "Unless you really think they wouldn't want me."

One of Abeo's charms, Donny remembered, was her lost puppy act. She'd fallen for it endlessly, feeding, sheltering, and sometimes supporting the little guy when he got in trouble with his boyfriends.

"Of course not," R protested. Donny had to keep herself from laughing aloud.

"Don't you move then," Abeo instructed. "I'll be right back."

When Abeo's door closed, Chick asked, "Are you sure you want to take her on?"

Donny added, "Don't act the martyr for us. Your info is bad. We're fine."

R studied their faces, then glanced quickly at the door to Abeo's room. With a quick stiff shrug, she said, "She's welcome on the land."

"So you don't have to ask the girls?" Donny asked.

"I think they'll agree with me."

"You know, I always thought you really ran the show up there," Donny said. Chick was rolling the crystal on her necklace back and forth over her lips.

"We make decisions collectively."

"But some votes are more equal than others?"

"A few of us have been on the land longer."

"I was thinking how your word must carry a lot more weight than some. How if you suggested it, some of those women might want to get involved in fighting to keep the commissioners from voting homophobia into the town charter."

"Women who want to work from within the system wouldn't be living on women's land."

"Women who live in this community have a stake in keeping it safe for themselves."

"The land is no part of this town's government," R said.

"But this town's government can make the land a lot more comfy."

"A few words in the boys' charter don't threaten me."

"Damn, woman, they'll encourage disrespect for you and what your land stands for. That's dangerous. If they see you standing up for yourselves here, you won't have to be fighting them off at your border."

"Donny, it's a waste of woman time to do battle with a group of old white men over whether they can make rules about us."

"But to make banning books legal? To make a law against letting us hold dances or meetings on city property?"

"I wouldn't do either in this town. That's why we have the land."

"Don't you get it? If discrimination is the law in small ways, it's open season on queers. If the town says it's scared of us, what does that tell people? What does that tell punks with blood-hungry fists? The same thing segregation tells African Americans! Would you ignore what's happening if they wanted to keep *The Color Purple* off the library shelves? Talk about denial, R. You are Ms. Denial her very own self."

R shook her head. "I'm not interested in debating this."

Donny took a deep breath and glared at her.

Abeo swept out of her room. Donny hoped she'd be able to hold her own at camp R. She hugged Chick and Donny, mopped her eyes with a pink bandanna, and presented herself to R, acting like a shy bride. R led the way out the side door in silence.

Chick shook her head. "Life's bizarre. This is not a scene I could have dreamed up."

"I think our Abe is dying to see what it'll be like with a woman."

"She hasn't yet?"

"Not that she's admitting it to me."

"Poor little Abe. She'll be back tomorrow."

"I don't know about that, babe. Lesbian politics seem to run higher in some women than lust. R may 'should' herself into this one because she thinks it's what she ought to do."

"Have you lost it, honeybunch? Her politics are as likely to get her into bed with a trans woman, as they are to get her to a town meeting."

Rather than say something bad about Chick's pal, Donny took Chick's hand and kissed the palm.

"You know R's not going to get into town politics," Chick said. "Why do you keep trying?"

"She gets me so mad. I guess she can afford to stay buried in those hills."

"She's not worth raising your blood pressure over. Save it for the straight boys."

Donny leaned her head against Chick's shoulder. "You're probably right. You always are."

They went to the side door to lock up, but Chick said, "Wait. I've got to see this."

Outside, they walked to the corner. Donny had half-expected Sheriff Sweet to still be crouched with Loopy, chuckling to herself at Abeo's newest escapade. An Alaskan robin hopped under the brush in a front yard, its white necklace still exotic to her after a lifetime of Midwestern birds. Pansies blossomed in a planter across the street.

For the first time in too long, Donny took Chick's hand. Between Chick's doldrums and her own crazy-ass fights with the bigots, there wasn't time or energy for each other. They stood with Loopy in the drizzling rain on Stage Street and watched the tall white woman stride over puddles while smaller Abeo darted around them. They could hear Abeo's chatter. She dangled a plastic bag stuffed with whatever she'd grabbed in the hurried minutes back in her room.

"Can you wrap your head around Abeo on women-only land?" asked Chick.

"I've protected Abeo from a lot of men, but she's on her own around R. Don't you wish you could be a fly in R's Honda?"

Chick laughed. "And who's going to protect R from Abeo?"

They put their arms around each other and went back into the store. Donny rushed Loopy up the inside stairs. She usually was careful to follow the health laws, but tonight keeping the mood was more important. She didn't want a replay of the time Chick's depression got in their way. She held the door open for Chick, caught her eye, and, without a word, they broke into giggles.

"Look at you!" Chick said. "I haven't seen you laugh like this in so long."

"You look good laughing yourself."

Chick seemed to shine. Donny realized that her breath felt hot as she drew it in. It seemed to burst inside her and send energy to her fingertips. She went to Chick, arms out, needing to press against her. Chick met her with her whole body. "It's been a long time since a lot of things," she told her.

They moved to the bedroom and shed their clothes. Donny switched off the light. In a major splurge they'd made the bed an island of warmth and comfort. Elsewhere, secondhand was good enough, including the store downstairs, where they spent most of their lives.

Chick had wanted flowered patterns, Donny solids. They'd stopped arguing when Donny made a quilt of solid squares and presented it to

Chick for their fourth anniversary. It was so thick and light she felt like she was pulling a cloud up over her naked self.

Their bed was where they came to feel safe and close. They never lay down and went right to sleep. There were always too many tales of the day to exchange, and plans to make for tomorrow. Tonight neither said a word.

Without preliminary she lay flat on Chick and rode her, rubbing pubic bone and breasts, shuddering at the thrill of Chick's wide softness pillowing her. She felt Chick's small hands on her back. Chick urged her up and down and faster, and then, when Donny let loose, wrapped her arms across her back and held her, rocked her, enclosed her.

There wasn't time for languor tonight. She lifted up and slid herself one way, then the other across Chick's damp body.

Chick moved her hips under her, like a sleeping thing coming awake. She liked to moan. Donny moved herself so she could touch Chick's face and breasts, so she could reach around and knead her buttocks the way Chick said felt so good.

After a few moments Chick's sounds stopped, but Donny kept on. She was going to make her feel better, damn it. Maybe, Donny was thinking, she'd insist on sex therapy every day, like a vitamin in winter to fight off the cold germs. There'd be no more failed lovemaking if she had her way.

She felt Chick's sob before she heard it, startled that Chick had been so ready.

Then Chick said, "I'm sorry, Donny."

Sorry? Donny thought, touching and touching.

"I'm so sorry."

That hadn't been a sob of pleasure—Chick was crying! Donny fought the impulse to give up. "I want you to feel it, babe," she whispered. "I just want to touch you till we take you there. I'll stop if you want me to, but give me a chance. You're feeling like my girl again."

"It's too hard, Donny. It's not worth the energy for a sixty-second spasm."

"You don't need any damn energy." Spasm? What happened to how close they'd feel, how high above the world? "This is like a present I'm giving to you. Would you say no if I gave you a diamond ring?"

"Oh god, Donny, what am I doing to you? To us?"

She lay beside Chick, touching all her places while the tears ran along Chick's cheeks to the pillow. "Don't you go getting water in your ears, babe, or I'll have to bail them out."

A smile quavered on Chick's lips. If she could only get her laughing again. Laughter took over Chick's whole body like an orgasm. Some couples fought and then fell into bed; she and Chick laughed their way to bed.

"I can see it now," Donny said. "Me working the store all alone, telling Clara you're so depressed you have puddles in your ears." The smile got wider. "Old Clara, she'd come storming up here with a Q-Tip the size of a mop and start sponging them out."

"She would!" Chick said and laughed.

Donny laughed with her and kissed her laugh and then was kissing on her all over again and Chick was moving those sweet hips, giving a weak moan, and her little hands were guiding Donny, no, pushing her south.

"Oh, babe," she said, breathing her hot breath onto Chick's groin, "you smell so good. Let me give you this, babe." Chick was letting her lap her swollen lips and bud.

"Oh, babe," she said again, mouthing the words right against Chick, feeling that little nest of graying fur trying to get in her way. She felt her big gal rising to her mouth now, felt her thighs strain to a warning stillness, and then Chick let out her deep cry and rocked back and forth as if to throw Donny, but she knew Chick didn't want her going anywhere. She hung in there, arms around Chick's thighs, her tongue teasing out all those feelings Chick had buried with sadness.

She almost laughed out loud in pleasure. Chick pulled her higher and held her again.

"Girl," she told Chick, "this is ours, you got that? If you start sinking again, these arms are going to catch you, and don't you forget it."

CHAPTER SEVENTEEN

The Trip

You're still the sneaky, power-hungry sex maniac I knew in San Francisco!" Chick shouted into the closed, musty-smelling space of her little-used car.

Patsy, a maroon '87 LTD, strained up a muddy switchback in the road. No, she thought, that would be too general. When she confronted M.C. in his home she wanted his wife there so she would learn how evil he was.

"You're stalking me, that's what you're doing, M.C., and I'm going to see your sorry ass in jail!"

Better, except that nervousness weakened her fury. The old Dead tape she was playing to mellow her out didn't seem to be working. She longed to have Donny by her side, but she still didn't dare tell her for fear of unleashing Donny the street scrapper. No way she was going to add to the scars on that fine old body.

The branches of the newer trees along the dirt road grew so low they clawed her roof as she bumped along, and she grasped the cool plastic steering wheel hard to avoid the small craters. She'd never have found this place if the Pensioners Posse hadn't already come to warn M.C. away and passed along good directions. Their crusade had worked for all of one month.

Why M.C. had retained his obsession with her since their flower-power days was as much of a puzzle as how both of them could have landed in the same tiny Northwest town twenty years later. It was obviously meant to be, but she couldn't see a way good might come of it, and she knew there was always good somewhere.

Whatever the circumstances, she'd come to the end of her tolerance. He wasn't the only cause of her depression, but swallowing her anger about his harassment made it worse. She'd forced herself to talk more with Donny, not about M.C., but about how she was feeling. Donny, such a wise little street punk, told her that when she'd been younger she'd found it healthier in the long run to get knocked around a little to get the mad out of her system. Chick wasn't planning any fistfights, but a good old confrontation might do wonders to reset her mellow button.

About two miles up she saw a huge barn-like structure and a smattering of abandoned-looking outbuildings. There were no cows, no horses or llamas, not even a goat, only three barking, rough-looking dogs in a chain-link pen under some cottonwoods by the barn. A flowering quince ran undisciplined along one side of the barn, and small wild irises dotted the untrammeled earth. The Scotch broom was blooming, giving the whole place a yellow tinge, like she was wearing yellow fog glasses.

She parked hood out and arranged her keys as weapons between her fingers, ready for anything. The dank air stung her nose with the smell of insecticide. What crop was being sprayed?

"I'm like a mountain," she chanted as she strode toward the barn, parka streaming rain. "I can do this."

It was a beautiful place, filled with vetch and mallows, monkey flowers and—was that a forktooth ookow? She stopped. Yes, and she'd been looking for just that shade of lavender for light summer overalls. R had taught her so much about flowers on their walks through the park in town. The park was teeming with wildflowers. Last year they'd walked about every week.

Could she do this?

In the years before her brother had been prescribed effective meds, she'd learned to fear mental illness. Martin's behavior had been unpredictable, but worse, she'd had no defense against his verbal attacks on her. When they were kids he'd seemed so reasonable when he had told her that his condition was her fault, that their parents' failures could be blamed on her. He'd elaborated on the nursery rhyme about stepping on a crack and breaking a mother's back, convincing her that a sick pet, a grandparent's death, a broken toy she'd watched him destroy—all were her fault.

Until she was ten or eleven she'd believed him and at the same time believed that she could make up for all that by taking care of him. Every day she'd made his bed in a room that smelled of rotting apple cores. Her mother had thought her devotion was cute. At eight she'd learned not only to heat a can of soup for lunch, while their mother and father were at work, but to bake Martin cookies and other treats. He'd thanked her with criticism or, worse, silence.

M.C. had always been wacko, but everyone had been wacko in the sixties. She might still be considered eccentric in her long skirts and tie dyes, her anarchistic worldview and just-get-by business style, but when M.C. smirked in her store window, she could see he'd been, or become, more unbalanced than anyone else from those dangerous days.

She stopped, astonished. Inside the barn was another whole structure, two stories high, lining the sides of the barn.

Nothing was painted or even plumb, but it looked sturdy, with windows hinting at an abundance of rooms. Brightly colored window frames and doors painted with the primitive flowers and stick figures of kids made it look like a *Laugh-In* TV stage set from the 1970s. The roof was punctuated with a half dozen skylights and covered a courtyard that held bicycles, a clothesline, huge stereo speakers, refrigerators, a freezer, stoves, grills, two woodstoves with long stove pipes, and two unpainted picnic tables with benches.

At the far end of one of the benches sat a lone middle-aged woman in a green-and-purple patterned Guatemalan jacket, faded jeans, and kelly green polyurethane clogs. She was brushing her long graying hair. As Chick got closer she could hear that the woman was singing a Beach Boys song in a thin clear voice—"Help Me Rhonda." It was eerie to hear the old music in this backwoods medieval hall. There was no sign of M.C.

The lyrics had become, "Help me, Donny," in her head, and she chanted silently.

"Hello?" she called, her free hand clutching at the crystal on her necklace. This whole place was full of bad vibes, and she didn't know if they all were M.C.'s.

"M.C. took the kids to church," called the singer, turning.

"Church? M.C.?"

The woman's vague smile disclosed gaps in her teeth. "You know how straight-acting the man's got."

Chick edged closer. Would her revelations shatter this fragile creature? She pulled her rain hood back and got her second shock. "Goddess! You're Pennylane, aren't you?"

The woman squinted a long moment. "Isn't that Earthbird from next door? It isn't. It's—Chick? Is that Chicago Chick? Far fucking out!"

Chick felt an impulse to envelop in a hug this living remnant of her past, but held back. No wonder M.C. had become so crazed about Chick. Pennylane was still his old lady. But it had been nothing. Chick doubted that Pennylane even remembered the night she had spent with Chick, tripping and making love until M.C. walked in on them.

Except for that one stoned session, Pennylane hadn't been a woman she'd been particularly drawn to back in San Francisco, but she'd been a constant in the park and at the concerts. She could feel the damp grass of the park under her feet and the strange mix of chill and heat that was the San Francisco air. Pennylane had been younger than Chick, not too far into her teens, and now looked washed out, but not old at all. Chick remembered Pennylane's intense, laughing craziness, a live-free-or-die defiance she'd flaunted. In retrospect, Chick realized that Pennylane had acted as if she had a compulsive need to challenge. She took on cops, business owners, rules, facts, street signs. She remembered when the city had initiated a campaign to stop panhandling in the Fisherman's Wharf area. It had been Pennylane who'd organized the brilliant zap action for the freakiest of them to distribute change to tourists. That had frightened the visitors more than the begging, and made the patrolling cops look silly. And here she was, in Waterfall Falls, all grown up.

"What a trip," Pennylane finally said.

"This is mind-blowing, seeing you transported here from the old scene. You ended up with M.C.?"

"I was a runaway. He was Robin Hood."

"I would have loved to see you around town."

Pennylane shuddered. "Too big. Too many people. Buy this. Do that. The freeway goes so fast. Here I have no newspapers, no TV. We don't even get good radio reception. This is world peace, right here." Lazily, she waved the old "V" peace sign. "Except it's probably time to start Sunday dinner. It takes a while for fourteen."

"That's heavy. You didn't have twelve kids?"

Pennylane's voice had a weary huskiness to it. Her fear of town sounded like burnout. Had she lost too many of her challenges? Chick wanted to hold and soothe this sputtering flame of a woman, but if Pennylane remembered their encounter she wasn't acknowledging it. "Three. My two oldest I sent away, and Luke's with M.C." She looked at Chick, eyes briefly clear. "Marly's the baby machine."

"Marly?" Chick asked.

"You'd split the scene by then. M.C. dropped me, got together with Marly for about six months, then came back. After we got married and moved onto the land, here comes Marly, carrying his first son. We couldn't turn her out."

The words flew out of her mouth before she could stop them. "So he's a bigamist, too."

"No," Pennylane said quickly. "He didn't marry her, only me. By the time Marly showed up I was tired, Chick. All that rebellion takes its toll. I was glad to share him. When he decided the three of us should get it on together I found out—you're still a dyke, aren't you?" At Chick's nod she laughed and continued. "I found that M.C. was not at all necessary." She narrowed her eyes. "But what do you mean *too*?"

Pennylane didn't look as if she needed to know M.C. was sniffing after yet another woman from the old days.

Of course there was a smell of insecticide, she thought; they spray the dope. It came from outside. Inside, weeds had found their way up through the floorboards. "Only that he's still dealing, honey."

"Oh, sure," Pennylane said with the most tired-sounding laugh she'd ever heard. "He'll show you over the farm. He's got weed and mushrooms all over the woods. The black choppers never pick up on them. We've got grow lights and drying rooms under here with huge fans. M.C. figured out how to rip off electricity from the electric company, you know. Not that the pigs would check out a vigilante's cellar. He never sells locally."

Pennylane chatted away, definitely on some kind of upper. Chick sat at the other end of the picnic bench. The skylights were so high above them that they faded into gloom this far down. The place could be a cavern. This was too strange. She'd seen Sheriff Sweet keeping an eye on the Deadheads who drifted through town on their way to concerts and the hippies headed for barter days and bluegrass fairs. She'd seen front yards hung with tie-dyed clothing for sale. This living space looked as if M.C.'s family had packed up the sixties and moved it whole to Waterfall Falls, then co-opted a little eighties law and order and studded it with some nineties churchgoing for cover. Poor Pennylane.

"That's why M.C.'s so respectable," Pennylane was saying, "to throw off suspicion. Especially since Bobby McGee, Marly's oldest, started making the meth and freed up M.C. to go make nice in town so there'd be no suspicion about us. Him living up in the woods with two chicks and a passel of kids was sure to bring attention our way. He told them Marly was his sister and he was rescuing her from her husband's beatings. I actually shipped my girls out so they could learn there were other ways to live. But Bobby McGee dropped out of school and learned chemistry. He even makes acid for the older crowd. He gets mucho cash for it. Here, I'll give you a couple of hits."

Pennylane rose stiffly, slowly. There were red marks on her throat. Chick couldn't hide her concern. "What happened to you?" she asked, putting the tips of her fingers to her own throat.

Pennylane said, "M.C. and me had it out again last night. He won't stop picking on baby Luke. He's four now. M.C. treats him like he's some kind of child devil. Somewhere he knows what I never told him about that baby's daddy." Pennylane's eyes drifted off. "You probably heard his daddy play at the old-time music festival over in Birdseye. He's there most years. That man picks a banjo like a cross between Jimi Hendrix and Segovia." She touched her neck, smiled her gap-toothed smile at Chick, and added in a boastful tone, "M.C. did this to me, but I blacked his eye."

Chick watched her pluck a huge multivitamin bottle from the table. "Hold out your hand."

"Thanks, but I swore off," Chick said, fascinated and horrified.

The bottle was full. Did the children help themselves too? M.C. was a total monster. He hit Pennylane and cheated on her and mistreated her kid; he left hallucinogens out where his own children could get them. If Pennylane had known enough to get her older children out, why didn't she leave? Immediately, she thought the poor woman probably had nowhere to go. She was strung out on drugs and had probably never held a straight job in her life.

"I'm hip, but stay for dinner. They ought to be back soon." Again Pennylane's gaze wandered off over some horizon Chick couldn't see. "I used to love to cook tripping." She looked as if she were contemplating slipping one of the tabs she'd offered under her tongue. "We grow our own food. I learned how to can. It's a groove, this country life. And as close to peace as anything I'll know on earth." She put down the jar of acid. "I gave up everything but weed."

Chick felt guilty at her relief that she couldn't confront M.C. here, in his make-believe world, with his agoraphobic wife, where he was cool, not criminal; Robin Hood, not a batterer; a father who couldn't turn away his old love, and suspected he'd been wronged by the birth of his wife's youngest son. This was The Jefferson Airplane's White Rabbit universe come bizarrely alive.

She'd slipped off her sandals, and now pulled them on with her toes under the table. She had to get out of there fast and tried to think of an excuse.

"I don't know, Chicago Chick. Sometimes I think I've come to the end of a long strange trip and it's time to move on. Sometimes I think I'll stay here till they carry me out. The trouble is, I don't know where I'd go or what I'd do once I got there."

"Your birth family, honey? Friends back in the Bay Area?"

Pennylane, obviously talking to herself, didn't answer. Chick wondered if she'd been looking in the wrong place for the good in this whole M.C. deal. She ran a finger across the rough gray wood of the table. Who said the good had to come to her because M.C. made her suffer? Pennylane was getting the worst of it. Over the years Chick had watched dozens of married women enter a kind of Underground Railroad unwittingly run by lesbians they hardly knew but fled to on their way to new lives, straight or gay. She'd come to Mister Cuckoo's land to help herself, but maybe she was really there to someday, somehow, help Pennylane. What an amazing trip, but not one she wanted to be on.

"Honey, I'm sorry, but I have to split," she said.

"So soon?" Pennylane's face lost its mellow, pleasant expression and turned worried. Chick felt pulled by guilt and by the need to escape. Did Pennylane think she'd brought a sack full of answers, and now was leaving with them?

"Will you come back?"

Instead of telling her that she wouldn't, couldn't be in M.C.'s space again, she found a piece of paper on the picnic table and wrote down the number at the store. "You call," she told her and held out her arms. Pennylane clung rather than hugged her. Her own embrace was tentative, like she didn't want to catch what this woman had. At the last, though, she gave Pennylane a good squeeze. "Know I'm there."

Pennylane pulled away, her tone alarmed. Had she heard M.C.'s car, or was she one of those people who couldn't handle an offer of help? It was probably neither. She'd more likely sensed Chick's ambivalence. "I've got to start dinner. Thanks for stopping by. Peace."

"Peace," Chick responded. The word tasted of her past. It evoked the sourness of green dope, the scent of sandalwood incense. There was a pressure in her head. Could she get a contact high from memories?

She hurried to the car, now anxious to escape before M.C. and his brood returned. Patsy flew from rut to rut, the string of multicolored worry beads on her mirror wildly dancing. She was on the blacktop and streaking toward town before she realized Pennylane hadn't asked her a thing about herself or what she was doing on their land. Chick might have been dropping in at her pad in the Bay Area to buy a chunk of hash, catching up since their last visit. Instead of helping her resolve anything, M.C.'s strange time warp threatened to mess up her mind even further.

It would do no good to confront M.C. or to expose him to his family. He was both their good king and their bad king and most significantly theirs, not vulnerable to an outsider's judgment. For them it would be like trying to sue a physician who was still treating you. M.C. had the power, right down to meeting their chemical needs.

She'd find another way to jumpstart a cure, one that didn't involve interacting with people crazier than herself.

CHAPTER EIGHTEEN

Curious Katie—May 2001

"Man, that Chick's a lot of woman," M.C. loudly confided to Katie, eyes following as Chick left with an emptied coffeepot.

He had arrived two hours earlier, reeking of weed, and removed his denim jacket to reveal a black T-shirt adorned with a Day-Glo image of Jim Morrison. Oh, retch, Katie thought. M.C., legs stretched across the booth, was almost supine now. He'd been calling to Chick regularly for coffee refills, especially, as his high wore off, when she had a clump of customers or was in the middle of some messy chore.

Pissed, Katie thought about punching the stop button on the Sony when what she really wanted was to punch out his lights. This was good stuff though. She had a feeling she might have more here than she'd anticipated. She was imagining the music she'd use on M.C.'s segments, maybe some old Led Zep. No, early Pink Floyd might display the interior of his mind better.

She'd done hundreds of interviews before coming to Waterfall Falls, but they'd all been to a formula, done more to make a neat package for couch potatoes than to extract anything deep. Now, though, she felt like she was hitting her stride. Even Spruce had talked her head off while hammering tar paper and shingles to the roof of the lodge. Katie had filmed her from the top of a ten-foot ladder that leaned against the flimsy aluminum rain gutter. This dude talked too, but it was all bad news, some of the most paranoid, judgmental, twisted thinking she'd encountered in her career.

"What's your prob, M.C.?" She took off her sunglasses and used them like a sword, feinting toward the man. "You came on like the gentle new-age man when we first talked. Am I getting Mr. Cro-Magnon on tape here or what?"

M.C. yawned widely and balanced a dental plate on his tongue, revealing threads of saliva. He snapped the plate back into place and asked, "Gross you out? I do that to my littlest girl sometimes. Scares the crap out of her."

Katie panned the store to chill, but couldn't obscure the memory of those dark nights. What was it about Waterfall Falls that took her so far back?

Her mom had dated a man for a while when Katie was seven. When Mom decided he was bad news, he hadn't agreed to meekly disappear. Had it been days or weeks that Mom woke her every night? They sat in the frigging dark and listened to him rattle the knob of the trailer's flimsy front door, bellowing threats and endearments and pleas until the neighbors called the police. She'd counted each blow of his fist on the door. She'd counted to thirty-seven one night. Eventually, Mom had gotten a restraining order, but she remembered standing night after night in her flimsy shortie pjs, hiding out of sight in the narrow hallway to her mom's bedroom, and trying to stop her mother, who sat on the floor, from shaking so badly. Mom's head was the height of Katie's chest, and she held it tight, her only comfort that she could comfort her mother. It was too frightening to see her mom shaking and helpless; she needed to make her strong enough to be Mom again, but it hadn't worked. From that day on, and maybe long before that (how could a little kid know) her mom had leaned on her.

Well, it had grown her up fast, and added some emotional muscle and sinew to her she might not otherwise have had.

She set the Sony down on the table and looked M.C. in the eye. "You've been so rude to Chick all morning. What's your problem?" She hated herself for it, but knew even as she tried to protect Chick, she was digging for more of a story. Expose the conflict, she'd been taught in a journalism course. What makes the subject tick, what makes him vulnerable, what's going to get the reader hooked? It was all about selling stories. Strip the subject naked and film him freezing to death, counseled one instructor. That's the real story.

Or was Chick the real story here? She'd never seen her so jangled and huffy. Chick was infamous for taking care of absolutely everyone around her, from old men smelling of cow manure to clueless baby dykes to gaggles of mothers with strollers and pooked-out bellies. She'd never seen Chick rattled before. It was a little scary around the edges to see her lose it.

M.C. was answering her, but he sounded like he was speaking from inside a fish tank, his mouth pouted like a fish's, the words rolling out slowly. Definitely Pink Floyd. She didn't want to feel afraid. She'd rather not feel at all than feel scared like this. When the crash came, she picked up her Sony without thinking and turned with it at her eye. A sense of invulnerability and invincibility, of being at one with this recording device came over her. It was the one time in her life, other than making love, that she had a sense of serenity. I'm in slo mo! She loved when she was nada but an extension of the camera. She counted to sixty, then to sixty again as she filmed.

Chick had dropped a glass coffeepot, smashing it. She grasped the plastic handle, a sharp edge of glass attached to it. "Get out!" she shouted. The customers at the counter stepped back from her. "Get out!" she yelled again, eyes fastened on M.C.

Katie wanted to go to Chick, to ask what was wrong, to sit her down and hold her until she calmed down. As she came toward them, Katie was aware of the great fear rising again within herself. She slowly followed Chick's progress with the Sony, panning the overhanging quilts for contrast, while she held her breath and struggled to kill the fear. Fifty-three, she heard herself counting, fifty-four, fifty-five seconds of tape. Chick was rushing M.C., but it was taking her forever to reach him. Chick's long jumper hugged the front of her legs as if pressed there by howling winds. Her cushiony face, a smile its normal resting position, looked stripped almost to the bone, and not red with anger, but pale with rage.

Again the Sony shifted as if on its own, back to the cluster of customers, shock and concern on their faces, holding very still as if they also feared to breathe. Where was Donny?

Fina, who had the clothing shop up the hill, shouted, "Madre de Dios, Chick, no!" Katie followed her with a steady lens as Fina rushed Chick and held her arm.

"Get out of here, M.C.," growled Chick. "I'm not taking your crap one more minute."

"Aw, Chick. I was goofing on you. You used to laugh at shit like that. Remember how it used to be—tripping all night down at the Marina, the old mob at Airplane and Crosby, Stills, Nash, and Young concerts. We were so happening. I dealt you breaks, gave you Sunshine. Remember that trip down at the beach? I told you what I wanted, had you pressed up close. Your knee about killed me. How could you do that to me in front of them all?" His voice was now angry instead of cajoling. "You walked out into the water like I was such a gross-out, you were never coming back. And you laughed at me with every step you took into that water; all the way out you were laughing at me. It took three of the other chicks to turn you around. Things were never the same after that. You took away my fucking manhood in their eyes, bitch, kicking me like you did. The other freaks were never tight with me again. They bought my dope, but they acted like I wasn't cool enough to be around. Me and my old lady blew town after that. Traveled a couple of years, bought my spread here. Nobody ever even looked us up."

Katie's arms were tired, and she rested the Sony on a shelf, still filming. Her whole being trembled with excitement, like a gong vibrating under its hammer. She'd never felt like this on a story before. So this sleaze came from Chick's past. Did she have a right to record this? She'd film now, think out the ethics later. This was too perfect—the micro town, the old hippies, the vigilantes, the merchants and the retirees in the background, and all the facets of the dyke-straight clash being enacted in front of her Sony. Her fear had been replaced by the concentration she needed to get this story. The Melissa Etheridge song "My Beloved," Katie's personal anthem, was loud in her head. Etheridge had a way of singing about love and politics that had turned Katie on to the connection between the two. Through Etheridge's music she'd come to see ways to make statements with her own work.

"You're one sick flashback," Chick was saying, but real low. Stealthily, Katie checked the sound level. "I know about your 'wives.' I know about your dope factory up in the hills and your Mr. Vigilante act in town. I don't know why you're still obsessed by me, but," Chick waved the sharp glass at him, "you're going to get over it starting now. Get out. Don't come back."

Katie watched through her camera, every bit of her focused on the scene. Fina grabbed Chick's arm, her other hand prying the coffeepot away. "Come over here, Chick. I'll find Donny."

"No!" Chick cried.

"Okay," Fina said, voice still calm, "Then I'll call Sheriff Sweet for you."

M.C. had scuttled backwards on his chair toward the window with an abruptness that acknowledged Chick's fury. Now he feigned calm, stretching as he slowly got his feet on the ground. "Chick is a good person," he told Fina, as if to apologize for her. He smirked. "We rub each other the wrong way. I get the funny feeling it's time for me to split."

"Let him pass, Chick," Fina instructed, pulling at Chick's arm. She took the broken pot and held it behind her. Hector White grabbed it. "Get him out of here," Fina told Hector.

"No sheriff, no Donny," Chick hissed.

M.C. whirled to the camera and growled. "I could give a crap about owls or loggers, but I have a message for Uncle Sam. Stay off my land. Life, liberty, and the pursuit of my happiness—women, highs, and carrying a gun—I want that guaranteed."

Earlier the man had put on a bashful country-boy smile. He'd been playing to the camera the whole time, and Katie had hated giving him a stage.

Chick lunged, dragging Fina with her.

Katie heard a screech. She shoved boxes of granola bars off a shelf as she secured her Sony, then ran to encircle Chick's waist from behind. M.C. slipped past them, white cowboy hat in hand, and sauntered out the door. She felt like hurting the arrogant shit herself.

Chick was crying now, bent over, her back rising and falling with sobs. Fina put her arms around her. Katie brought a chair. She couldn't stand to see Chick like this, felt completely hopeless that anything would ever be right again. The man must have been tormenting her a long time for this to build up. Had Chick told anyone? Why hadn't Donny intervened?

Katie was shaking, damp with a chilly sweat. The room lurched like a ship over a storm wave, like a small trailer house being stormed, a man launching himself at it with his shoulder over and over until she thought it would tip. She felt her stomach roll and heave. She ran to the bathroom and vomited into the toilet until she was weak and her throat felt ragged. She flushed again and again as if the memories were swirling down with the water. God, she'd wanted to forget her mom's ex-boyfriend, that enraged stupid bull charging them.

Someone had swept up the broken glass when Katie, sweaty, legs unsteady, returned. Chick was replacing the granola bars on the shelf. Everyone else was gone. She looked around for the Sony.

"Your camera is behind the counter," Chick told her. Chick picked up a green goddess figurine and studied it. "I'm sorry I'm not more serene. More like R."

Katie had been going for her Sony, but turned back, a flash of anger shooting through her. "Don't wish that on yourself, Chick. You have a fire in you she never had." Chick looked at her and she realized how she sounded. "I can't believe I said that." She shook her head. "I love R. She's so intense."

But it was true. Upset as she'd gotten over Chick's rage, Chick came by it honestly. R's passion felt cold, drawn from some intellectual or political premise.

"Intensity and passion don't equal love, do they?" Chick said, watching her as if for signs that Katie finally got it, whatever it was.

If she and R made love tonight—and that had seldom happened after the first few weeks—she would watch for real passion. But she already knew it wasn't there. R sought an orgasm like she ate an apple; both were pleasant experiences and nourished her. Casting R back into the darkness and steadying herself against a shelving unit, she asked Chick, "What was that all about? I never heard you bitch out a living soul before."

Chick reached to enfold Katie in a hug. She could feel Chick trembling too. In a voice hoarse with crying Chick said, "Being nice to some people is like offering a treat to a dog. It doesn't make them go away. It only teaches them to come back for more. Once upon a time I tolerated that man, because he was central to a group of women I dug and because he sold us drugs. My mistake. You're smart to keep that camera between you and the world, Katie Delgado."

It segues me out into the world, she thought. Then she switched into automatic interview mode. "Is he an old squeeze? This isn't the first time he's bugged you, is it? What's the story?"

Chick pulled away. "On the other hand, curious Katie, because of your camera, baring my soul doesn't feel cool. For your information, though, I've been a woman's woman since day one."

"Truth? You're not safe period around that guy, Chick. I've interviewed convicts less spooky than him."

"I've never lost it like this before. I wanted to maim that troubled man."

"Troubled! He's a live bomb." Katie shuddered, though she felt steadier now.

"But if you tell Donny," warned Chick, "I'll have to break a coffeepot on you."

"Never! I'm not looking to expose my friends."

Or was she? Damn, why had she been so quick to pledge silence? She was the mirror to this little world, and Chick was reflected like everyone else. She was a mirror wherever she went. A reporter's job was to watch and never take on what she reflected, but look how she'd reacted today. On the job she'd always arrived on scene after the violence, as part of the cleanup, to try to give a sense of, even make sense of what had happened. Today she'd seen her first real violence and she'd been catapulted back inside the fragile skin of metal that had sheltered her and her mom.

Watching Chick defend herself against M.C., where had the objective journalist gone? She'd held the Sony, but essentially wasted the film. This really wasn't something she could show the world, she thought with regret, except for M.C.'s mocking words. But she knew she'd play the Chick scene in her mind many times over. Had it mirrored her and her mom? No. Chick had gone on the attack, had altered Katie's reality. It was in Katie's memory bank differently now, right next to Mom and herself cowering.

"Katie?" Chick asked, taking both her hands. Chick's hands were warm, her own embarrassingly clammy. "Give me your word this will stay between us. Donny would lose it over something like this."

"I'd never use it," she said, wrestling with the need to use such great footage for the story she wanted to tell.

"Not just the film, Katie. I'm serious about not wanting Donny to know. She's up at Dawn Farm again today working."

Chick sounded unsure of her. Well, du-uh, she thought. Chick had good reason. So Donny was up at Dawn Farm. Did she need to know Chick was in danger—from M.C. and from her own fury? She followed Chick to the counter. Did she need to tell Donny? No. It wasn't her job to protect Chick, just like it hadn't been her job to protect her mom. Why in hell had her mother wanted a seven-year-old to protect her? Hadn't that been asking a bit much? If Chick needed someone to take care of her, she could decide that for herself.

"Your secret's safe with moi," she said. "There are things I want to use on this tape or I'd give it to you to destroy."

Chick had taken the camera out from under the counter, but only now did she pass it over. As Katie accepted it, she knew she would keep Chick's trust. She didn't quite understand what had happened inside herself today, but earth-mother Chick—she wanted to call her Mama Chick—was totally central to it.

"I want to crack open the secrets of this little town in the worst way. Scratch the women's land story. I can do a docu-drama about the heart and soul of a small town." She felt so alive talking about this, but switched into her Chatty Cathy newscaster voice. "Waterfall Falls, afraid of corruption by the new casino, seethes with its own self-destruction. The druggies, the retirees, the farmers and loggers and jobless mill workers, the gays, the Native Americans, the Mexicans, the welfare-to-work families, redneck hippies, professionals, tourist-gamblers. America's melting pot is at meltdown in Waterfall Falls."

Chick gave her another quicker hug. "Save the world with your journalism, sweetie, but make sure you edit me out."

Chapter Nineteen

Burning Ambition

The day was brimming with sunshine and the promise that seemed to inhabit Fridays. Jeep's breath came in steady frosty puffs as she skated past the idle mill to work. She'd shoved her fiddle inside the old canvas rucksack she used to transport it, then secured it tightly to her back with bungee cords. Band rehearsal was tonight.

"Excellent day!" she burst out as she entered the noisy classroom. The volume seemed to go up a notch every day that they got closer to the end of the school year.

Arlene Hardy, the other teachers' aide, came in behind her, but the teacher, Dottie Yankel, was, as usual, already there. She was applying the brakes to a little girl's wheelchair. Jeep got busy taking off baseball caps, helping the blind boy find his coat hook, soothing one of the autistic boys. Poor little guy, he was revved up and rocking already. She wasn't at all sure he would make it to a regular classroom.

Her favorite pupil arrived late. Luke's big sister led him by the hand to Arlene, then veered off to a regular classroom at top speed. On the way she cried, "This is my Auntie Marly's magic coat!" She was holding the long, oversized multi-colored cardigan up and out on her arms as if it could give her flight.

"Does your aunt know you have it?" Arlene called after the girl, but got no reply. Arlene muttered to Jeep, "Probably not."

Jeep waved to blond, round-faced Luke, and he grinned, clapping his little hands without sound to some intricate rhythm he seemed to hear ceaselessly. Sometimes she wondered if he didn't talk because the sounds in his head were too loud.

On her break midway through the afternoon she hung with Dottie.

"I could never get into this part of your job. You're always catching up on paperwork."

"You've got to clean up the poop."

She laughed and stretched. "This afternoon is being really intense on cleaning up messes. Hey, how come when someone messes up, you clean up? Shouldn't you clean down, or maybe they should mess down? Anyway, I'll bet this is the most fragrant zone in Waterfall School."

Dottie smiled and nodded, obviously giving her only half an ear as she worked.

"That's okay," Jeep said, talking as much to herself as to Dottie. "I'm never depressed at work. Here I can forget I'm not on the fast track to concert violinist or even first violin in the Lucky City Symphony. Which was not exactly my life goal anyway."

"You've got time to come up with a burning ambition," said Dottie, who wasn't much older than Jeep, but was the most together person, next to Cat, Jeep had ever met. Well, except she was kind of a dumpling and needed to lose the Coke-bottle glasses.

"Tell that to Mom and Dad." She took her harmonica from her pocket and turned it in her fingers as she spoke. She loved the feel of the thing, the cool metal and the wooden holes against her thumb. "Every week I call from the pay phone at the trailer park so they know I didn't do a bunk with some UFO cult. Does it help? No, they say I'm throwing my expensive education and scholarships out the window. My buzz cut embarrasses them. The only thing they like about this job is that I ditched the nose stud and three earrings because the kids got so bumptious with them. Worse, about once a month they ask if, you know, I've *changed*. Meaning switched to boys. No freakin' way."

Dottie wrote and smiled, shaking her head full of drab, heavy hair as if in sympathy. When she looked up, it was with an appraising eye Jeep hadn't seen since her interview. "Jeep, have you ever considered the field of music therapy?"

"Me? No, I've always been into performing. There was a girl in the dorm who had a double major in music and psych, but I thought she was kind of, like, making up the music therapy thing."

"It's pretty new as a recognized therapy, but it's being taught at a number of schools now, including one a couple of hours north of here. It could be a good skill to have when performing is slow."

"But what is it? I mean music is therapy. That's a given. But do you play? Teach? Do—what does Chick call them—hootenannies?"

Dottie, still filling in forms, smiled at her papers. "I don't know much about it. It's probably all those and more. I've wondered if some of the less verbal pupils could learn to express themselves through instruments or by singing."

"You mean like Luke?"

"Like Luke and all the little Lukes who come through these classes. You know, he's not going to make it into kindergarten if he doesn't start talking here. I couldn't recommend him for that."

"So what then? He repeats preschool? We get him for another term? Breaks my heart."

Dottie put down her pen and gazed out the window. Jeep could see that a deer was helping itself to a meal of new leaves from the lower branches of a young sapling. It's typical of life, isn't it? The more successful we are at our jobs the sooner we lose the pupil." She looked Jeep in the eyes for the first time. "You can't get too attached to them, Jeep. It'll only break your heart when they graduate or—worse—don't make it."

"What happens if they don't?"

"It depends on the reason." Again Dottie's eyes strayed to the window, and Jeep smiled to see two fawns barely old enough to have lost their spots stroll up to their mother. One nuzzled her belly, the other nibbled on a bush. "Some do repeat the class. Some wait out kindergarten or find a church preschool because we don't have funding to support a special-ed kindergarten. They start in special-ed first grade. That's the biggest measure of our success—how many succeed. A few are institutionalized or placed in foster homes because their families either can't or won't care for them adequately. And then, of course, these children are at risk. Some get sick, some die."

"Which children?" She hadn't thought much about her job beyond coping with each day in the classroom and finally getting some money in her wallet. Her sister Jill had mainstreamed, no problem, and she'd assumed most of these guys would eventually. But the thought that Luke—"Who could die?"

"Yancy Dillard. Jennifer Schwane. Little Jaquelle Ruiz. Their problems are not merely developmental."

"Holy shit. And who might get institutionalized? Not Luke? He's not going to die, is he?" Her hands suddenly hot, she blew on them, though this never worked to bring their temperature down.

"I understand his home situation is not the best, Jeep. There's a suspicion of little kids running wild and possibly having access to drugs despite the father's very public law-and-order stance. Luke's older siblings—he's from a huge blended family—have been in trouble. Two were sent to live with their grandparents. They're smart kids. The state intervened, convinced the mom to get them out. Something's wrong there. I think the mom is an old hippie or something. Very vague, hard to get information from."

"But his sister's okay."

"She was in here for two terms and is barely hanging on in first grade. ADD, hyperactive, and deeply marked by a childish father who seems to tease and taunt her unmercifully. Unless she's making these stories up."

"Aw, Dottie, don't tell me these things. Luke's love on two feet."

"I know, I know. And when I see you interact with him, with all of them, you're real good, Gina—Jeep, sorry. You're Gina Pauline on the paperwork."

"But Dottie, that's, like, too weird. I never thought about going into this work forever."

"Didn't you tell me in your interview that you had an autistic big sister?"

"Jill. But shouldn't that make me want to run in the other direction?"

Dottie peered at her. "Did you love your sister?"

Jeep nodded. She tried not to think about Jill and, after all these years, pretty much succeeded. "Then I hope you'll give the field serious thought. A talented adult can save a life. If not Luke's, then someone else's. I have no idea what the job prospects are for music therapists, but if I had the funding I'd get one in here without hesitation."

"I don't know." Jeep's mind was in overdrive. Rug rats? More student loans? Years of heartbreaks? Jill had been heartache enough for a lifetime. "How about you?" she asked, more to distract herself than to challenge Dottie. "Have you ever thought of making a radical change? Like getting a buzz cut?" She ran her fingers though her own hair. Did the woman know she was queer as a Susan B. Anthony dollar?

"Um-hum."

"Why don't you?"

Dottie looked out at the kids, rubbing her chin with a pen. "I'm not brave enough."

"That's honest."

"I'm supporting my mother and my little brother. He's graduating with honors from Greenhill Community College this weekend. Can't afford to lose this job over a haircut." Dottie looked back down to her paperwork and sighed aloud, as if she could hear Jeep thinking that

Dottie was scared of a lot more than a haircut. "Do you have your fiddle today? The kids might like to hear you play."

"I could get into that, no problemo!"

"I know. It's what makes you a kid magnet. Go get 'em, Pied Piper."

The children watched as she plucked the strings to tune up. She started with a simple bluegrass piece, roaming the classroom. "Go Sara!" she encouraged as the little girl danced in her wheelchair.

Another child sang nonsense words. Grinning, Luke beat the table in perfect syncopation. A kid magnet. I like that, Jeep thought, and then felt a pang so sharp she stopped, swallowed, and took a few deep breaths, before she could put bow to string again. She missed the kids, the three sibs who had come after her and Jill. Her parents had never trusted her with them and had let her stay alone in the room she had shared with Jill while the little ones slept in the other upstairs bedroom together.

She shook her head slightly to bring her eyes back into focus and wondered how Luke would accompany something more complex. She switched to a lively Vivaldi concerto. Luke's mouth became an "o" of astonishment. He watched her every move. The other children grew restless, but Luke lifted his arms and mimicked her, obviously mesmerized. He kept time with both feet. His smile returned, beatific. Jeep got totally choked up, watching Luke's transformation. She was going to miss him all summer, but Dottie had recommended that he come back for a second year since he'd started in January rather than last September. Luke's reprieve.

For the rest of the afternoon Luke held an invisible violin under his chin, playing it with an orange crayon. Jeep was all quivery, like when she fell in love hard.

After school she asked Cat, "What do you think it means?" She tossed her board into the bed of Cat's pickup.

"The kid's a child prodigy? He's a cute little dude." Cat twisted to back out of her parking space. "Want to eat at the A&W?"

"Okay, but I mean it was kind of like a throw-away-your-crutches experience, Cat."

Cat backed out of her parking space in the school lot and gave her a warning look.

"What?" Jeep asked, although the look felt protective.

"Maybe all the stimulation he gets at home is from church and the TV, and here you come playing church music he doesn't have to sit still for."

The burger place was down the street. It always came as a shock to her that this A&W still had carhop service. She leaned over Cat to the teenaged girl in a brown and orange uniform. "Stacy" was stenciled on her pocket. "Can I get a double Velveeta burger and a float with coffee ice cream?"

"You sure can," Stacy answered.

She felt like an old letch, but the girl was cheerleader-pretty, with an adventurous look about her.

The promising smell of burgers grilling and potatoes frying had them both superhungry. Cat was halfway through her first Coney Dog when Jeep brought the subject up again. "Music is awesome, Cat. You know what I'm saying. Listening to it, playing it, feeling the vibrations through my fingers. Until today, though, I never really thought about using its super powers. Healing powers. Luke might never talk, but music does."

"Now you sound like your friend Rattlesnake." Cat's smile was teasing.

"R? My friend? No way!" she protested. "Dottie said to check out music therapy. I'm thinking if I had the moves, what couldn't I do for some kid?"

"Jeep, I know Dottie lives and breathes her work, but I get indigestion mixing school and chocolate milk shakes, especially on a Friday afternoon. Can't we be passionate about something else right now?"

"Whatever. I'm thinking out loud." She slouched into her seat and sucked on her straw, bummed. She had to remember that Cat wasn't Sarah and didn't want to hear every thought in her head. Donny would give her a ride to the county library tomorrow. She'd research music therapy on one of their computers.

Cat crinkled up her hamburger wrapper and said, "I promised one of my old high school friends that I'd stop at her garage sale. Her daughter's one of my all-time favorite kids. We can still make it if you're willing."

"Sure," she said.

Maybe Cat had been right to stomp on her newfound dream. Poor Cat was the one who had to listen to all her enthusiasms. Last week she'd been stoked about med school to cure the kids. The week before, she'd been researching orchestras in Seattle. The truth was that she wanted to do all of it. Was Katie right? Had they been drawn to

Waterfall Falls to, like, find their capital-P paths? Life seemed like such a little scrap of time that she wanted to do it right. Why wasn't there someone she could ask what choices to make?

They climbed the hill on the west side of town—Cat's side— turning onto streets she hadn't known were there until they reached a dead end cut from the side of a cliff. She got out of the truck and saw the whole town below her and the maze of streets they'd driven. Cliff Street began as a stately cypress-lined boulevard down where Cat lived. Her place was one of a row of large homes built early in the century by prosperous merchants, bankers, and city fathers. At the next level, where power shovels had begun to dig for new residential land, like some twentieth-century version of the gold rush, a dozen houses crowded together on each street. Here at the crest claimed by the new town gentry there were only four homes, well-insulated by green plots of land that backed onto thickets of a tiny thinned forest of evergreens and manzanita bushes. A water tower was surrounded by barbed wire.

"Zowie," she said as Cat came up behind her. "The town pretty much starts at Natural Woman Foods and crashes to a stop at the casino."

"Waterfall Falls, my personal minitown," said Cat with what sounded like great satisfaction.

"Have you ever considered living somewhere else?"

"Not seriously. I spent four years at Western Washington U in Bellingham, and it never felt like home. I love being able to see the whole town at once by driving up a hill."

"Yeah," Jeep said, shivering a little in a mountain breeze, "it feels good, like it's a place I can wrap my mind around. But it's still the whole world, isn't it?"

"Minus war and natural disasters except for forest fires. Those are nasty."

"Auntie Cat!" cried a plump-cheeked little girl with long dark hair.

"Hi, Gretchen. Hi, Gretchen's mom. This is Auntie Jeep. She teaches at Waterfall School too."

"I get to go there next year," Gretchen told them. And not, Jeep thought, looking from the child to the large new house she was growing up in, not in a special-ed class. Was she way off, or were most of the kids in her class unlikely to live in a place like this?

"We were about to pull everything inside for the night," Gretchen's mom told them. "Haven't had even a looky-loo for over an hour. Do you need anything special or are you visiting?"

Jeep noticed a bass fiddle in the back of the garage. She said she'd take a look around and managed to make herself linger over Christmas decorations, small appliances, and neatly folded sheets that smelled strongly of fabric softener. Cat was looking through the children's books, chatting with Gretchen about which ones to buy when Jeep, making her tone as casual as she could, pointed at the bass and asked, "Do you store this thing out here?"

"I'm afraid so." The woman held out a hand and said, "I'm Myra."

"Jeep."

"Jeep as in the car?"

"Yes, but short for G.P., my initials."

"Oh!" Myra lowered her voice and her eyes sought the child. "Not Gretchen Patricia? That's my little girl's name."

"No," Jeep assured her, thinking, 'Don't worry. Your girl won't grow up to be a dyke with a crew cut. If you're lucky.' Oh yeah, she thought, this upscale little enclave looked down on more than the town.

"My husband's father played in a big band in the forties and fifties. We hauled the bass down from the old place in Greenhill when they moved to Arizona. A lot of this garage sale is my attempt to get rid of their old household items."

With all the critical concern she could muster, hands glowing like coals of embarrassment, Jeep asked all in one breath, "How long has it been here? I hate to think what the damp winters and dry summers do to the wood—not to mention the strings." She sniffed for mustiness. She had a feeling the minute she touched the bridge it would collapse. "May I?" she asked and stepped to the instrument. She plucked a string and it snapped, almost lashing her face. "I'm sorry!" she said.

The bridge listed, but didn't fall. She could fix that with the right tools. She had some of the glue her dad used in his repairs. All those hours spent watching him bring old instruments back to useful lives might pay off yet. He repaired all of the school district's instruments and kept pretty busy with all the musical entertainment in town. His father had done the same thing before him. Her little brother was being prepped to join in the business. She'd kind of thought the sign would one day say Chs. Morgan and Daughter, but then the Jill thing happened. Oh, well.

Cat's friend was exclaiming, "It's not your fault. It needs a good home with someone who'll take proper care of it."

"It does," Jeep said, moving away from it. "We could use it in the band, but I can't keep it in a tiny trailer." She laughed. "Or lug it across town on my skateboard." She was watching herself set up this negotiator stance and was surprised that it came so naturally, although she shouldn't be, given all she'd learned at Sami's shop.

Sami had started leaving her alone in charge of the shop from day three. That was how long restless Sami could stay indoors. She had to see her business connections, she had to score, she had to buy something for the shop; any excuse, and she was gone. Sometimes Jeep wondered if Sami chose all her lovers by how good they'd be in the shop. Gawd. She got disgusted with herself at the thought she'd stayed with Sami a year and a half. The woman was a cokehead and ran a sleazy business, not to mention that she was probably seeing other women half the time when she was out of the shop. Sami sucked in anything that came her way and moved through the world saying mine, mine, mine.

Then, before she beat herself up totally, Jeep remembered the shop. That's what she'd fallen in love with; Sami was a nuisance factor. While there, she'd learned by trial and error what to offer someone selling their sax or bootlegged early Miles Davis collection and what to come down to when a customer made an offer. She'd learned fast how to read faces and how to say no, and more about what was a real problem with a used instrument and what was a minor ding. She'd even learned bookkeeping. Most importantly, she learned what she'd be able to fix herself and what Sami would have to pay an expert to repair.

Slowly, as if an idea was forming in her mind as she spoke, Cat offered, "You could store it at my place. I never use the old dining room except for our rehearsals. I might even learn to play something like that if it's living there. Right now," she told Myra, "I play the harmonica and sticks."

"Well," Jeep said, and silently reviewed her finances, "I have about $25 to my name after the rent, laundry, food, and change to call Mom and Dad, but I could pay $10 a month."

"In the shape that's in I don't think it would take you more than three months to pay it off," Myra told her. "My father-in-law would be pleased that you rescued it."

A bass fiddle for $30? Ka-ching!

"Will you teach me to play?" Cat asked.

"Seriously?"

"Seriously. I'll go halves on the bass and store it if you'll teach me. You could come by and play it anytime you wanted."

"Deal!" They paid Myra, who threw in a mildewed bedspread and army blanket to wrap the instrument for the ride downhill. Jeep secured it with her bungee cords and brought the skateboard up front.

"I've never seen you this excited," Cat said as she maneuvered carefully out of the driveway.

"Boy, oh boy. What a deal. A new instrument for peanuts, to fix and to play and to teach and to have in the band. That's like about four Christmases in one."

"And it got your mind off school. And off your little pal."

"Now that you mention Luke—"

"Did I speak too soon?"

"No! I mean yes, you did. It was your bass lessons that got me thinking about how if I could pick up a drum pad, cheap, I could teach Luke to play. Just some practice exercises. He's got a way excellent sense of rhythm."

"Ask the music teacher. The school may have one."

"Du-uh. I never thought of that. And maybe a place to practice? If they don't go for it, I can call it music therapy. Who do I talk to?"

Cat laughed. "Go to the music room at the very end of the blue corridor. Wynn Schneider is the music guru."

"Am I kind of like, nuts, trying to do stuff for this kid? What if the parents object? He'll drive them around the bend banging on anything that makes noise."

Cat pulled into her driveway. Two band members were already seated on her front porch. She looked at Jeep with steely eyes. "These parents may not even notice. It is never nuts to do stuff for a kid, amigo. Not ever."

"Got it. Music lessons. Full speed ahead, Sulu."

As they got out of the truck the mandolin player called, "Need to practice, Cat! Let us in!"

Cat slowly shook her head. "Lesbians. The neighbors are going to worry about property values. Do you need help with the bass?"

Jeep had already gotten out of the car and was attaching the violin to her back. "I'm all over it."

Cat walked backwards, shaking her head again as Jeep mounted the bass on her skateboard and started rolling it toward the steps.

CHAPTER TWENTY

Donny and the Raiders

"Hey, Don, you taking Abeo back to the Ridge?"
Donny whirled, dropping her flashlight with a clatter in the gutter. "Shit!"

"Hush up, Jeep!" said Abeo in a loud whisper.

"Don't wake Chick!" said Donny.

Jeep, skateboard under her arm, joined them at Donny's pickup. "What's happening?"

"What're you doing here? It's midnight," Donny asked, damning small towns. "You can't keep a secret from one side of the street to the other around here."

"I go for an interview at the music therapy school tomorrow. I'm too hyped to sleep so I came to hang out in your garden with the other gayfeathers."

"You have some very weird friends, Don," said Abeo.

"What can I say? I don't have a garden of my own. When I was a kid that's where I used to hang out to get away from everybody."

"Only one thing we can do," Donny said. "We better take you along. Abeo?"

"Better another guilty party than a witness."

"Wha—" Jeep yelped as they hustled her into Donny's little pickup, one on each side of her, skateboard between her legs.

"Here's what's going down, little buddy," Donny said as she turned toward Mule Butte Road. "I'm getting my girl back tonight."

"Dude? Clue me in? I thought I saw Chick at the store today?"

"I told you I was worried about her. She hasn't been my laughing lady for such a long time."

"You said she had a blue outlook. I thought that was temporary."

"For months, Jeep, months. I thought it was her time of life, you know?" Jeep nodded. "Your ex, Katie, found out this fucker she knew in her hippie days is messing with Chick."

Abeo explained, "Pulling shit like shadowing her, making rude remarks, starting scenes at the store."

"Why didn't she tell you? Or the sheriff?"

Donny shook her head.

"Because she knew Donny would try to kick the stuffing out of the guy," Abeo said. "And she was right. The sheriff wouldn't have kept it from you."

"I could kill his ass. He calls himself M.C. He thinks he can mess with my girl? I am tired of white boys acting like they own the world. I am tired of asking politely for them to stop. I am ready to take one of them out."

"Chill, Donalds. You're going to crash the truck before we take care of him if you don't calm down." Abeo turned up the volume on the Temptations tape Donny had been playing. Donny switched it off.

"Is that where we're going? To kick the stuffing out of him?" Jeep asked, sinking back into the seat. "I don't think I want to know about this."

"Don't worry," Donny said with a sour glance toward Abeo. Nobody was going to shut her up, especially not this little two-faced retired dealer. "We don't have to get violent. His setup, from what Katie found out, makes him easy to get at. We're going to permanently remove him from decent society, right, Abe?" They slapped hands across Jeep.

"Katie always was a primo investigator." Jeep sighed. "So he's, like, stalking her?"

Abeo said, "Exactly like."

"And we're going to blast him into space junk?"

"I like your style, Jeep," said Donny, with a laugh. She felt tight as a fishing line pulling in a catch, as much for sneaking out on Chick as for this operation itself. "I was all for dynamiting him, but girlfriend here persuaded me otherwise."

Abeo smoothed down an eyebrow. Donny thanked god that Spirit Ridge had a no-fragrance policy or Abeo would give them away with the first breeze, the way she usually piled on the perfume. "I am so brilliant," Abeo said. "M.C. is Lord of the Drugs in this valley and covers himself by being in that vigilante group. We're going to feed him live to his own vigilantes."

"And rescue Chick too? That's beaucoup de cool!" Jeep said with her little bray of a laugh.

Donny waited for Jeep to ask the question.

"Can we get in trouble for this?"

"Joan and me set it up. Nothing to worry about."

"Child," Abeo said, "it's bad enough we have to be all smashed together on this ratty old seat without you bouncing up and down on it."

Donny took the truck as far as she dared up M.C.'s dirt road. Every time she pressed on the accelerator she revved up her own fury. Rocket fuel, that's what had been flowing through her veins since she found out. It explained everything—why Chick had seemed to be hiding something, why she'd return from her talks with R looking like she'd been crying. Donny had tried to take R's head off every time the woman got near her, but it wasn't R; it was this asshole M.C. Why hadn't Chick said anything?

She still didn't know the whole story. Katie had been interviewing M.C. for that documentary she wanted to do, and M.C. had talked about this dyke chick he wanted to put in her place. She'd been the only woman he'd wanted back in the late sixties who wouldn't trade him sex for drugs. She'd be normal by now, he'd told Katie, if she'd given him a chance. Now he had kids growing up in this town, and he wanted them to know their dad took a stand against queers. The town council was one thing, but this chick was his personal mission. Katie had finally realized that he'd meant this Chick—with a capital "C."

Donny hadn't said a word to Chick. It would only be worse for her if she had to worry that Donny would get herself in trouble over it. She'd lain awake nights thinking about what she'd like to do to him. Tonight she'd ruin the man legally.

Two days ago she'd followed M.C. from town and driven brazenly up his road. She'd come this far and found the narrow clearing she backed into now. She'd crept into the woods enough to see that Katie was right; M.C. wasn't exactly growing cobra lilies back here. It had been easier in daylight, but a clump of fire pokers grew at the edge of the clearing to mark the spot. Tonight her anger had a nervous edginess to it.

She whispered, "Don't slam the doors." She didn't want the dogs she'd heard the other day to sound an alarm. Maybe she should have told Chick where she was going.

As they crunched and crackled their way into the brush, grabbed by blackberry brambles each tried to hold back for the next, Jeep whispered, "I've heard some of these growers booby-trap their land?"

"Then be careful and don't blow up your cute white butt," Abeo suggested.

"Cute?" Jeep echoed, craning her head back toward her bottom, acting like this was fun.

"Quiet." Donny stepped carefully, but without any light on this overcast night she cracked every twig in her path. She didn't know if she was shivering from the night chill or from nerves. Her biggest worry was that M.C. would catch them before they could do any good. She sensed the next clearing before she saw it. "Yo, ladies, look at that."

"Reefer in the raw," Abeo pronounced. "What's this wire?" Donny followed it with the beam of her flashlight along the trees they'd be passing through. "Shit. This could be very bad news."

"Maybe he knew we were coming," suggested Jeep. She sounded terrified now. "Maybe he's got a plant at the cop shop."

"I wouldn't be surprised," Donny joked. "It looks like he's got plants everywhere else."

Jeep poked her in the side. Donny smiled—she was really as excited as Jeep. This would fix things for Chick. If, she thought, this really was all that was bothering her.

"Shine that thing along here," Abeo ordered in a rough, grim whisper. Deftly, she made her way to a tree. A shotgun barrel poked out. Abeo disarmed it, then slipped it out of the crook of branches and held it up like a trophy. "You're right, Jeep—booby trap number one. I hope this is the only one."

Donny said, "That wasn't here when I was up here before. I'm starting to get the willies." She definitely should have told Chick where she was going.

Jeep was staring at Abeo. "How'd you learn stuff like disarming a trap? I didn't even hear you move."

"'Nam," Abeo replied as she swiftly, noiselessly emptied the gun. "Special Forces. Two tours. When I was a man-child, I had a lot to prove."

"Stop gawking, Jeep," Donny told her, although she didn't blame the kid.

Abe had come out in Nam, of all places. He'd returned to Chicago when he was only twenty-four and launched himself into the gay life like a man granted a reprieve. He'd told Donny that a Vietnamese lover had taught him he didn't belong over there and he'd soured on the military, blaming macho egos for the killing. He'd found and encouraged what he called his feminine side. Jeep saw only the contrasts, while Donny had watched the transition. And the drug addiction he came home with. And the dealing even after he—she'd kicked. Damn, Abe had been through rough times. Who was she to be judge and jury over his particular sins? Abe may have dealt, but she'd worked for him off and on even before the trip west, not to mention stealing from him. And now it was Abe's know-how and guts that made her feel like she could handle this. Sometimes she wondered what Abe could have been without the war, without drugs.

"Let's boogie," she told them.

"Haven't we seen enough to get him?" Jeep whispered, slipping back behind the two of them as they crept toward the outbuildings.

"The cops need probable cause to come on M.C.'s land. After I checked this place out the first time, Sheriff Sweet called our friendly State Trooper Bruce, told him what's going down. Joan's well-connected, for all her quiet ways. Knows how to bullshit with the guys. We arranged for Abeo and me to stumble on everything we could tonight while we got lost looking for a place to camp. Bruce will bring up the rear with his gang as soon as I give Joan the high sign." She pulled a cell phone from a pocket in her overalls and held it up. "I won't get much of a signal out here, but the call will work. I tested it."

"You hope," Abeo whispered as they crept ahead.

Donny thought she would pass out from fear when she heard a loud squawk in a bush to their right. Her breath came like she'd swum across Sweet Creek at flood stage. Why hadn't she told Chick? What would Chick think when they told her about finding Donny's body out here?

She managed to form her mouth around the word "Wha," when great flapping sounds came from the same bush. She knew she would laugh later at the image of the three of them frozen in midstep, but that was only if there was a later.

"Turkeys," Abeo said in a weak voice.

"Turkeys?" Donny repeated. She noticed that Jeep wasn't saying a word.

"Wild turkeys," Abeo explained, straightening as the flock fled behind some manzanita bushes deeper in the woods.

"They must have been out foraging when I came before." Donny giggled. "Oh, lord, don't get me laughing now!"

But it was too late. Jeep said, "We got spooked by a bunch of turkeys?" and then she was laughing too and holding both hands over her mouth. Abeo was both shushing them and trying to quiet her own escaping giggles.

"Look." Near the clearing Donny pointed out the barn-like structure, shed, and rusted campers she'd scoped out before. The sight of the place sobered them immediately.

"It wasn't good enough to call this in when you were here the other day?" Jeep asked.

"What was I doing here, spying for the sheriff? It's easier to say we're lost at night. And now we have three witnesses, not only one."

"Wait. Do I want to be a witness?"

"Do you want to help rescue Chick?"

"Count me in!"

Ahead of them, Abeo stopped. She was sniffing the night air like a hound. "Meth," she said, all business.

"Where?"

"This closest trailer must be a meth lab. Or the shed. I know that smell." Abeo had let her voice get gruff. She glanced at Donny. "An evil friend of mine was in the business."

Donny said, "Uh-huh."

"There's nothing worse than a reformed speed freak," Abeo confessed. "And here I am depriving hundreds of their source. I'd better be well rewarded in heaven."

"You must have friends in high places if you think you're going to get into that club."

"High is the word, bro. Now if you'll excuse me, I'm going to look in the window of that shed."

They were whispering and keeping low, but Donny felt so righteous at that moment that she was certain she could stride right onto the property, invincible. She was glad she hadn't given Chick something to worry about.

Abeo scuttled back. Small and nimble, she must have been a gem in the Vietnamese tunnels. Donny already knew Abeo was tough enough to survive anything, even R. She'd probably charmed at least the socks off the women up at Spirit Ridge.

Abeo showed them an empty iodine bottle and foil packets.

"Meth?" asked Donny. Abeo nodded.

"This is a major big deal then," Jeep said. She took one of the iodine bottles and stared at it, open-mouthed, as if it could tell her something.

"Looks like they process and package the dried weed in that first shed," said Abeo. "The meth lab is in the second trailer."

"You saw the weed?"

"Enough to keep your whole county stoned for a month."

Donny was satisfied. She pulled out the phone. "Wait. Where's Jeep at? I forgot we shanghaied her."

They looked uphill through the trees in time to see Jeep jogging toward them. Without warning, she went down. Donny saw the flash through the trees behind Jeep before she heard the blast. The dogs went into a frenzy of barking.

"Sweet Jesus," cried Abeo. "That's another one!" They ran toward her, then saw that Jeep, bent, clutching her side, was coming back downhill. She fell against Donny. Abeo pulled Jeep's hand away. "No blood, Don."

Jeep's face was the color of someone in shock. "It hurts to breathe," she gasped. "I was—looking for the dope."

Abeo took off, running crouched low, up the hill to the site where Jeep had fallen. A light came on at the complex. The dogs filled the night with howling.

"Oh god, oh god," Donny heard herself whine. "We've got to get out of here! Where's Abe?" She remembered then to hit the buttons on the phone, fumbling, disconnecting, dialing again. Was it connected? "Help," she whispered into it. "We set off a trap!" Was that a voice at the other end or static?

Jeep was still bent over, breathing in shallow gulps. "I don't think my ribs are—broken. But you go ahead. This is all my fault."

There was too much happening. She'd lost control over it all. Chick would kill her if she got Jeep shot. Was Jeep shot? Was M.C. coming for them? Had someone warned him to set traps? Did her call get through to the sheriff? Did she have to tell Chick about this? Where the hell was—

Abeo appeared out of the trees with the shotgun. She grabbed one of Jeep's arms and Donny grabbed the other. They took off, forcing a whimpering Jeep to run between them.

Donny said, "The fastest way out is straight down the driveway."

"No cover!" objected Abeo, but they plunged on.

Donny's knees felt spongy. Chick would be mad as hell if she got not just Jeep, but them all killed. She lifted the phone and tried to find the numbers as she ran. The dial tone sounded like a rock concert. M.C. must be after them by now anyway.

Jeep gave a hoarse protest. "Can't run any more!" but by then they were at the truck.

Abeo laid the trophy shotgun in the truck bed and shoved Jeep inside the cab, diving in after her. "I hope to god you didn't puncture a lung, child. We should have taken you to stay with the sheriff."

"Stop!" shouted a male voice. Far back in the woods another shot rang out.

She was almost in the truck. The key was almost in the ignition. This felt like one of her slow-motion dreams where her legs are too weak to go fast.

Another shot, another voice, closer, shouting. "You're dead meat!"

She raced the truck backwards and overshot the edge of the clearing because her foot punched the accelerator instead of the brake. Abeo held onto Jeep, anchoring them both. She straightened the steering wheel and shot out of the ditch downhill. She could see headlights jouncing up and down ahead of them.

"There's your cavalry!" Abeo announced.

"We've got him!" Donny hooted.

Trooper Bruce's car stopped. Donny braked and leapt out, rushing to it. She heard herself babbling about the meth trailer, the grass crop, the trip wires. The trooper talked into his radio. Within thirty seconds police vehicles streamed around them and up M.C.'s road. The woods looked like an airport, thick with searchlights. She even saw Johnny Johnson—the sheriff must have deputized a bunch of people for this operation. Wouldn't Johnson about have a coronary when he saw they were arresting a brother vigilante.

Jeep was in the car holding onto her side, eyes wide and fixed. "I'm sorry I blew it," she said.

Donny looked at the pathetic mess in front of her, surprised she didn't feel angry. "You're a kid. Kids are supposed to do dumb things."

"This poor baby," said Abeo, "got her ankle caught by a trip wire and fell onto a rock."

"A sharp rock," Jeep added.

"We'll wake up Doc Wu. Make sure nothing's broken."

There were shouts up near the buildings. Donny felt a little light-headed from the running and the letdown after all the fear, but she was most aware of the need to pee. "I'll be right back," she told them. This time she took a flashlight from the truck. She didn't want to squat on poison oak.

She was tucking her shirt in, flashlight off, practicing what she would tell Chick, when she heard movement up behind her. "Abe? Jeep?"

"Yo!" called Abeo from the truck.

She swung around, switching the flashlight on, and there he was, M.C. himself, crouched, weaponless, as startled as her. They both froze for seconds and then he turned and ran, stumbling, through the brush.

"Here!" she screamed to Abeo as she took off after him, knowing it was a lost cause, wondering how he'd eluded all those cops. This was like the old days of bar fights, but now she wished the cops would show up. Where was her anger when she needed it?

She could hear Abeo entering the tree line behind her and M.C. breaking branches off the grove of little manzanita bushes he'd run into. They grew thicker here and slowed him down. She knew she had only one chance. This was the motherfucker who'd been making Chick's life miserable. When she got close enough she launched herself at his back. He fell into a bush with her on top, then heaved up and crushed her against a trunk with her arm at an odd angle. She cried out, hanging on with the other arm, and then Abeo was over them, one shotgun trained on M.C., the other under her arm. M.C. went still.

Abeo raised one gun and discharged it into the sky. Pretty convincing. M.C. didn't know there wouldn't be anything in either gun now. Donny crawled away from M.C., leaning on her good arm. By the time she straightened up next to Abeo she was laughing despite the pain. "Do you believe this shit?" she asked.

"Yeah," answered Abeo. "Now I know why you think country living is so peaceful."

CHAPTER TWENTY-ONE

Button, Button

Chick wasn't behind her counter when R sought her out this time. She was at the back of Stage Street Mercantile where she'd come to get the plum corduroy fabric she'd ordered from Betty, an octogenarian who still ran the ancient family store. Chick had gotten worse after her trek up to M.C.'s enclave. Donny had suggested that she keep an antigloom list to help cure her depression. If something made her happy it went on the list and she'd do it, buy it, eat it, or find it. Making bright, soft clothing was right up there in her top ten. She ran an index finger along the yielding ridges of the corduroy.

"What are you turning this into?" R asked, fingering the fabric.

"Luxuriously large overalls." She swiveled, arms open, to embrace R's narrow shoulders. R's clothing smelled so strongly of a fabric softener Chick coughed and stepped back. So much for back to nature. "How are you, sweetie?"

"I've always admired your skill."

"It's more of a necessity than a skill." She forced herself out of the trance she'd been in at the button drawers.

This store had a hush to it, absorbing everyday town noises she wasn't aware of until she was inside. It smelled like her version of heaven, crammed with fabric and craft supplies, sewing notions, and old boxes of faded oddities like hatmakers' forms. She definitely needed to get the buttons on her antigloom list. She'd fill a glass jar with bright purple and red and sun-orange and key lime green and smoky blue buttons. She'd fill a dozen glass jars and line the windowsills upstairs. The thought made her smile.

"Finding the kind of clothes I like," she told R, "is truly difficult, and finding them in my size is impossible. I can get denim overalls like Donny's in a men's size, but I don't know how Donny can stand that stiff denim with the steel fasteners. What do you think?" She held the oversized coral-colored buttons to the purple.

"I'd use black," R replied without hesitation. "This looks gaudy to me."

Chick gave a warm gurgle of laughter. "Of course it's gaudy. I live for gaudy." She noted R's charcoal cape, her black high-water pants, and pilling navy turtleneck.

R looked toward Betty, who was folding and wrapping patterned remnants with quick, big-knuckled hands. There was a tiny TV on the counter, and Chick could hear a news story about Jenna Bush's drinking problem. Why didn't they leave the poor lamb alone? She'd drink too if she had that man for a father.

Dropping her voice, R said, "Donny told me you'd be here."

Chick grew more alert. She'd sometimes wondered if R didn't hang out longer at the store than a weekly restocking trip called for. And R never said no to an invitation for a cup of espresso. She seemed to know when things would be slow and Chick alone.

"Is something wrong? Is it time for us to come rescue Abeo from the lesbians? Or, on second thought, to rescue Spirit Ridge from Abeo?"

"Not at all." R surprised her by blushing. "I find Abeo fascinating." She held Chick's eyes with one of her intense green-eyed gazes. "I wanted to know how you are. Has Abeo's absence made a difference for you?"

"No, she wasn't a problem. I've thought some about you worrying over us. I don't think my depressions have anything to do with Donny and me. Some of it has to do with fifty coming on like a big neon sign saying, 'Get it together, you won't live forever.' But Donny loves me the way I think everyone wants to be loved. I feel so fully loved that I feel whole in a way I never did before. Does that make sense to you? It's as if now that it's finally all right to be who I am, I can be me in the world, doing what I'm meant to do."

R asked, "Which is?"

"Oh, R, it doesn't matter. I do everything from a foundation of love, and it makes me feel better and better about who I am and who I do it with."

"What a romantic," said R, shaking her head.

"There's nothing wrong with being a romantic. Donny once pointed out to me that I feel loved best when I'm giving love. When you run a store that sells whole foods, you can do it because that's what's hot this decade, or you can do it because you care about your customers. Once you get to be you there's no limit to the love you can hand out like the guy on the ice cream truck with his goodies."

"And does Donny get her investment of love back?"

"I can't help but do that. She fanned the flames and I'm a walking, glowing chunk of charcoal!" She thought for a moment. "I've seen this happen, though, where one woman loves another this well. The lover blossoms and thinks she has to move on, not realizing that she needs what and who she's already got. No, being loved like this may have set me free, but it's a freedom to grow in place, not to wander. I'd never find this again. If some fever moved me on, I'd only damage myself by trashing Donny and what she's given me."

"What a bunch of hokum."

"You think so? It may be hokum, but it's good hokum, hokum I can live with. We may not be in top form now and then, but more good times are right around the corner for Donny and me."

"Right around the corner." R shook her head. "I don't think in terms of straight lines and angles. I live in a spiraling world where good and bad blend instead of alternating."

"You're the most literal person I've ever met, R. It was only an expression. Why would you prefer curves anyway? They don't give you time to stop and sneak a peak at what's next. I need to know if it's safe to go on." A horn blared outside, a seldom-heard sound in Waterfall Falls.

"As if we have a choice. We always go on."

"Don't make it sound like such a downer. Determination is a good thing." She slid open another wooden drawer. "I personally am determined to find the perfect button. Wow. I've never seen anything like these." They were pink, with spiraling purple lines. "Do these have your name on them or what?"

"I've been meaning to mention how much I like the name of your store."

It took her a minute to make the leap to R's thought. She was hard to follow sometimes. "We named it after Aretha Franklin's 'Natural Woman.'"

"I don't think I know it."

"Oh, wow. Did your husband keep you locked up?"

R looked like she was sucking on a lemon. "He didn't have to. Heterosexist society did a fine job. I remember Helen Reddy's 'I Am Woman,' which I thought was more brassy seduction than radical challenge."

"I suppose 'Natural Woman' was about surrender, but what a great dance tune."

"Tell me about your name. Chick? How did that happen? It's such a derogatory term for a woman."

"I was a preemie, so small my mother said I looked like a fuzzy chick. Dad insisted on crowning me with his mother's name, Cicely, so it was either Sissy or Chick. It's a reminder of how much they loved me so I've always liked it. I almost changed it when I was a teenager, but decided to turn myself into a high femme chick instead."

"When I moved here from the city, I took a name that echoed my inner self."

"R! You don't see yourself as a poisonous reptile, do you?" That horn went off again. Not M.C. Chick's stomach clenched with dread. It couldn't be M.C., unless—had he made bail?

R went on in her deep monotone. "The snakes live communally, at least in cold weather. Otherwise they're solitary, even secretive. I'm told that I intimidate, or rattle, people. It's an honest name."

Donny would be nodding her head a mile a minute. Chick's wanton sympathy welled up with a warmth that replaced the chill of her recent sadness. She laid a hand on R's arm. "You're too hard on yourself, honey."

"Honesty is hard. And—" R turned her face away. Was she going to cry? Chick was horrified at the thought that this prickly, proud, and sometimes all-too-venomous community cornerstone might melt like a wicked witch right in front of her. "You've always been so accepting."

Chick took one of R's cold hands in her own and felt herself jump at the third honk outside the store.

R was too self-absorbed to notice. "I feel that you're another powerful woman and my only real peer in this area. I know what some women think of me and of my name. I respect my namesake. Rattlesnakes wander. The females don't go far, but they do go. It's simply part of who they are."

There were tears on her cheeks. Chick hugged her again, rocking her slightly. She could see the store's front window over R's shoulder, but a floral fabric display was blocking her view of the street.

"There are women who don't care for me. I know that," continued R, stiff in her arms and reeking of that fabric softener smell. She must have come to town to do her laundry. The thought of R using a fabric softener bugged Chick. It didn't fit. "Yet occasionally one comes into my life who glorifies me." She pulled back, but Chick didn't let go.

"Katie's a glorifier. It's flattering, but not enough. She only comes home late at night, and I need someone who's there for me all the time."

R's face was dark pink, almost the color of the spiral buttons Chick fingered on their card. "I'm surprised Katie puts her camera down when she comes home at night," she said with a laugh.

R gave her a surprised look. It occurred to Chick that she might have taken up with a journalist for reasons beyond Katie's personal charms. Calculated reasons. R's face relaxed into its accustomed passive expression, the one Donny called her what-me-worry? mask.

"At first our connection felt so deep. Katie wouldn't let me out of her sight. She claimed I was a lesbian land pioneer, that she wanted to document my life." R sighed. "Katie documents everyone's life, including her own. What I thought might at last be love as I'd never before experienced it was her unsustainable universal enthusiasm. She falls in love weekly," she said, making a clicking sound with her mouth, "sometimes with a woman, but as often with an idea or a thing. Currently it's this community profile she's doing, interviewing anyone who'll talk to a camera. She has no time for me now."

Chick closed the button drawer with more force than she'd intended. R hadn't been worried about how things were going with Donny—she'd come looking for Chick today because of her own distress. This was rattlesnake honesty. She had to smile at the depth of R's self-deception. What a character. "Where's Katie during the day?"

"She's off somewhere, everywhere while I meditate, work on the land, write in my journal, weave, spend time with my land partners. Today she filmed the men and your Donny doing something to reinforce Kimama's roof."

Chick shook the buttons toward R. "Katie's vibrant and ambitious. Did you really expect that she'd simply settle in your isolated world, adapt the schedule of a recluse? Of course she would make a life of her own. She's used to a high-pressure career and a social life in the heart of gay America." The horn rang out: shave and a haircut, two bits. Chick's heart pounded. "Who is that out there?" A car lurched into sight. It wasn't M.C. It was someone driving R's Volvo wagon. An impatient someone.

"And lately I've been spending time with—"

"Abeo?" Chick exclaimed. "What's Abeo doing out there in your car honking?" Since when did R tolerate someone rudely summoning her, not to mention commandeering her car?

R's face turned that spiral button dark pink again. She made a kind of fluttery gesture toward the window and turned back to Chick.

"I didn't want her with us at first, but I couldn't turn away the only black lesbian I've ever had on the land. Yet nothing about her is lesbian. She isn't really a woman, yet sometimes I think she's more womanly than I am. I abhor her and—" she looked pleadingly at Chick, "she's so profoundly spiritual." She looked quickly away.

"Abeo? Spiritual?" Chick stifled a laugh. "She's got your number, Miz Rattlesnake."

In an excited tone R confided, "She sang with a church group before she transitioned. She sang for me. I was moved, thoroughly moved."

Wait till Donny hears about this. "Of course you were. Abeo's playing you like a symphony. But I'm not sure that's all bad. Look at you. You're like a prism today, honey, flashing colors at me. I've never seen you so animated."

"I'm uncomfortable with these feelings of excitement. There's no depth to them. This half-man in women's clothing comes along and I'm rattled!" she said with a flustered laugh. The horn blasted. "I need to go."

"Ciao," Chick said, envisioning Katie crying over an espresso when she learned she'd been supplanted. She'd have to have her over for dinner, let her know she had friends. "Enjoy yourself, sweetie."

R pressed her hand. "Thank you." Her odd friend let go and hurried to the door. "I feel like a kitten chasing milkweed."

Kitten? Chick thought, knowing it was mean to laugh at the ridiculous notion of R as a kitten. Ah, but laughter was on her antigloom list, so, once the door closed, she let it explode out. Betty looked shocked.

"Dynamite buttons!" Chick told her, holding up her find.

She hoped to the Goddess R wasn't thinking of changing her name to Kitten for the sake of honesty. Donny was going to wet her pants laughing over this. She took the pink spiral buttons and the plum corduroy yardage toward the cash register.

"Outrageous," she said.

Poor R, always a little pathetically ridiculous in her dogmatic and pompous lesbian-feminism, was hung up on a trans woman. Chick stumbled over some loose linoleum, her insides reacting as if she'd nearly fallen down a long hole into an alternate world. Then she laughed aloud again. This was already an alternate world—her depression was missing. It had lifted before, so she expected that it would return, but maybe the ol' happy list was doing what prescription drugs hadn't. She was suddenly desperate to keep feeling this way. Cool it, lady, she told herself. R had simply reminded her how good it felt to be Chick.

"Life," she told Betty, "is a kick."

CHAPTER TWENTY-TWO

Familyville

Jeep sat on Cat's front porch in the fancy part of town. She'd gone with Cat to see the new film *Pearl Harbor*. Not for the movie, but for the air-conditioned theater; the trailer was sweltering. She fingered her bruised ribs to test for lingering pain, lay her hands on them like their warmth would finish the healing. Doctor Wu had predicted six weeks of pain.

"I almost fell over when I made the connection, Cat. Chick's stalker turns out to be Luke's dad? I mean, soap opera city!"

"Welcome to small town living, Jeep. We'd have figured it out sooner or later, whether old M.C. skipped bail or not."

This was the first day the temperature had gone over ninety degrees, and they were catching whatever breeze they could in the old cushioned wicker chairs. Cat's fat part-Siamese cat, Lump Sum, lay on his back, all four paws in the air, and George the gentle pit bull panted at Cat's feet.

"How could a mother and father just leave their kid behind at school like that?"

"Luke's better off running with a fugitive family? I'm sure," Cat said, as she stretched her legs across the top step. She was sucking the fluid out of honeysuckle blossoms, one after another. "You positive you don't want any, Jeep? Tastes like honey."

"You know, if Muriel did that, I wouldn't be tempted, but you make it look like such a decadent thing. I'll bet some of those politicians Donny hates would ban honeysuckle." She took a flower and touched the tip of her tongue to its nectar, then started laughing. Cat joined her. "It's like we're playing a joke on familyville. Doing this totally erotic thing in broad daylight."

Cat drank from another flower. The cat waddled over and yowled. Cat said, "Come on, Lump Sum, cats don't like honeysuckle." He flicked his tail at George, then collapsed down onto one hip and watched them pick blossoms and lick.

"Shouldn't he be on a diet?"

"I've tried. He doesn't let me sleep. He doesn't allow me to have any privacy. I always give in. He's not my fault. I inherited him from Mrs. Schmidt across the way." Cat was rubbing Lump Sum behind the ears. "I promised to take the beast if she died. I was sure she'd outlast him. Wrong."

Jeep gave him a vigorous back scratch, thinking about poor Luke. "Seriously, he's the only one they left, Cat. Didn't they know a little kid would feel geeky?"

"Hey, maybe you're identifying too much."

"Maybe I am. And maybe that's what it takes to care."

Jeep stood and surveyed the street. It was dinnertime and she could smell all-American food smells—charcoal-grilled beef, onions, some kind of potatoes. Cat lived alone in this big western home built by her great-grandparents, founders of the local bank. Jeep imagined the other houses peopled with happy, happy families.

Thinking of her own and of Cat's disrupted family, she said, "It's always a lie, isn't it? Even the alternative family's bullshit. If the family's the basis of our civilization, we're in deep doo-doo."

"Watch what you say, we're inside familyville."

Cliff Street had kids in almost every house, and Jeep knew that under those blonde corkscrew curls of hers, Cat had dreams of filling her house with some of her own.

"You know what I wish? I wish one of these families wanted to adopt a little kid, adopt Luke or at least be foster parents. The children on this street, you know they've got a head start in life. Or the woman up the hill, Gretchen's mother. That family could use a son. What about it, Cat, you could talk to her."

"They already have a couple of boys. I don't know where they were the day we bought the bass."

"Then who?"

"How about you?"

"Right. I was the one who changed the subject every time Sarah got into naming our kids."

"You'd have to make some big changes yourself. And like you always say, your trailer isn't big enough for you and your laundry."

"Keep dreaming."

Then, with even less inflection than usual in her country-slow speech, Cat added. "So you and Luke could move in here."

First she laughed, but a glance at Cat told her she was serious. "Uh—*hello?*"

"You could, Jeep. It's so big George and Lump Sum and I rattle around like jumping beans in a giant's hand."

George's ears picked up at his name, but she never opened her eyes. Cat was always so practical in her drawling purposeful way, like she knew the Rules of Life. But the truth was that Jeep had been kind of peeking at scenes of living with Luke in her imagination, kind of poking at herself to see how that might feel. And she might, once or twice, have pictured herself as the perfect roommate Donny had told her Cat was looking for. If she did somehow figure a way to get the authorities to let her raise Luke, could Cat be right? She seemed so certain about what she wanted.

"They'd never let me have Luke. Besides, I don't know if I want to live with a child. A boy-child."

"You want him."

"No, I don't. Yes, I do. I'm incredibly nuts about Luke." Jeep became aware that she was spinning a wheel on her skateboard and stopped. "You think they'd let a dyke raise him?"

"It's about two dykes, girlfriend." Cat held up two fingers.

"Two dyke friends and a little boy. The state would swallow that?"

"You might need to get a haircut."

"Ditch the buzz?" Jeep said with alarm, feeling the prickles of hair with her palm.

"Maybe some nice, conservative, anti-gay family will take him in and teach him hymns."

"Okay, okay. I'll cut it."

"We'd take Luke to parades. You'd teach him music. I'd play softball with him. We'd feed him."

"And he'll grow to mongo proportions. What about puberty? Adolescence? Talk about majorly alternative lifestyles. It'd be like living with an alien."

Cat had the mockingest grin on her face. "You mean a big, smelly teenage boy with acne and a yen for girls?"

"Gross."

"Even your fiddler hero—how do you pronounce his name?— Yitzhak Perlman was a kid once."

"Negative. He just started small."

Cat's chuckle was appreciative. "Luke could turn out gay."

Jeep shrugged. "Or bi, or become a Buddhist monk. Do you think they'd let him stay with me?"

"If you lived in a house like this, maybe."

"What's in it for you?"

"How about a family?"

"Wasn't one family enough?"

"Mine wasn't." Cat's voice grew even softer. "Or maybe it was and I want more of what they gave me before Mom split with her aging Baja beach boy. Maybe a grandson other than Lump Sum would bring Dad back from the bank in Tokyo."

"Look, Teach, you may not have to worry about such minor matters, but I don't earn enough coin to qualify as a parent."

"Together we do."

"It'd be like marrying you, Cat. I am through with love." Oh, dude, she thought, those words will come back to haunt you. It was true. Though she harbored fantasies about Cat and every other appealing dyke in town, in the end she couldn't imagine herself being lovers with any of them. After all this time she couldn't imagine herself with Katie either.

"This isn't about hormones. Imagine raising a child with any of your exes."

"I was in bed too much to pour a rug rat's cereal." But as she said the words, she thought of Sarah again, of how she'd talk about all the kids in the world needing homes. She hadn't wanted to hear it then. Sarah would flip if she knew I was even thinking about taking on a tiny tot, thought Jeep.

With a sweep of her arm, Cat said, "It's here for the taking, amigo. This is something I've wanted for a long time. I can't do it with the woman I love, so it's time I got some other kinds of love into my life. I have a home to offer, you offer companionship, help around the house, someone to share bringing up a kid with. It's not perfect for either of us, but today, I like it." Cat was silent for a minute or two, then said, "Who knows, maybe my s.o. might get comfortable enough to hang around a house that had more than one single woman living in it. Checking up on Luke, or something."

Jeep hadn't been able to eat since hearing about Luke that morning, yet she felt like she would spew. "Cat, I'd be stuck here into the twenty-second century. Me, Jeep Morgan, in Waterfall Falls, the only place in America so backwards it never noticed the Y2K crisis. I couldn't even go back to school for music therapy without a long commute in a phantom car. I couldn't join a big symphony if I wanted to."

"You'd work it out. You already have a student training site. You said you don't want the classical roadie insecurity, and in these parts old-time music runs a close second to country-western. Your audience would be right here."

"Say you're right. Say I've stumbled onto the best thing in the world for me—palatial home, survivable job, ready-made audience. Where's my life? I mean, how do I get to sow my wild oats if everything's all settled? Hell, I felt like I was dying in Reno, like my life was a paint-by-numbers canvas all laid out."

She kicked the concrete step planter which was filled with pansies and more pansies, some in colors she hadn't known existed. The two stupid madrone trees in the terraced front yard rustled, fully leafed in the middle of winter, but now nearly bare. Dry Creek ran through Cat's property, and this time of year it tumbled swollen into the conduit that took it under Cliff Street. It was too hot here in summer and rained all the rest of the year. Law and order was big, too many of the dykes were downwardly mobile. Except for Cat.

Slow-moving sexy Cat who'd never seemed inclined to make a move on Jeep because she had a secret beau she didn't live with. Did Jeep want to be part of the family Cat hoped would lure her beau home? Did she want to eat dinner every night with a woman who was spoken for?

Back in Reno, sitting at the dinner table with sweet Sarah night after night, the wildness would rise up in her, a taut straining as if she were growing wings and poised to use them. Instead she poured it all into her fiddle, like a live wire feeding the strings the juice of her personal riot. It had never occurred to her that anyone would pick up on her vibes when she'd landed a temp gig with a small all-boy band.

The night the woman approached her, she'd been as totally wired as her electric fiddle. Sweat rolled into her ears, along her rib cage, and made her quick fingers slick. Then her solo had ended. The cowboys and their women at the Stompin' Inn yelled for more, but she'd already given them more, so she'd faded back to her seat while the boys took over with harmonica, banjo, and guitar.

She hadn't known how easy she'd had it when she'd played pop tunes for gamblers. The locals only gambled for fun. They were too alive to sit around, and many could be found at The Stompin' Inn roadhouse on a Saturday night, always asking for more. The dancing started up again, and Jeep joined the boys in "I'm A Man of Constant Sorrow."

Bluegrass music zapped everything out of her. It was a heart thing. She'd drag around the gift shop the next morning like she had a hangover, finally holing up in the back office to work on the books. She wasn't sorry. It had been a matter of piling this Saturday night gig with a mostly country-western band on top of full-time work at the hotel, or leaving Reno, leaving Sarah, leaving everything she knew to find another way to do music.

At about 10:45 the bartender yelled for Jeep. That had been the deal; the band would try her out as their replacement fiddler while the regular guy was in the pokey for his umpteenth DUI, but, because the owner was also their banjo player, he wanted her to double as bartender between sets so he could rest.

"What can I get you?" Jeep yelled to a customer even before she was behind the bar.

She threw herself into a whirlwind beer-drawing, drink-mixing dance. It was weird; that night, for some reason, every time she set a drink on the bar her eyes met those of a woman with blonde-streaked dark hair. She'd noticed the woman watching her while she was playing. Each time it happened, she felt that visual touch like a vibration low in her belly. She thought the orders would never stop. Finally, the first surge of drinkers was settled and the woman was there, giving Jeep a smile and a knowing look. She was saying something. Jeep strained to catch the woman's soft words.

"They should pay you enough for your incredible music so you don't have to work the bar too."

In this rowdy crowd of het men and women she sounded like a spring day out in the desert when the cactus plants got all dressed up in flowers. Or like night, by the lake, kissing.

"You're into old-time music?" was all Jeep could think to say.

The woman smiled. She didn't leave a tip.

The next Saturday night she was there again, though the place was so crowded it took a while to spot her. Jeep introduced herself as she handed the woman a bottle of Calistoga water over the bar.

"Lara," answered the woman, extending a hand to be shaken.

She was thin in the graceful way of dancers, but too tall to be a show girl. Was she part of this mining and ranching crowd? She'd admired the backcountry kids in high school. A lot of them had the

Basque blood of the early settlers and looked like some kind of classy imports, dark, strong-featured rebel types.

Jeep rolled a Calistoga bottle of her own on the back of her neck to cool down and played the next set half-watching Lara, who wore a red Western shirt. The black yoke emphasized her breasts, the pearl buttons shone under the house lights. She was alone, resting against the jukebox, long hair spilling past her shoulders, a small pair of wire-rimmed glasses hanging from her mouth by the stem. Jeep found her eyes frozen to the woman. Was Lara beautiful? Sexy? Better than Sarah? Temptation? Her true soul mate?

Jeep felt so inexperienced—she'd only been with Sarah and Mindy. And she felt completely dweebed out in her fiddling suit—black jeans, robin's egg blue Western shirt buttoned to the neck, and a black sheep's head slide on a white bolo tie—the band was called The Black Sheep Boys. When they'd given her the tie they told her she'd have to settle for being one of the boys because they weren't changing the band's name.

After the next set she worked even faster to get everyone served. The owner of the inn, who was also the banjo player, flicked a white bar towel at her and told her, with a look at Lara and a wink, to vamoose.

Lara was at the far end of the bar. She'd speared the lime wedge Jeep had given her with a toothpick and was sucking on the pulp of the lime. Jeep was thinking this whole scene was like some corny Bogart flick. Lara turned with a beckoning move of her chin. Jeep followed her outside.

They leaned against the fence at the back of the parking lot, each with two fingers hooked in chain links, smiling small smiles at each other. Cigarette smoke drifted over from the smokers on the porch.

"Lara," said Jeep. "For the song?"

Lara nodded. "My mother still thinks *Dr. Zhivago* is the greatest movie ever made."

You sure are something out of a movie, she almost said, but swallowed her words before she embarrassed herself. She looked away. Men dressed like cowboys laughed and smoked in groups along the front of the club's Western facade.

"I should be inside."

"Inside?" Lara picked up Jeep's free hand. "Fiddler's fingers."

"Inside with the band," she stuttered, knowing full well what Lara was saying, or not saying, and that the band wouldn't be on again for nearly half an hour.

"I came to hear you play."

She rumbled through her mind, searching for something cool to say. "Gracias. Do you play?"

Lara let her smile linger long enough for Jeep to understand the double entendre she'd made, then answered, "I'm a court reporter."

"Like for the newspaper?"

"No," Lara said with a gentle laugh. "Like for the court. I'm a glorified typist."

"Cool."

"I do it freelance. Can't stand nine to five work."

"That's deadly."

"The gift shop isn't you." Lara smiled at her surprise. "It took me a while to remember where I'd seen you before. I worked in the casino kitchen when things were slow last year."

"Cooking?"

"You could say that."

Why was it that everything she said came out sounding like a come-on? "Working the shop bought violin strings," Jeep explained.

"And flowers for your girlfriend?"

"Sarah's allergic to—" She wanted to take it back. She wanted to run to Sarah. She wanted to go play her violin. She turned to fade into the sunset, but Lara's hand, strong, trapped her wrist, both yielding and anchoring.

"My girlfriend goes ballistic over flowers. I'll bring her some tonight," Lara said.

What was going on? Maybe Lara just wanted to be friends? The thought brought immediate relief and then vast disappointment. "She doesn't like this music?"

"Yes, but she gives me my freedom."

"Sarah's an architect, but she works at the hotel too, in HR. Days." Oh god, she'd done it again. She sounded like she was announcing that she was available.

"Uh-huh."

This time Lara walked away, but her hand stayed gently around Jeep's wrist and pulled her along. She knew she could break away and end the temptation. She knew she'd never be able to blame anyone but herself.

Lara led her to the other side of a VW Vanagon which looked like it had seen a lot of road, to the privacy between it and the wooden fence around the dumpster. Jeep put the side of her forefinger to Lara's warm, smooth cheek. Lara smelled like fresh-baked bread—did she still cook? She heard her own shallow breathing. Lara slowly turned her head until her lips touched Jeep's finger. Jeep's eyes wouldn't stay open. She drew a long breath through pouted lips and, feeling troubled and dizzy all at once, watching Lara's eyes, kissed this stranger who was no stranger. She hadn't anticipated that Lara's thin lips could be so symphonic.

"You'll think I'm a groupie," Lara said.

"You'll think I'm sex-starved."

"Are you?"

"From the minute I saw you."

They climbed into the back of the van. It was neat, clean, surprisingly warm for this late hour. Most of it was taken up by a foam pad covered with a slightly scratchy blanket in a Navajo pattern. There were closed purple curtains on the windows. They undressed, half-bending under the low roof. Sensing that Lara had done this before only made her more excited.

The cool palm of Lara's hand admired Jeep's angular hip. She shuddered at Lara's touch, and each touch was more disastrous to what she'd thought was her marriage than the last.

Lara's hair was an inverted bowl of yellow over dark brown. Jeep was fascinated by this new body, so hyper-sensitive to the least touch compared to—no, she couldn't think about Sarah now.

It wasn't long before she plunged her fingers inside wet Lara.

"Fiddler fingers," Lara told her. "Long as a comet's tail. Oh. And that hot."

Jeep floated in Lara's space, floated into Lara, sucked up by feelings that felt like meltdown. "Can I survive away from you after this? You're kind of like a space suit, oxygen and all. I wish I could wear you."

Lara kept bucking against her fingers, faster and faster, slamming the heel of Jeep's hand against herself, her demanding hips riding high, her vulva gasping. Jeep was light-headed with lust, and her fingers threatened to slip out. She lowered her mouth to the damp pubic curls, ignoring everything she'd learned about safe sex. One thrust of her tongue and this goddess was pounding the broad-striped bedspread as if they were inside a house on a solid foundation.

"Sweet fingers," Lara said, taking them into her mouth. "I can't wait to do that to you."

Jeep kissed her, pressed closer. It wouldn't take much.

Lara laughed. "But not tonight. I need to go."

"What? Now? Why?"

"When can you get away? I'd like to hang out with you some more."

"I'll tell Sarah we're having a rehearsal." Of course she'd lie.

"Saturday morning? Eight? Up the Truckee? There's a gravel road past the cell phone billboard. A red sign says No Dumping."

"Woo-hoo!" Her memories of Mindy and the river were enough to make her accept without hesitation. "I'll find it." She took one more rebel kiss. She asked, "Are you?"

"Am I what?" The smile was permanent in Lara's eyes, a self-mocking, worldly-wise, playful, drawing-in amused look that didn't stop. What Jeep wouldn't do to have been-everywhere eyes like that. She was forever being taken for a teenaged boy, with her open face and her flattop.

"A groupie."

"I've never done this before except with Karen."

"Karen?"

"My Sarah. Later, Fiddler."

Jeep was ultra-aware of the seam of her jeans as she walked back through the sting of cigarette smoke and reeking alcohol, through the straight couples dancing to a slow jukebox song. She felt like a walking, talking don't-ask-don't-tell poster child.

"Lara," that most romantic song. Lara, who wasn't about romance at all, only sex, but had turned Jeep's life into a lesbian Harlequin novel.

When the group started to play the next set Jeep saw that Sarah was there, waving from a table. Her bow crash-landed on the wrong string. After the break she signaled that she needed to use the restroom, where she roughly washed her hands and lips. She looked in the mirror and found that Lara stood behind her. They were alone. Lara slid her hand to Jeep's breast, and in the mirror they both watched her index finger circle the nipple.

"Sarah's here," croaked Jeep.

Lara whispered, "Sweet dreams," and was gone.

"Wassup?" Jeep asked when she reached Sarah's table. She loosened her bow for the night. "You're usually asleep by now."

"I wanted to hear you."

Jeep fidgeted. "It was great to see you out here."

"Thanks. You've been feeling far away lately. I thought maybe I wasn't showing enough interest in your music. You practically started a fire burning up those strings just now."

"I know you like it better when I play Lalo or Resphigi."

"No, Jeep. I enjoy listening to whatever."

She spotted Lara leaving, wanted to go after her. "No!" she cried. "I mean you don't have to like it because—"

"What's wrong, Jeep? You're so jumpy. Should I go?"

"No!" she cried again. "Everything's cool. Everything. I mean, the band's been so hot, it's hard to come down afterwards. I usually don't see you till I get home."

"I understand. Do you want to take a walk?"

If she saw Lara out there, in the night, wrapped in the darkness instead of her arms—"No!"

"Okay. Chill out, Jeep, okay? I brought something to show you. I finished it tonight." It was a Polaroid, the model of their dream house assembled on their kitchen table.

Jeep stared at it. She stopped herself from bouncing the bow on her thigh.

"This isn't a good time, Jeep, is it? You're preoccupied."

"Yes! It's perfect! The time, not the house. I mean, the house too." The owner plinked a few high notes on his banjo and she checked the bar. Mobbed. "I've got to get to work," she explained with relief. "Are you going to stay?" She knew Sarah saw right through her, saw her hoping she wouldn't stay.

Sarah shook her head. "I'll see you after work tomorrow."

Her voice sounded so sad that Jeep thought she could reproduce it on her strings.

"Pick it up, Jeep," the bartender told her, holding out a rubber basin.

Gradually, as she collected empty glasses, she was taken over by a fantasy of Lara, out at the lake, leaning against her pickup smoking, then inside the van, naked and waiting. In the few moments they'd talked Lara had said she was taking classes at the college, art classes. Lara and Karen were going to have rug rats. None of her plans had included Jeep. Yet how could Jeep resist when her life was like a river, quick with snow melt, herself the roof torn from a submerged dream house and hurtling downstream.

"You take it, Jeep," the owner had said, giving her the reins, handing her the towel when she'd finished dunking glasses. She'd poured and served, poured and served that night, and felt as intoxicated as the barroom crowd was with alcohol.

"Cat to Jeep. Cat to Jeep. Are you still with me, Jeep?" Cat was saying, a hand on her arm.

Jeep snapped back to the present fast. "The band! Who would take care of Luke with us at rehearsals, performances?" she asked.

"We'll appoint aunts and uncles. And grandparents. You get two of each and so do I. They'll love spending time with a kid who goes home after a few hours."

"Chick and Donny," Jeep said. "Chick'll want to undo what M.C. did to Luke and teach him spirituality. Donny'll want to break him in on fishing poles and building. We could have holidays together. Do you think Luke would start talking?"

"With his tendency to autism? Dunno. He'd have you, amigo. The one who unlocked his closet."

"And helped to get his folks busted."

"Kids shouldn't have closets."

"At least he doesn't take after M.C. Maybe, like, the stork brought Luke, dropped him off, and the M.C. crowd took him in? That might explain why they left him behind." She faced Cat and gave the skateboard wheel a fast spin. "Did you ever think about how there could be no other word on the planet for stork except 'stork'? It's like Chinese. It's a picture of the bird. You hear it and you see a stork. Unless you're Chinese or maybe Russian. Maybe they think the same thing about their word for stork. Do you really want housemates? Me and Luke?"

Cat looked at her with a smile. "Did anyone ever tell you you're nuts? Well, you are and yes, I really do."

"Me, with a son. I don't much like males, Cat. I wouldn't be doing Luke any favors."

"You sure like this boy."

"That round beaming face. I never knew a kid like him." Her spirits lifted. She grinned.

"His smile's like yours, Jeep. B-i-g."

"We have to get him out of that care center. It could set him back—" Jeep laughed at herself. "Further than even I could."

"I'll talk to Joan. She'll know how."

"Joan?"

"Sheriff Sweet."

"You're in with her?"

"You could say that," Cat answered with her mocking grin as she smoothly pulled herself up by the stair rail. George was instantly awake. That's when Jeep realized why she'd been thinking of Lara. Cat moved like her. Cat had her seductive silence, her economy with words. Was this going to be erotic torture, living with Cat, or an ending of some kind, a way she could learn to like a woman without jumping her bones?

Was the sheriff Cat's closet lover? That would explain a whole bunch of things. "Why do I get the feeling I'm going to get real familiar with Sheriff Sweet?"

"First we have to move you in here."

"Can I borrow your car? It'll only take one trip to empty the trailer."

"I guess you decided?"

"Shee-it!" she said. Then, thinking she'd have to quit cursing around Luke, she clapped a hand briefly over her mouth. "I did?"

CHAPTER TWENTY-THREE

Casting

"This is trey cinema vérité," Katie said. "Why is it so dark in here? And so hot? R? Abeo?"

The two remained silent. A single candle on the floor cast their great shadows to the batiked sheet on the wall behind them.

Kate had been over at Hector and Clara's all day, following them around on their acreage while Hector mended the fence that kept his sheep in and Clara tended to the beloved peacocks and peahens which she raised to sell, but so reluctantly she had a yard full of them. Het the Whites might be, but they had a warm, clean old wood house, established routines, and a sometimes rancorous, always lively interaction, like something she might want for herself some day. She smiled into the darkness. Poor adorable Jeep had admitted to wanting to be married to her, but Jeep was far too agreeable to be happy with a woman as scrappy as Katie knew herself to be. Part of her thrived on conflict, enjoyed confrontation, was always ready to fight the good fight.

She felt as much an outsider coming back to the darkness of Spirit Ridge as she'd felt at the Whites'. The silence and camping-out feel of the Ridge was a downer. She had to admit that to herself as she'd approached R's yurt. It was the largest of the little homes on the land, and had niceties like an indoor sink with a drain to take water outside, though no running water, and a built-in couch-bed downstairs, where Katie slept when R wanted her own space up in the loft.

She was a little surprised to see that Abeo was there, sitting next to R, on the couch-bed. She'd been totally blown away to hear that Abeo had come to live on the land. Trannies were cool, but she had not imagined the mostly separatist land women, and especially the man-hating R, would want to live with one. Truth? The thought of an M to F trannie kind of creeped her out. Like, was there still a man in there? A wolf in sheep's clothing?

R had covered the big bird, so the yurt was quiet except for the music in her head—maybe the *X-Files* theme—something a little spooky anyway. The air was nearly solid with woodstove heat, way hotter than R normally kept it, but she still felt chilled. The place had that vegetarian food smell so unique to lesbian kitchens, a highly spiced, carefully herbed meatless food smell that made her want to gag. Or maybe it wasn't the smell that was gagging her.

"Wassup, Abeo?" she asked.

She'd learned right away that R wasn't someone who wanted hugging and kissing, even after a long day apart, so she smiled her hello across the room as she set down her equipment and took off her leather jacket. The land women had objected to that, to wearing the skin of an animal, but it was so kickin', Katie tried not to think about where it came from. If she dwelt on that kind of thing, she'd never eat another steak.

R and Abeo were now talking low. She wondered if there was something left over she could nosh on, and trained her flashlight over the countertop. A vase held gayfeathers, that purple flower Donny and Chick grew out in front of their store, like their own personal gay flags. R and her guest had been eating brie with hunks of bread, and carrot sticks. And chocolate-covered strawberries. She hadn't seen those foods in R's cabin since their first days together. It must be R's take on guest food, she thought, a little smug that she was no longer a guest in her home.

"Okay if I mac out on some of your cheese and bread?" she asked, sampling it.

R said, "Bring it over here."

As she assembled a plateful—one strawberry, two, three, four—they whispered more. It sounded like R was importuning Abeo. R, who asked no one for anything, drew what and who she wanted to herself. What could she admit to needing from this *maricon*—no, from this trannie?

She'd sat down and taken a bite of seeded baguette when R, her voice fluidly imperious, said, "Katie, we want you to film us."

"Cool. Bring up the lights. I'll shoot as soon as I get supper down."

"Making love," R added.

Anger flushed her body until it burned. "Run that by me again? No, never mind." She stared at R, looked at Abeo, then back to R. "Is this your mellow mode of giving me my walking papers, R?"

"I told you this was the wrong way, Snake Lady," said Abeo. "You don't tell somebody this shit like saying you're going out for a quart of homo and the daily rag."

Katie pulled her gaze away from Abeo, who really did have a skin color she'd love to film. "You two are—" She didn't want to show or know how shaken she felt. "You're—"

"We're two feathers blown together in the breeze," R said. "There is no *we*. What I'd like you to film is a trans male-to-female lesbian and a female-born lesbian making love for the first time."

"Why?"

There was a pause, then R explained in her fluid hypnotic voice, "I believe it's important, Kate. Stripping the mystery will lead to acceptance."

Wind blew through a gap in a window held to the wall with a hook and eye. The candle went out. Katie remembered what R had told her about her first woman lover, the eleven years they'd been together both during and after their marriages, R's expectation of forever and the quick surprising death of Birch from brain cancer. How R claimed that her heart had gone away with Birch into an unexpected kind of forever. There'd been no process, as there was for a living ex-lover, to reclaim her heart. None.

So this was what was left for R, solemn semiritualized physical intimacy that evolved from her politics. She'd sensed it in their own lovemaking, the purposeful give and take that dampened what she felt. If it had dampened R in the right places, that would have been cool. It was—she couldn't tell if it was her or if nothing turned R on. She'd be shaking with lust, and R would have on her smile, all Mona Lisa.

Katie pitied her and recognized what she should have seen right away—that no one was home. Had R ever wanted or even tried to recover her heart so it would be available to give again? Maybe she should be kind and satisfy this new craving of R's. Who was she to put R down for her carnivorous ego? Wasn't it always about our own egos? If she chose to be kind to R, wasn't she actually trying to gain favor with her? Didn't it all come back to keeping our look-goods intact, whatever pretty words we used?

She heard a plastic lighter flick. Abeo brought the candle back to life with a yellow disposable.

It took a minute before Katie found her TV studio laugh—her canned laughter, she called it. "I've heard a lot of wild projects, girls, but this one's beyond weird. You want me, your lover, to film you taking a new lover?"

"Would that be a problem for you, Katie?" R had a way of asking something with a tone of such intense caring that a negative response became an admission of ineptitude and weakness.

Katie tried not to take the bait. "I don't know. It would be an experience. But *me siento mal*," she added, knowing they wouldn't understand that she was saying she felt bad. She thought of the material she couldn't use from Chick's attack on M.C. "Since it's so important, what if I show it for, say, educational purposes?"

"No. The images will be of our bodies. It would belong to us, although we might choose to show it."

"Now I'm an unpaid hired camera. Are you sure this isn't your way of telling me to fade?" she challenged, sugaring her voice to sound like her bitchy Aunt Luz. Her dad had disappeared, but his family had stayed around and kept tight with her mom.

"Move out? No," exclaimed R, her voice infinitesimally louder. "I want you to stay, Kate. And I want Abeo to join us."

Abeo looked small. She was biting her lower lip and toying nonstop with a yellow scarf tied around her neck. To hide her goddamn Adam's apple, thought Katie. Abeo smiled apologetically at her.

"So we're going to be a threesome?" Katie asked, trying the concept on.

"I suppose that could happen," R replied. She went silent, eyes toward the ceiling, like a supplicant asking for celestial guidance. "Yes. I'd be open to that. But for now, I'd assumed we'd interact one on one."

"Oh? Like Abeo on you? Me on you? You, R, being the operative word?"

"Whatever spirit moves us," R answered with smugly pursed lips.

"Fuck that shit," said Katie, and she realized that she'd shredded the bread on her plate into little pellets of dough, and knew that she'd counted all fifteen of them over and over.

Emotions shifted inside her. One—anger, two—hurt, three—pride, four—rebellion, five—revenge, six—pain; she felt like a damaged kaleidoscope.

The candlelight burnished Abeo's dark skin. She wore a mint-green vee-neck sweater and black ladies' slacks, the kind with a permanent crease. Her hair was covered in a patterned yellow and black scarf that almost matched the scarf around her neck. She'd told Katie she was forty-six, but there wasn't a gray hair in sight or a line on her delicate triangular face. There was an athlete in that transformed body. She guessed Abeo could probably give as good as she got in bed.

Is that what R wants, Katie wondered? Or was it the novelty? The audience? She realized that she didn't know a thing about what made R's brain click and whir. Tonight she questioned whether R even had what she needed to learn. Was this business with Abeo the mark of a deeply spiritual woman, a woman who possessed true serenity? Of someone who professed to be at one with the universe? Or was R at heart an excitement junkie like Katie, who wore her mantle of composure to cover this up?

There was R's need for frequent new lovers, a need Katie had hoped would subside for a few years at least. The argumentative nature that kept everyone around her in a turmoil of decisions, changes, and efforts to please her. There were her projects in the community, which she'd start, then abandon to underlings who practically fawned for approval at her follow-up visits. There were her disappearances to unknown rendezvous. For all they knew, she was reporting on the lesbian-feminist underground to the FBI. That would be enough to feed an excitement jones.

If R turned out to be a fraud, where did that leave Katie, the almost big-time sophisticated journalist who'd given up her TV career to do what she believed in? Oh my god, she thought, that's what I've done. I've gone all idealistic on myself.

But R was no fraud. The woman was as sincere as she knew how to be. Katie wondered how far she had to go to learn what R could teach her. Did this adventure with Abeo have something to do with being open and accepting? God, she was so confused.

She was reminded of a brown-skinned Latina she'd loved to distraction for three months. How they'd danced in Connie's single bed—sisters, twins, two halves! The nights had been bright with fierce music. They'd played Gloria Estefan and Kim Carnes until the lyrics were imbedded in her brain for life. Connie's hair chopped and dyed— yes, mint green. They'd been sixteen, sweet sex-crazed sixteen. And the girl had gone straight.

That interlude had made her half-crazy. All she could do afterward was pace—around the trailer, around the park, around school and the neighborhood, though she'd had to curb that when men tried to pick her up. She'd fling herself to the floor of the trailer, cheek against the rough braided rug, and lie there, not daring to rise until the flood of pain had passed. Her skin had felt flayed, her heart scored, she'd been insane. "So you're having a breakdown," from one of Melissa Etheridge's songs, filled her head when she thought back to that time.

No! She thought. Not again. She would not let R take her down into a mental snake pit like Connie had, like others had since then. Like poor sweet Jeep almost had until Katie ditched her guilt and adopted R's policy: everything happens for a reason which will be revealed some day.

This was not a ride she wanted to be on, this plunging roller coaster of emotions. No! She had work to do. She had a name to make for herself so she could keep working, so the man in his many guises, corporation or non-profit or government, would pay her to accomplish her goal. She would tear the hypocrisy off the face of Amerika. Like Melissa Etheridge sang—she'd talk about how the bigots paid their dues and never had to get their hands dirty, paid some crackpot organizer to rid the world of queer vermin, Hispanic vermin, the plague of dark-skinned vermin. All those people who didn't see her, Katie, because she was not like them. But she saw them, all right. Oh, yes, she saw them for what they were, and with her Sony she was going to show every hateful sneer, lustful leer, every bald spot, every hair on the bellies she despised. It was what she'd been born for, and she was damned if anyone would sidetrack her, even R. Love the spirit, leave the danger alone, she told herself.

Abeo was a fucking man. She didn't believe his trannie bull. He was only another man chasing sex or a mother or a new turn-on, and she was damned if she'd watch the moves of a man in a woman's body, submit to the touch of a man released from a male body. She would not encourage R's fascination with this new kink.

Or should she film it, she asked herself. If she said no to this, would R shut her out? I'm screwed either way, she told herself. Either I give her what she wants or I lose what I want. How was this different from the world she'd left? Couldn't she avoid compromise anywhere?

Damn R. She had no business messing with people's hearts like this. Truth? Maybe she should capture what she saw and turn it loose on the world some day. Show up this craze where boys thought they were girls and girls thought they were boys, as an attempt to make sense of gender and try on different bodies now that unisex clothing was an ancient rebellion.

She thought of Jeep's appealing innocence and how she'd wanted to protect her. No, lesbians were vulnerable enough. Transsexuals too. They didn't need one of their own queer ilk exposing them, explaining queerness away. She wanted nothing to do with this one. They could have their fun. She had enough on her plate. She would not cower. If R blasted her out of Spirit Ridge, she'd have a strong clue that R didn't have what she was looking for.

"You've told me, R, how you like to go over every edge you come to."

"So you'll do it," R said, eyes on Katie's hands.

"We have different edges. You don't ask me to go over yours, and I won't ask you to go over mine. Deal?" Like a sleepwalker, Katie turned away, picked up her jacket and the Sony, and walked to the door.

"I'm drawn to the unique," R called to her back, as if afraid that Katie was criticizing her. "Change is challenge. I like my challenges."

Kate turned back to the room, to the candlelight's macabre shadows. This entanglement would gut her. No, she thought. No, no, no male flesh would touch hers. She felt sick to her stomach.

"I'm a living, breathing woman, R, not some forbidden fruit to be tasted, not a wild thing to be imprinted. You enjoy your challenges, but I'm going to accomplish what I need to, not do the wild thing with every player that comes down the pike."

When the chill evening air hit her she wondered if, without a witness, R would play out the scene. There's something wrong with this picture, she thought. Did R pick me or my camera?

CHAPTER TWENTY-FOUR

Second Story

Y ou okay?" Chick asked in a mumble as Donny eased out of bed.

Donny bent back, nudged the crystal necklace over, and left a kiss at the hollow of Chick's throat. "I can't sleep worth a damn tonight."

"Full moon," Chick said before she turned her face back into her pillow.

Donny was hot and itchy and damp in hard-to-reach places. She tiptoed into the sitting room overlooking Stage Street. Almost silently, from long practice on these sleepless nights and from years of doing shift work, she opened the window high. Chick was right. The moon was showing her stuff, clouds like wispy gray scarves floating across her face. The windowsill was wide enough to perch on. She looked down at Stage Street in the white moonwash. Beyond it the freeway was almost empty, one car buzzing by like a bug in a hurry.

It had been a month since the M.C. bust. Chick hadn't even known Donny had been part of it except that she had to make a statement and, because she was so often a contact in the bigot battles, the whole thing was all over the papers.

"I know Joan appointed you deputy so you can do drug prevention talks, but why did you get involved in all this rough stuff?" Chick had asked, looking completely baffled.

"I wanted to help," Donny told her, but didn't say that it was Chick she'd wanted to help.

Chick had put her arms around Donny and held her close. "That man was dangerous."

"Not as dangerous as letting him do his thing."

Chick's hold tightened. "I'm glad you didn't get any more damaged than putting a second joint in your shoulder."

The emergency room doctor had popped that sucker back in, and, aside from some lingering soreness, M.C. might never have fallen on her. And while Chick wasn't one hundred percent, she was laughing more, and touching more.

"I'm so glad," Donny said. With Chick, it was never the details that mattered. They had too much respect for each other—and that wordless thing, trust—to need to know everything. What did the talking, Donny thought, was their love.

Damp as it often was here, and hot as menopause often kept her, tonight's warmth was soothing. She recalled a day, at least a dozen years ago, that had felt something like this. She and Denise Clinkscales had lived in a railroad flat on the South Side of Chicago.

"Where're you taking me for our anniversary tonight?" Denise had asked. She had a Sylvester tape playing and was wiggling her bottom to the beat. "Three's my lucky number."

Except for the music and Denise's hot-to-trot energy, the wide-windowed apartment sometimes felt peaceful after the streets. Denise kept it shining clean and neat as a magazine ad. Donny had come home from her job as graveyard fry cook. Her whites were spattered with grease, her hands smelled like old pan drippings, but the apartment smelled like fresh clean clothes.

"Out? Why? So I can show you off?" She pulled the slip Denise had drying on a black wire hanger across the bedroom door to her nose and breathed in the soap smell. "I love all your frilly stuff hung up to admire."

"You think I'm doing this for you, woman?" Denise replied with a swat. "Get your hands off before I have to go down and wash it again." That was one reason they'd taken the place despite the elevated rumbling by non-stop—a communal washing machine in the basement. "Where you going to take me for our anniversary, honey-boat?"

"To this bed of ours."

"We do that every morning, woman."

Donny slipped to the other side of the room and pressed herself to Denise's round butt. The iron gave off a damp steaming-wool smell that took her back to her coming up days. "You complaining?"

Denise, tall as Donny, was able to rub her nightgowned bottom against Donny's tummy. "You haven't taken me out," she went plaintively on, "since New Year's Eve. Six months, honeypot."

Donny let go. "Don't you love staying home?" She went to the window and thrust it up, dislodging paint chips from the sash. Daylight fell in. Balmy air, such as she smelled maybe once a year in Chicago, flowed over her face like an angel's cloud. A jet made a clean getaway overhead, its roar buffered by the cries of kids on the street. She thought she could smell the lake. "Look at that sky! Our own second-floor place on top of the world, Dee. We don't need some borrowed room or a crowded dance floor any more. We have our privacy and our cuddle-down time." She spun around and struck the lead dance position, arms out. "You want to dance? Come to The Don! We'll dance till night!"

Denise ignored her, ironing Donny's other set of whites so hard the ironing board shook.

"Don't you go sulky on me, Dee. Why can't we have a candlelight dinner—or breakfast—and fool around?"

"I want to go out on the town before we lose our friends! We never leave this place. If I didn't go to the beauty college I'd be jumping out of my skin. This is nothing but four walls, woman, and a sooty old sky, and those trains! Sometimes I think I'm going to get a gun and shoot those trains off the track."

Donny collapsed on the sofa. "Ouch!" She scooted off the damn spring that she hit every time.

"Why don't you want to take me out?" Denise pushed. "You ashamed to be seen with me? I'm ugly now?" She leaned over the sofa. "You afraid somebody's going to give me pretty things and lure me away?"

The woman was swinging at her heart with a sledge hammer. "Somebody could do that? Tempt you like that? Someone who's not putting all her cash into this apartment?"

"I'm not saying what will happen if we don't get out of this place once in a while."

Shaking her head, Donny said, "I'm too tired. It takes me a week to catch up on my sleep after we go out, you know that. Let's get a picnic lunch at the store and go eat it at the lake. You can call in sick to the school." Subway cars rolled by at full creaky speed. She could see the people hanging on straps, swaying.

"I can't call in sick. My state tests are coming up. Besides, that's not my idea of celebrating, Donny Donalds, and you know it. Once a week, that's all I'm asking. I'm compromising." Denise walked to the side of the room where the small stove and refrigerator stood. "I've got some nice greens and that leftover chicken for your lunch. Or do you want an omelet before I leave? Sit down, I'll make you one."

The sky had looked smaller from across the room, its blue hemmed in by white window frames. That, Donny remembered as she sat 2,000 miles west at the window over Natural Women Foods and looked down on empty, dark Stage Street, was the beginning of the end with Denise Clinkscales. But it had lasted long enough to give her a taste for permanence, something she hadn't had since her father, a shoe repairman and hotshot at the church, had tossed her out on her ass at sixteen for being an abomination.

Chick snorted, a high sleeping mound back in their bed. It was only two o'clock. At five every morning but Sunday, Tuesday, and Thursday, Chick slept in while Donny started the day's baking. She'd run a hand along the patchwork quilt that lay over Chick on her way out. She'd made that damn quilt as fine as her mother could have. Their friends at the Waterfall Ladies' Quilting Club had taught her.

She stifled a laugh. The Don in a ladies' club! She should have sent a picture to her evil father. Her and the old white country ladies who held down their permed hair with baseball caps from diesel shops. And a picture of her presenting Sheriff Sweet with the quilt they had all made for the jail fund-raiser. They liked Donny. They loved teaching. And they loved that her and Chick made them mad money by selling their quilts, displayed on the rafters at Natural Woman Foods.

Two truck rigs, rattling empty, blasted through the sound barrier this quiet time of night. A car with a hole in its muffler whizzed by the trucks. Hurrying fools. There wasn't a thing wrong with going slow and staying put. Down on the sidewalk the flowers in planters exhaled their fancy perfumes up at her.

"What happened to my Don Juan?" Denise had cried that hot Chicago morning, putting on her perfume before she left for school.

Donny had come to like the time she had alone after Denise left. She'd switch to an Ahmad Jamal tape, read the paper, putter, walk the neighborhood, daydream about saving up enough after Denise finished hairdresser school to buy a little travel trailer and see the world.

"You're a mean dancer," Denise reminded her, "a jazzy dresser. You're The Don!"

That was the morning she'd realized that she didn't want to be The Don, not anymore. The Don had been a wild thing, born raging to get out from under her father's heavy foot and away from the frosty bitch, her mother, who didn't have time in her day for an oddball kid.

"What am I supposed to do with this child?" her mother would ask the ladies at the church, or sometimes just a mother in the street who had a little girl in beribboned pigtails and a dress. Mrs. Donalds would complain, "Her hair's like my mother's. It won't grow long enough to put up, and when I put a skirt on her it looks like a dirty rag before the day is out." She would look accusingly down at Della, hands on her hips. "I can't dress her in anything but her brother's hand-me-downs."

Donny didn't see a problem. She loved her brother Marcus Junior's soft, old elastic-waisted pants and striped jerseys. The minute her mother tried to humiliate her by ordering her to put them on she'd feel free. It was the Sunday dresses that felt humiliating.

"Donny?" Denise said, putting her face up close. "Is anybody home?"

"I'm here," she said, but as Denise went back to clattering over at the stove, she'd found herself in a clammy sweat. Her mother had been so pretty. She'd had a laugh like a little girl's giggle and had used it often. At the church the ladies loved her. She'd volunteered for everything, dressed to the nines in the latest styles. Mama had sewn all her own clothes, first pinning fabric to rustley tissue-paper patterns, then cutting with big pinking shears. She could sew any of the other women under the table and often wished aloud that she'd been blessed with a little doll of a daughter she could dress up.

The women teased her momma by asking if the lost-looking little girl who followed her around was hers. "That's Della," Momma would say, "a poor little motherless ragamuffin we picked up on the streets." Then she'd laugh to show she was joking and pat Donny on the head.

She could remember the feel of her mother's tentative touch, like someone feeling in the dark, afraid of what she might find. In time, she'd learned to recite the poor little ragamuffin response before her mother could, grabbing the church ladies' laughs and getting hugged.

"Sometimes I think you don't care about me, Don," Denise was saying from the stove.

"Of course I care," she replied. Denise, now, she did love to show off her tall handsome Donny. She'd made Donny two dancing outfits, elegantly butchy, and she kept their clothes pressed right down to jeans and polyester uniforms. Donny felt so proud to have this pretty woman on her arm. All her girlfriends had been lookers, but flighty, more interested in a wild time than in settling down, more in love with the idea of Donny the charmer than with Donny herself. Denise had outlasted them all. "I'm tired, is all."

"You're always tired these days. You feeling okay?"

"I'm getting old, woman."

Denise looked away real quick. So she was worried about their age difference too. Getting up there scared Donny—who would love her? At the same time she looked forward to it. Her Grandma and Granddad Weatherbee had been old, and she'd never known happier people. They'd had a little this-and-that shop where Donny's mother would leave her while she did her fund-raising or brought food baskets to shut-ins. Grandma and Granddad always let her do some little job, very carefully pricing and piling pomades and small boxes of rice up on shelves. They let her wait on customers and make change by the time she was six, and she'd worked with them right into her early twenties, along with whatever job she had, when she wasn't out partying. They weren't making ends meet by then, and the landlord wanted more rent. Grandpa got prostrate cancer; Grandma died soon after. They'd always been laughing with each other or with the customers. People with little money came in to buy things they hardly needed, just to hang out and laugh.

"Dee," Donny had said after arguing all through their morning meal, "go out on your own tonight. Have a fine time. The Don's hanging out a while, and then she has a date with the clean sheets. You took up with an old dog too tired to maintain a thirty-eight-year-old's speed. I swear I'll take you out to celebrate next time I get two nights off in a row."

"Forty-five isn't old, Donny," Denise had said. She'd gotten all dressed up for school in tight black pants, a scoop-neck white pullover, and a pink smock. "You'll feel friskier when you wake up."

Yeah, Donny had thought, and Hank Aaron didn't just beat out Babe Ruth's home run record. She had kept busy all morning fixing the drip in their shower, then fallen asleep half-scared, half relieved to know she was going to lose Denise.

Now she was fifty-seven. Chick loved her the way she was. Whatever messed with them—women, moods, bigots—there wasn't an endless road in front of her any more. She was finally playing for keeps. It had taken a while, but she had come to see that what Chick was going through didn't have a thing to do with her. Chick still wanted her, and Joan had been right. She'd said, "Sometimes all you can do is stand aside while they go through their changes."

Donny remembered answering, "You think I should try to get her to talk about it? I'm scared if I do, she might jump ship because she feels crowded."

"It's better to leave her alone and hope."

At the time she'd told Joan, "I don't know if I can do that. You know, I've been lucky enough to have been over the rainbow more times than I can remember, and I've chased more rainbows than I can count, but here, with Chick, I'm under the rainbow and we're the pot of gold. I won't risk losing her when, if I do something, anything, it might help."

She shut the window on Stage Street, then padded to the patchwork quilt and snugged her back up against Chick's for a few more minutes of rest before the alarm went off. Maybe for their anniversary she'd whip up one of those spice cakes Chick loved so much. It would be nine years next week.

CHAPTER TWENTY-FIVE

Grandma Chick

Don't forget to grind more beans for the espresso monster!" Chick called from the front step.

"First things first, babe. Look at all these outdated tofu wieners and sprouted breads," answered Donny from the frozen case, waving her away.

Chick stepped onto the sidewalk, a freed woman. She poked a finger into the soil in the wooden planters to test for moisture. Donny's signature portulacas were gorgeous and bloomed in a rainbow of colors. Soil always smelled like spring to her, but it was full-fledged, mind-boggling summer now, hot and dry. There was plenty of snow pack on the mountains, though, so they might not have to suffer through forest fires this year. That was the worst of living around here; every couple of years the air turned yellow with smoke, and you couldn't go outside without smelling the burn.

Today she was going visiting on her afternoon off like a regular citizen and not a lesbian hippie who'd sold out and worked in a store sixty plus hours a week. She couldn't get over having become respectable. Of course, being respectable out West was different from being respectable in the Midwest, but who's counting, she thought. They weren't getting rich off the store and, until the seniors had started coming in, hadn't known if they would make it, but now they were comfortable enough to consider buying the building they were in.

Donny had told her she was taking the transition from outlaw to capitalist pig too hard. "The world isn't all black-and-white like you and me. It's not like you're selling insurance or wedding dresses."

"Still, I'm a little bit uncomfortable with all this. I probably need to accept what I am—a small businesswoman," she'd told Donny. She'd been doing their quarterly taxes, looking for write-offs to reduce their income.

"Every time I turn around you're giving away cash to some vagabond or to a stranger collecting for charity. And babe—"

"Hush. I'm trying to find the receipt for that check I wrote to the Girl Scouts."

"—you never have to be worried about turning into a *small* businesswoman."

With a laugh, she'd reached to smack Donny's rump, but she didn't feel that cheerful. There were times she had to wonder if her depression wasn't the symptom of some kind of growing pains, if that's what you called them in middle age. She was growing a new self, and that had to be painful.

She plunged across Stage Street. Through the plate glass windows of Mother Hubbard's Cupboard she caught sight of Sheriff Sweet raising a coffee mug in greeting. The sheriff's big spotted mare Gal was tied outside, next to a planter of lupins, snapdragons, and spicy-smelling carnations. There were a lot more horses downtown since the sheriff had taken to riding Gal. It made up in local color for some of the traffic from the casino. The tribe had their own police and state-of-the-art security vehicles for casino problems.

"Hi there, Marshall Dillon!" she called to the sheriff, letting the screen door slam behind her. She hadn't seen Joan since the Fourth of July concert on the green. "Nice barbershop singing last week. Whew! Who's been trying to burn this place down?"

Mother Hubbard, smudged apron tied like a girdle across a plump middle, gestured to a blackened patch of wall. "Grill fire."

"John on the road?" Chick asked, nimbly spinning a blue vinyl stool with one crooked finger, peeking to see if the sheriff noticed her peach-painted nails. John Hubbard usually worked beside his wife.

"He's hauling logs over to the coast today. With the casino taking all my tourist trade, somebody's got to keep food in the Cupboard." Mother Hubbard laughed at her own joke.

"Did you save the town, Sheriff, and put out the fire?"

Sheriff Sweet took a slug of coffee and tipped her hat back. She had the black hair of the local Native Americans and the cornflower blue eyes of her leggy California mother, a frail beauty whose various illnesses had brought her to Natural Woman Foods for herbal boosters when she'd still been able to get around.

"Not much a good cup of black coffee won't cure," said the sheriff.

Chick looked at the dark drippings down the front of the grill. "I see you doused it with the stuff."

"She about put it out too. I didn't even need to use up the fire extinguisher," said Mother Hubbard.

Chick's heart always got a little fluttery around the taciturn, mysterious sheriff who'd been beanpole Joanie Sweet home from college for the summer, shooting hoops in her driveway one day, and disappeared down south to college the next. Five years later she ran for sheriff when her dad, injured during a chase, turned in his badge to care for Mrs. Sweet. The sheriff's smile always spoke of secrets she'd never reveal, but Chick, had she and Joan been free, thought she knew how to get them out of her.

Mother Hubbard scraped loudly at the grill.

Chick announced, "I'm trucking up to meet my grandson-to-be. That is, he'll be mine once my friends get the paperwork approved. Jeep and Cat are trying to adopt him and they've asked me to be one of his grandmas. Can you believe it? I never expected to do the grandma trip."

"Congrats," the sheriff said with a nod of approval.

As if the sheriff didn't know the whole story from Cat. As if Chick didn't know the sheriff and Cat were in the hottest closet in Waterfall Falls.

"Catch you later!" Chick said. Sweaty-faced Mother Hubbard winked and went back to work. Joan sipped her coffee and watched her. Chick gave her a once-over and answered the secret smile with one of her own and a quiet, "Yum." She hoped the sheriff heard, though she knew better than to expect acknowledgement.

Up sunny Cliff Street she stepped, humming a little Pooh Bear song: "Yum, yum, a hot bum on that one. Yum, yum."

Goddess, she felt good. It was only in the mid-nineties today; a lick of light wind cooled her damp forehead. She always looked forward to the four o'clock summer breezes to cool things down, but four o'clock wasn't anytime soon, and she planned to enjoy this little sweat lodge of an afternoon. She wasn't even going to give her depression the time of day. If it showed its nasty head she'd slam it with a laugh or gulp air into her lungs like someone rescued from drowning. "Exercise and deep breathing," Dr. Wu had instructed her. "Breathe in peace, breathe out your cares."

"Señorita Cheek!" her friend Fina called from the doorway of Fina's Finery. They'd met at a Chamber of Commerce meeting and become friends in the drumming group that met after hours in the back of Natural Women Foods.

Chick bent to hug the warm little fireplug and smelled baby talc. Her nerves twanged with anxiety at the thought of babies. She'd never been drawn to them. But little Luke was four. "Any new Guatemalan vests? Donny's birthday is coming up."

"Next month, Chick, I promise, if I have to go down there to get them myself. I ordered some Donny's size." She held her hand up high to indicate Donny's height.

"And Hernando?" They liked to joke about their two "old men." Fina was an ex-biker mama, retired from the Angelino gang she'd run with.

"He looks so slick the way the casino's dressing them up in old-time dealer clothes, like a gambler in a Western movie."

"That casino's putting a bunch of beans in some local pots."

"Thank God," said Fina, blessing herself. "After all the years he couldn't get work because of his leg when he sold firewood off the truck. Where are you going in such a hurry?"

"I'm checking out my grandson today!"

"Did they give him to your friends already?" Fina asked in a shocked whisper. She gestured Chick into her shop doorway under a pink and yellow donkey piñata. "It's official?"

A logging truck laden with thin, uniformly sized trunks from a tree farm shifted gears to climb to the freeway entrance. Diesel fumes filled the air.

Chick explained. "Not yet, but foster parents don't grow on trees, especially when the kid is a disabled four-year-old with parents out on bail and on the lam. I'm so freaked over who he'll act like. Forget me being Grandma if he's a strutting little banty rooster with M.C.'s conniving mind and a rank brown ponytail like his. I'm not even sure I can live with him looking like Pennylane. I remember her when she wasn't much more than ten years older than Luke is now."

"Never mind," Fina said, shooing her along. "You go meet the kid. He'll be your greatest love no matter what he looks like. Take it from me. It broke my heart when my daughter married a redheaded gringo. But their kids? I'm nuts about them."

"I'm not helping to unleash another M.C. on the world."

"No grandson of yours would dare to be an M.C.!"

"This is true," Chick answered smartly, doubting her own words.

She didn't know whether to sail up the next block or to creep. The closer she got, the more nervous she felt. Why hadn't they asked her to be an aunt? That would have been more in line with where her head was at. Jeep and Cat had intended to bestow a great honor by making her a grandmother, but was that how Jeep really saw her the first day she'd stumbled down the steps into Natural Woman Foods? Had she made herself ridiculous flirting with a kid who looked at her and saw a crone? Inside, she felt like a kid herself.

At the Rocket gas station old Regis Rice came gimping over. "How's my favorite big gal?" he shouted. "Can I fill your tank today?"

It was windier up here by the freeway, and noisy from logging trucks and triple-trailers making time on this straightaway. Chick was glad for the bulk of her long dress and quilted, puffy jacket near this retired satyr who reeked of tobacco. Still, at least old Regis thought she was chasing material just as much as Donny did.

She laughed as usual and yelled back, "I'm not driving, Regis!"

"Oh, I can do the driving, big gal."

Poor old goat. She waved him off, amused and not amused all at once. He couldn't hear a thing she said, so they always had the same exchange. What if Luke grew up to work at the BP station, a slick grease monkey who sold cheap chains to drivers headed over the pass and raised the price when it snowed? Chick would struggle by on a walker twenty years from now, old Regis gone, and an oily guy in a BP cap with M.C.'s face would call her Grandma. She couldn't deal with it. No way, she swore, lifting her own tangle of still honey-brown hair off her sweaty neck.

She was already in the freeway's dank shadow, and she almost turned back. Would Jeep and Cat pull a trip like that on her, introduce an M.C. clone with no warning? If they even saw the resemblance—Jeep had only seen M.C. in the dark in the midst of much confusion, and Cat probably only saw him in the papers when the police were looking for him. Gulp that air! Walk faster!

The traffic thundered overhead, and several purple foxgloves waved at the end of the overpass. Something nagged at her. Was the remembering part of her brain drying up? Had she destroyed something with all those hallucinogens? Pennylane, M.C.'s wife, had mentioned the child's daddy—that the boy had never heard his daddy pick guitar—or was it a banjo that he picked? Jeep said the boy had his father's musical genes. It sounded as if she could stop worrying. M.C. wasn't his birth father. With a little luck the rest of his genes would overshadow M.C.'s influence as a father figure. Some people shouldn't be allowed to raise kids.

Still, it was an honor to get appointed Grandma. Jeep and Cat had invited her, Donny, Clara, and Hector—two sets of grandparents. They'd made a little ceremony of it, presenting fancy handmade certificates and taking pictures so Luke could have them when he was older. This was better, like Grandmama-to-be Donny said, than letting a speck of DNA decide who was family.

Chick emerged from the shadow of the overpass and continued under the wicked blazing sun around a grassy curve. The incline was steady as she entered the moneyed part of Waterfall Falls. She could see Cat's grandparents' home almost at the crest of the hill. The grandfather was a banker, she'd heard. That would give Luke a running start—money for music lessons and a good college once he was cured of not talking. And he would talk. She imagined an M.C. junior in a dark crew cut and double-breasted pinstripe. Would he look like his banker side or like an underground gangster? Or like his birth father? She'd ask Jeep if she could get a photo of him.

By the time she reached the retaining wall that shored up the proud houses, she was wiped out. She paused to catch her breath and pat her face dry with a pink bandanna. The garages here were all at street level, made of concrete that had cracked over the years. Next to Cat's garage seventeen steps led to a landing, then another eight to the porch. She grasped the hot rail, but let go of it fast, and climbed. Sweat ran down her back. She hoped she smelled all right. The house loomed above her, washed pink stucco with gray-blue trim. Two large windows were set to either side of the dark wood door. Living room and dining room, she guessed, dark and cool on a summer's day, but gloomy in winter. The house seemed a little overbearing. Maybe she should have waited until Sunday, when the store was closed, so she could have come with Donny. She could turn around and go back.

Then the door flew open. There was Jeep, bouncing on the balls of her feet, a humongous smile pushing her cheeks up till her eyes were almost closed. Her newly spiked hair looked incongruous in this neighborhood. A small blonde head peered out from behind her, one hand clutching Jeep's black jeans. No, this child looked nothing like M.C. and barely like Pennylane. Luke's open face was round, not sharp-featured, and his broad smile was entirely Jeep's.

"Blonde?" Chick exclaimed. She quickly touched her own light hair. "My grandson is blonde?"

Jeep reached around and tousled Luke's hair. The boy grinned and ducked. "Come out and say hi to your Grandmother Chick."

In that moment Chick felt something new in the vicinity of her heart that reminded her of the way vanilla ice cream must feel under a flow of hot fudge sauce, a surge of warmth and a sensation of melting. Luke looked so helpless. Here was someone that truly didn't know how to do anything for himself.

"I never got to care for such a small person before," Chick said. "He's beautiful."

Luke hadn't yet come out of hiding. "He's a pretty cool bean, aren't you, dude? Let's go inside so you two can get used to each other."

Released, Luke ran ahead of them. A large cream-colored cat with patchy brown markings flung himself down at Chick's feet.

"That's Lump Sum," Jeep explained. "He thinks he's hungry. Ignore him."

Chick laughed. "He looks like a Lump Sum."

"When Cat inherited him his name was Simba."

Luke cast a shy glance back when he reached the first door.

"You need to practice now? Go for it, dude." Jeep turned to her. "Was he stoked when he saw that drum pad. We leave the sound very low because he's in here every chance he gets."

Jeep, despite her hair, seemed to have grown up by a decade. Her energy was smoother, more self-assured now.

"Luke plays drums like his grandmother? Does Luke know what he's doing?"

"I've taught him one riff which he's still learning. Little kids like to do their own thing, though, and Luke's majorly inventive. Sometimes he plays along with the radio or a CD, but mostly he's, like, an explorer. He'll play a simple beat, listen, repeat it. That's the uncanny thing. The kid can remember his moves and repeat them over and over, even the next day. I talked to my dad about it, and he says that's way prodigious."

Jeep started to move away from the door, but Chick laid a hand on her arm. "May I stay here with him and watch?"

"Your call. I'll go chill in the kitchen. George probably wants in by now." Jeep started to leave, but turned back. "Are you sure you're cool with this? You look like you never saw a rug rat before."

Chick forced herself to look away from her grandson. "This will sound very strange, Jeep, but I don't think I really ever did."

CHAPTER TWENTY-SIX

Game Plan

I've always been this way, out of bed in the morning like a junkie for daylight. My mother says that on the way to my first day of kindergarten, I led her to a classroom of grown-up third-graders. I skipped a grade, did college in three years, and I guess I'm still in a rush."

Katie was changing cartridges, fumbling a bit in her rush to get everything on tape. Already she was looking forward to the weeks she'd spend editing. She'd found a tiny soundproofed studio with all the equipment she would need in a revamped garage up in Greenhill. The guy had agreed to rent it to her for a full month whenever she was ready because he had a day job and could only use it nights.

Clara White said, "You're one of those type ace personalities they talk about on the TV." She was squinting as if watching bright electrical charges orbit Katie's head.

"You don't get many of those around here," Hector White commented from his recliner by the woodstove. He hadn't moved since she'd arrived. On this second day of shooting, in the scene she thought of as The Indoor Life, she decided to tape him on his chair, his wife across the big kitchen the way they really lived instead of mashed together on the sofa. The TV was going, Hector half-watching "Live with Regis."

"Why do you say that?" she asked, film rolling.

Hector pushed the recliner back with a groan. Now he was man of the house, not the nervous creature who cracked his knob-like knuckles alone with her out in the meadow where his sheep grazed and he couldn't look straight at the camera.

"A person gets out in the woods, puts his whole self into taking down a big old spruce—a person does that for a few hours and he's in another world. There's no place out there for hurry-up."

"Cool."

This was excellent. Hector had retired from logging when the industry began its slide downhill. Last time he talked about how, like a lot of the guys, he'd worked for years with a bum knee and decided, the next time he hurt it at work, he'd put in for workman's comp and buy whatever livestock he could with his retirement. The insurance people, he'd told her, had hassled him, but he bided his time and eventually they came through. Never used a lawyer either, he bragged—lawyers were for people in a god-awful rush, and he got a couple more sheep instead of paying lawyer fees.

"My son lives in Portland," Hector said today. "He tells me he feels the same when he jogs as I used to in the woods."

"A runner's high?" Katie asked, jotting a quick note to herself to ask how the Whites felt about environmentalists.

"There you go. When I falled trees for a living, it was what being in a church is supposed to make me feel. The preacher down at the Community Bible Church is always saying we should get high on God, not on liquor and drugs. Where's God if not in those trees?" he finished, pointing out the window. "Speaking of church, listen to this one. Did Adam ever have a date with Eve?"

"No, just a fig leaf?" Katie joked.

"Close, but no banana. It wasn't a date, it was an apple."

"What are you blaspheming about now, Pa?" Clara called over the water running into the kitchen sink. Dishwashing suds rose steadily, their sharp perfume striking at Katie's nostrils.

"You're like me," she said. "Work's a mission."

"I don't know as a person would say it exactly like that," Hector answered.

"When I'm into it. Tripping over cables, clock ticking, crew running around like the sky is falling. It's a zoo. I stay there until I'm off the air. It takes me hours to chill."

The cities seemed so long ago. Even her arrival in Waterfall Falls seemed a distant past. Since then Jeep had turned into a mom, she'd watched a town get strung along by its own vigilante, she'd taken and lost a new lover, and she'd learned a bit about who she really was. She felt as old as Yoda without the wisdom.

It wasn't that she hadn't been around, or that the combination of R and Abeo was a big deal in itself. She'd had fun and loved with abandon before coming to Waterfall Falls. The day after she'd refused to film R and Abeo, she had forced her journalist self to ask R what had happened with Abeo. R claimed that Abeo had never removed her own clothing or allowed R to touch her in any intimate way. Katie's anger had turned to puzzlement.

R had been wrapped in a woven Mexican blanket, eyes aglitter with the reflected light of her oil lamp, remembering aloud the whole shitty scene. "We fell on each other like beasts," R told her. "I've never experienced anything like it." Toto gave an anguished caw under his cloth covering. Katie had felt as stripped and ripped off as she had when she'd slipped from the cabin the night before, leather jacket and Sony in hand, and cleansed her lungs with damp, pine-scented air.

Hector brought the recliner down like he was crashing an airplane. "You know what the first step is before Henry Mancini or even old Beethoven could write a tune?" He paused. "It's me, cutting the timber that makes their pianos."

She'd managed to put the Sony back on him just in time.

"I don't know why these blockhead environmentalists can't understand it," Hector fumed. She wouldn't have to ask her question after all. "They wave signs—what's the poster board and the stakes that hold it up made of, if not wood? They plan their foolishness in meetings— what do they think the chairs and table are made from? They look out the window at the forest—and let me tell you, there's plenty of forest left—that window frame they're looking out of is likely pure wood."

Clara jumped in, clanging pots, "And for what? So some bird doesn't have to move? I love the birds. There's swallows galore who nest under the eaves of the garage right now, making a mess. But it's the loggers who have to move if they can't put food on the table for their babies. Those birds have taken good care of themselves since the beginning of time. If they disappear, maybe it's God's will. Tell those green people we're all going to disappear sooner or later. Maybe it's time for those trees to make space for some other things to grow."

"What about your grandchildren?" Katie asked. "If you cut all the trees scientists say the whole eco-system—"

"Echo-schmeko," Clara replied, vigorously scrubbing a pot. "My grandkids need those jobs more than some bird does."

Hector said, "I'd rather my grandkids work in the woods instead of cooped up in some factory making chips for the damn computers. What the heck kind of thing is that anyway, chips? Why are we fighting with the Japs over who gets to make fancy chips? Wood chips are good enough for me."

"You won't find wood in one of those computers," Clara scoffed.

Katie had seen long trailer-trucks bearing cages of wood chips on I-5 and supposed pressed-wood furniture was made from them. "I did a special on silicon chips," she said, and was surprised as she explained them at how much she'd retained, especially about the dependence of the West Coast on the little devices.

Clara ignored her husband and turned to Katie. "Listen at her go, Pa. If TV's what rings your bells, honey, what are you doing in Waterfall Falls? I remember when you first came to town with that spike-haired girl. You were at Chick's place looking like somebody off the TV."

Hector let out a roar of laughter. "That's what she is, Ma! Somebody off the TV!"

Clara dunked a pie plate. "You think I don't know that? But she wasn't in New York City. She was here in Waterfall Falls, makeup, funny clothes, and all."

"New York!" exclaimed Katie, turning off the Sony and settling at the kitchen table. "In my dreams." But her silent voice knew this documentary might get her where she wanted to be in the end. Katie Delgado, the filmmaker's filmmaker, the bright star from Southern California via the rural Northwest.

This place had changed her fast. She'd traveled here wanting to rewrite the script that had ruled her all her life. She'd imagined a never-ending music festival where free-loving women cast off their clothing and played hard. She'd imagined her own spirit thriving in the nurturing mountains. On the way north she'd stopped at Mt. Shasta and, after she sent Jeep to walk around the town, had waited for her cloud crown to lift, and to lift her to a spiritual level she'd never before experienced, but neither happened.

Instead she'd found R's world, with its court of loyal handmaidens, more intense in its way than TV land, lit with the flickering wisdom Katie was struggling to learn. This women's land business was so effing weird. Only through her Sony did she begin to see the patterns and purposes in a way of life so alien to her. In the city she'd thought that to be truly alive she must be a perpetual-motion machine. By following R's mellowed-out style she'd planned to blend the old into a new Katie, but R's was a strangely purposeful peace, like she was acting a part. And that made Katie wonder if serenity and ambition were complete contradictions.

She grabbed a dishcloth. "May I dry?"

"Of course. He'd never pick up a hand to help."

"Aw, Clara. You tell me I'm a clumsy oaf around the house."

"I'd rather have my dishes whole, thank you."

"Who trimmed back your honeysuckle this morning in this heat? I don't know why she encourages that weed. Sometimes I think I'd rather have the poison oak. At least she'd let me get rid of that."

"You be careful what you wish. I remember that summer when all you'd talk about was the heat, heat, heat and how you wished for a snowy winter. That next winter we stood and watched those cedars we had out back bend under the weight of the wet snow and the wind during the night. We got the kids up and took them to the living room and told them we were having a slumber party in case any of the trees came down on the house. Nothing fell on the house, but they came down in the pasture where it was more damp. Trees fell for two days after that storm."

"And you're still giving me credit for that storm. Just call me Father Nature."

What a contrast there was between Hector's geniality and Clara's disagreeable manner. Yet Clara kept their home so bright, with pink plaid curtains tied back from the big one-pane windows, gleaming pink and cream linoleum on the kitchen floor, and a cheerful red plastic tablecloth. Now that the suds had settled Katie smelled again the warm fruit of the pie Clara had earlier pulled from her freezer to heat.

"How do you two do it?" she asked, her life suddenly in deep focus: R and Abeo, Clara and Hector, Katie halfway between the two. "How have you stayed together for so long? How did you know this is the one?"

She'd been fascinated the first time she'd watched R sit in a circle spilling her struggles to the women around the bonfire. She'd thought, "I've finally found her."

Rituals were a really good idea, a seasonal review like TV sweeps, letting go of the bummer stuff and dreams and good intentions. It could be that preparing to talk was the most valuable part of the women's circles, making a time to think about the season past. But the actual sitting in a circle—truth? The thought made her itchy. She wasn't made to be still hour after hour like at school. It was bore-ing. If she could keep a camera in front of her face—then she'd be doing something.

Smoke had stung her eyes at the equinox bonfire, but still she'd watched the gray-braided head. When the gourd had passed to her, R had intoned her loneliness, her struggle to accept that she would not again be partnered. She must have spoken of the triumphs and troubles of the season past—they all did—but Katie hadn't heard that. She'd sprung into rescue mode, her liaison with Jeep doing a fast fade into ancient history even before she'd broken up with her.

Her leap had ended in R's bed. Before R, sex had been a romp. With her it was a form of holy exaltation, a spirit union that needed accompaniment by a slow trance music number. Gawd, she could not believe she was thinking such cheesy thoughts and that this walking bottlebrush of a straight woman, Clara, should bring them out in her.

Clara patted her permed hair, her eyes on a crowd of photographs that sat on a small electric organ: babies, graduations, weddings, grandbabies. Katie counted twenty-six frames, and some were collages. "You don't want to hear about all that nonsense before we were married."

Katie had finished dryings the dishes. Now she stopped sorting silverware to exclaim, "I do!" She tapped an index finger on the worn wooden drawer and wondered if Hector, loving Clara and the home they shared, had crafted it. "I have this huge need to know how so I can do forever myself."

R hadn't wanted forever.

Katie sometimes found herself wandering the land while Abeo consumed R's attention. It was called women's land, but R owned it like she'd come to practically own Katie. She remembered the tour R had given Jeep and herself when they had first arrived. R showed off the terraced gardens and sweat lodge as if they were her accomplishments and not built by volunteers. The women who were the land's real caretakers now took care of abandoned Katie. The land women seemed fascinated and paralyzed by Abeo's strangeness, difference. They were obviously trying not to walk on any politically sensitive eggs—or unborn chickens—and were like kids pretending so hard they weren't staring at a disabled person that they never saw the person at all. They drew Katie in from the night, gave her chamomile tea, and chastely shared their beds. Their eyes turned mournful when they looked at her. She might have been widowed. She felt humiliated, an outcast taken in by a strange feudal tribe. On those days she did not leap out of bed eager for life.

Katie dried the twelfth piece of silverware before she slid the drawer shut and went to the pictures. "Cool!" she said, pointing. This might get Clara talking. "Your wedding picture. You were way young."

Clara hadn't exactly been good-looking even then. "That's an excellent dress." Casually, she aimed the Sony at her.

"It wasn't fancy, but it was white. Nowadays just anyone marries in white. Then it meant something."

"Meant a *lot* to Clara," muttered Hector.

"I can identify." For the first time in her life she could. R had told her that their bodies were sacred, to be shared sparingly, respectfully. Remembering that, a few nights after Abeo had arrived, she'd stormed into R's cabin, desperate with the pain of rejection, intent on reminding R about her beliefs. Abeo had quickly covered herself with an afghan, R shielding her as if Katie were dangerous.

"We'll go up to the loft," R offered.

Katie had wailed, "I need to talk with you. Alone!"

R, smiling with a frozen-looking sympathy, seemed to grow into her own looming shadow on the cabin wall. "Look at you."

It was hard to keep sharp, living from tent to cabin. The few clothes she'd come with had grown too large and too city for the land. Her leather jacket, belts, and shoes had finally gone into storage along with her TV drag. She wore clothing the land women shared with her— sweat pants in every shade of purple, layers of short- and long-sleeved political T-shirts, and at night, flannels and thermals, sweats, even a striped homemade wool watch cap because she was so cold all the time. She could have bought her own clothes, but she was doing a dissolve into an entirely new Katie, and she simply didn't know what to buy.

R said, "You're letting yourself go, Kate, obsessing like this about my life. Why aren't you working? You're one of these people who is her work. Why are you haunting me instead?"

Haunting! Was she a little girl with lice and hand-me-down clothes, ashamed of a new kind of poverty she couldn't name? What a babe in the woods she'd been. No more, Goddess willing, was she going to let R twist her reality.

Hector shot back his recliner. "It hasn't been all hearts and flowers by a long shot. Look at this." He held up one of his few tufts of hair to reveal the knot of a white scar over an ear. "A flying skillet."

"Clara?" Katie asked.

"None other," Hector responded.

"Tell your part, Pa."

"I raised a hand to her. I truly never would hurt her."

"You never came home worse for the drink again, did you, Mister?"

Clara turned to Katie. "The boy and his sister could have seen him stumble around here, reeking of it, pawing at me. I put a stop to that."

"You never thought to leave each other?"

"You'd be a poor woman if you gave me a penny for every time I thought to drive him out of this house he built," Clara answered.

Hector thrust his chin up and his chest out. "She's a little spitfire all right."

"So you just—"

"Stayed," said Clara.

"No matter what."

"Maybe because," Hector said with a knowing nod.

"Did anyone ever, like, come between you two?"

Clara and Hector did not look at each other. The room felt chilly. Katie hugged herself.

Hector moved to the woodstove, opened the flue, then poked inside the heavy door with an iron rod, and set two pieces of wood on the coals. The house was so well insulated and shaded by carefully pruned, healthy trees that they kept the stove going even in summer. "There were months at a time I'd go logging in Alaska, Washington, Idaho. A person might make a mistake."

Clara scrubbed the sink, shaking Bon Ami like it was a fast-acting poison. "Men. He always came home."

"Say, I forgot to tell you this one, Katie. Which side of a church does a yew tree grow on?"

She smiled at silly, irrepressible Hector. "I give up."

"On the outside!"

"Don't laugh," Clara said. "It only encourages him."

Katie went to the window. A peacock was displaying the magnificence of his tail, and the peahens were ignoring him.

It wasn't simple. Even straight people had an uphill climb. Still, the way Clara and Hector were living had alerted her to dreams she hadn't known she had, just as R had made her aware of a startling passionate spirituality in herself that was propelling her beyond her old ambitions.

Waterfall Falls was not the kind of place she'd imagined herself doing the discovery thing. Had she ever made a decision to stay in this place? It was so odd, how she'd gotten here—just a week off after all those interviews, on the way back to the Bay Area to find another job and get sucked into the expensive city life—just a week to visit Jeep's friend Solstice, then another week. Then, because she was between jobs, camping out at the library in Greenhill and forcing herself to send out resumes, while the thought of returning to a studio became more and more repugnant, and the hold this place had on her got stronger. Her little radio ate batteries like a kitten drank milk. She'd thought she was in R's thrall, but really it was the mountains, the beating heart of something, something they called the Goddess at Spirit Ridge. It was so close to the surface here she felt like every time she touched a tree or let icy water in a creek run through her fingers, she was touching the soul of the universe.

Someday, she had dreamed, she and R would tell young women in pain about how they'd "just stayed," meaning together. Now she would tell them how it was to have stayed on alone, how she'd begun to feel bigger and even powerful, and had prepared in Waterfall Falls to take her place in the big world where, like Chick, she would neither cower nor pretend to be something she wasn't. But imagining that day, she felt a pang of such aloneness she had to sit back down. Goddess, she needed—what? who? These two could show her the way if she could get them to open up a little more.

"You're not giving me much of a game plan here," she urged.

Clara barked, "Could be because life's no game."

CHAPTER TWENTY-SEVEN

Silk-hand Butches

Donny and Jeep burst through the door of Natural Woman Foods like puppies playing. Their clothes and pants were soaked. Donny's fragrant string of fish dripped on the floor as she and Jeep fenced along the aisle with their rods.

Chick, inspecting the ears of corn balanced on her lap, laughed so hard an ear went tumbling to the floor. Donny feinted around Jeep and rushed back to kiss Chick full on the mouth, picking up the corn and depositing it in her lap in one economical swoop as she did.

"You taste like cinnamon roll, Donny Donaldson. Is that why I was two short this morning?"

"Yo, R!" Donny said over her shoulder by way of a greeting, as she clattered after Jeep up the old wooden stairs in the back to the apartment. For a moment there was quiet in the store except for whirring refrigeration units. Then she heard the blast of music upstairs. Donny had fallen in love with the singer Mary J. Blige and had to hear her every minute of the day.

"They bring the spring inside with them," R said softly.

"Butches are outrageous! You can't help but love them."

"Where does Donny get the energy at her age?"

"She'll live to a hundred. Her mother's seventy-six and still working. I plan to be around as long as Donny. I don't want to miss a minute of her."

"I'm glad Abeo slowed down before she got to me."

Chick studied R's pale face and the dark smudges under her eyes. "Do you feel as dragged out as you look?"

"Tired, very tired."

Chick had told Donny as they lay late in bed this last warm summer Sunday morning, "R's not someone I love being around. She reminds me too much of my mom and her tight-lipped don't-let-the-anger-show depressions. I'm drawn to R's spirit. She's like some kind of bird that's not born to fly, yet keeps trying. I think it's why she's such a good teacher. No one knows the mechanics of flying better than a creature without working wings. Even if we didn't connect that way, R's so melancholy, how could I turn my back on the poor woman?"

"You're all soft underbelly right now, Chick. You don't have enough ups in you to be giving any away to that downer. You watch your precious self, okay?" Donny had advised.

She could hear Donny and Jeep scraping chairs and dropping shoes overhead. "I suspect there's plenty of fish for dinner. Can you stay?" Donny would never forgive her if R took her up on it.

"I don't eat flesh," R said, pulling her chin back as if offended. "Abeo's with Dr. Wu getting her shots. Afterwards we'll go back up the mountain."

"Shots?"

"Her hormones. She's difficult to be with when they start taking effect."

Chick laughed. Donny was right. R was draining, but spending time with her made Chick more sure of her own mental health than anything else she did. "It must be like PMS. What a trip for her. In the old days, when I still got PMS and did dope, I'd get stoned and clean house for hours or eat nothing but sweets for days—or both. If I had acid, I'd save it until I started bleeding. Mellowed me right out. I was Sweet Creek, my cramps were the point in the pond where the waterfall hits—heavy water, but it whirlpooled like coming. Did you ever notice how close cramps feel to orgasmic spasms?"

"I had a total hysterectomy at thirty-two after my second caesarian. And a husband who demanded my orgasms in a way that took the pleasure out of them. He wanted to think of himself as a good lover."

"Wow, heavy shit. I can't imagine you under some man's thumb, or believe you did that whole era as a housewife while I tie-dyed American flags. Now you're living the revolution and I'm a capitalist pig! Life is too strange. Don't you love it?"

"All too much," R said without explanation. She had few words during her visits. She always sat at the small scratched maple table by the window, hands locked around a mug of organic coffee, a weary look on her face.

Chick was drawn to her like a healing magnet, offering pastries, putting on the verbal equivalent of a floor show. "I talk too much when you're here, R."

R's laugh was so faint she could barely hear it over a Manhattan Transfer CD. "Your world amuses and comforts me. Somehow, I feel part of the stories you tell."

"I wish you could've been part of that kaleidoscope time." Chick ran a fingernail through a shallow split in the table to clean it out. "From what you've told me, the Jefferson Airplane probably hurt your ears. There I was trying to keep Woodstock alive forever, and you thought *Sesame Street* was the revolution, right? I was freaking out on magic buttons because Jimi and Janis crash-landed, and you were taking tranqs so you wouldn't fly."

R's smile lingered as she sipped her coffee.

Chick remembered younger photographs of herself. "I lived in two different worlds. During the days I hung out with long-haired bi girls, getting stoned in the sunshine, drinking wine, and watching the fog eat San Francisco block by block. They always left me by nightfall for their male musicians and dealers. I'd drift to a barstool, listen to Anne Murray, and dream that a real lesbian like Donny would lead me to the dance floor." She clapped her hands once and laughed. "Now *I'm* the real lesbian, can you dig it?"

R put down her mug and folded her hands.

"They were something in those days," Chick continued, "the bar dykes. Then it was passing butches. Now it's Name That Gender." Her insides fluttered with the grand memory of being a brand-new powerfully feminine lesbian. "The boys on the streets wore granny glasses and love beads and flowing manes, but the butch girls in the bars wouldn't be caught dead in such sissy-wear. They'd curse out the draft dodgers and wolf whistle at the gentle generation. After all, gays have been into free love from day one, and we never got a Broadway musical out of it."

R's laugh was more an exhalation of breath. She covered her mouth as the laughter became a cough.

"I used to close the bars. There was one hole-in-the-wall near the Marina that held Christian services on Sunday afternoons using a drunken minister. The straight owners made up for supplying queers with a place to dance by offering us a way to salvation. Then there was the hotel bar in the Tenderloin where married ladies who dared wandered off from home while their husbands worked late. You would have liked that one."

"I wish I'd known a little more about myself then."

"I was having too much fun for introspection. Were you dancing to "Bennie and the Jets" at straight living-room parties while I did tribal group dancing at gay-lib bashes? Did you even know Elton and Bernie were an item?" she asked, flicking a wrist, pinky first, in the air. "We loved it."

When R smiled at her out of intensely focused eyes, Chick went on. "I was selling classified ads at a newspaper. Practically our whole department was gay. I remember one holiday party when the manager, a tiny sassy butch who wore button-down shirtwaist dresses, got tipsy. We danced in the hallway to an eight-track of Isaac Hayes. The two queens from the mail room screeched with laughter. The few hets looked like they wished they could have a liberation movement and have that much fun too."

She looked away from her memories at R's eyes and thought she'd never seen a sadder face.

"I would have liked to meet one of your fairy-tale butches."

"They're all around you. Sometimes, R, I feel like I got it on with one after another of those dynamite silk-hand butches back in 1969 and lay around stoned to Jethro Tull for ten years until it was time to disco with the gayboys under the light-throwing balls. Then I got up, found a disco-butch, and danced for another decade."

They both looked out the window at the sound of a police car. Joan Sweet sped by, blue roof light strobing. A century ago, she thought, the sheriff would have been a man urging speed from his four-legged mount. And she, Chick—what would she have been? A bar owner with a string of girls upstairs? She'd heard that had been the first use of this building, before it became a feed store.

"Poor R, did you really miss the decadent decade? The Allman Brothers, Taj Mahal, Joy of Cooking. Who cared what was playing as long as it was slow. Or faster than the speed of speed. 'I Will Survive,' 'Voulez Vous Coucher Avec Moi,' the Village People—Goddess! The music never ended, and we ended the seventies with Meg Christian and Holly Near in Berkeley blowing us all away."

Again, she looked out the window. It was early afternoon and Stage Street was deserted. The saloon smelled of sawdust and spilled beer. Her ladies of the night were resting upstairs in preparation for the cowboys on the cattle run coming through later. One of the girls, Cassie Ann, was her bed warmer, though Chick yearned after the widow

Hortense, who had pulled on her husband's old pants and taken over the running of the family spread.

She brought herself back to thoroughly twenty-first-century R. "What can I recommend as a pick-me-up?"

"I've tried them all."

"Maybe it's time to see a doctor."

R scowled. "They've done me enough harm."

"Medical doctors?"

"The caesarians I mentioned?"

Chick waited for a caustic criticism.

"Unnecessary. I don't know if the ob-gyns were reimbursed more for them by the insurance companies or if they feared malpractice suits, but I know now the procedure was used more often than circumstances warranted. It infuriates me to have been denied natural childbirth for the convenience of this patriarchal so-called health care system."

"Still, something could be wrong, R."

"Oh, something's wrong all right. But you don't carry anything that can shrink a lump in my breast, do you?" R held her left breast up like she was offering a piece of rotting fruit.

Chick felt the goose bumps rise on her forearms. She'd lost an old Chicago friend to breast cancer not four years ago and, 2000 miles away, hadn't been able to be there for her. What was a bit of depression to this?

She rose from her seat and moved to the other side of the booth to engulf R in her arms and hold her to her chest, all too aware that she needed the hug as badly as R must. "You poor baby. When did you find out? How big is the lump?"

R didn't struggle at all. She might even have relaxed her stiff neck for a moment to lay her head against Chick's softness, or, Chick thought with a silent chuckle, R might only have been finding a more comfortable position. Poor proud R wouldn't admit to a weakness if— if it killed her. She rocked her a little and then, because an unfamiliar customer was parking outside, let go.

The door opened, letting in the noise of the freeway and reminding Chick that there was a world outside this pod of bad news. The customer was a traveler wanting a cold drink, cookies, and directions. When Chick returned to the booth, R was cleaning her glasses with a napkin.

"I noticed it about three months ago. It was a little smaller than one of the giant marbles my sons had as kids. They called them jumbos."

"And now?"

"I can't tell. It may have grown some or my memory may have shrunk the original."

"Pain?"

"No, it's not painful. The glands under my arms are tender, but they're far from the lump."

Her own breasts ached. Now it was R who was alone and naked on a rocky mountaintop crag. "Has Abeo felt it? Katie?" She could not quell this urge to rescue every hurt creature, but really, whose life could she save other than her own?

R looked out the window toward the sky. "Katie would want to do a documentary on living with breast cancer. Abeo's wonderful." She spoke even more slowly than usual. "I believe she *is* a woman trapped in a man's body. There's some sort of acculturation that takes place as we are raised as women, however, some nameless intuitiveness, that she lacks. If I told her, she'd turn into a round-the-clock nurse in bed and out. That would be the only way she could express empathy, solidarity, understanding. Whereas you simply threw your arms around me and held me. And then you asked the right questions—because you're also at risk, so you know what to ask. I'm sure Abeo would be perfect for an HIV positive person, but I imagine even your silk-handed butches would understand better than Abeo."

"Oh, especially a butch. She'd feel it right here," she told R, touching her fingertips to her solar plexus. "She'd have the double whammy of being unable to protect a femme against something nasty and knowing it could happen to her too." She wanted R to get off her high horse about butches and femmes and to understand before it was too late. "I don't think anyone on earth is more sensitive to women's pain than a butch lesbian. Except maybe a femme, of course."

R looked blank.

"So you haven't told either of them?" She couldn't imagine not telling something like this to Donny. She would want all the support she could get. When R shook her head, Chick said, "Whatever works for you, sweetheart, is fine, but you're still describing a good-sized lump. Aren't you scared?"

"Not as frightened as I am of the medico-pharmaceutical establishment. I trust the Goddess to bring me healing."

"R, the Goddess expects us to take care of ourselves."

"I don't smoke or drink or expose my breasts to X-rays."

"Do you keep your fat intake low?" She was being a nag. What else could she be when she felt so helpless?

"Of course. Nor do I wear a bra or antiperspirant."

"And your family history?"

Her expression as flat as ever, R said, "Radical mastectomies were all the rage when my mother was diagnosed. They took both her breasts, burned her with radiation, poisoned her with chemotherapy, and she took insufferably long to die."

"You're not bitter."

"I'd rather die sooner with all my sacred parts than have the man's technology chip away at me for years."

Chick kept herself from throwing her hands up in disgust. R was a fool, but she could think of nothing that would change her mind. "Vitamin A is good. How much C do you do?"

"Whatever I get from fruit and greens."

"You need to be taking 5,000 to 10,000 mg. daily."

"Where are you finding your information?"

She rolled her necklace's tiny green crystal between her fingers, wanting to give it to R for healing, but it had been a gift to her from Donny, and she needed its energy. "In between Western novels and lesbian romances, I read nutritional books."

"By women?"

"When I can find them."

"Even the books by women draw their information primarily from male sources. We know who profits from their expensive therapies, herbal or not. No, this is between the Goddess and myself."

"I don't know if you're brave or crazy. I'd be in surgery so fast I'd ask Donny to wheel in my gurney."

"In the wild I would heal myself or die. This," R added with one hand on her breast, "is benign. I practice validations continually."

"I'm getting you to a doctor."

She heard the side door slam. Jeep passed the front window, obviously avoiding R, the snake who'd stolen Katie from her. Chick watched her push into the street on her skateboard, a damp spot on her purple backpack from the wet fish. She waved without looking at them and headed down toward the freeway. Mary J. Blige and her electronic sounds thumped upstairs.

It was a terrifying thought, but Chick wondered if by next spring Jeep would need to avoid R—if R might be gone.

CHAPTER TWENTY-EIGHT

Garage Sale Dandy

A ren't you the garage sale dandy!" Hector exclaimed.
The phrase stopped her dead—almost the words Sarah had used about her. Way cool. "What do you think?" she asked. She planted a dusty brown fedora on her head, set her harmonica in her mouth, and danced a mock soft-shoe.

Hector cleared his throat, his face went red, and he pitched his voice high. "Co-ol!" He gave Jeep the high five she'd taught him. "And look at young Luke, all decked out in his Sunday best."

With his helmet and knee pads, elbow and wrist guards, Luke wore skateboarder grunge shorts and a Teletubbies T-shirt. He insisted on wearing his gear and carrying his miniboard whenever they went out.

Since she'd gone on unemployment, she and Luke spent their afternoons bopping around town. Not making a living was driving her bonkers. The school had let her finish out the term, but wouldn't renew her contract as long as Luke lived with her. And there were fewer jobs out there than the last time she'd been hunting. At least Luke, a foster kid, had medical coverage. So afternoons they'd visit Chick and Donny, then the playground. It helped when Clara and Hector picked them up Fridays, treated them to lunch at the Dairy Queen, and took them to garage sales up the mountain roads.

Sometimes she looked at Luke and was startled by the amazing road he'd led her to. If Spruce, the local Tarot maven, had read her cards and told her this was next on the agenda she'd have said Madonna and child was one thing, but Jeep and child? No way. But stranger things had happened.

At band practice the week before she'd been talking with Muriel, who claimed no knowledge of The Storm.

"You are so out of it, Mur," Jeep had said. "The Seattle Storm? The WNBA? Women's basketball? Do you even know we have a women's league?"

Muriel had turned the tables and scoffed, "So you're into boy games too?"

"Get real. You're the one sharing the land with a trannie."

"You mean Abeo? Spare me! One of these days, I'm going to put a list of who's who at women's land on your violin so you stop getting us all mixed up. She's not at Dawn Farm—she's R's partner!"

Jeep felt her hands burn. "R's partner? Did Katie and the Rat break up?"

"No one broke up. It's Katie and R *and* Abeo now."

"Holy holodeck, that's disgusting."

"You're going to bring up a male child and you think that's disgusting?"

Muriel had hit below the belt with that Katie news. Katie with a trans man? There was no way. The land women were focusing on Katie, the newcomer city girl, when it was R acting so weird. Somebody needed to tell them that Katie was pure lesbian. In San Francisco it had been Katie always steering them to women's spaces, Katie avoiding the Castro because there were too many men there, Katie putting in her time in the straight media world so later she could go out on her own and do women-only documentaries or whatever. Even this story she'd heard Katie was working on, the environmental thing, you could bet the women in it would turn out to be the heroes, no question. She smiled to herself. If Katie was spending time with R and Abeo, it was for the story angle. Katie's camera was kind of like a semipermeable barrier. She looked at everything through it, but only took what she needed. She was going to change the world for women.

Jeep really believed that. She'd never known anyone as focused as Katie was—like twenty-four/seven. She was honest as fire and pure as music. How could she not have fallen for Katie after sleazy Sami?

"I don't believe it about Katie and Abeo," she found herself saying aloud at odd times and stopped herself now as Luke brought her a yellow Pokeman that looked kind of like someone's dog had chewed it up. He picked up and smelled every musty old thing he saw until he tentatively circled a set of toy trap drums.

"You going to be the little drummer boy?" Hector asked. "Brump-a-pum-pum."

Luke gave him his sunny smile.

"You should have seen him up in Portland. I think when he gets old enough he's going to run away from home and join the Lions of Batucada, not the circus." Luke started dancing the samba at the reminder. She danced with him and told Hector and Clara, "Did you ever hear them? Brazilian music, up tempo to the max."

"Tell Grandpap to buy you those drums, Lucas," Clara said, shaking out an old white tablecloth trimmed with strawberries. "I had a cloth like this when the kids were young. Ruined in a picnic. Looks like I should have waited and sold it instead of cutting it up for rags."

"He's already got Jeep's blue ukulele and our Sonny's penny whistle," Hector complained.

"And a real drum pad at school," Jeep added.

Hector said, "Hey Luke, why did Johnny tiptoe past the medicine cabinet?"

Luke ducked his head and grinned, hands resting on the skin of a drum. He looked like he could tell Grandpa Hector was going to crack a joke.

Hector laughed and answered, "He was afraid to wake the sleeping pills!" Luke brushed soft applause on the drum.

Jeep handled red salt and pepper shakers in the shape of two hens. Mother Hubbard at the restaurant across from Donny and Chick would love them, but a dollar was too high to pay at a garage sale. Now if these were in an antique-y kind of shop, she'd charge three bucks and come down to two for regulars.

"Course, you could always resell the drums, Jeep, if he lost interest. Growing boy like that, you could open a store with everything he'll lose interest in."

"A store called Garage Sale Dandy?" she asked, distracted. "Hector, this will fit that light fixture you showed me."

Hector took the glass globe from her and turned it in his hands. "Dang, but you've got an eye for these things, Jeep. I looked right at it."

She was thinking that she might as well open a store except for the capital it would take. Count them—twelve employers had turned her down for a job this week alone. The over-helpful woman at the employment office told her it was because the tourist season hadn't started and the government wouldn't let the loggers cut so their business was down. Depressed, Jeep said she'd be glad to clean rooms at the casino hotel, but they didn't hire her either. She ran her hand over her hair. She could've supplemented cleaning work with music lessons and bought up every secondhand instrument that came her way, then resold them on eBay. At this rate she'd have to go to the music therapy program up north and try to live on whatever grant they gave her. Her hands started chilling up.

She actually missed Sami's music shop in San Francisco sometimes, and the freedom to look the way she liked to look. She'd probably have to straighten up if she was going to school. School had never exactly been her favorite thing. She'd hated sitting in a classroom when she could be playing music.

Luke patted the drum skins with his hands, Pokeman forgotten on a card table stacked with old cookie tins. There were no drumsticks, so every once in a while he'd sound the cymbal with a flick of his fingers. She saw in the little furrow of his brow the concentration it had once taken her to capture a melody, to make a song with her bow.

"Don't you already have that one?" complained Hector, as Clara set the tablecloth by the seller's cash box.

Clara clucked at him. "How much do you want for the drums?" she asked the seller.

"Oh, those drums!" the woman said with a laugh. "Thank goodness my daughter's moved on to basketball. At least that noise is outside. What do you think is fair?"

Luke patted and brushed with his little hands. He found the foot pedal of the bass drum and made a respectful thump. This was primo timing. Muriel had agreed to try rehearsing with Luke in the room—how liberal of her, Jeep thought, since Luke lived where they rehearsed—and Jeep suspected Muriel might be coming around again. Luke was entranced by the band's music. He had his drum pad and would silently play along. Jeep always tried to keep focused on the band, but now and then slipped over to correct Luke's hold or tell him he was a dynamite drummer.

"We can pay four dollars," said Clara.

"Oh, I'd have to get at least ten."

"It'll cost you that to take them to the dump. Five dollars."

"Eight."

"Six."

"They're yours."

Jeep soaked it up. She was learning from old skinflint Clara. "This hat," she said, holding out the fedora, hearing the tentative sound in her voice, "says a dollar. Will you take fifty cents?"

The seller looked at Clara and Hector hefting the little set of drums toward the car. "You're a lot like your mother, aren't you? Seventy-five cents."

Jeep let the woman's mistake go, started to put the hat back, examined the shakers, started to put them back too, then offered, "A dollar for the hat and these old shakers."

"Oh, I suppose I can take that."

Bingo, another deal! Bargaining had seemed so mysterious a process. Her parents had pulled out the checkbook and paid the asking price. Now she did deals like Clara. But garage sale dandy? Dream on, girlfriend. She really could hawk music stuff on line, though. If she had a computer. She'd left her computer with Sarah. When she'd abandoned civilization to drive out West with Katie, she'd thought she'd make enough money to buy a laptop. Maybe Sarah would ship it to her. Maybe she didn't have the guts to ask.

They moved to their next stop, Jeep playing with the shakers, Luke keeping an eye on the drums. As much as she'd needed to get out of Reno and see the world, this was the happiest she'd been since she left. And as much as she'd wanted to have great romances—first with Lara, who'd simply disappeared, then sleazy Sami, then restless Katie—great romance hadn't lived up to its billing, though Katie had been fun while she lasted.

A few months after she'd arrived in San Francisco it had come as no big duh to her that, as revved as she was about the band she'd joined—a folksy-bluesy-bluegrassy group, half men and half women, that mostly played Oakland and Berkeley spots—and as revved as she was about the band getting an interview with the TV station's evening news magazine, she was more revved about Katie Delgado the reporter, a short stick of dynamite in a long red sweater and black tights that made her think for the first time of the allure of legs.

"Jeep," the bass player had called from his van when the interview was wrapped. "The bus is leaving."

"Catch you at rehearsal," she'd answered, waving him away.

Duane tilted his cowboy hat down to his muttonchops and aimed his fingers like pistols at her. She'd suspected the guys had appreciated the reporter too.

"Where's your next gig?" Jeep asked the reporter.

"Down at the Embarcadero."

"I'd love to watch."

"I don't think so."

"Why not? You have a take-no-prisoners policy?"

"It's the insurance—the station has a take-no-passengers policy."

"Put me on then. I'll run the picture machine," Jeep said.

The reporter, who had a little edge of toughness to her, dashed toward her car, saying, "My cam jockey's there by now."

When the woman closed her door, Jeep felt suddenly like a too-tight string that had popped. Like a dumped lover. But no one had dumped her. Why was she crooning to Ms. Dynamite? Her despair must have shown. The woman hit the down button for her window.

"I'm a quick study," implored Jeep.

They were face to face, the reporter's hand on the shift, her ride running. The woman looked startled, like she'd never seen her before that moment. "I'll bet you are," she told Jeep, making a quick circle with her index finger.

"Yes!" Jeep exulted, slapping the hood as she loped around the car. She was in.

The reporter darted the little white Ford, station logo on its sides, into traffic, and back bass filled the interior.

"Yo, it's my woman! Deborah Harry is a goddess," Jeep shouted over the din.

The reporter smiled.

"I didn't catch your name," Jeep fibbed.

"Katie."

"I'm Jeep."

"What kind of name is that?"

"It's the kind that comes with a long story."

"Start talking, then, Fiddler."

She did, never taking her eyes from this fine-looking woman. "My family called me G.P., for Gina Pauline, but my sister Jill, she talked—well, she kind of like ran it together when she talked. G.P., Jeep—get it?"

Lowering the CD, Katie said, "That wasn't very long. Tell me who Jeep is."

Feeling like a motormouth, she went on. "I was born in Reno, just outside Reno, really, where it looks more like the railroad stop it was before all the glitter."

Katie wound in and around the traffic, cursing out the other drivers. She made a come-on gesture with curled fingers.

"I was in the school orchestra, did the street-music-prodigy scene.

The family was big enough that we'd play music together a lot. We'd go to the old-time music festivals in Nevada and northern California. There were these booths, bearded old guys giving lessons for the weekend, or workshops, so I started taking my violin. It was slick, learning from the old-timers. I went electric in college, way electric, and kind of fiddled my way here."

Katie gave her a glance. "Where do you live?"

"You do not want to know, believe me." Jeep described Sami and the shop. "The woman is way bizarre. I don't know why I stay."

"You don't know where you're going, that's why."

"Story of my life." How did this stranger know?

Katie complained, "We may never make this interview."

They were stuck in traffic, inching along. She'd liked the sound of that word, we. "Want me to see if there's an accident ahead?"

Katie shook her head no and fumbled in her bag for a cell phone, then pressed some numbers.

"Hey, that's so cool—you can call the traffic helicopter?" she asked when Katie hung up.

"The station. It's a tipped tanker. They want me there in case it's a hazmat spill."

"You go, girl! Am I glad I'm riding shotgun."

"When we get closer I'll need you to take the wheel so I can get an interview. They're filming from the sky. Damn."

Other cars were on the shoulder at the exit. Katie came to a halt.

"Ditch the wheels, Katie. We'll run."

"And get tossed in jail for obstructing emergency vehicles? No thank you. Talk. Distract me. I'm going to try something."

Katie slowly honked her way toward the median.

There were better ways to distract Katie, thought Jeep, but she was enjoying getting listened to between the horn's insistent bleats. Sarah had known everything about her. Lara and she hadn't talked. Sami never stopped talking.

"So," Jeep went on, "my dad repairs band instruments for a living. And my mom gives piano lessons. My brother plays bass; my little sisters play harmonica and mandolin. Mom sings. Dad does any wind instrument you can name, plus he fiddles too."

Jeep looked over at Katie. Was she listening? "I'm embarrassed, talking so much about me," she said. When Katie didn't answer, she thought, what the hey, and started talking again.

"We had this, like, poster-board-size backyard and, get this, a big old ranch house—the real thing—from the 1800s, and out front we were on top of a long rolling slope. We watered the hell out of the grass, even though it wasn't ours. Dad wanted it to look like a park. When we were little, my sister Jill and me rolled down that sucker over and over till we got dizzy. Then we'd stagger around pretending we were drunk. Summer evenings the whole family would take our music stands and go out on top of the slope—Dad built a white gazebo, like our own personal band shell—why do they call it a gazebo anyway: gay-gaze-bow? Anyway, we'd play Sousa and stuff. Music was the best time with my family. Learning to work on instruments with Dad was when we were closest. Sometimes the neighbors would straggle over to hear the Morgan family band, featuring Gretchen Pauline Morgan on the old-time fiddle. Sometimes they'd barricade themselves in their houses or pick that time to mow their lawns—especially," she laughed, "when us kids were learning to play."

Katie was on the median now, half on the narrow left shoulder, one set of wheels on pavement, the other not. Diesel fumes pumped into the windows from the stalled trucks. They still weren't in sight of the spill. Jeep noticed that Katie's nose was pierced, although she obviously didn't wear the ring during work hours. She had been thinking of doing some piercing someplace subtle.

Katie glanced at her, eyebrows raised.

"Uh, I lucked out playing fiddle. Last summer? Me and Sami went to Michigan. You ever been?" Katie shook her head no. "Yeah, well it's real retro. Like a hippie orgy or something, but you'd think those women had never seen a dyke fiddler before. Not even Martie Seidel, but you wouldn't expect The Dixie Chicks to be at Michigan.

"So Sami has this booth? She sells women's music crapola: G-clef candles, double women's symbol guitar straps, Ani DiFranco T-shirts, shit like that? And I'm giving lessons to any dyke who can operate a bow. I split covering the booth with Sami. She didn't have a clue where I went or who I was with. Babe week. I was totally high, I mean totally, on those women."

She realized they'd been stopped for a while. A patrol car with flashing lights blocked the median. The cop was directing traffic into one lane. Katie called in.

"The station got somebody else there," she told Jeep, scanning the traffic. "My interview left for the airport. Tell me when that cop's not looking."

"Now."

She was flung hard against the passenger door as Katie did a u-turn into oncoming traffic.

"Aw-right!" cried Jeep.

Katie sped up. "We might catch him before his flight."

"Who is this guy?"

"I didn't tell you? That archeologist who found the burial ground in Nevada. Is that near where you grew up?"

"Nevada's a big state. Everybody thinks it's the gambling towns, but it's like anyplace else. There are even a bunch of gay bars, but I don't drink and I don't smoke and I didn't much like what or who I saw there. Why should I go hide in a dark smelly place because I'm gay? I want a gay national park. I want to change Lake Tahoe to Sweet Honey Lake. I want a gay resort!"

Katie stomped on the brakes and triple-parked. "Drive around. I'll be right here when I'm done."

Jeep humped over the stick shift and sat checking out the spiff dash that did everything but spit ice cubes. She got Madonna's "Like a Prayer" booming and slid around a huge tourist bus disgorging a lot of deeply tanned middle-agers in trendy outdoor gear.

She hadn't had a car of her own since her Chevy Spirit died in the parking lot about three weeks before she left for the Bay Area. She should at least have had it towed to the junkyard when she left Sarah. Had it been late-blooming hormones driving her? She felt caught up in a dyke indie flick. Glamorous career girl with pierced nostril meets girl from the boonies with available heart. If she and Katie hit it off she'd hang around—that she knew without knowing Katie. Katie and Jeep. She liked it.

Katie drove them back into town in the early twilight. The fruit tree blossoms were ice cream colors, and front yards streamed with flowering bushes. Katie had taken off her sunglasses. She was sleek. Dark hair, dark eyes, skin a shade those eagle freaks from the tour bus just spent thousands to get during a two-week vacation.

"Where do you want me to drop you, Jeep Morgan?" Katie asked.

"Wherever you're headed is fine. I'll get home from there."

"Is this a trick to find out where I live?"

"You think I'm that crass? I can use a phone book."

"What made you so sure I'm gay?"

"My gaydar went off."

"Like you have one of those gadgets in your pocket."

"No, a chip implanted in my hypothalamus," Jeep joked, but realized her hands had heated up. Something was going on here.

Katie let go and really laughed for the first time. "Thanks for taking over the car and not getting into a twenty-vehicle pileup or wandering onto a runway. I would have missed the archeologist if I'd had to park."

"Thanks for trusting me with it."

Katie looked long at her, until the traffic light turned green. "That's so weird. It never occurred to me not to."

"I don't suppose you want to rescue me from Sami."

"I don't think my girlfriend would like that."

"Girlfriend?" Her voice sounded pathetic. She cleared her throat. "I should have known you'd be taken."

On Dolores Street Katie used a remote to open a garage door under a pink stucco building. There was a red Honda in one of the two spaces.

"Where are we?"

"My place. You can come up for a while. Tanya's a software guru and thinks it's more important to get her company to IPO status than to keep me happy."

"Woo-hoo!"

Katie's Honda had been small, but that didn't matter. When they packed it a month later, Jeep hadn't had much more to put in it than when she'd left Reno with Sami.

Hector White's car was a little different from Katie's. He and Clara mostly used the big old pickup, but they also had their Sunday car, a 1978 white Plymouth Fury Hector kept under a tarp and polished regularly. They used it to go to the garage sales because, Clara said, "We've got a regular family again."

After the garage sale, after they'd managed to fit the drums in the trunk, they drove across town where Hector pulled into a parking space outside Waterfall Convalescent Center to make their weekly visit to Clara's older brother, Jack. Luke darted from the open door to look for drumsticks under the plum trees. The ground was covered with a confetti of white plum blossoms.

"It's kind of criminal," Jeep told them, "that there's no place in town a little dude can buy a set of drumsticks. If I ever get the chance to play store again, I'm going to carry them. And used computers. I know enough to do basic troubleshooting, and I'd keep one for myself." She'd need an eBay name—garage sale dude would do it. No, garagesaledandy.com.

"They need to be smooth, Luke, or you'll break the skins," Jeep advised as he waved knobby pine twigs at her.

When they entered the building, Hector gave out big orange daylilies from Clara's back garden. Patients, staff, visitors, he didn't care. Hector offered them to whomever caught his eye until he ran out.

"Hello there, sunshine!" an old woman in a wheelchair called to Luke, waving her daylily.

Jeep took Luke into Lillian Levine's room. If the hallways smelled like canned soup, this room was soaked in some astringent deodorizer. Lillian introduced her dolls to every visitor who stopped by, and she always had a lollipop for Luke. These were people who could use more music in their lives, but she couldn't see going to school for two years when she could come over here once a week to play and have a sing-along. These folks would dig on old-time music. She put her hands to either side of her face to cool them against her cheeks. She hated making decisions.

At Room 314, Clara greeted her brother Jack by shoving a paper bag at him. Jack looked furtively around, then slipped it under his pillow.

His roommate Jethro wheeled over. "I'm going to steal that goody while you're in the john, Jack-ass," he threatened, winking at Luke. "Me and Luke here are going to eat every last crumb."

Jack raised his arms defensively, but Jethro wheeled away, laughing. "If I could collect all the marbles your brother's lost, Clara, I'd sell them at my shop."

Clara, silent as her brother, handed the other bag she carried to Jethro.

He brought his caterpillar-like eyebrows together. "Clara, you ought to open up your own bakery. Cinnamon and sugar—this smells like heaven. Nobody cooks like you anymore."

"Thank the Lord," Hector said.

Clara shot him a glance, but he was watching Jethro cut up the coffee cake. Luke got the first piece.

Jeep let the buttery crumbles dissolve in her mouth, dreaming she'd devote a counter at Garage Sale Dandy to Clara's baking. No, that would compete with Donny's baking. Except Donny didn't use sugar or white flour. Maybe Garage Sale Dandy could sell the unhealthy stuff.

Jack held out his hand. Jethro cut him a big piece. They watched Jack wrap it in a handkerchief and put it in a dresser drawer. He left the room.

"I don't know why you still visit this nutty brother of yours," Hector said, wiping his hands on his baggy jeans.

"I'm all he's got in the world." Clara gave the same answer every week.

Hector replied, as usual, "Because he's driven everyone else away."

"Give us a few years and you'll be exactly like him," Clara sniped back.

Jeep felt a chill in her hands. That was a sucky thought. She was needing these people too much to lose them.

"Here's a good one for you, Jethro. How can you make a coat last?" Jethro tapped a foot and looked toward the ceiling, pretending to ignore him until Hector gave in and announced, "Make the trousers and vest first!"

"I don't know who's nuttier, Clara, your brother or the man you married. Did I tell you my brother was up here Tuesday," Jethro said. "The fella he hired to manage the shop took off with a day's receipts. John's ready to sell the place out from under me. That's two managers since I came in here. I've got a second operation scheduled now that my weight's down, but he won't even advertise for someone else to run the place."

"You're looking to fill a job?" Jeep asked. She held her breath. Luke drummed on her thigh with his little sticks.

"Why? You know somebody?"

She looked at Clara, then at Hector. Luke went still and grabbed her waist, burying his face in her sweatshirt.

"What's it take?"

"It's not hard. He'd have to be honest, add and subtract, dicker for good prices, buy what would sell." Jethro laughed. "Why? You think you can persuade Hector to drop his fishing rod long enough to do a lick of work?"

"And if nominated I will decline!" Hector said with enthusiasm. "It's our Jeep who's looking for work."

Luke held tighter, shaking his head against her. She stroked his silky light hair. "It's okay, dude. It's okay. We'd still be together."

"Work? I thought you were a fiddler."

"Big whoop. There's no cash in fiddling. I'll run your store for you, Jethro. What do you sell?"

"Whatever I can get."

"He's a junk dealer in town, Jeep."

She kept herself as still as she would if she spotted some huge bargain at a garage sale. "A used store?"

"Well used, my dear. I started it when I retired from the navy, twenty-three years ago. I had all this treasure I picked up in my travels and no wife or family who wanted any of it. So I rented that little place next to the pharmacy, Jethro's Jumble?"

"I can't picture it."

"Locals don't go there," Clara said, "but the casino tourists like useless junk with steep prices. Little china dogs and ratty fur jackets."

Jethro defended himself. "These Californians are getting a deal."

"These Californians wouldn't know a deal if it walked up to them and punched them in the nose," Hector said. He turned to Jeep. "You think you could stand waiting on them?"

"You said I'd be good at it."

"She's learning. We take her and the boy to the sales with us."

Was this something Clara and Hector dreamed up? Was this why they brought her and Luke to see Jack every week, so she'd meet Jethro? "Jethro," she asked, stroking Luke's hair faster, "do you sell musical instruments?"

"I don't go out looking for them, but I have a little of this, a little of that. And old 78 RPM records—Les Brown and His Band of Renown? Count Basie? Clara, do you remember 'One O'Clock Jump'?" He wheeled his chair jerkily back and forth in a little dance.

Clara gave Jeep a push toward him.

"I've managed stores—a gift shop and a music shop. And I can repair musical instruments," Jeep said, dodging the wheels of the chair. "I can add and subtract and dicker and spot a bargain. Would the manager get to go out and buy stuff?"

Jethro wiped his hands on his robe. "I used to hit all the garage sales I could before I opened the shop. And people knew to bring me good items, not the leftovers." He paused and studied her. "I couldn't pay much."

"Can you go over minimum? I've got Luke to take care of now."

Clara leaned down to Jethro's face. "You can afford to pay her good, Moneybags. She hasn't got two thin dimes to rub together. Do you want the boy to wear rags?"

Jethro stitched his eyebrows together. "There's a whole apartment over the store I won't be able to use, not with this leg and back. I'll put a trailer in the yard when I get out of here. You could have the apartment for part of your pay."

"Leave Cat's place?" She shivered.

Clara zeroed in on Jethro again, eyes narrowed to angry slits. "That boy is being raised with all the advantages. Why should they pack themselves into some old man's musty apartment? Catching Rinehart is the other foster parent, Jethro. The family that started this town? That owns the bank?"

"We'd want to keep living in Cat's house. But we could use your upstairs to sell something. Maybe that's where used musical instruments could go?" She closed her eyes and saw everything. "We could have little concerts, take a percentage of the gross. And set up Clara's Home Baked Shelf. Could I give lessons there when the shop's closed?"

When she opened her eyes, Jethro and Hector were looking at each other, and Clara was dusting her brother's spotless mirror.

"Eight-fifty an hour. That's what I paid the men for minding the till. And five percent more of sales above last year's, month by month."

"Can I use your phone? I need to get the school bus to let Luke off at the store next week."

CHAPTER TWENTY-NINE

Honeysuckle Falls

I swear, this is hotter than back home, Don," said Abeo. "I break out in a sweat walking to the john. Jane."

Donny drew open the front room drapes and lifted the windows wide to let in the night air. It felt like it had dipped into the eighties after going over a hundred degrees in the late afternoon. She'd had to persuade Chick she'd survive alone before Chick had given in and gone to Movie Night at the Grange Hall to see the Kim Novak revival. Donny was coming down with a summer cold and wanted to get under the covers no matter what the temperature. "It's all those hormones you're taking," she told Abeo.

"Say what?"

Donny smiled to think that Abe had these say-what days too. "You know it's this heat day in and day out. The place is going to burn up one of these summer days. Even my gayfeathers dried up early. Now that honeysuckle, it'd be two hundred degrees, and they'd still be out there growing a foot a week. You know what Clara said when I asked her how to keep them from taking over the whole garden?"

"Move. She told you to move."

"I told you that before?"

"No more than half a dozen times, you old fool."

"But look at all the plums on my tree out back. I may sell some there's so many. Here," she said, offering a bowl to Abeo. "Have some." Abeo waved them away but Donny bit into one. "This shit is good. Take your mind off the heat. At least it's not humid."

"I'm getting tired of it, Donny."

"I thought all those women battling to get in your bed were what was making you tired."

Abeo threw herself on the couch. "I kept reading about how lesbians stay together. How lesbians are monogamous. How lesbians take care of their sisters. How men are cruel and fickle. I knew I could find my true love here, a simple countrywoman."

Donny sneezed. "You are the backwardest child I have ever known. Lesbians aren't made in simple. Why didn't you try the classifieds, instead of dive-bombing the women of Waterfall Falls?"

"City girls are so snooty. And these country sisters think I'm exciting, a little glamorous compared to hauling in the wood and bathing in cold water. Like you say, they're trampling each other to get in my pants. My skirt. Which is off-limits anyway."

"There isn't any such thing as a stone femme, Abeo."

"You wrote the rule book, Donny?"

"I had the best teachers. A stone femme would be like—what? A butterfly that didn't flutter," she decided.

Abeo, on Donny's recliner, said, "Oh, I flutter all right. Maybe not how they expect, but I can still flutter."

"Did the surgery leave you anything to flutter with?"

Abeo gave her a strange look. "Donny? You're still my brother, right? Can you hush your mouth about something?"

"Abeo, is this anything I want to hear?"

"I hope so, because I need to talk to somebody about it."

"You never did know how to shut your mouth longer than five minutes," Donny agreed, ticking off a list of Abeo's slips in her head.

Abeo hesitated, inspected the ceiling, then blew air out between pursed lips. "I haven't been brave enough to have my bottom surgery."

This wasn't anything she'd expected. "I'm not hearing this. You lied to me again? And about something as important as this? You came into my town and pulled a scam like this on me, on Chick, on our friends?"

"Watch your blood pressure, Donalds. Don't have a stroke on my account." Abeo looked wary. "I needed a trial run where everybody and his boyfriend wasn't watching my moves."

Donny turned her back and opened up the drapes again. Craning her neck, she could see some of Blackberry Mountain to the north and east. That mountain was one solid mother. She wished she were that solid and still. Thelonius Monk was doing something mellow, and she listened for a while, longing to be out blackberrying with Chick and the dog. Loopy would be using her soft mouth to pull blackberries from low branches. Chick had taught her to do that, nights down at the deserted park with the dog where they'd feed each other berries and go home kissing in the dark with their purple lips.

More and more these days she seemed to want to be in the world differently. Why fuss over what sex Abeo was? When was she going to stop getting upset that he didn't know how to get through a day without lying?

She fished the bandanna out of her back pocket and blew her nose. She was too old to be flinging herself into rages all the time. She couldn't keep it up. Sometimes she was able to leave behind whatever got her going by walking the trail out to the falls or daydreaming that she was walking it. She could hear the sheriff and Gal clomping along behind her, taste the gritty dust of a hot summer day like today. She imagined being the first settler to follow the roar of the water, blazing the trail and getting her first look at the giant spill.

The sight of Honeysuckle and Waterfall Falls took her breath away every time she saw them. There were actually two of them, both plunging falls. Honeysuckle came over a long ridge maybe seventy-five feet up. The second waterfall was underneath it, only about fifty feet high and fed from underground springs. This was the waterfall's fall.

The postcards they carried at the store showed them in profile, but didn't really capture two distinct falls. Even together they were no Niagara. On the other hand, she'd never seen Niagara, and she could go see Honeysuckle and Waterfall Falls any time she wanted. In summer, when the valley was scary dry and the creek just a shadow of its swollen self, neither falls disappeared completely.

There was a way to get behind both of them, stepping on the wild spearmint that thrived along the way, then wiggling between some boulders and around a great old tree stump. Finally she'd drop down onto a smooth rock ledge about as wide as the queen-sized bed at home. She'd stroll right behind the wall of water, get goose bumps from the wet vapor that settled on her arms, listen to the rough and tumble. It shielded her from the bad news of the world. If the sun was shining, there would be a rainbow of light dancing before her. On the best days, there was a double rainbow. That was such a thrill, especially when Chick was with her.

When she was under the falls she couldn't believe the things she let get to her. There was that time with the sheriff when she'd been so mad at—what—that Abe had ratted her out? That Joan knew she'd spent a few months of her life as a drug courier, even as a penny-ante dealer for a few months? Hell, she was mad at herself for stooping so low. Then there'd been all the times R had infuriated her. The antigay crowd still got to her, though they'd backed off a lot since the nineties.

She'd given so much energy to those damn bigots—why did she get all hot and bothered over any of it? Next to the falls and the mountain, everything was so much bullshit.

What used to seem like a major deal was now water over the falls, water sliding with a steady thunder into the deep pool she'd played in with Chick when they'd first arrived. They needed to get back up there, back to their peaceful spot, be blessed by the chilly spray and the smell of clean air. She'd never understood that peace was something she wanted until she'd gone under the turmoil of the falls and found it.

A log truck upshifted on its way to the freeway. The house still smelled like their fish dinner. "Tell me this isn't true, Abe. I knew it didn't sound like you to mutilate yourself, but then to say you had? Honey, when it comes time to get what you're after, you do not leave prisoners, do you?"

"I thought, with me being so girly all my life I'd be a natural. But the idea of boy-girl sex—I can't tell you how nasty that seems to me."

"Isn't that what you've been doing?"

"Maybe I've been exaggerating a little. And if I'd found my soul mate I would have done the surgery if she'd wanted me to."

"Abraham—forget me calling you by that woman name—you don't walk into a women's community looking for sex. Especially with the most political women you could have found."

"That's where you're wrong. I feel like Christopher Columbus. These women are a new world to me. You think they'd hate me if they knew I was still Abraham?"

"You have betrayed their trust—my trust—and insulted them. I am not taking you back up the mountain. You're looking for love in the most dumb-ass place you could find."

"You don't think R truly loves me? She acts like it, kicking Katie out of her bed, not seeing other women. She told me she felt most loved when she gave love. Everybody on the land told me how different R was. They said I'd turned her into a homebody. And then, when I told her, she did an about-face so fast I'm still spinning."

"You told that woman?" Donny pulled out her now-wet bandanna and sneezed into it. She was really getting sick, she thought.

"I thought she loved who I really am. She had a good line of bull about loving the woman, not the body. I was even thinking about being a man again and marrying her."

"The biggest separatist in town? That's all she is—a line, a walking rule book. I thought she moved here to get away from men."

"The woman freaked out on me. All of a sudden she's after me for thinking like a man when I know damn well it was Abraham, not Abeo, she wanted. I've been sleeping in the barn, entertaining all the ladies, one by one."

"All?"

"A mess of them at Spirit Ridge and Dawn Farm."

"Don't tell me all. I don't want to hear about feminist sluttiness."

"I was trying to give this thing a chance," Abraham whined, "before I gave up and went back to find a boyfriend, but you're on the money. They wanted to talk, to help."

"The other women don't know about—"

"They don't know shit. I wanted to at least fool around with them to see if one might be husband material. They acted like I was royalty and they were some kind of knights of honor. And no, these women don't understand the first thing about trannie stuff. They may be big bad revolutionary queers, but they're also a bunch of nice white girls mad at the world and living in the woods where they can make some rules that don't leave them out. Rattlesnake's rules don't always sit right, but they come closer to what they think they want. And they're too well brought up to ask me for surgical details."

"And you're too polite to tell them the damn truth?" Chick would laugh about that.

"They were curious enough to see how it felt to hang with a gender freak like me, but sometimes I think it's as much because I'm black that they're curious. And talk? You'd think I was some kind of psychotherapist. Would you like to know what I learned in all those intimate hours of talking? They're like men, Donny! They only want to feel loved. I mean, why did I go through all this? I already knew that in the dark, we're all just looking for a loving touch."

"R hasn't copped in public to you being half-man?"

"I think she's embarrassed."

"I'd say it's time to shove off, Abe."

"It's for sure getting too hot around here for me, but how can I go? I don't have a job. I don't have anyplace to live. I don't even have the fare back to the city."

"Chicago."

"No. The Bay Area. Chicago wasn't the same after you left."

"Don't blame it on me that you had to get out of that town too. San Francisco's always been your second home."

"I could hitchhike, but that's not very safe for me."

Donny knew now where all this had been leading, but for once, she wasn't doling out money for a score, a clinic visit, a bus ticket. "Is that where you want to be?"

"Yes. No. Maybe. I don't know anymore, Donny!" He'd begun to cry. Donny gave him the bandanna from her back pocket. "I thought at least one of these women would be like you. Steady and strong and loving, an Adonis of a momma and a daddy all rolled into one. Chick is so lucky."

Abraham pitched forward onto her shoulder, and Donny held him while he cried. Adonis? Abe must want more than fare home to be flattering her like that.

"I am so tired of life in the hysterical lane, Donny."

"What am I going to do with you?" she asked, but an idea had come to her. It wasn't like there were no men in Waterfall Falls.

"Rescue me before R tells them and they come after me with double-bladed Amazon axes!"

"You want to be rescued? Okay, I'll rescue you. Come on." She propped Abraham up, grabbed keys, and marched him out to the truck. "I love you, brother, but why am I always doing crazy things with you in the dead of night instead of catching up on my sleep?"

"It's only nine thirty."

"I should have been in bed an hour ago; it's a baking day tomorrow." She stopped to write a note for Chick, something she wouldn't do in front of just anyone, but then Abe had been in school with her all those years before anyone had heard of dyslexia. The teachers had diagnosed Donny as a troublemaker because of her frustrated rages over being unable to learn.

"I remember when you'd be starting your day at nine thirty at night. You're getting old, Donalds."

"And glad of it. At least it's only you still getting in trouble, not the both of us."

Once in the truck and on the county road she felt more calm, but she knew she still had anger to talk out. She thought Chick would be cool about what she was doing. "The sheriff and I were talking about you a while back while we were trying to catch some fish."

Abraham abruptly stopped crying and looked at her over the bandanna. "Don't you be telling any sheriffs noh-thing you know about me."

"Abe, it was the sheriff telling me about you."

"I don't even know that woman. What's she talking to you about me for?"

"About the bust in Portland. About my name coming up. Joan has a friend in the department up there."

Abe went quiet.

"And then you had the nerve to ask could you stay with me a while. And now this."

"You're the only gay family I have left, bro."

"Because you used us all up. Because you used us till there was nothing left to use."

"You're scaring me. Where we going anyway? Where you taking me?"

Donny let him stew for a while.

"Don?"

"The sheriff told me about the two-spirit people in native culture. Men who lived like women. The tribe didn't make these dudes choose which they wanted to be."

"You mean she thinks it's not fucked-up to live two ways at the same time?"

"They were holy men, babe."

"Do you think I should go back to being Abraham in pearls instead of Abeo in the woods?"

"Do I think you should stop beating yourself up over who you are? We all have our own wars to fight, but you recruit a whole army to fight yours. Do I think helping you find some peace would save a whole lot of heart and headaches for a whole lot of people? I'd say so."

"But I'm so old now. You know how guys are when someone like me gets a little ripe."

"Are you having a midlife crisis too?"

It took another five minutes of listening to Abraham try to explain to himself why he had to choose between being male and female before Donny put the truck into second gear and climbed the long dark driveway, fragrant with horse droppings and sweet hay. They were halfway to Blackberry Mountain, at Harold and Joe's home.

The manufactured double-wide that had belonged to Harold's father sat atop a cluttered knoll. Chaparral, grayed tree stumps, a small pyramid of tires, and an uncovered, unstacked heap of firewood appeared in the foggy murk of the headlights. She told Abe where they were going.

"Donny, no! You can't bring me here! These boys knew me in the city when I was a svelte and beautiful boy. I am so ashamed."

Harold had left Waterfall Falls to live in San Francisco. When his father died, he'd inherited thirty acres and moved home with Joe.

"You were never svelte, lady. You need a reality check, and these boys will give it to you."

Lights blazed from every window. The front half-deck and steps were littered with boots, axes, cartons, and an old pink wing chair. There was a huge hydrangea bush packed with blue blossoms that concealed the end of the deck. No one was in sight, but when they slammed the truck doors, a voice called, "We're out back!"

"Yo! It's Donny Donalds and Abeo!"

"Go on in. We're in the hot tub!"

Abraham gave Donny a coy look. "I think I'll take a stroll out back."

"Abe, you stay with me. As far as they know you're still a trans woman."

"Just a peek?"

"I don't know why I thought you'd change. You never intended to go all the way, did you? You wanted to lose the extra hair and grow your chests." She studied Abraham in the porch light. "And try it with women."

"I was curious."

"That's too queer."

"No such thing," Abraham said, trotting up the steps after her.

The inside of the house was dark from paneling and woodstove soot. An ancient collie-like dog limped to them and sniffed, then shuffled back to the hearth. Classical music pumped from the boom box CD player set at an open window.

"Close your eyes, women!" called a voice at the back door. Donny turned to the TV where one of those Japanese cartoons that baffled her flickered its colors across the screen. She could hear the men pulling on pants and shirts in the kitchen.

"Well," said big Harold in his breathy voice, "isn't this a wonderful surprise! Give me a hug, Donny. It's been too long. Up at Dawn Farm, wasn't it?"

Joe padded barefoot behind him, sucking on a joint. He handed it to Abraham.

"Exactly what the doctor ordered," Abe said.

Donny waved the thing away and watched Harold scowl at Joe. Joe shrugged and grinned, then took another toke.

"So this is Abeo. I've heard all kinds of things about you." He squinted at Abe. "My, you look familiar."

Donny was tired and her head had begun to ache, but while Abraham and Joe got into the cartoon, exclaiming at the colors, mocking the story, she and Harold went into the kitchen and sat at the cluttered table. She told him everything.

"I mean," she finished, "I've known this child since I wore skirts and he wore a tie in grammar school. It doesn't feel right to pay for his bus ticket and hustle him out of town. At least he had hope when he got here."

"Hope for what?"

"For answers, Harold. He had to find out if this trans thing was a fit for him, and he had to do it where nobody knew him, where he could be his new self."

"And now he's more confused than ever? His little experiment isn't exactly working, and he's got himself stranded between genders and worlds?"

"And styles. He's acting like a fucked-up queen. Look at him. That's how he's always solved his problems."

"Dope?"

"And liquor. And falling in love."

"Do you want a cup of tea?"

She'd noticed the slug of dirty mugs in the sink. Harold and Joe had hooked up to the electrical lines without the help of the power company, but they hadn't gotten around to putting in a hot water heater. "I'm okay."

They sat silent. The TV droned on.

"I don't know what to do, Harold. Abraham's a grown man, but I feel responsible for him. I always have. Chick says I'm wasting my energy."

"So it's not only Abraham's problem."

"He's become a community problem."

"Oh, I don't think so, Donny." Harold leaned toward her. "The community will swallow or spit up whatever comes near it, like a sea creature feeding. You've watched this happen a hundred times. Maybe Abraham's fate isn't in your hands?"

"I know it's not!" she snapped, then sneezed. "But he's never known which end is up. His mother told me that first day of school to take care of him because he wasn't as tough as the other boys. I'm still trying."

"Okay, okay, don't get your knickers in a twist. I'm trying to help here too."

"Shit. You're right." She'd let her anger take over again. Maybe she loved it as much as she loved poor Abe. Maybe she should put it in the shopping bag with Abe's stuff along with intimidation, high blood pressure, and the old fears that made her flare up, and send it away with him. That would be the greatest gift she could give Chick. "I treat him like he's still in his kindergarten smock. But I can't walk away from the man. He's in white boy country here."

"You might have to."

"Does that mean it's Greyhound time?"

"No, not yet. I have another idea."

"Which is?"

Harold put a finger beside his nose and squinted at the table. "I'm thinking we may have someone who needs to go to the two-spirit gathering Labor Day weekend."

"Great minds think alike." She sneezed again. "I was talking to Abe about this two-spirit idea. He's lived at such extremes, Vietnam grunt to wannabe dyke. It's like he's at war inside himself."

"But most of us come to terms with it by this time of life."

"I'm afraid Labor Day may be too far away for him."

Harold frowned at her. "Donny..."

"Got it. Let go. Cut my losses and run."

Harold stood up to hug her. She craned her neck and caught a glimpse of Abraham, snuggled against Joe, still watching TV. The movement made her realize that everything in her ached. Was this the flu?

Harold, arm on her shoulder, firmly led her to the door.

CHAPTER THIRTY

Rooftops

Y ou should've been butch, you're so stubborn," Chick told
R, leaning into Patsy's passenger-side window where R sat,
arms folded, eyes angry. "You're as bad as Donny. I got you this far,
now let's truck on up to the doctor's office."

It was weird being with R in the blasting dry heat of the Greenhill
Clinic parking lot instead of the woods, or tiny Waterfall Falls. Greenhill
was a lot larger than their country town—20,000 people, not 1,400. R
had brought her shepherd's crook—for protection, she'd claimed—but
Chick could see the woman was wobbly on her feet. Was that culture
shock at being out in the world or the cancer?

If R had breast cancer. The thought gave her a queasy feeling, and
the lump, big as it was, might yet turn out benign. R's sore underarm
might have nothing to do with cancer. Yet there was no escaping R's
mother's history.

The clinic was enormous, its air-conditioning a relief. She held
onto the crystal necklace to help her through this. R had to register
and fill out a bucket of forms. Her earrings, three flat circles each,
were never still. She was surprised to learn that R got Social Security
Disability and Medi-something or other.

"They can buy guns or feed me," R replied peevishly when Chick
noted aloud that the despised patriarchy supported her. "I consider it a
supplement to my alimony."

"No shit. You still get alimony?"

"Not officially. I put him through Wharton School of Business,
didn't I? The feds don't know, but he'll repay my services for the rest
of his life."

"Generous ex. That's a lot of cash."

R looked up from the medical history questions. "I'm not greedy. He
can well afford the little I ask for." She huffed out a laugh. "And generosity
had nothing to do with it. He was a coward pure and simple."

"A coward?"

"I know too much about his wild days, and I was too close to his parents for his comfort."

"You blackmailed him?"

"I'm really offended by that term, Chick. It's very racist."

"I don't mean it that way, you know that."

"I may, but would a woman of color?"

"Not—" she started to say, but understood that, aside from the truth of her objection, R was using the argument to deflect more questions. The woman might not be as emotionally frail as she appeared. It was pretty ridiculous to call her a racist when Donny was the most important person in the world to her.

When R turned in the completed paperwork, they were sent to a second-floor waiting room crowded with patients and frenzied staff. They took chairs facing a listless little boy, some parents comforting a squalling infant, and a middle-aged woman who restlessly flipped through a magazine and ignored the old woman beside her.

"I have to admire your friend Jeep," said R.

Chick suspected R was trying to distract herself from her surroundings. "Why?"

"Taking in a boy-child is not a popular choice in this community. I watched her with Muriel at a gathering last week. She was trying to defend what she was doing to Muriel."

"What," asked Chick, "does Muriel have to say about it? Luke is such a gentle kid."

"Exactly what Jeep told her. Muriel wanted to know how she could say that about a male child?"

"Jeep must have been pissed off."

She thought about scrawny Muriel and her wild curly hair. Muriel played an adequate washboard base in the band, learned solely, as she frequently announced, so she could play music with women. Jeep had told Chick that the addition of a bass fiddle in the hands of another band member had Muriel edgier than ever toward her, the only professional musician in the band that Muriel had started and, although she called it a collective, now led. Muriel was being silly. Jeep didn't want to lead any band. All that booking and getting people to rehearsals and finding replacements—uh-uh, she'd said, not for her. All Jeep wanted was a chance to play music. So she sparred with Muriel, both of them stepping on each others' toes, backing off and saving their relationship by laughing at themselves.

"This is what comes of playing your Grateful Dead music," Jeep quoted what Muriel had once said. "Right," she'd told Muriel, "I love Luke because I listen to the Dead. I can see that connection, no problem. Real clear."

"Jeep is clever," R told Chick now. "She offered to make Muriel Luke's aunt because Muriel loves her blood nephew." R shook her head. "Then Muriel was all over the child. Why is it so difficult for women to live their principles?"

"Luke is a special little boy," said Chick.

R seemed to loom over her, although she'd done nothing but turn toward Chick. "You think having a disability makes him different from other man-children, don't you?" R accused in a whisper. "That's a typical ablest mistake."

"R, Luke happens to *be* different, and even if he wasn't, even if he spent his time mugging two-year-olds for purple dinosaurs, he deserves love as much as any living creature." That was an idea Donny preached. She thought even R deserved love, though she was adamant that it didn't have to be herself giving out the love.

"Yes, but in the right place. Look at us. He's in our space, taking up our words and thoughts and energy."

"I know my memory isn't what it once was, R, but didn't you bring this up? I don't think I did."

Lesbians are so nuts, she thought. Seps were ancient history, like from the seventies. Sure they had to keep men away while they did their thing, whatever that was. But this was a new century. Time to get on with it. You couldn't change anything if you hid in the backwoods. She admired them in some ways, but the handful that were left looked kind of pathetic, like some navel-gazing backwards culture making its last stand. Not Luddites, but maybe Luddettes. You had to love them.

"What good does it do to hide out in the mountains, R? I mean, we've been there, done that, two decades ago, haven't we?"

"You can live in their world," said R. "I can't. Won't."

"And the other land women?"

R shrugged. "We're not all separatists."

"Everyone needs safe space."

Chick saw such a mixture of defiance and serenity in those eyes that she felt glad for R, glad she had her sanctuary. Maybe keeping guys out wasn't such a fossilized idea. Goddess knows, she needed a space like that herself.

"Let's move where we can look out a window at least," R said, leading the way.

The day was bright and around 102 degrees, but mill smoke made the sky more a hazy white than blue. A view of rooftops and backyards, full clotheslines, scratching dogs and toddlers splashing in little plastic pools stretched maybe three-tenths of a mile to the foothills south of the city. On the way north she'd seen several groups of people in rafts, Tahitis, and inner tubes going over riffles on the mostly tame, brown, half-empty Elk River. This section of Greenhill was a mix of duplexes, old two-story homes, and crazy-quilt add-on cottages. The town had been built around Greenhill Wood Products, one of the last of the great mills in the state.

R was looking outside too, picking and picking at a loose thread on her cuff. Chick stopped her and felt the chill of R's hand. "Isn't that a homey sight? I can almost smell the clean laundry."

"Home doesn't look like that to me anymore. I want to see nothing but old-growth forest from my windows."

Chick sighed. R, who had agreed to go to the clinic only after Chick had done the work of finding a doctor who would see her, didn't know how disagreeable she sounded, but Chick wished the woman would make an effort to be pleasant. Deep down she was good people, Chick told herself, although sometimes talking to her was like blowing up balloons for a kid with a slingshot.

"My earliest memory," Chick said, automatically going into her cheerful mode, "is of watching my mother hang clothes out to dry on the rooftop of our apartment building. It smelled so good up there—like the country, my mother said. The sheets were bleached white and the wind lifted them like kites. Martin was terrified of the roof. He'd wail all the way up the narrow stairs and glue himself to the door." She looked at R's face. It had the same pale hue and sweaty-looking shine to it as Martin's once had—the look of fear.

R gave no sign of hearing, but Chick went on with her memory-lane trip. "I was maybe three years old. I knew from cowboy and Indian movies that you waved white flags to surrender—and yes, I know those movies were racist too. I was convinced my mother left white sheets flapping in the wind to tell God he should send my daddy home from World War II."

She patted R's still hand as she had Martin's. "I'd run back to Martin over and over, to get him to come look. The poor little guy had nightmares of Daddy walking off the edge of the roof to get to the war and of himself falling off as Japanese bombers attacked us. When my mother talked about the war, she said God was on our side. I pictured this god bending over the rooftop, his cheeks all puffed out, blowing at the sheets. He was not a nice god. I was mad because he was playing some ego game using Daddy as a toy soldier. Bombs, weeping women, little kids like us were no more than pebbles in a creek to him. No wonder I grew up wanting to make love, not war. Do you remember the Dylan song 'Masters of War'? 'You that only built to destroy, you play with my world like it's a little toy'?"

The infant's irritating yells crescendoed as the parents changed her diapers on a cushion between them, peppering the air with baby powder. R, sitting with her proud posture, looked stiff. Her hand had taken no warmth from Chick's. The woman was an ice statue, Chick was thinking, completely shut down. It wasn't like breast cancer was a death sentence any more, she wanted to tell R. On the other hand, R had apparently been fooling around with self-healing for months.

"Go on," R urged in a strangely tiny voice, like Martin's at bedtime. "It's never as dark while you're talking," he'd say. R was only the second person she'd told this story to. Donny had been the first.

"I always got my mother's god mixed up with the landlord of our building, an old guy who collected the rent in a Cadillac, skimped on coal for our furnace, and told us that going up to the roof without Mom was against the rules. We had to go up. We could see the lake from the roof. That's where God and Daddy were fighting the war, somewhere over the water."

R turned to face her. "You have a remarkable memory from that age. I was born long after the victory, but I remember stories about the end of the war—all the shouting and relief, as if men would really ever stop fighting completely."

"After the war my father turned out to be nothing like the pictures Mom had all over the apartment. He'd gotten bald and scrawny and glum. He apprenticed with Mom's plumber uncle. When somebody asked about his job, he'd say, 'I'm still cleaning up the messes of this world.' Martin wouldn't let Daddy near him for the longest time. He screeched like Daddy was an enemy soldier."

If only R would say she was scared, squeeze her hand, break down and cry. But no, she was as uptight as Martin had been, hanging on to her and hanging onto her fear. No matter what she did, no matter how much time she'd spent trying to make Martin happy, he'd always needed, needed, and needed, and she had always failed him. She never seemed to fail Donny.

The waiting room was becoming even more crowded. These establishment doctors, she thought, were always over-scheduled and would probably only refer R on to specialists. A woman in white came out of the back with a clipboard and glanced down at it. R withdrew her hand. She seemed to pull even farther inside herself, but the call was for a mother with three preschoolers. The noise level in the waiting room immediately went down.

Feeling a familiar helplessness, Chick kept telling stories. "Our parents bought the house Grandmom had been renting, and we moved in when I was ten. I have a picture of Martin and me. He was scowling and fragile-looking. I was chubby, smiley little Cicely, my arm around Martin. I wore a homemade navy-blue Easter coat with lace at the cuffs and collar. I remember the deliciousness of those bright yellow, spongy marshmallow chicks we'd get in our baskets, and the little milk-chocolate bunnies laid out against fake green grass."

R came out of her frozen stupor again long enough to look at her, head back, eyes narrowed, arms again folded. "Were you a happy child?"

The question startled Chick. "I tried to be. It made everyone around me happier if I was. I mean, Martin's behavior made my mother so unhappy, I tried to make up for him."

"And you did everything you could to make your mother happy. That's why Katie calls you the Earth Mother of Waterfall Falls," R said with sarcasm.

"Does she? Is that a bad thing?"

"It is if you're doing penance for having a mentally ill brother. I would counsel you to let him go. It's an old story, yet another man draining yet another woman."

"Martin is not just another man. He's sick and he's my little brother." She got up and went to the window. Donny understood this part. Maybe she should fake R out and stop taking care of everyone right now. Let R find her own high-and-mighty way home.

She stayed at the window several minutes, the sound of the clinic too loud and irritating, surprised at her unaccustomed anger. R's words, like a dentist's probe exploring decay around a raw nerve, wouldn't go away. Her head was as bad, refusing to abandon R without setting up another ride. She couldn't storm off and send Abeo back for her in Patsy now that Abeo seemed to be in permanent party mode at Harold and Joe's, another bad scene. Abeo had even quit coming to help out at the store.

When she went back and sat next to R she said, "I still feel best when I'm taking care of the world, but now my world is smaller and I get to pick who's in it. I like being an earth-mother type. I wish, if it's going to be my karma, that I could be better at it."

"Stop belittling yourself, Chick." R's brow was furrowed, her look cross. "You give enormously of yourself. It's no wonder you're depressed, the way you tear yourself down while the rest of us thank the Goddess you're here for us. You've made up for not curing your brother a thousand times over. We know that Chick equals love, but is it love or is it some kind of insurance so you won't ever fail your impossible tasks again? Martin's not stalking you any more. Let it go."

"You think my brother stalked me?"

"Emotionally, yes, that's obvious."

"You think my depression comes of feeling like I failed to cure my brother?"

"And everyone else in your world. As my mother used to say, that's as plain as the nose on your face. Look at Donny's temper. I'd find living with that much anger depressing."

"She never turns her anger on me. It used to be hard to watch because I was afraid it was hurting her."

"Used to be?"

"The things she might have blown up about a year ago don't set her off any more. I can see her forcing herself to shrug and moving on to something else. Later she'll work on whatever it is, but sometimes she won't even bother. It's like she found some common sense lying out on Stage Street where somebody dropped it, and she picked it up and put it in her pocket."

R gave her a funny little smile, then turned away and was soon picking at her sleeve again. Now Chick's head fought what R had said. Had she set herself impossible tasks in early childhood? Had caretaking become some kind of survival technique for her? It was true; anyone would feel depressed in the face of all that futile nurturing.

A woman in white emerged from an open door. "Rosemary Harris?" she called. Chick was startled when R rose. She said nothing, but to hear R of all people called by such an ordinary name?

R stood, leaned on her stick, and looked down. Chick had a vision of a tree after an ice storm, R's powerful aura falling from her with the crackle of icicles melting.

"Do you want me to go in with you?" Chick asked.

R's eyes were huge in her thin face; she looked like a person in shock.

"Ms. Harris?" encouraged the woman in white.

R closed her eyes for a long few seconds, then lifted her chin and slowly shook her head. The look on her face was of pure affection. "No. You don't need to go through this. See if you can take care of my friend Chick for me, will you?" R turned to the woman in white and followed her through the door.

The baby sputtered to silence, the daughter crisply turned another magazine page, the clothes in the backyards rose with the breeze. Chick didn't want to think about R in the examining room, resisting medical help or, even worse for R, surrendering to it. With an older partner, she had to think how it would be to watch Donny go through this. She looked out at the clotheslines again. Greenhill had its white sheets hanging too. She was thinking how nice it would be if she could remove the clothespins from her sadness, such an old useless feeling, let it fly off like a sheet of surrender over the town, out beyond the mountains where it could disintegrate into the sea.

Could it be that easy? Would she fall apart without the fabric of depression shaping her, or would she plummet into schizophrenia? She'd been dressing up in tie-dyes, bright colors, soft, protective flesh, and cheerful words all her adult life, but had never been able to give up this under layer of gray. Now she was more together than she'd ever been, practically a crone, and she had Donny, the store, a good community, even a fairly stable income. What was she waiting for?

A little girl of four or five sat next to her mother, head bowed over a Golden book. She seemed to sense Chick looking at her and raised her eyes. Chick smiled. She was a sturdy-looking freckle-faced kid, with big glasses, short unruly hair, and an earnest expression. Would her mom expect her to care for a sick little brother? What about Luke? The thought made her angry. She'd cream anyone who ever again tried to burden her grandson with adult problems.

"Take care of my friend Chick for me," R had said.

She went to the little girl and told her and her mother, "I have a grandson your age who likes me to read to him."

The child offered up her book almost before Chick finished talking.

"She's greedy for stories," said the mother. "I have to ration them or I'd never get anything done."

"Would you rather I didn't?"

"Be my guest."

"Once upon a time," she began when they'd made room on the couch for her. The little girl stuck her thumb in her mouth and wiggled in close.

Chick felt a laugh surfacing. While it might not look like it to R, she couldn't be more content than she was right now. This was taking care of herself. But, oh, what about her Donny, Jeep and Katie, Abeo, and poor, poor R?

CHAPTER THIRTY-ONE

City Girl / Lesbian Woods

The longer she stared at the candle, the wider and more colorful the halo around it grew. Katie found herself wondering if this weird phenomenon was related to rainbows, and she tried to remember exactly what refraction of light was about. Then, bored out of her skull, she dowsed the candle. Meditation sucked even with a vanilla-scented candle, and it was, after all, fire season. These woods were so dry it wouldn't take much to get a fire going that would burn for weeks. She switched on her headset, but the only music without static was country-western. She was not in the mood for suicide music.

"Okay," she said aloud, "it doesn't suck, I can't do it." She lay back in the dark on the used mat she'd bought that morning at Jethro's Jumble. "Secondhand. As if. Try thirty-second hand."

She was probably one of a long line of women who'd attempted the impossible art of meditation on this thing. R had led her down the very last garden path. Impressing a woven pattern on her buns was not Katie's idea of time well spent. She was going to have to find her own way of getting in touch with her spiritual side. If her feebly Catholic childhood hadn't ruined her for life. Crapola! She'd led Jeep to *her* new life, but had lost her own way. Sometimes she felt as empty as film with no image.

What was that rustling sound she kept hearing? She held her breath and listened to the night outside the dark cabin. This was M.C.'s land. After crashing here and there at Spirit Ridge, she'd turned down all the sympathetic offers to split housing costs—and beds—on a more permanent basis. She wasn't about to stay where she had to watch R and Abeo together. She was no crunchy-granola, open-relationship martyr type. It was too weird and painful for her taste. She'd heard talk that Abeo had moved in with some guys far out of town, but found that hard to believe. Even if Abeo had left, R felt wrong to her now, sullied and clay-footed.

She'd gone to ground here to concentrate on interviewing the non-gay population. Minus M.C., who'd gotten himself on the wanted list not long after she'd taped him the first time—she still considered the tape where Chick attacked him out of bounds. So she was lonesome, but she'd been lonesome even living with a lover, so no big deal. Staying here meant her money would last a lot longer.

Leaving Tanya in San Francisco had been a piece of cake compared to getting eased out of R's heart by a trans party girl. She felt like she hadn't made the grade with R. She was ashamed of her spiritual failure. Back in the Bay Area she and Tanya had agreed that there was nothing left after they'd both worked sixteen/seven the whole time they'd been together. She wondered if Tanya's IPO had gone well. She was so out of touch up here, she wouldn't even know if the whole high-tech bubble all of a sudden burst one day. Natural Woman Foods was on line, so she'd taken her laptop down a couple of times at first. But Jeep hung there, and Jeep didn't exactly act overjoyed to see her. She'd stopped going to the store where she'd at least gotten news of R from Chick. It felt better editing out the news which only tormented her. R was obviously not giving her a second thought.

Jeep and Cat. She'd seen them together, and still couldn't imagine the combination. There was no chemistry there, she was sure of it. Yet she'd heard from Clara and Hector that they were legally adopting the kid together? That was quick. The land women were on their oh-so self-righteous high horses about that. Like Jeep didn't have the sense to keep a boy-child off the land where he wasn't wanted. She'd be more of an older brother to him than a mom. Jeep had been the most playful lover she'd been with since her teens, her and her word play and sudden bursts of music. She'd sing, she'd drum on anything, she'd make whistles of willow leaves and start doing the samba in the middle of a Wal-Mart, marking time to the Musak with baby rattles. She missed that, but Jeep didn't have much of an attention span for anything other than music. Even making love kept her focused only so long, while she liked to linger and find her way deeper inside the spirit of a woman.

Could it be that this was her own kind of meditation, this flitting from thought to thought, this taking *time* to think, to dream up the scripts of her life through flashbacks and a long lens? God, lying here, too warm to get a fire going, no distractions, she felt like she could really breathe for the first time in years. She filled her lungs and smelled musty earth, wood, fire—mushrooms grew in wooden boxes under the shack, waiting for a harvester. The lousy radio reception out here—was this a good thing?

Tanya had been three years of occasional fun while their thing lasted and what she'd needed after Una. What was it with her and these older spiritual types? Una had been an Irish witch. Seven buoyant, breathtaking months of love and then Una had jumped on her heart with both feet. In spiked heels. She'd thought Una was it, the love of her life, her soul mate. Wrong.

Maybe she wanted to *be* these women, not be their lovers. Maybe getting her heart shattered a few times was like some kind of lesbian spirituality apprenticeship. What was next? Journeyman level? If she wasn't at the journey stage out here in these isolated, isolating woods, where was she supposed to be?

A fragmented thought buzzed her brain. She should be back in the city doing her career hooked up with a solid butchy woman like Jeep, only more simpatico and definitely not younger. She remembered R's words, "Women mate with many things, Aster. The land, for example." Was it her fate to have a camera as her only mate? "Intensity and passion don't equal love, do they?" Chick had said. That was the difference she was looking for? R was all about a cold intensity and passion, both for the land and for her lovers, that came from the mind and had nothing to do with love. Katie wanted Chick's all-heart passions, but was she capable of them or was she like R?

Whatever, she wouldn't give up. She'd felt led to these mountains, and she wasn't leaving until she finished whatever it was she needed to do, just as she'd felt led to choose a camera back in her teens and hadn't stopped probing life with it since. One of the old women in the trailer park had hired her to clean her place. Then she'd needed someone to drive her to cancer treatments and arranged to teach Katie to drive in exchange for the rides. Finally, when the woman had to go to a nursing home, she'd given Katie her husband's old Argus C3. By that time Katie had two other regular cleaning jobs and with the money she earned bought film. Her high school had a darkroom. She started selling photos to the local paper. In college she got use of a video camera by volunteering at one of the TV stations. They hired her after she covered a big deal sports and drugs scandal. Working for a San Francisco station had been her big goal, but by the time she'd gotten there, the challenges were getting old. Ambition didn't rev her up any more.

She felt like she'd learned here that she could use the camera to move into another realm, to do more than record images of people. She could search people's souls, film their worlds through their own eyes, and splice it all together to make—what? More than a documentary, something as alive as her subjects that could take on a life of its own and even move these mountains. She wanted to find her own power, nothing like R's; she didn't need that draining, controlling power. She wanted to use it to be a mirror. Only if she were clear enough could she reflect others' light. The work she was doing now was her spirit in action, and the camera fed her spirit. She'd needed to get out of R's sphere. R's treachery had been draining her. She'd known M.C.'s land and its buildings lay abandoned, so she'd decided to squat.

She'd been in this one-room shed over a month now. The police had confiscated most of M.C.'s equipment, but there were still cases of plastic bags stacked against one wall. She'd helped herself to the preserved foods she'd found in a shed smaller than hers and learned to operate—and cook on—the *diminutivo* propane stove. The woman at the hardware store had taught her how to pump up the gas lantern she'd bought. There was already a cot with more blankets than she could use in this hot weather.

The hardest part was going without a bathroom. Presumably there was one in the big complex down the hill, but that was padlocked. It might as well be as far as the next rest stop on a desert interstate. She rolled over and pushed herself to her feet, achy from lying on the flat floor. The door creaked as she opened it onto the dark stillness of the forest. At least San Francisco had lights.

In her head, perhaps to distract herself from the chilly little toilet excursions, she'd been playing with writing a humorous short video she'd been calling "City Girl/Lesbian Woods." It would begin with the sound of pine needles falling—a peaceful silence—in the dark. Then the fears would intrude on her character's peace. She would take a distant flashlight approaching along the forest floor and turn it into a majorly petrifying scene. She would play with sounds: the catch of raccoon claws on tree trunks, deer brushing against wet branches, the primeval screech of a startled night heron in the wetlands.

As she grabbed the roll of t.p. she kept in a closed coffee can outside the door, she contemplated a Scrooge-like character, a lesbian with ghosts. All the women she'd abandoned would drift through the mist to terrorize her. The character would feel haunted and vulnerable as giant trees dripped loudly around her, but she'd face her ghosts, yell back at their taunts, prod the empty shadows with a sharpened stick. Donna Quixote, she'd call her, a victim of her own loving.

So involved was she in her script that when the hand clamped over her mouth it seemed part of the story line. She tried to move out of its grip, but an arm came across her collarbone. Oh my God, she thought. We're not taping in a studio! Her bladder let go. She was dragged backwards by someone strong, someone wearing a heavy denim jacket, someone who thought Katie was Fay Wray. If she could get purchase on the heel of his hand with her teeth...

She caught some flesh and bit down hard. The flesh tasted like a chemical. What was this, an alien invasion?

"Shit!" he cried out, letting go.

She scrambled away on hands and knees until she hit a wall of bare, scratchy bushes. Despite her terror she thought, story of the century—if I live through it.

He grabbed at her. She kicked the fucker, but her clog flew off and her foot sunk into something creepily soft. He was heavily bearded, long-haired, and wore a layer of flesh like a cushion around himself. She rose to a crouch, then lunged toward the cabin. He tackled her. She squirmed and kicked and bit and butted, and then she saw his face.

"*Madre de diosa*! M.C.!" He'd blown up from the wiry guy who'd run from the police.

He squinted toward her. "It's the little dyke moviemaker! What the fuck are you doing on my property?"

Gross. He had old garlic breath. "House-sitting, you dumb gringo. Is this the thanks I get?"

"Who asked you to? You're causing me big trouble, woman."

"Let me go, dude." She was amazed when he did. She talked fast. This is what she did best, this thinking on her feet, riding an adrenaline spike. "I can leave. I was never here. You were never here."

"Right, and let you rat me out to your cop sister?"

"Sheriff Sweet? I've never even met the woman."

"She's still a sister of yours." M.C. played the flashlight over his property. "Maybe you did do some good here. Everything looks okay."

The man's clothes reeked—she had it now—of meth-making chemicals. "Where did you go? I never got to interview your family."

"That's all you care about, your interview?"

"No," she said and saw it all at once.

She wasn't here for the stories in Waterfall Falls; she was here for her story. R had not rescued the women at Spirit Ridge; they had never needed rescuing any more than she needed it right now. They wanted a mommy to take care of them and she, thinking they had found one in R, wanted her too. But R was no mommy, she was a power glutton. Katie was here to learn that she needed neither.

M.C. wrapped a bandanna around his bloody hand. "You have teeth like a fox, you little bitch," he said with a wimpy grimace.

Yes, she thought. I have good strong teeth and can take care of myself, can protect myself even against you.

But M.C. wasn't witness to her revelation. "What about us?" he asked. "We're busted. The pigs get me again and it's sayonara, baby, because this isn't the first time they've shut down Mission Control."

"What are you, brain-dead? You came back here for what bonehead reason?"

"I'm making one last humungous batch of meth, to set myself up in Mexico. We've got the police scanner on so we know where everybody is. The cops stole so much of our equipment, but they didn't find my stash of chemicals." He held up his hands, red with dirt. "Buried it up the mountain on the property next door. Those old people never walk out that far."

"It's true then? You manufacture? I didn't believe them."

"That bother you, reporter lady?"

"It puts a whole new spin on things, dealer man. I thought I was documenting an old hippie turned vigilante logger, but I have plenty of loggers. You were using that holy roller church and the vigilantes as cover, weren't you? What a story! How do you really feel about living in Waterfall Falls? Why did you settle here—"

"I settled here because it used to be mountain-man territory! The old-timers and the crazed Viet vets wanted to be left alone. I did my thing. The first Sheriff Sweet was a good old boy, easy to handle. His deputies looked the other way for a little stash. Now, with all these retirees from down south moving onto the land, building their fucking rustic castles copied out of *House Beautiful*, acting holier than thou, and with that new Sheriff Straight-Arrow-on-the-Job-and-Crooked-Arrow-off-Duty...Don't get me started. I have work to do."

M.C. gave her a shove toward the cabin.

"Hello?" she objected.

"Get in the shack, *Tortillera*, and mellow out. I see your door open or your car move an inch, and you're a dead dyke." He picked up a shotgun he must have tossed away to grab her. "The sheriff will think it's a hate crime, or a gal-pal quarrel. Get in," he repeated, gesturing with the gun.

"Fine. Whatever. You don't have to go postal on me. I'm wiped. I'll put what you said on tape while it's fresh, then crash. I'm not used to fending off attackers." She pushed the door open and asked over its creaking, "I could keep myself awake if you'd, like, let me film you while you're cooking? I'd edit your face out of the final story."

"Are you shitting me? Story, story! You're going to get yourself killed for a story."

His face lost its hurried look, and she watched as his ego considered the lure of mondo-risk fame. "What if I blew us sky-high? You willing to take that chance?"

She couldn't say no now.

But he did. "No, you're the one who's nuts, not me. You stay right where you are and write your story—as long as you make sure I'm long gone before you move on it. And don't forget for a second, I'm going to have one of my boys on lookout. If he sees you move outside, I'll be on you."

"*Tu madre!* You'd risk blowing up your sons? No wonder you left the little guy behind. How could you do that?"

"He's not mine. I got it out of one of my old ladies before we split—she had him by this guitar player who came through town. The kid's probably some kind of musical genius, another Jakob Dylan. But he was fucked up, wouldn't talk. I told her, you can come with me or you can have the kid. Well, the kid's not going to score for her, but she's been moaning and bitching ever since." A car drove by on the road far below them. M.C. listened until its sound faded. "She's down there taking care of business now. I decided, if she finds him, she can keep the little mutant, if that'll shut her up."

"But he was in the papers."

"No shit?"

"Someone's trying to adopt him. She can't go in there and steal him back."

"She's his mother. She has a pretty good claim, and she's going to take him back," he said, mimicking her. "Is that a problem for you? It wouldn't cost but a minute to tie you up and leave you hoping somebody comes looking for you before winter."

Who would? God, nobody, she thought.

"Not to worry," she told him, her wet jeans cold now. Did she smell like a public urinal? Whatever. She'd deal with it. "The country is about freedom for me too. I'll be asleep before you start your work. Oh, and M.C.?" she laughed. She would not let this man intimidate her. "Have a good life—preferably in another galaxy."

He gave her a last half-smiling, half-threatening look and lumbered up the hill. Gaining weight was a killer disguise, she thought with admiration. Maybe she could use that on film some day. He'd scared her big-time, but at least she wasn't bored.

Katie creaked the door shut as if she'd gone inside. She stood still and hoped the shadows of the trees, swaying slightly in the low wind, swallowed her. She tried to come up with some inspiring movie-theme music, but all she got was Disney, the lyrics lost to her childhood except something about whistling when you're scared. Well, she couldn't exactly whistle, could she? If she was going to walk out of here, she'd have to do it before M.C. alerted his kids. God, she did smell like an outhouse. She started counting. At one hundred she would move.

She could see the lights up in the big trailer as she crept, shaking badly now, barely breathing, while blackberry bushes stretching across her path clutched at her ankles, into the woods.

CHAPTER THIRTY-TWO

Two-Spirit

Sheriff Sweet hasn't used her siren since the Garrett girl had her baby at Mother Hubbard's restaurant," Donny said, watching with some alarm as the police car zoomed north on Stage Street. Her scanner was silent.

Abraham stepped back out of the bus shelter where he'd either read every word of the Greyhound schedule or was avoiding talking to Donny. "As long as R didn't send her after me."

Donny surprised herself by feeling only mildly annoyed at him. "I don't know why R wanted you back in the first place, as messed up as you are."

"I am messed up."

"First you're a flaming South Side queen, then you claim to have your amputation and come here to be a lesbian, next thing I know you're all boy again with Harold and Joe. You never even told me you'd gone back to R, and now you can't wait to get away from her again?"

Abraham's whine hadn't changed since he was six. "I was set to tell you at the potluck that I'd moved back to Spirit Ridge, but you never showed up and you know R doesn't have a phone."

"I was too sick to lift my head and you want me to go chasing after you?"

"What did you have, some kind of spring flu? You look like you lost weight. You're too skinny to start with."

"No more than I've lost worrying over you all these years. It was a summer cold. Knocked me on my ass."

"I would have helped out at the store if you'd gotten word to me."

"Jeep came in every chance she could."

"Now there's a messed-up woman. What is she thinking of, taking on that little boy? No lesbian in your community will get in five feet of her except Cat. She'll be single forever."

"Maybe single suits her."

"Maybe, but you know how she strikes me? She feels like a woman already claimed. Like she's given her heart away, wanted or not. I hope it wasn't to Katie. Her passion is her camera."

"Abe, how come you know so much about how Jeep should live her life and not a damn thing about how to live your own?"

"Ain't that a bitch? I'm thinking I'll go back to college and get my counseling degree."

"I've heard that one before. Tell me what I should be doing."

"Oh, you're doing it, Donalds. I don't know why a tiny burg without a gay bar to its name suits you, but this is the Don's town now. You've got your fingers in every pie—the small businesses, the Sheriff's Department, the gay people, the old ladies' sewing circle, and the politickers. You've got the nicest woman you've ever been with, and she even knows she's lucky to have you. You've got land women friends and faggot friends and straight friends. You can fish your heart out here like you always wanted to. You're home, Donny."

Donny looked away, eyes wet. She didn't trust her voice. It was all true, and she hadn't thought about it all at once like that. Her Chick was the greatest treasure on earth, plus she had so much else! Gram and Grampop were surely looking out for her up there.

"The only thing that worries me about you, Donalds, is your temper. You're getting too old to let every little thing spike your blood pressure."

Abe was all in black tonight, with purple flecking on his tissue-thin scarf. Behind him was a signpost the Chamber of Commerce had donated to the town. Surrounded by a disk of earth thick with dahlias, wooden arrows sprouted in every direction listing far-off cities and their distances from Waterfall Falls. Istanbul, one of them read, 6,400 miles. Why would anyone want to know how far she was from Istanbul unless she wanted to send a fool like Abe there?

Donny said, "That Greyhound is late."

There was the sound of another siren, this one approaching from Greenhill. She glanced at Abraham. He had that coy, weasely look she found so annoying. She hoped he wasn't running from the law. At least tonight that look didn't throw her into a rage the way it used to the first fifty years she'd known him, but it still pissed her off. Abe's call had come at 10:00, when she and Chick had cut the light.

"You have to come get me out of here!" Abe had whispered into the phone.

"Where're you at? What kind of trouble did you get yourself into now?" Donny had asked.

"I'm at the pay phone outside the Mule Butte General Store on the way to town. I walked down here and I'm ready to collapse. Come get me, Donny! I have to catch that 12:40 bus!"

"Abe, I'm tired. Chick's tired. Why have you stranded yourself this time?"

"R just told me she's got the big C."

"Say what?"

"I can't take care of another terminal! They were reason numero forty-five why I tried women. I loved my boys, but they died on me, one by one. Come and get me out of here, and I'll never ask another thing, I swear!"

Donny knew she wasn't getting the whole story. R announces she's dying and Abraham runs out on her? Not likely. She covered the mouthpiece and turned to Chick next to her in bed. "Why didn't you tell me R's cancer metastasized to her bones? How long did the doc give her?"

Chick stared at her, lurched out of bed, and grabbed the clothes she'd only a few minutes ago taken off. Wrong way to break that news to Chick, Donalds, she chided herself. She could see Chick getting whiter in the face.

Abe's voice grew shrill. "It's in more lymph nodes than I thought you could have. I can't stay here, Donalds. She's got all of you to take care of her. I need to go find a family that will take care of me. I'm not doing this again."

She repeated the details to Chick.

"And Abe left her?" Chick asked while she struggled with her socks.

"And you left her?"

"Don't be saying it like that. She had a meeting of the women up there to announce it. They're all bawling and hugging on R and each other. It's a mess. I said I was going outside to pee. That was a long time ago. I'm standing out here in the rain in nothing but somebody's rubber boots, pajamas, and R's rain jacket. You need to grab the clothes I left downstairs so I can change in your car. You can have whatever money I left at Spirit Ridge, and I'll send the rest of what I owe you for the ticket."

"Easy, Abe, easy. I'll be right there." It was either that or answer a frantic knock on the door after he hitched a ride—or got arrested.

Chick, pulling on socks, asked, "Where's R? Why didn't she tell me the results?"

"From what Abe said, R's at Spirit Ridge." Donny held her arms open. "I'm sorry, babe. She threw me. I thought you knew about R and hadn't told me."

Chick hesitated. "No. I have to keep going. If I feel your arms around me I'll cry. I don't want to cry. R doesn't need me crying all over her."

"Come here." Chick laid her head on Donny's shoulder. "I'm so sorry about your friend. I thought you went to the clinic with her."

"I did. She must have gone alone for the results. I kept asking if they were in and telling her I'd drive her up there. Poor, stupid R, the hardest part. Poor, stupid, proud R probably didn't want anyone to see her freak out. I'll bet she never did go. I should have known. She probably fought with them to find out over the phone since she'd already decided she was going the natural way."

Donny held her tighter.

"First we become grandparents, now we've got someone dying. What's going on, Donny?"

"We're grownups, babe."

"That's all? This is what it's going to be like from here on?"

Donny thought for a moment, remembering Abraham in short pants, herself in a white dress at some do. Remembering her first girlfriend, plump little Angel, and kissing for hours behind the high school, listening to the Chiffons, the Ronettes. Remembering the long evenings patrolling the museum, the long dawns disco dancing, her brother coming out of jail that first time when she felt so hopeful about him, Martin Luther King's speech, the Panthers, riots and fires, drugs all around her, and drive-by shootings and hot summer picnics on the lakefront playing Frisbee and pickup basketball and the Cubs losing every time she went to see them play and her first gay pride march and driving west with Chick.

"What is it going to be like, babe? It's going to be me holding you. You holding me. That's how it's going to be."

Chick leaned back and smiled. Her eyes were like blue water in the sunshine, like the blue of the pool under the falls. They'd finally gotten back to the falls again last Sunday. The sun had burned and burned till it got so hot in town they were desperate for relief. They'd driven up quickly, and had not dallied on the trail. It was dinnertime and they were alone. They'd walked the curving path, climbed over fallen trees, and crept around boulders to stand behind the falls and watch the water's unending dive into the blue pond. She'd intended to picture herself tossing all her anger in, watching it whirl and sink and flow downstream forever, but she'd forgotten to do that in the relief of the moment.

That feeling of peace came back to her now as Chick said, "For the rest of our lives, honeypot. And don't you forget it." She gave Donny's cheek a quick moist kiss, then dashed to the bathroom.

So Chick had gone up to Spirit Ridge while Donny followed along the dark wet roads behind her to the closed general store where Abraham skulked to the truck.

Now in front of the sign to Istanbul, Abe looked up from under her eyebrows at Donny, all coy. He seemed to have forgotten R as soon as Donny showed up to whisk him away.

The glow from that hugging time with Chick had faded by then. She asked, "What the hell were you doing back with R? I thought I already rescued your ass when I took you to Joe and Harold's?"

"R said she missed me. She was so down I couldn't say no, but she didn't tell me about the cancer. I think she wanted me around because I told her about nursing my boys. I think she wanted her own personal hospice nurse." Abraham hugged himself. "I can't do this again."

"Don't start crying now. The last thing I need is a hysterical queen on my hands."

If her reaction was any indication, Chick was going to be a handful herself. She'd probably want to bring R to their place to die. Donny could hear Chick now: "We're a straight shot to the hospital, honeypot. I can look in on her between customers." But she'd seen it before, Chick taking in some needy stray who would as likely as not rip them off before leaving Waterfall Falls. This would be an emotional rip-off, with R going off to lesbian separatist heaven, leaving Donny catching up after a hundred extra washes in their little laundry room in back of the store and Chick grieving.

"You can't tell the land women what I told you about me, Donny. They'll turn on her."

"Bullshit. They'll rush to take care of her all the faster."

"No. I've listened to them go on about men. They'll leave her alone to die! You have to swear on your Mama's grave that you won't say anything."

"Your big brother Donny has no need to protect all those bare-ass little gals playing Tarzan. They can take a dose of truth about their guru-ette."

"You swear."

"I don't hold back from Chick."

"Will she go running off at the mouth?"

Yet another siren was arriving. She reached in the truck window and ratcheted up the volume on the scanner, but there was silence. That troubled her all the more. Something was happening the sheriff didn't want broadcast. What a stupid fool thing to ask about Chick, as if she would broadcast someone's secrets.

"Fuck this shit. I need to go find Joan. She may need help." Immediately, she told herself, easy, girl, and breathed deeply.

Abe pushed between her and the truck. With her face close to Donny's, he whispered, "You have to understand, girlfriend. R's got enough without confessing that she's—"

"Straight? Abraham, I do not want to hear any more," she shouted over the sirens. It was two state cops, taking the corner of Stage and Cliff on the edges of their wheels. She noticed that all the sirens cut off as they left town to drive east up the mountain. "What the fuck's going on? It must be a car wreck."

"Lord, don't let it be that bus. I need to—"

"To what, Abraham? To go mess up somebody else's head?"

"She wanted me, Donny. She said she was more a political lesbian than a sexual one. She was studying the two-spirit idea, starting to look at herself that way. Now she'll never have time to find out who she is."

"I'm not talking about R's head. It's mine that's confused."

"Hell, you only have the one spirit, and it's pure diesel dyke."

She almost snapped "I know that" at Abraham, but found herself smiling instead. "Aren't I lucky," she said.

The scanner in her little truck came alive. Nine-eleven dispatch was calling for Sheriff Sweet's deputies. Man, did she hate being a deputy on the same team with Johnny Johnson and his friends, but somebody had to back Joan up when they went overboard.

"I've got to go."

Abe lunged at her and mashed her in a hug.

"Abe! I thought you got rid of your sandpaper chin."

Abe looked panicky. "R says the hormones are bad for me."

"Son of a b. It sounds like the two spirits inside Abraham Clinkscales are getting to know each other pretty well."

"You're not mad at me, are you?"

Abraham was the most infuriating person in her life, but it was true, he'd done more than his share of caretaking. HIV had been his second Vietnam. And gender confusion had turned into a gay national pastime in recent years. That must have been irresistible to his lost soul. She heard herself thinking beyond anger. "Why would I be? Lots of queer folk come up here to find themselves. I'm glad it's working out for you."

"It is. I'll be back for the two-spirit gathering. If they have an opening at the Gay Bay Area Youth Center I'm going to take it too, residential, graveyard, whatever they need, and I'll finish my degree. This time, Don, I'll do it. I think I've got something these kids can use. Thanks for everything, man."

"Be careful who you call a man. It's not safe to take anything for granted these days."

While the scanner tripped over its channels, Abe looked to be studying her face before laughing. "You crack me up, Donny, you really do. You were such a wild young thing and now you're such an old fogey."

Donny let herself laugh too. She'd only looked wild from the outside. It had been home she'd been looking for all her life, and she'd woman-hunted with the wildness of desperation every time she lost one, not realizing that a woman was only part of the foundation. It had taken Chick, the store, the old ladies, and the politicking—and even this crazy-ass, out-of-the-way, mostly white hick burg out of a Western—to make her roots grow.

"The bus will be here any minute. You cool with me taking off?"

"Very cool. I need to go home."

"Let me know." Donny looked at Abe's groin. "About everything."

As she slid her flashing light onto the roof of the truck, she recognized that for all the aggravation of the evening, she still felt good. Wait till she told Chick that she hadn't blown her fuse once.

CHAPTER THIRTY-THREE

Garage Sale Dandy, The Shop

The call came as Jeep switched off the computer. She reached for the phone across her broad oak desk. The sight of it always made her smile. What a total find it had been at that estate sale. And the computer was one of a lot of twelve she'd found at an online auction site. She'd sold every one of them within three weeks of their arrival except the one she kept. The money bankrolled a nice selection of used instruments. The desk still smelled of the lemon oil she'd rubbed into it.

A small business loan had covered everything she'd needed to set up Garage Sale Dandy, including the refurbished laptop. She'd been working at Jethro's Junk a couple of months when Jethro came back to work. He'd lost the weight he needed to for his back operation and felt fit enough to skip the surgery. Meanwhile, she'd been so successful at bringing inventory to the shop, both from scrounging around the county with Clara and Hector and from the internet deals, that she was crowding him out. Since Jethro lacked the ambition to do anything but go fishing and talked incessantly about retiring, they agreed things would work more smoothly if, instead of Jeep managing his shop, he let her use the upstairs gratis for Garage Sale Dandy and paid her a wage when she filled in for him downstairs. All this had been way too fun to even think about music therapy. She had gone ahead with giving lessons to three people so far, in three instruments, and was working on her first repair. None of this was what she'd dreamed of, but it sure felt good.

Luke had spent the day with her, except for Pollywog Day Camp, but Cat had him tonight. Jeep, who'd been without a computer for so long she'd reverted to a techno-peasant, needed the time to get her spreadsheet program under control, and to enter some new CDs she'd ordered for customers reluctant to travel to the nearest mall music shop up in Greenhill. If MP3 didn't knock her out of the loop, she was pretty certain her little business would work. Bookkeeping was a downer. Why did they still call it bookkeeping anyway, if you did it on a computer? Compu-keeping? Spreadsheeting? Accu-comping?

She'd been buzzing along high on dreams and adrenaline and only realized it was so late because Jethro's clocks were all chiming eleven downstairs.

"Chill," she said calmly to Cat on the phone. This was no more than a blip in her perfect stratosphere. Luke was safe somewhere. "So Luke's not in his bed. Maybe he's in the music room, sleeping under the drum set. He's done that before." She listened to all the places Cat had searched, then, doing a 360 on her worry meter, told her, "I'm on my way."

Her skateboard wasn't going to cut it. She was a little anxious to get home and couldn't use the board once she reached the hill. Chick liked to hear the sound of Jeep's skateboard going by the store late at night; the neighbors wouldn't. She rang Chick's number to see if she or Donny could give her a ride, but only the machine answered. No way they were out anywhere—they crashed early, like most everyone else she knew in this town. It was a country thing. No one else lived close enough to make getting a ride worthwhile. The truth was that she liked to have Donny or Chick around in a crisis. They were Luke's grandparents; they'd know what to do. She thought of another grandparent and called Casino Cab. Waterfall Falls had never needed a cab before the casino went in.

Hattie the cabby arrived in the alley as Jeep was locking the back door to the shop.

"You have an emergency?" Hattie asked when Jeep dove into the front seat beside her.

She felt her anxiety rev up as she answered, "Luke's missing."

Hattie responded by backing non-stop out of the alley instead of weaving through the dumpsters and discarded display racks. If Hattie was that worried, maybe they should call the sheriff. Hattie had raised more kids that anyone Jeep knew. Hattie's live-in great-grandson, born with cerebral palsy, had been in Jeep's class last year. Jeep figured Hattie was at least seventy, well beyond the age someone should have to drive a cab or raise a kid, but Hattie claimed she couldn't sleep nights anyway and loved getting out and meeting the people she called "those dumb clucks from Greenhill who couldn't find anything better to do with their cash than give it to the tribe." Her nephew, whom she'd raised, was a tribal bigwig at the casino, so what Hattie wanted, she got.

Donny's truck was at the Greyhound stop. She was standing there with Abe under the drugstore's neon mortar and pestle sign. The bus was southbound this time of night; maybe Abe was having an emergency too. Jeep's fingers ached with cold. Her mouth tasted like aluminum foil. The needle on her worry meter jiggled like a compass in a meteor storm.

She grabbed the ceiling handle when Hattie slammed on her brakes to avoid Sheriff Sweet. Siren shrieking, the cruiser was rounding the corner of Stage and Cliff in the other direction.

"I've been saying all evening," Hattie drawled as if she wasn't doing fifty through the blind underpass, "there's something in the air tonight. Dark of the moon."

"The little guy's a sleepwalker," Jeep explained, as much to herself as to Hattie. "Cat's house is so big he could be anywhere. One time we found him curled up sound asleep in the attic on a pile of old afghans stored in Cat's grandmother's hope chest. At least he left the chest open." She blurted out, "That kid rocks my world, Hattie."

"The young ones do. It's a dangerous world for them. If it isn't sharks at the seashore, it's terrorists in the cities. You let me know when he turns up," Hattie said outside Cat's place. She wouldn't take money, but Jeep laid it on the seat and took off up the steps at a run.

Cat looked so fragged Jeep didn't have to ask whether Luke had shown up yet. Her blouse was untucked, and her hair had gone all flat in the back. She guessed she knew what Cat had been doing this evening and that she'd been doing it with Joan. There was a huge charge of electricity between those two, and they didn't get much chance to drain the energy. Like Hattie the cabby, Cat knew kids better than Jeep did.

"Is this why the sheriff went through town like the aliens had landed?"

"Joan was here all evening until her squawker went off. She said it was about cleaning up unfinished business. I looked in on Luke after she left and saw he wasn't there."

"When did you last see him?" Jeep asked, propping her board in the hall closet.

"We were watching TV. I'd put Luke to bed at eight, checked him at nine thirty. He was fast asleep. I wanted to close the window, but you know how he is about keeping it open. I think he wants to make sure the tooth fairy gets in when he's older."

"You don't think he went out the window?"

Cat put an arm around her and they hugged quickly. "It was only open a crack. I brought George inside. He was barking out there like there were burglars jimmying every window and door. I was getting nervous."

They started a methodical tour of the house with George at their heels. Lump Sum, disturbed in the living room, followed as far as the kitchen. Jeep willed herself to go slowly. She didn't want to involve the whole town if Luke was only well-concealed. "You checked the basement?"

"Only four times."

"The attic?"

"Let's look again. The light's so poor up there."

"I'll grab the bigger flashlight." When she climbed the narrow stairs she immediately smelled it. "Cat?" she called back. "Why does it smell like dope up here?"

Cat's head appeared at the opening. "I noticed that. I thought it was time for an airing. You think it's dope?"

"Oh, yeah."

"George, stay," she commanded. "Wait for us right there."

Jeep went to the small dormer window at the north end of the attic and opened it. "Don't you usually keep this window locked?"

"Always."

"Look at this. Somebody—" she picked up a scrap of thin white paper and some ash. She smelled it, mystified. "Who in hell would be dousing roaches on your attic windowsill? Luke isn't old enough to know what weed is, much less smoke it. Or is he? You're the teacher. Tell me the preschoolers are getting high."

"How long has it been there?"

"Cat. It's clean paper. The smallest draft would have blown it away otherwise. Rain would have disintegrated it."

"This is creepy. I'm going to try Joan again."

"I have a feeling she may be up to her ass in alligators, Cat. She was heading east at warp speed."

"Shh," Cat said.

"What?"

"Shh!"

She didn't hear anything, but the attic was weirding her out. This was normally dead space. Not tonight. Were the spirits Katie always talked about flying? Katie. It felt like decades since she'd been with Katie.

"Luke?" she called softly. "Lukie? Come on out, dude. You're not in any trouble."

They both stood very still for longer than Jeep thought she could tolerate. That's when she felt the chilled air. This was way wrong. Where the fuck was it getting in? From the trap door to the roof? The door, reached by wooden rungs nailed to the east wall, normally was fastened tightly with a block of wood that swung in and out of place on a nail. The wood was in its open position, which could mean the door had been closed from outside.

"Holy holodeck," she whispered, pointing. Cat moved swiftly toward the ladder. "I'll check the yard," she told Cat. "He could be lying out there with a broken neck!"

Instead she stood frozen in place, staring as Cat heaved the door upward. It had been built with an overlap to prevent rain from getting inside, and that made it even heavier. The night air smelled of wide-open dangerous spaces. Cat could need her help here. Yet every second might count if Luke was injured. How could he have lifted such a thing by himself? Why was she so paralyzed?

Cat was half-out, supporting the door with her left shoulder. "I'm going on the roof, Jeep. Would you hold this thing open?"

She found the fast-forward button in her brain and shot up the rungs on the wall, catching the door as Cat eased it onto her hands. "Be careful," she whispered, not because she was afraid Luke would hear, but because she was afraid. Now that she held the rough wooden weight of the door she knew he hadn't lifted it. Not alone.

Hattie had been right; it was the dark of the moon. She could hear Cat scrabbling along the rooftop more than see her. Then there was a sharp intake of breath.

"Who are you?" Jeep heard. Then, "Let him go!"

"Cat!" Jeep cried.

"Come to me, Luke." Cat said. "Who are you!"

Jeep heard a small voice, but couldn't make out what it said. Another child? A woman? Then it was clear.

"My mama!"

She'd heard enough of Luke's whispery baby-talk attempts at speech to recognize it. A flicker of relief was erased by alarm. His mother? Here? To do what? Kidnap him? Was it kidnapping to take back a foster child? Maybe, if she was a fugitive, Jeep conjectured, trying to understand the implications of it all, but it had never been clear if the mother actually was charged with anything or if she'd run away with her drug lord. At that, an enormous sense of loss came over her. She felt like a horn player who'd lost her lip, a pianist with broken hands. The mother would take the boy. She was going to lose him.

Cat persuaded mother and son to come in off the roof. Jeep relinquished the door and backed slowly down the rungs. It might not be tonight, but she would lose him. He'd spoken aloud for his mama. Maybe he always had.

But of course, she supposed that's what children were about: the over-the-top joy of them, the rearing as best you could, the letting go. It was all happening kind of fast for her taste, but even if they fought the mother, or kept Luke until the mother was free, or raised him until he went off, which he for sure would, with a ragtag band lucky enough to find a drummer as fine as Luke was going to be, she was going to miss him big-time. She'd make the mother take his drums. She'd tell her to give Luke his music.

Then she'd vamoose to Reno. Go back home and help out with her nieces and nephews when they started arriving. She'd buy instruments from gambling musicians down on their luck and peddle instruments to them when they'd won enough money to get to their next gigs. Maybe Luke's band would come through town some day. Maybe he'd remember her. She and Sarah could have had a rug rat of their own by now. Or a slew of them. As a joke she'd given Sarah a turkey baster for Valentine's Day their second year together. Jeep doubted Sarah had gotten rid of that, even though she went on about overpopulation and how she wanted to adopt. Unless maybe she'd found someone else to use it with. She couldn't believe how wigged out she got every time that possibility came to mind.

She didn't know for sure, but when she'd called Sarah last week, Sarah acted single. It was Jeep who had to say, "There's someone else in my life."

Sarah said, "I could have figured that out."

"No, not like that," she'd replied and told her about Luke and how she and Cat were co-foster parenting him and about the sheriff and living with Cat. She could feel Sarah loving the boy through the phone lines and realized she might never have gotten involved in this Luke thing if Sarah hadn't taught her about the importance of adopting and the crime of overpopulation. She'd never thought of that stuff before Sarah.

"It's not that I want or need a kid in my life, it's that Luke needs someone and he's so special.

"I've made some changes too," Sarah eventually told her. She'd stayed in personnel, but moved to another hotel. With all her old enthusiasm she told Jeep, "It's like architecture. I get to take all these different elements—people—and create a functional structure—the department. I love meeting all the applicants and employees and hearing their ambitions and seeing myself in them."

She wondered if they would have ended up making the same kinds of decisions if she hadn't left Reno.

Jeep brought herself back to the present. They were all in the living room. Luke wouldn't leave his mother's side, but petted George with his free hand.

"Hey, dude, where's the smile?" Jeep teased him, but he only grabbed tighter to his mother's bright Mexican patchwork jacket. Jeep felt like the enemy.

The woman was short and thin, with long graying brown hair and some missing teeth. She sat on the couch with Luke.

Another siren came down off the freeway, and she realized that she'd been hearing the whooping and blaring for a long time.

"My name is Pennylane. I came in the back door," the mother was saying, in answer to Cat's questions. "It wasn't very locked. I know how those store-bought locks work." She brought Luke so close to herself on the couch he looked like a piece of her.

He'd never given a hint that he missed his mother, Jeep marveled. She'd thought he was content, and yet here he was, obviously not about to let the woman out of his sight any time soon, even though she looked and acted like she'd stepped out of a time machine from the nineteen sixties. What did a kid know?

"I heard you talking in the kitchen with the woman pig," Pennylane continued. "So I went down the hall and looked around." She smiled down at Luke, and Jeep could see where he'd gotten his beaming smile. "My baby was asleep in a room. I saw all the Leap Frog and Harry Potter and Matchbox stuff you got him. I thought about splitting because you're giving him a good life, but then I tripped on a cat that was lying on its back right in my way. I must have made a sound without meaning to because he was out of the bed and on me whispering, 'Mama, Mama,' and I thought my heart would break like it did when I left him behind."

That dumb Lump Sum, Jeep thought. The woman was lucky George hadn't bounded to greet her.

The woman composed herself, wiping her eyes with the back of her hand. Jeep gritted her teeth to hold in her anger—where had this soft heart been when she'd abandoned Luke. She tried to hand Pennylane her bandanna, but Luke took it, opened it, swiped roughly at his mother's face, and went back to pinning her to the couch like a proud young wrestling champ.

Pennylane's voice took on a tough edge. Jeep guessed her accent was from some not-quite-Southern state, like Missouri. Pennylane told Cat, "You were in the living room, watching the TV. Luke was a good boy and stayed in his room while I checked." She'd been talking mostly to the floor, but now looked Cat full in the face. "You were kissing that woman in the pig uniform. She's the sheriff here, isn't she? That's when I decided I wasn't leaving my little boy behind. I may be a loser, but I can do him better than dykes."

"Better than love?" Jeep shot back. "Love and music and sane, sober people who think he's a total miracle?"

The woman looked at her like she'd been doused with ice water, but then went on with her story. "I was trying for the back door when your sheriff girlfriend rushed into the kitchen and out the back door herself. She would have caught us if she hadn't been in such a hurry. Luke led me up to the attic. Pretty soon I heard his name being called. There was no place to hide but the roof."

"That wasn't a safe place to take a little kid."

Pennylane hissed, "And this house, with what goes on in it is? Are you her girlfriend too? Don't you say a word to anyone about me taking Luke or I'll go to the newspapers with what I saw. She won't be sheriff long."

"And you," Jeep found herself saying, "will be taking a time-out in the ladies' slammer. Don't you know the police are looking for you? Then who'll give Luke what we can give him?"

"His aunt Marly and me, that's who! She's got two little ones he's been raised with. They're still safe back in Mexico. It's only M.C. and me who had to come back. We've got unfinished business."

Luke suddenly let go and shook his head with such mondo movements Jeep said, "Luke, stop! You'll give yourself whiplash."

It was Cat's turn. "You're not taking this boy back to that atmosphere. You're lucky he was born as whole as he is with all that drug activity. Look, even he doesn't want that."

The mother was silent, watching the boy. She held out her arms to him, and as he hesitated she blurted, "You think I don't know that? Come here, Pumpkin. I know M.C. blew it with you. I know the others picked on you bad. I couldn't stop them. They made him worse, if you ask me. Every time he opened his mouth the kids were copycatting him. He has this sweet little lisp. They were jealous of you from the first, my poor baby, my favorite, and Marly's so stoned she doesn't kick their little asses for them. You've always been like an angel come to earth, with that out-of-sight smile, haven't you? They couldn't deal with your loving nature. Pretty soon he stopped talking except when we were alone, like he took some kind of, like, vow of silence to protect his incredibly sweet self."

She looked at Cat, then at Jeep, her eyes like those of someone trapped. "I never knew what to do. I thought leaving him behind he'd be free of the drug life, but I missed you so bad, Luke. I don't care what I have to do. I won't freak out on you again."

"Even," Jeep asked, filled with guilt that she was using this as a threat, but desperate for herself and for Luke, who'd have no chance at all if he went back to that family, "even if it means getting clean?"

Pennylane looked at her, the anger hard, then smoldering, then draining from her eyes. "Yes. I'm ready. I had my last toke up in your attic. For the longest time it hasn't been doing nothing for me but frying my brain. Things have been over between me and M.C. for years except the insults, the hitting, and the drugs. I didn't know where to go, what to do!"

The woman stroked Luke's blond hair, and he closed his eyes like someone too content to stand much more pleasure. "I'm sorry I got so hateful about you being queer," she said, not looking away from Luke. "The truth is, I sometimes think me and Marly would be a lot better off without M.C. He's not much of an improvement on nothing at all, teaching the kids to make shit and peddling it. When I was stoned all the time it was funny, but not any more. I got Luke's half-sister out." She dropped her voice to a whisper, as if Luke couldn't hear her. "M.C. was bothering her. She's staying with my folks in Oklahoma and going to the community college. My first is over in Africa in the Peace Corps. I'm so proud of him. They'll turn out okay, no thanks to me."

"But you stayed," said Cat.

Eyes cast down, Pennylane replied, "But I stayed." There was a defiant lift to her chin when she looked up. "What would I do in the straight world? At least Luke got a better daddy than my others did."

Astonished, Jeep said, "Wait. You mean M.C.'s not his father?"

"Oh, no. Only Luke and me knew, but M.C. guessed not long before the raid went down. His real dad's Trevor McKinnon, the banjo player for True Harps. I played Luke his tapes since before you were born, right, Luke? It's old-time—"

"McKinnon rocks!" Jeep exclaimed, and told Cat, "They are like the number-one group in the world, and McKinnon—he's from Ireland, right?—he's so fast you can't see his fingers move. Luke," she said, kneeling by him, "you're your old man's sprout all right. You came by your talent naturally."

"I know he has rhythm," Pennylane said. "Every chance he got he'd be tapping out a tune with a spoon or a stick. Drove M.C. nuts. I'd have to stop poor Luke."

"I always heard M.C. was a few fries short of a Happy Meal. This is super news. Luke's been, like, in charge of keeping the beat around here. You want to show mom your skins, dude?"

The boy's sunny disposition reemerged, and he pulled Pennylane after him into the music room.

After a moment they heard Luke's steady beat and swish on his small traps. Then the piano started up, and the mother was playing a hesitant rendition of the Beatles' tune "Michelle." Luke picked up the rhythm.

Cat had tears in her eyes too. "We'll have to help them," she said.

Jeep nodded. "Maybe we can stay in Luke's life. Don't they have some kind of get-out-of-jail-free card if you rat somebody out? Do you think we can get her to tell Joan about every indictable thing M.C. ever did?"

The phone rang. Jeep went to watch Luke and his mom, both touched by and anxious about the reunion.

The mom called to her, "I haven't forgotten everything!" She launched hesitantly into an old Neil Young song.

She felt like a trapdoor had opened under her, and she was being held up by nothing more than a swirl of smoke. Music wasn't enough, she thought. She might live with Luke, take care of him sometimes, but she'd just lost half of the center of her life. Again. Be real, Jeep, you know what you need. Its time to get serious and chase Sarah Teitel. Could be she's just another dream, this one made of regrets. Could be I've been trying to fill up her place in my soul with these imposters. If

Sarah was interested, they could start a family of their own. Maybe I'm ready now. Or not.

Cat joined them in the music room. "That was the sheriff. Pennylane?" Pennylane stopped playing and turned to her. "I have some news for you. The sheriff caught up with M.C. on your land, packing up meth supplies. Two boys were helping him."

Pennylane shook her head. "Marly's two oldest."

"All three of them are in custody."

"Stay with me," lisped Luke.

Pennylane took him in her arms and rocked him. "Oh, my baby boy, I will. We'll find our way together, won't we?" She looked up at Cat. "What I wouldn't do for a big fat J right about now, but you know—" She extracted a small baggie of dried weed, papers, and a silver roach clip from the back pocket of her jeans and handed them to Cat. "This won't be real easy after all these years, but he's more important than getting high. I'm ready to get over it. Would you flush it? You won't have to tell the sheriff, will you?"

Cat tossed the bag over to Jeep. "Tell her what?"

CHAPTER THIRTY-FOUR

The Center of the Universe

It was September first, but it was still summer, the hot high summer that bleached the grasses and parched the creeks, that left the population of Waterfall Falls limp and sweaty and longing for the first rains. The rains might come any day or might wait until November. The weekly paper reported that the snowmelt on the mountains was long gone. The only sign of fall that Chick could feel was the cooling of the nights and the news of lightning strikes that started forest fires.

The men who harvested the forests welcomed fire season because there would be work. Every few years one of them would get caught setting a fire that might rage for weeks. If he got away with it, he'd hire on to fight the fire and then to log out the burned woods. Still later, he might be one of the planters who dug holes for saplings, or he'd get a job counting the salmon whose habitat was disappearing with the logged trees.

Sheriff Sweet had two teens in the jail for arson. The sons of a laid-off chain puller in a mill, filled with resentment at environmentalists and sheer summer boredom, they'd been setting fires along the railroad tracks for weeks.

Donny had baked well before the heat of day. Chick was sharing a sticky pull-apart with her, Cat, and the sheriff before opening the store. The building still smelled strongly of cinnamon and held chilly air from the night before.

"I'm glad we didn't waste any more bait today," Donny announced after they'd polished off the whole pull-apart.

Joan didn't answer, but accepted a refill of coffee from Chick.

"From what you've been saying, there isn't a fish left in the valley," Chick said, pouring the last of the coffee into her own cup. She went over to the sink to put on a fresh pot, but she was still in earshot, and she could see Cat's foot running up under Joan's uniform leg.

"The water's lower than I've ever seen it," Donny said. "I think it's that clear-cut up above. Soil can't hold much water or snow with no root system, and the fish skipped Sweet Creek this year. Soon there won't be any shade left to sit under if the creek dries up and can't feed the cottonwoods."

Cat said, "It's going the way of Dry Creek outside my place this year."

"Not much else dry in that neighborhood," muttered Joan, sliding her glance toward Cat.

Chick and Donny laughed while Cat made as if to slap the sheriff's hand and said, "Joan!"

The sheriff wiped her lips with a paper napkin. "Pretty bleak," she commented. "I've been wondering if Old M.C. was dumping waste chemicals in that water last winter and killing the fish."

"You think?" Chick asked, rejoining them.

"I wish you'd had an excuse to shoot the critter," Donny mused.

"If I'd known then how abusive he'd been to little Luke or that he'd taught his own kids the fine art of chemistry and dealing, I might have found an excuse." Joan stretched her legs out and tipped back her chair before she went on. "We've got him on charges of possession, manufacture and delivery, endangering the welfare and supplying a minor, maintaining a place where controlled substances are used, booby-trapping, skipping bail, eluding and assaulting an officer, and two counts toward the three-times-and-you're-out law. Prison won't be enough punishment for a sleazeball like that."

"How about impersonating a human being? Doesn't that add twenty years or so?" Donny asked. "Can I recommend it to the court as head honcho of the local DARE? I should at least have used the pepper spray when I tackled him."

"There you go."

"At the very least," Chick agreed. She gave Donny a kiss on the top of her head. "My hero."

"One more stalker bites the dust," said the sheriff with a chuckle.

Donny wiped her hands with a blue bandanna. Chick could see from her eyes that she was trying to hide a proud grin. Cat briefly linked her arm in Joan's and hugged it to her. Joan peered out the window toward a lone cable guy getting into a van, his back to them.

Loopy was outside, chewing on a back toenail while a couple of retired guys walked from Mother Hubbard's to their pickups.

After the second arrest the whole sad story of her and M.C. had to come out, but Donny had never admitted to knowing about the stalking before that. Chick had gone along with pretending she didn't know Donny knew. She saw no harm in letting Donny feel like her secret savior.

She'd been blown away when she realized her tailspin of depression was starting to slow after they locked M.C. up again and the judge refused to set bail. That week, for the second time that summer, she and Donny finally went up to the waterfalls. They had closed the store and powered up Blackberry Mountain in Chick's V-8 LTD. At odd moments of the day Chick had packed them a picnic supper of apples, cheese, pecans, and chocolate. When they reached the trailhead, Donny slid the backpack of food onto her shoulders, and Chick carried the bottle of sparkling grape juice wrapped in her plaid car blanket.

There had been no one at the falls when they arrived, and they had walked, Donny first, to the ledge behind the water slowly and silently, as if approaching a temple. If ever she had found a power spot in the world, this was it, she remembered thinking. The smoothed and slightly concave rock wall, scooped out by eons of water, offered the suggestion of an embrace. Before them the two streams of water, still lively, but diminished by the dryness of the season, fell through the evening light like beaded curtains forever twisting into whirlpools.

"Look at them," said Donny, "taking on the world together."

"And apart," Chick added, mesmerized by the sight. "They only merge at the pool."

Donny spread the blanket and they sat. Chick opened the grape juice while Donny set out the food, cutting chunks of Swiss cheese, then peeling and slicing the apples with her penknife. While it wasn't full enough to roar, the falls filled their embrasure with sound. Every move they made seemed to be part of a deliberate ritual, filled with import. This was like tripping, but now love was the trip, love as she'd never imagined it could be.

Donny presented her with apple and cheese on an orange, oversized napkin from last Thanksgiving. Chick passed over a plastic wine glass of bubbling juice. They raised their glasses to each other and drank until the glasses were empty.

Donny squirmed on the cool rock as if, thought Chick, she was getting ready to make a big speech. "Chick, maybe I didn't always say everything I should have these last few months."

She refilled Donny's glass and said, "Shhh. Maybe we don't always need to."

"I never lied to you. I need to be honest with you and with me. Things just don't always make it into words. Does that sound crazy?"

"Oh, wow, not only doesn't it sound crazy, you're saying what I'm thinking." She laughed. "Unless we're both crazy."

"Babe, we already know that!" Donny replied, stretching her arm to catch waterfall spray in her glass. "But, you know," she said, frowning, "I could learn to talk more if that's what we need to keep us going."

"I was just so afraid that—" Chick said, hesitating to bring up Donny's temper when she knew Donny was working on that. "I was just afraid," she finally said, "of everything. That shut me up too. But I never stopped loving you or wanting to be with you."

Donny slid closer. She whispered, "Good, cause I'd drag you back and rope you to me if I had to."

She looked up through her lashes and asked, "Front to front?"

Donny raised her eyebrows and looked cocky. "I don't think I'd need the rope in that position, babe."

Laughing again, she'd asked, "Is it getting hot under here, or is it just me?"

They'd gone home soon after that, completed their nightly chores, and climbed under the covers, naked. Their lovemaking was slow, deliberate, and more cautious than usual—as if it was the first time. Loopy finally figured out that if she was going to get any sleep that night, she needed to be in her basket, not with them.

More and more, since the night of the waterfalls, Chick felt a bubbly mellowness coursing through her, like she was a mountain pleasurably tickled by waterfalls. Some days she was down, but not as low, and more days she was up, but not as high. She was scheduled to be off the Prozac completely by the end of summer. Although she'd never gone to the sheriff to complain about M.C., fearful that between her hippie past and uncloseted present she'd made herself a target for a crazy like him, apparently Joan had heard, probably through the Pensioners Posse. The whole situation was in good hands. Now she needed to let it all go.

"I wonder where Jeep is," she said. "She never misses a pull-apart day."

Cat said, "She took my truck up to Eugene to pick up her friend from Reno."

"I completely forgot." She felt that little anxious stab that reminded her she was letting her age show. "It's a good thing we still have hot young items like you and the sheriff around, to remember things."

Cat and Joan's eyes met. Chick looked at Donny and fanned herself.

The sheriff moved her gaze from Cat to scrutinize Chick briefly. She said, "You're not over any hills yet that I can see, Miss Chick."

"That was the right answer," Chick told her. "Sometimes I try to remember what it was like to have a memory."

Joan eyed Donny next. "I hope Jeep's out-of-town friend isn't anything like yours."

"Abraham? If nothing else, we taught him that San Francisco is his real home," Donny said. "He can be as trans or gay or none of the above as he wants to be and always fit in."

"Abe didn't do anyone harm," Chick said.

"True," admitted the sheriff, "but he was about ripe for some kind of trouble. You don't live someplace like this without either fitting in real quick or getting spit out like a piece of gristle that can't be digested."

Cat lightly slapped her hand again. "Lovely image at breakfast. They're going to encourage you back across the street to Mother Hubbard's."

"I'm still getting lunch there. I hear more. Besides which, bean sprouts hurt my belly."

Outside, there was the sound of a car with a problem muffler passing slowly on Stage Street. That would be Fina, come in to town to open her shop. Not a minute later, Chick heard a great rattling by the parking spaces around the corner. There was a timid tapping at the side door.

"Sounds like Pennylane in her rattletrap retired-post-office jeep, reporting for her first day of work," Chick said and got up to let her in.

Donny chuckled. "Sounds like she got wheels to match her crazy homestead."

"Penelope, initial C, Bispo, according to the computer," said the sheriff.

"Italian?" Donny asked.

"Portuguese-Irish is what I hear. You're real good to give her work. I was all for keeping her locked up to teach her a lesson."

"Like the judge said, she's had her lesson," Donny proclaimed.

Chick had watched Donny take most of a week to accept the rehabilitation plans for Luke's mother. Donny, after all, had been in on both busts of Penny's soon-to-be ex-husband, M.C. She'd taken a flying leap onto his back that night they recaptured him, banging up the same shoulder that had just healed after the first capture. How that skinny butch of hers had managed to handcuff M.C., Chick couldn't picture.

"I pretended I was at least ten screaming and kicking dykes saving the world from this scum," was the only explanation she'd gotten. "I was my whole gang back in Chicago, only I didn't do as much damage."

Donny had blamed Pennylane as much as she did M.C. until she'd learned that the boys, a couple of meek but nasty kids, weren't Pennylane's, but Marly's sons. It helped that Cat had drug-rehab connections who got Pennylane going immediately in Narcotics Anonymous and as a patient in town at a satellite of the rehab center up in Greenhill. The caseworker assigned to Luke was the partner of his school principal. Small town living was a gas. It had been a relief when Donny had come around, as Chick had known she would—she'd needed her to do her figuring-it-all-out fast so she could set things up.

Having a job guaranteed that Pennylane could stay in the community. Accepting the offer of a home with Cat and Jeep solved their problem too. They got to keep Luke. The court wouldn't grant Luke to Pennylane for a long time, if ever, but was allowing them to live together on a trial basis. Jeep, in her excitement, joked over and over that they hadn't lost a son, they'd gained a mother. She'd taken to calling Pennylane Wendy and introducing herself as Peter Pan.

"The Goddess works in wonderful ways," she said to Pennylane as she let her in. "Stay, Loopy."

"I'm so nervous I'm going to forget everything you teach me, Chick."

"Nervous about working at Natural Woman Foods? There's no need. If you were tough enough to survive what you've gone through so far, you can do anything." She led Pennylane to the back room and showed her where to leave her coat. "Okay?"

Pennylane did look even more pale than usual, and when Chick took her hand it was damp with nervous sweat.

"I've never worked for a living before, Chick, and my mind is still kind of foggy."

She'd confessed this more than once, and Chick had reassured her the same way she did today. "Yes you have. You've baked, canned, cleaned, kept your shelves stocked, and even done some sales work before. You've got all the skills to work here."

"Selling drugs doesn't count!"

"Of course it does. Not that I'm recommending it as a career path, but I think you had to deal with tougher customers than we get here, handle bigger money, and be real careful about quality. What is that expression Jeep uses? You've got the right skill set." She looked up at the big old wall clock that advertised horse medicine. "We need to boogie. Put this apron on because you need to pull produce out of the cooler and make the case look pretty. Donny? You want to show Pennylane the ropes?" Donny's elbow was still in a brace. "You came along just in time. Donny still can't do much lifting and reaching with that shoulder she keeps injuring."

"Good, I don't want any charity." Pennylane's tone had a resentful edge to it.

Chick smiled. "We need you."

The sheriff nodded at Pennylane on her way out and laid two dollars on the counter. She said, "Miss Chick, thank you for breakfast."

She knew Joan was too young to have watched Matt Dillon and Miss Kitty flirt on the TV show *Gunsmoke*, but she felt like Miss Kitty when she replied, "My pleasure, handsome."

The sheriff smiled and shook her head, then put on her cowboy hat as she passed through the door. A few minutes later, Cat hugged Donny and Chick, saying, "I need to get to work."

"Can't you and Joan even walk out a door at the same time?" Donny asked, leading Pennylane back in with a basket of tomatoes.

"Leave her alone," said Chick. "They need to do what they need to do."

Cat explained, "Joan says all it takes is one careless minute and some Orange County transplant will have an impeachment petition with four hundred names, and we only have nineteen hundred people in Waterfall Falls."

By late morning Chick needed to prop open the front and back doors to let out the heat of the late-morning sun. Donny had gone to the bank for change, leaving Pennylane to fill the bulk bins. Pennylane was well-dusted with chickpea and soy flour and more cheerful now, if hesitant with the customers. Chick began to dream of taking a vacation with Donny while Pennylane ran the store. The woman, after feeding all those people for so many years, knew her hippie health foods.

Katie bounced through the front door, holding aloft a check. "I got it!" she cried. "My friend in New York gave me the go-ahead to do *Funeral for a Forest*!"

"That's amazing!" Chick said. "Our Katie's going to do a TV documentary?"

"For a network, girlfriend. And they're giving me money up front so I can live here, live the story!"

Chick admired Katie's spunk, the nervous energy that seemed to force her to create. Poor Katie got put down a lot for placing her life, all their lives, under scrutiny, but wouldn't this work to their advantage in the long run? Maybe it would, as Katie thought, save the trees to have their plight personalized, so people all over the country would learn to care.

"I'm still a sixties kid," she told Katie, taking a warm, petite hand in her own. "I believe you'll make a difference."

"Oh I will. We have to tell people the story. What do they know about it, living in the cities or on the plains and being fed this propaganda about renewable resources and retraining? They don't understand that this is their land that's being converted into bucks for big business, that their grandkids won't have any resources if we let things go on the way they have."

Pennylane came up to the counter and wiped her hands on her apron.

Katie stepped back as if to see Pennylane better. "I didn't know you had a new helper."

"This isn't any old helper. This is our new sidekick, Pennylane. Penny, meet Katie."

"I know you," Katie said. "Your picture was in the paper."

"For all the wrong reasons," Pennylane said. She hid her gap-toothed smile behind her hand.

"I thought that dim judge was going to treat you like a felon when it was obvious your husband ran you. That's a tough one, needing the dude's drugs."

Pennylane sounded sullen again. "I like to think I had something to do with my first forty-three years."

"Why? Most women don't." Katie looked at Chick. "I have to fess up to your helper, Chick. I mean some of this is my fault."

Chick had been wondering how to give Pennylane this awkward bit of news. "Because you called the sheriff when M.C. threatened to hurt you?" she asked.

"I turned him in—Penny? Is that your name?"

Pennylane nodded and looked at Katie for a long moment. "I guess it's like Chick says, the Goddess works in wonderful ways."

"The Goddess?" Katie said slowly, as if tasting the word.

With a shy laugh Pennylane said, "M.C. has tainted enough lives. I'm glad he didn't hurt you too. He was a pretty desperate hombre by then."

"Oh. I'm too tough and wily for any old dealer to mess me up." Katie looked at Chick. "When does Pennylane get a break? Want to have a latte with me, Penny?"

"As if I could stop Katie-energy. Watch out for this woman, Penny. She's insatiable for other people's stories. Two lattes coming up. On the house—to celebrate your project, Katie."

"You're a TV writer?" she heard Pennylane ask as they moved to a booth by the window. "That is so far out there. Where do you get the courage?"

And Katie's urgency as she said, "So are you really into this goddess stuff?"

Chick went out in front of the store and stood on the covered sidewalk, breathing in the smell of hot dust. She didn't hear the snort of trucks accelerating or the frequent whoosh of the cars pushing eighty up on the freeway. She didn't see the gas stations up the hill or their lighted signs, only the faded gray stair-step storefronts as they might have looked a hundred-odd years ago. The cafe, Fina's Finery, the store that sold jeans, saddles, and riding gear, could have been there back then. Outlaws might pull into town any minute. She'd come to look forward to the days Sheriff Sweet rode the length of Stage Street like a U.S. marshal charged with keeping the peace in a wild frontier town.

A hot flash crept through her body, radiating out from under her rib cage. That heat, combined with the noon sun, was like a sauna, moist yet dry, unbearable yet cleansing, a feeling she dreaded and at the same time reveled in. The Goddess must be making all the arrangements, she thought. I couldn't have chosen a more satisfying place to live.

The town and its people, with its smattering of dykes, could not have been more commonplace or more rare. It drew modern-day pioneers like the land women and bandits like M.C.; it produced Claras and Hectors, Cats and Lukes, Rs and Joans. Was there another place in America like this, or was this like every place in America, only her size, so she could grasp it, understand it, embrace it. She got teary with love for Waterfall

Falls, her home now and her homeland. She could feel another scrap of her sadness float up over the mountains toward the sea.

Inside, Katie and Penny's heads leaned together over their table. Chick was chuckling again when Donny returned from the bank with the change bag.

"What's so funny?"

"People. Here goes Katie again, this time interviewing Pennylane for her film."

Donny followed her eyes. "And she'll probably paste her in right with M.C., just as if she taped them together."

"Kind of like real life, the way things fall in place," Chick said, slipping a hand under the bib of Donny's overalls.

"Like my mama always said, will wonders never cease." Donny squirmed against her hand as Hector and Clara pulled into one of the diagonal parking spots in front of the store. "Looks like Luke's other Grandma and Grandpa are here."

"Did you ever wonder if this store's become the center of the universe?"

"Isn't it?" Donny asked with a straight face.

Chick smiled. "I suppose the planet could do worse."

"It's the kind of day I expect to see Mr. Bigot himself, John Johnson, come in here with a white flag."

Clara's strident voice preceded her. "Where's that paper you've been having all those women sign up on to take care of the lady with the breast cancer?" When R started needing care, lesbians from women's land all over the state stopped by to ask how they could help, as if this was the attack against which they'd planned to circle their covered wagons all along. Chick had finally blocked out a month on a piece of notebook paper and told them to sign on. Clara added, "I don't see why I shouldn't be allowed to help."

"Maybe she wants her own kind around her at the last," Hector suggested.

"And maybe she shouldn't be so fussy. Her friends would probably like some time off. Where is it?"

Chick pulled a clipboard out from under a stack of order books under the counter. "As long as you're of the female persuasion, I don't imagine R will object."

Donny gave a grunt. Her attitude toward Pennylane might have done a turnaround, but her opinion of R hadn't improved. Chick suspected Abe might have shared some state secrets Donny didn't find to her liking but was too honorable to reveal.

"Okay, let's try this one, gang," said Hector. "When does a ship tell a falsehood?"

Donny groaned. "Get it over with, Bob Hope."

"When she lies at the wharf!"

"Cut!" Katie said, jumping up and taking off her sunglasses. "I knew there was something I came here to tell you."

Chick felt cold. "R's not worse, is she?"

"Who knows? Sorry. I got distracted by my New York call. R's gone."

"Gone?" Donny repeated.

Chick felt like an earthquake was shaking the Valley.

"Gone," Donny went on, "like dead or like split?"

"Like she has blown this taco stand, people." Katie gestured toward the freeway with her sunglasses. "Her ex-husband came to take her away at the crack of dawn, complete with her two grown sons to load up the truck. She took her wigged-out macaw so you know she's not coming back."

"But, R?" Chick protested. She felt around for the stool she sat on to do the books. Donny slid it under her. "This can't be happening. She talked about her husband and their sons like they were something she'd cleaned out of the litter box."

Katie said, "She hadn't changed her mind on that as of last night when she came by the cabin where I'm crashing, but this morning, before anyone else was up, she went with the men. They had an SUV. It made a lot of noise coming up the mountain, then backing to her yurt. I watched the women move out of their spaces in nightclothes and stand staring. The mist was hovering over the ground. They looked like ghosts. No one said a word. R didn't even look at us."

"Now we know," said Donnie, "who all those secret rendezvous were with."

"Check," Katie agreed. "Her bouncing baby boys. Count them—two."

"This is too strange," Chick said. "I can't take it in. And you, Katie? You're back at Spirit Ridge?"

"Once Abeo left and R got sick, I lost my attitude fast."

Clara's eyes followed from speaker to speaker. Hector had taken off his hat and was scratching his bald spot.

"Go on," urged Chick. "There's got to be an explanation."

Katie rubbed together thumb and index finger. "Dinero. Hubby has the big bucks to finance a cure down in Mexico. There's also a guy in New York she's trying to get in to see. He does curing with nutrition."

"But," Chick protested, well aware that the messenger couldn't change a thing, "she'd accepted that she was going to die. She was looking forward to her personal audience with the Goddess."

"I guess she changed her mind."

"What, Donny?" Chick asked. "You look like you're choking."

"I'm not surprised, that's all. I'm just not surprised." Donny let out a quiet laugh. "Some women can't give up on men. And some men might be worth going back to, right, Hector? What's going to happen to all those women on the land?"

"I hadn't even thought of that." Chick glanced at the clock. They'd get a flood of customers come noon. Thank goodness it wasn't senior citizens' day or they'd be swamped by now. Half an hour to get it together.

"You have to understand," Katie said. "R's a panicked woman. She told me last night that she may have to sell the land if her ex runs out of funds and she still needs therapy."

"Sell the land?" Chick exclaimed. "She can't do that. Too many of you depend on living there."

"At her pleasure," said Donny in a tone both sarcastic and disgusted. "She has no use for it anymore. It served her purpose only as long as it drew in volunteers to help pay the mortgage, or keep her company, or to get one of her projects done."

Chick spoke sharply. "R gave back as much as she took."

Donny turned sad eyes on her. "She did. But the equation's changed now, ladies. She resigned as prime taker."

Katie asked, "Do you really think R's that much of a user?"

Donny answered, "I do. We all are, sometimes, and we all have reasons to let ourselves be used, but I think R's the hustle queen. Does that mean I'd vote for M.C. as chief dogcatcher over R? She raised my blood pressure now and then, but on a scale of one to ten, with M.C. being a 10, I'd say R was only about a two enemy-wise."

"I have to admit I'm going to benefit," Katie said. "She asked me to come back to Spirit Ridge rent free and help Dorothea take care of things. That's the other reason I'll be able to do this script; the cash advance wouldn't have been enough by itself."

"Poor R," said Chick. "I hope she finds her cure. Whoever or whatever she really is, wherever she got her money, how she left—she made a place where women could be themselves. Whether she was one of us or not, she gave us ourselves."

"God love her. She wanted to change the world like the rest of you girls, didn't she?" Clara slowly shook her head. "Life kicks the legs right out from under us just when we think we're in charge."

Chick grabbed onto Donny's arm and held it tight between her hands. "Thank you, Goddess," she whispered, astounded by the joy and wholesomeness she found in her life, "for everything you've given me."

"For what you've created, my little chickadee," Donny said. "It's good because you are."

Chick squeezed her eyes shut to keep back tears. "I do want to be good, to do good," she whispered, pleased at this discovery. "For us and for all of them." She released Donny's arm and gestured to their friends talking among themselves.

Pennylane went back to the disordered health-and-beauty shelves. Chick felt hopeful about her industriousness. The woman really wanted a new life for herself. She didn't see Cat's truck arrive, but she heard Jeep doing her donkey laugh somewhere outside.

Less than a minute later, Luke burst through the open front door calling, "Mama!"

They all watched him bolt across the old wooden floor, a crayon drawing in his hand.

"You'd think he hadn't seen his mother in a million years," marveled Clara. She told the group at the counter, "Jeep must have picked him up from school on her way back from the airport." Without a break she rushed right on. "I've read all sorts of good things about that apricot pit cure. I only met the woman once or twice, but whatever else she's done, she sounds ornery enough to beat cancer."

"A-men," said Hector. "If looks could kill a man, I'd be dead and buried ten times over by that one. I think her husband should apply for sainthood."

Maybe, Chick thought, Luke wasn't autistic at all. He still didn't say much, and that mostly when his mother was near. Maybe he'd grow into a quiet man. There was nothing wrong with that. She had to laugh at the contradiction—a quiet drummer.

Jeep, her Natural Woman Foods baseball cap turned forward for once, was pointing out the step down into the store. She was beaming over the head of a dark-haired young woman wearing a long corduroy jumper, a scoop-necked T-shirt, and clunky platform sandals. Chick noted the familiar way they moved with each other and had no doubt they'd be sharing a bed again very soon.

That, she thought with a jolt of finality, is who Jeep needs.

Jeep stared at Katie with that mouth-slightly-open, out-of-focus look of hers long enough to remind Chick that the two hadn't seen much of each other since their breakup. Jeep's Sarah, for that's who she must be, looked first at Jeep, then at Katie, and blushed. Chick liked this new gayfeather for that.

"Sarah, honeybunch," she said with her arms open. "Welcome to Waterfall Falls!"

SHERIFF JOAN SWEET

Endnote

They said I was an athlete, they say I'm a cop, but I say I'm a friend, a loving friend of women in a certain town, in the town where I was born, where I hope to end my days. The town is Waterfall Falls, a tourist stop along rural Interstate 5 well north of California. I patrol the streets downtown and the county roads that stretch into these mountains.

My dead little town whose sidewalks roll up of their own accord at dark would be all lit up from the stadium lights when I played softball here. We took the state championship that year. Whistles, cheers, the yelling, the kids in Nikes, the bleachers full, and later, the traffic stopping when they saw me on the street. I was fast, but I wanted to be more than that.

These mountains are bigger than I'll ever be, and older, and stronger. They range around us like a silent tribe of protectors. Their ancientness, their stubbornness, their Zen being-ness bring a serenity I've found nowhere else, though I long for it inside me.

And who am I? Who am I to forget to be humble, to dare to put our mountains into words? I am an Indian dipped in white blood, a child of this land and of the bigger world, one whose natures war with one another like most Americans. My blood is divided like the two forks of Sweet Creek that flow around Blackberry Mountain. Sweet Creek was named, after all, for my great-grandfather Thomas Sweet Water.

The cop patrols the Indian. The athlete runs from the white girl, although I don't know why sometimes, because we were all one family until some crossed the ice. The friend knows this twin creek rages through her friends. I watch them and see myself, though I feel very different from them. I watch them and know I am one of them, yet I am of this mountain, and I am descended from those who once were the original strangers to this land.

When I am not patrolling, not controlling the people who live here or visit, I sit in my office next to the post office, in this old brown wooden building we call the town hall. I sit here at the computer I use to track records and criminals and travelers. I sit here with my yellow paper pads and write the stories of my friends.

The Indian is an oral storyteller. The European is a writer. I put my friends in words to understand myself and to understand this life we live, though I've yet to understand either.

Still, I like the stories which I'll show someone some day. Cat probably, if I stand the test of time with her, and the kid in my life, Luke, so they know what treasures they are, are to me and to the mountain that cradles them in her hilly arms.

I'll never forget what Donny told me one time.

"I believe," she said, "that Chick loves me right down to this great big conflicted heart of mine which used to go off every which way like Sweet Creek when it turns into waterfalls. Because she does such a fine job of loving the dizzy old thing, it stays in one place now, almost as peaceful as those hills."

That was the day I realized, it's not about the waterfalls. It's about the mountain.

About the Author

Lee Lynch has been proudly writing lesbian stories since the 1960s when, under various pseudonyms, she was a frequent contributor to *The Ladder,* the only lesbian publication at the time. Since then she has published a dozen books including *Toothpick House; Old Dyke Tales;* the trilogy *Dusty's Queen of Hearts Diner, Rafferty Street* and *Morton River Valley; The Swashbuckler; Home in Your Hands; The Amazon Trail; Sue Slate, Private Eye; That Old Studebaker; Cactus Love;* and *Off the Rag: Lesbians Writing on Menopause,* edited with Akia Woods. Her stories and essays have appeared in *Lesbian Texts and Contexts* edited by Karla Jay and Joanne Glasgow, *The Persistent Desire* edited by Joan Nestle, *Lesbian and Gay Studies and the Teaching of English* edited by William J. Spurlin, and other anthologies. She has written reviews and feature articles for *The San Francisco Chronicle, The Lambda Book Report, The Advocate,* and other publications. Her syndicated column, *The Amazon Trail,* has been running in lesbian, gay and PFLAG papers since 1986.

She is employed in the social services in the Pacific Northwest.

Books Available From Bold Strokes Books

Sweet Creek by Lee Lynch. A celebration of the enduring nature of love, friendship, and community in the quirky, heart-warming lesbian community of Waterfall Falls. (1-933110-29-5)

The Devil Inside by Ali Vali. Derby Cain Casey, head of a New Orleans crime organization, runs the family business with guts and grit, and no one crosses her. No one, that is, until Emma Verde claims her heart and turns her world upside down. (1-933110-30-9)

Grave Silence by Rose Beecham. Detective Jude Devine's investigation of a series of ritual murders is complicated by her torrid affair with the golden girl of Southwestern forensic pathology, Dr. Mercy Westmoreland. (1-933110-25-2)

Honor Reclaimed by Radclyffe. In the aftermath of 9/11, Secret Service Agent Cameron Roberts and Blair Powell close ranks with a trusted few to find the would-be assassins who nearly claimed Blair's life. (1-933110-18-X)

Honor Bound by Radclyffe. Secret Service Agent Cameron Roberts and Blair Powell face political intrigue, a clandestine threat to Blair's safety, and the seemingly irreconcilable personal differences that force them ever farther apart. (1-933110-20-1)

Protector of the Realm: Supreme Constellations Book One by Gun Brooke. A space adventure filled with suspense and a daring intergalactic romance featuring Commodore Rae Jacelon and a stunning, but decidedly lethal, Kellen O'Dal. (1-933110-26-0)

Innocent Hearts by Radclyffe. In a wild and unforgiving land, two women learn about love, passion, and the wonders of the heart. (1-933110-21-X)

The Temple at Landfall by Jane Fletcher. An imprinter, one of Celaeno's most revered servants of the Goddess, is also a prisoner to the faith—until a Ranger frees her by claiming her heart. (1-933110-27-9)

Force of Nature by Kim Baldwin. From tornados to forest fires, the forces of nature conspire to bring Gable McCoy and Erin Richards close to danger, and closer to each other. (1-933110-23-6)

In Too Deep by Ronica Black. Undercover homicide cop Erin McKenzie tracks a femme fatale who just might be a real killer…with love and danger hot on her heels. (1-933110-17-1)

Stolen Moments: *Erotic Interludes 2* by Stacia Seaman and Radclyffe, eds. Love on the run, in the office, in the shadows…Fast, furious, and almost too hot to handle. (1-933110-16-3)

Course of Action by Gun Brooke. Actress Carolyn Black desperately wants the starring role in an upcoming film produced by Annelie Peterson. Just how far will she go for the dream part of a lifetime? (1-933110-22-8)

Rangers at Roadsend by Jane Fletcher. Sergeant Chip Coppelli has learned to spot trouble coming, and that is exactly what she sees in her new recruit, Katryn Nagata. The Celaeno series. (1-933110-28-7)

Justice Served by Radclyffe. Lieutenant Rebecca Frye and her lover, Dr. Catherine Rawlings, embark on a deadly game of hide-and-seek with an underworld kingpin who traffics in human souls. (1-933110-15-5)

Distant Shores, Silent Thunder by Radclyffe. Doctor Tory King—and the women who love her—is forced to examine the boundaries of love, friendship, and the ties that transcend time. (1-933110-08-2)

Hunter's Pursuit by Kim Baldwin. A raging blizzard, a mountain hideaway, and a killer-for-hire set a scene for disaster—or desire—when Katarzyna Demetrious rescues a beautiful stranger. (1-933110-09-0)

The Walls of Westernfort by Jane Fletcher. All Temple Guard Natasha Ionadis wants is to serve the Goddess—until she falls in love with one of the rebels she is sworn to destroy. The Celaeno series. (1-933110-24-4)

Change Of Pace: *Erotic Interludes* by Radclyffe. Twenty-five hot-wired encounters guaranteed to spark more than just your imagination. Erotica as you've always dreamed of it. (1-933110-07-4)

Honor Guards by Radclyffe. In a wild flight for their lives, the president's daughter and those who are sworn to protect her wage a desperate struggle for survival. (1-933110-01-5)

Fated Love by Radclyffe. Amidst the chaos and drama of a busy emergency room, two women must contend not only with the fragile nature of life, but also with the irresistible forces of fate. (1-933110-05-8)

Justice in the Shadows by Radclyffe. In a shadow world of secrets and lies, Detective Sergeant Rebecca Frye and her lover, Dr. Catherine Rawlings, join forces in the elusive search for justice. (1-933110-03-1)

shadowland by Radclyffe. In a world on the far edge of desire, two women are drawn together by power, passion, and dark pleasures. An erotic romance. (1-933110-11-2)

Love's Masquerade by Radclyffe. Plunged into the indistinguishable realms of fiction, fantasy, and hidden desires, Auden Frost is forced to question all she believes about the nature of love. (1-933110-14-7)

Love & Honor by Radclyffe. The president's daughter and her lover are faced with difficult choices as they battle a tangled web of Washington intrigue for...love and honor. (1-933110-10-4)

Beyond the Breakwater by Radclyffe. One Provincetown summer three women learn the true meaning of love, friendship, and family. (1-933110-06-6)

Tomorrow's Promise by Radclyffe. One timeless summer, two very different women discover the power of passion to heal and the promise of hope that only love can bestow. (1-933110-12-0)

Love's Tender Warriors by Radclyffe. Two women who have accepted loneliness as a way of life learn that love is worth fighting for and a battle they cannot afford to lose. (1-933110-02-3)

Love's Melody Lost by Radclyffe. A secretive artist with a haunted past and a young woman escaping a life that has proved to be a lie find their destinies entwined. (1-933110-00-7)

Safe Harbor by Radclyffe. A mysterious newcomer, a reclusive doctor, and a troubled gay teenager learn about love, friendship, and trust during one tumultuous summer in Provincetown. (1-933110-13-9)

Above All, Honor by Radclyffe. Secret Service Agent Cameron Roberts fights her desire the one woman she can't have—Blair Powell, the daughter of the president of the United States. (1-933110-04-X)